Silenced Whispers

A Novel

Afarin Ordubadi Bellisario

To my grandmother,
Fatima Madadoff Radpay, and
my aunt, Sorour Ordubadi,
whose love and wisdom
have shaped my life.

Book design: Adam Hay Studio, UK

Cover: Shirin Neshat,
Whispers, from Women of Allah series, 1997
Ink on LE silver gelatin print.
© Shirin Neshat
Courtesy of the artist and Gladstone Gallery

Hardback
ISBN: 979-8-9900044-6-7
Paperback
ISBN: 979-8-9900044-1-2
eBook
ISBN: 979-8-9900044-0-5

And the night, the clock, and the moon;
Tell you pensively,
"One must fall in love and stay;
One must shut the window and sit";
Behind the wall, someone sings.'
"One must fall in love and go;
The Winds are passing by …"

A. M. AZAD

CONTENTS

A Historical Background

By the start of the nineteenth century, the once mighty and prosperous Iran was struggling with a sluggish economy, an antiquated military, and an archaic way of life. Over the next two centuries, the country lurched to modernity amid internal conflicts and foreign meddling. But it was in the first two decades of the twentieth century—before, during, and after WWI—that a new Iran was truly formed. The pivotal era began in 1905 with the Constitutional Revolution that terminated the absolute monarchy and ended with the ascent of Reza Khan, the founder of the Pahlavi dynasty, in 1925. The legacy of those decades still impacts Iran and beyond.

The Grand Vizier Amir Kabir had embarked on remaking Iran in the mid-nineteenth century. He focused on breaking clerics' hold on the court and monarch, reining in foreign powers, and exposing Iranians to modern science and technology. To that end, he established the first school of science in Iran, Dar-al-Funun, sent Iranians to be educated abroad and encouraged entrepreneurs to bring technology to Iran. His efforts cost him his life.

With Western science and education came Western ideas of democracy, secular laws, and social change, especially in the status and role of women. In the early twentieth century, the quest for a representative government led to the formation of a parliament, the Majles.

The nascent democracy was endangered from the start. In the Majles, advocates for secular law and adherents to Islamic law, Sharia, clashed, and the conflict spread to the streets and turned violent. At the same time, the rival colonial powers that were busy exploiting Iran's natural resources—England and Russia—opposed any reform that threatened their interests. Further opposition came from reactionaries—frequently allied with one or both colonial powers—who profited from the status quo. Domestic corruption and conflicts, combined with foreign power grab under a weak central government, destabilized Iran at the onset of WWI.

This book is the fictional tale of individuals caught in the turmoil of that era. The historical events depicted in this book, including the Russian invasion of Northern Iran and the women's march to the Majles in protest, are real, as are the women's societies advocating for women's rights and democracy in Iran.

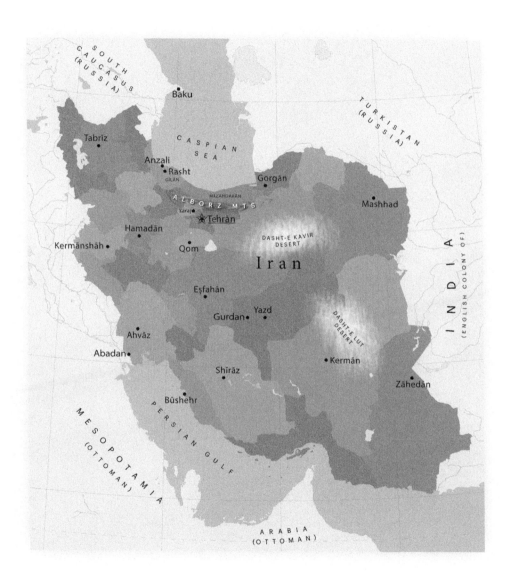

PART I
Awakening

If you come to my house, my kindhearted,
Bring me a lamp and a portal;
Through which I can gaze
At the commotion of the fortunate alley

F. FAROKHZAD

1

January 1909, Gurdan, Iran

"How could you?"

Gohar froze midway across the living room, then turned slowly. Framed in the doorway stood her accuser, the woman who had raised her from infancy: Qamar. In fourteen years of living with her, Gohar had never seen the old woman's round, gentle face so hardened with rage.

Sweat drenched her loose blouse. How much did Qamar know about what had happened the day before? Would she beat her? Qamar had never hit her, but she had no qualms about smacking her own daughters or ordering her husband to cane their sons. That Gohar was a foot taller than Qamar wouldn't stop her, either. She scanned the small room for cover. But neither the beat-up cushions on the floor nor the low table holding a samovar in the corner offered any protection.

She tightened her grip on her teacup and mumbled a greeting.

Qamar stepped forward, plopped down on the threadbare rug, and slapped a folded paper onto the floor. "Sit down," she barked. Her narrowed, fiery eyes burrowed into Gohar.

Gohar paled. The paper was the letter her friend Kavous had dropped in the alley the day before when the local tough guy—a *luti*—chased him. The luti must have taken it and given it to Qamar. Gohar sat at the edge of the strip of sunlight pouring through the doorway, her back to the wall, her head bowed.

"Do you remember what happened to the butcher after the mullah caught his daughter talking to a man?" Qamar leaned forward. She smelled of fried onion and turmeric.

Gohar shuddered. Even after he sent his daughter away, the butcher had lost customers, his wife had been ostracized, his son's engagement had been called off, and his other daughter had been beaten to a pulp by her in-laws. Soon, the family had vanished.

What if Qamar kicked her out? Gohar wasn't even her kin. A beating, she could endure. But survival was a pipe dream without family in a desert town seven days horseback ride from other towns.

What had she done? Correspondence with a boy—no matter how chaste—was trouble in a place where houses had no windows to the outside, and doors had separate knockers for men and women. When women heard a man knocking, they covered themselves and hid.

She grasped the medallion on her neck—her only keepsake from her mother. Engraved with a Qur'anic verse, it protected her from all calamities.

Qamar wagged her finger. "How long has this been going on?"

The boy's white skullcap had first piqued Gohar's curiosity three months before when he passed the alley while she watched from the rooftop. It was the kind only *Gabrs,* the followers of Zoroaster, wore, and Gabrs seldom crossed Muslim neighborhoods. She had tossed a pebble at him. He'd lifted his head and smiled. His narrow olive face looked harmless, with only a hint of hair above his full mouth. She'd smiled back.

But Qamar had no way of knowing who the letter was for or what was in it. No one in the area could read except for her and the mullah. And Qamar would never pay the meddlesome man to read it for her and spread the content around the neighborhood.

Gohar raised her head. "What do you mean?"

"I mean, how many love letters has he left you?"

She met Qamar's eyes. "How do you know it is for me, Naneh? Or that it's a love letter? Shall I read it for you?"

Qamar stared back. "What else would a man write to a woman?"

"How should I know? I don't get letters from boys."

"Did you write back?"

The note Gohar had left Kavous in the crack in the wall had not been discovered. Silently, she offered a prayer of gratitude to Fatimah, daughter of the Prophet—May the Lord bless him and his family. She would light a candle at the neighborhood shrine.

"Of course not, Naneh dear."

Qamar tucked an unruly strand of hennaed hair under her scarf. "Worst of all, he's a Gabr," she fumed. "Doves with doves, hawks with hawks; Muslims with Muslims and Gabrs with Gabrs; everyone with their kind."

Gohar wanted to blurt out that Qamar herself never missed a chance to chat and giggle with the Gabr confectioner or encourage him to give Gohar candy and sugar plums. But she kept quiet.

A torrent of words poured out of Qamar. "You must have done something. Otherwise, how would he know there's a grown girl in this house? You are not a child. People would gossip if they saw a man leaving you a letter. You can close the city gate, but you can't shut people's mouths. We are lucky that the luti was there to save our honor."

Qamar's softening tone emboldened Gohar. "Maybe the boy was going to the post office and dropped the letter when the luti scared him."

"Don't be fresh," Qamar grumbled. "The luti saw him with his own eyes bending down to leave the letter in our wall."

"Maybe he was trying to tie his shoes," Gohar offered.

Qamar rolled her eyes. "And maybe the shah was my father."

Once Qamar was gone, Gohar rushed to her room, leaving her untouched tea by the samovar. Outside, the winter sun shimmered through the leaves of the ancient, gnarled tree that dominated their tiny yard. A breeze cooled her burning face as she sped through the veranda that connected all four rooms of their mudbrick house.

Though only large enough for her to lie down and separated from the veranda by nothing but a faded curtain, her room was her sanctuary. It was the only place she had never shared, even when the house overflowed with Qamar's four sons and two daughters. At the back of her room, in a storeroom stacked high with extra bedding and out-of-season clothing, was an old, velvet-lined wooden trunk hiding her *tar*.

She grasped the musical instrument by its long, narrow neck, took it out, and clutched it to her chest. The touch of the well-worn skin of the tar's double bowls calmed her instantly.

The tar had captivated her from the minute she found it inside the trunk in the cellar. She was surprised to find an instrument played by female *motreb*s at weddings and circumcisions in the house she shared with Qamar and her family. Qamar loathed musical instruments and derided merrymakers. Nonetheless, Gohar had felt compelled to take the tar out, twist its pegs, and pluck its strings to make a sound.

Fearful of Qamar burning the instrument if she knew about it, Gohar had kept it hidden and played only when no one was around. Luckily, Qamar's husband, Amoo Ali, was busy at his greengrocer store every day while Qamar ambled through the market or chewed the fat at weddings and funerals. Soon, Gohar had mastered the familiar melodies and invented new ones. The tar became her friend and confidant, her respite when she was anxious, her tongue when she was lost for words.

She cradled the instrument and leaned on the wall in the dim light from the narrow window near the ceiling.

The disaster had struck the previous afternoon. Gohar had climbed the tree in their yard to reach the roof, as she often did while Qamar napped. Nothing seemed out of the ordinary in the alley. The cobbler was hammering shoes in the shade of a wall, and the cutler was flirting with a woman in a flowery chador. In front of the coffeehouse, emaciated dogs fought over a bone while a storyteller entertained men smoking hookah on carpeted platforms.

There was no trace of the mullah or the self-appointed guardian of local honor, the luti. No one would report her to Qamar for being on the roof. She sat on the sloping straw-clay surface. A draft ruffled the tail of her scarf and whirled softly in the wind-catchers—the slender towers that dotted the neighborhood, harnessing the wind to cool the houses.

The ribbon of hills to the east marked the path of the caravans that once brought Chinese silk and Indian spices to Gurdan, the oldest city in Iran. Nowadays, the rare convoys that reached the town brought cheap Russian-made cotton and English-branded tea cultivated in India. Beyond the hills, the desert stretched boundless and wild. Only tamarisks kept the sandstorms at bay.

How glorious it would be to fly—to sail over the ocean of sand and see wonders she had only heard about: snow-capped mountains, rivers full of fish, forests bursting with flowers.

Kavous's white outfit caught her eye as he weaved through a mob of barefoot boys chasing a wooden wheel with a stick. What would be in his letter today? A report of excursions to a Gabr village marked by a pair of cypresses or a fire burning for fifteen hundred years? An account of mischief at school? Everything he wrote was new to her. Excited, she waved. He smiled.

Suddenly, from the corner of her eye, she saw the luti rise from a platform outside the coffeehouse. How could she have missed him? Her heart sank. He wasn't keen on stranger boys—especially Gabrs—frequenting the neighborhood.

He pulled on his cloth shoes and fetched a wooden stick. His eyes, cruel and narrow, scanned the rooftops as his beefy fingers grabbed the handle of the dagger tucked into his sash. He followed Kavous. Terrified, she silently pleaded with her friend to turn around.

Oblivious to his stalker, Kavous bent by the crack in the wall to replace the letter Gohar had left him with his own. The luti lowered the club. The boy grabbed his shoulder, cursed, and turned. At the sight of his assailant, Kavous dropped the letter and bolted.

The luti gave chase. A gust of wind blew his felt hat away. His shaved head glinted in the sun. Under any other circumstances, the sight of a bowlegged bald man in a short robe and billowing pants racing after a boy would have made her laugh, but now all she could picture was Kavous lying in the dirt, blood oozing out of his throat. She prayed to Fatimah, the Prophet's daughter.

As it turned out, Fatimah—or luck—was on her side. Kavous, twenty years younger and fifty pounds lighter than the luti, easily outran him. He disappeared past the bend in the alley before the luti could touch him. The man didn't follow. Gabrs had their own tough guys, reputed to be much stronger than the luti and his cronies. Panting, the luti spat on the ground and vowed loudly to kill the boy if he ever dared to set foot in their neighborhood again.

She slid down the tree, oblivious to the branches tearing through her thin pants and bloodying her legs. In her room, she sat on her rolled-up bedding, trying to calm her racing heart. There would be trouble if the luti could connect her to the incident and report it to Qamar or Amoo Ali. But how could he? He hadn't seen her on the roof.

That evening, Qamar had looked skeptically at Gohar hammering at a sugar cone to break it apart. "Watch your fingers," she'd said. Gohar never volunteered for chores. Qamar never asked.

Amoo Ali had been equally startled when Gohar offered to carry the carrots and turnips he had brought home down the broken steps to the kitchen. His sallow face had opened to a rare grin, revealing the last of his tobacco-blackened teeth.

Shortly after the evening call to prayer, a knock on the door had surprised them. "There is a man at the door," Qamar had said, covering her plump body with her flowery blue chador. "I hope no one's sick." Then she sent Gohar to her room.

In her room, Gohar had overheard Amoo Ali invite the luti to their seldom-used sitting room, the largest in the house and the only one with a door. She had felt sick.

Gohar caressed the strings of the tar. She hadn't been beaten or banished, but she had lost a friend. Kavous could never return to her neighborhood, and she had no way of reaching him. The loss hung heavy on her heart. She longed to play, but with Qamar so close, she dared not risk her last companion.

2

January 1909, Gurdan

Qamar stayed home for days, praying late into the night. The furrow lines on her forehead deepened, and calluses formed on her fingers from counting the rosary. Distressed, Gohar quit climbing the tree and volunteered to read the letters the neighbors had received and write replies. That endeared her to women tired of paying the mullah to read their intimate letters and putting up with his inane and unwanted advice.

At night, the swirl of wind in the desert reminded her of Kavous's tales of the royal princesses. She pictured the noble ladies, tall and regal on white horses, fleeing the marauding Arabs. At the edge of the cliffs, their horses neighed. Then, the mountains wept, taking the women into their bosoms.

One afternoon, Gohar overheard Qamar confide in her eldest daughter.

"Believe me, Gohar didn't mean to harm us," Qamar said as she sewed. "She didn't know any better. But I had to fill up the bottomless well of that bastard luti's stomach to keep him from blabbering all over the neighborhood."

"What did he want?" Qamar's daughter asked indifferently as she nursed her youngest.

"What do lutis want these days? Free food. In the old times, they guarded the honor of the neighborhood and asked for nothing. But now they're no better than thugs."

"You know best, Naneh," Qamar's daughter said. "But if you want my opinion, you are too lenient with Gohar. You should smack her like you smacked the rest of us. Drill some sense into her. You shouldn't have hired a tutor. As the mullah says, teaching a girl to read opens the door to Satan."

"You know that wasn't my idea," Qamar said.

The woman responsible for hiring the tutor was a princess Qamar had nursed. She had been a friend of Gohar's mother. Gohar had met her only once, five years before, but the tears in the woman's sad green eyes still haunted her. The princesses in Qamar's tales never cried, except when trapped in a witch's spell.

Gohar knew nothing about her parents. Qamar claimed she didn't know them. She had taken in the infant Gohar after the princess's mother, Noor—a Georgian concubine of a past shah—had asked her to. And as generous as she was in embellishing stories of the princes and their steeds, Qamar was a miser when it came to Gohar's family.

Every detail of visiting the princess in the governor's mansion was still vivid in Gohar's: the thrill of meeting her mother's friend, the joy of taking a droshky—an unusual splurge for Qamar—the vastness of the reflecting pools in front of the estate and the intricacy of the plasterwork that had distracted her and caused her to trip on the carpet.

But it was the princess herself who had made the most enduring impression. Enchanting in a peach crepe-de-chine dress of a design Gohar had never seen before, she had surprised Gohar by embracing her tightly and kissing the parting of her hair. She was visibly dismayed to learn that Gohar was illiterate.

After the visit, Gohar had hoped to hear more from Qamar about her parents. But the more she prodded, the more indignant Qamar became. Finally, out of fear of hurting or antagonizing Qamar, Gohar had stopped asking.

A month later, a messenger had brought a dress with a full skirt and lacy collar for Gohar and money for Qamar to hire a tutor. The outfit was from *Farangestan*—*Farang* for short—the mysterious land that her tutor—when he was appointed—would call Europe, where *Farangis* lived. Gohar had worn the dress until it fell into tatters.

The whining of Qamar's daughter brought Gohar back to the present. "But *you* let her read useless books all day," she said. "She can't cook, or sew, or clean. No wonder she gets into mischief. You ought to marry her off, and soon. She's already fourteen. In two years, she'll be a spinster."

Gohar glanced at the haggard face of Qamar's daughter, already old at twenty. What had happened to the vibrant girl who smiled constantly before marriage? She recalled the apprehensive look on the faces of local nine- and ten-year-old brides, dollops of blush plastered on their cheeks, some marrying men older than their fathers. It was a blessing that Qamar deftly avoided the matchmakers lurking in the public bathhouse.

"But to whom?" Qamar said, exasperated. "I can't marry her off to a baker or a butcher. She has to marry her own kind, and her kind wouldn't even look at a no-name, no-dowry girl living in this neighborhood."

But who was *her kind?* Did he, like her, look different from others? Gangly and flat-chested, with an unruly mass of auburn hair and a pale oval face, Gohar had none of the feminine attributes celebrated by the poets: voluptuous curves, a round face, and supple black hair. Only her eyes, shaped like almonds and black as a moonless night, drew praise.

More importantly, whoever he was, would he beat her black and blue, as Qamar's sons-in-law did to their wives, or be meek and mild, like Amoo Ali, who obeyed Qamar unquestioningly?

Qamar continued. "Even if a proper suitor comes along, she needs a male guardian to agree to the marriage and negotiate a contract."

"Oh dear. You mean you still don't know who her guardian is?"

"How would I? I haven't heard from the family since the princess visited."

"Then you'd better find out before we have a disaster on our hands."

Gohar glanced at Qamar's grandchildren fighting over a homemade doll in the courtyard. Despite their frequent squabbles, they were lucky to have each other.

"Easier said than done," Qamar snapped. "How am I going to find the family? I have no idea where Noor is. The old Shah is dead, and his harem is gone. She could've gone back to Georgia."

"What is she going to do with her life if you can't marry her off?"

"I wish I knew, my dear," Qamar sighed. "I wish I knew."

3

February 1909, Gurdan

The wind gusted across the narrow alleys as Gohar and Qamar hurried through the predawn darkness. *Ta'azyeh*, the enactment of the martyrdom of the Prophet's grandson, Imam Hossein, started in the late afternoon, but the women's section in their local *tekyeh* filled up long before noon. Everyone was eager to mourn the Imam on the anniversary of his murder in Kabala, on the tenth of the holy month of Muharram, Ashura.

Gohar covered her mouth with the corner of her chador to keep out the specks of sand. The pageantry of Ta'azyeh always lifted her spirits despite its tragic ending, and crying on this holiest day of the year purified the heart, compelling the divine to grant her wish and restore Qamar's spirit.

When Gohar and Qamar arrived, green flags fluttered outside the black cloth–covered tekyeh. They elbowed their way through the horde of women in black, towing sniffling children. Near the raised platform in the middle of the tekyeh, Qamar's friends wiggled to make room for them on the earth-packed floor. The spot was perfect: close enough to the stage to see the performance but far enough to escape the dust kicked up in the action.

The morning dragged on. Qamar dispensed advice on remedies for colicky children and the necessity of newborn boy's urine to dispel the curse of a jealous co-wife. Gohar munched on dried mulberry and dreamt about Tekyeh Dowlat in Tehran, where, according to Qamar, hundreds of chandeliers illuminated professional stage sets where trained actors performed. Here, oil lamps lit a makeshift stage where worn canopies depicted the combatants' camps, and a beat-up sofa represented the court of the evil King, Yazid. The neighborhood men portrayed the heroes—the Imam and his entourage—and villains—Yazid and his army.

At noon, the children of the wealthy served cumin-laced rice with tiny meatballs piled over flatbreads. The smell of saffron and lard filled the space, blending with sweat and rosewater. Women chewed noisily and gossiped. Some ate while nursing babies. Qamar wrapped her and Gohar's leftovers in a cloth for dinner.

Finally, drum rolls and trumpets heralded the arrival of the performers. Behind a large wooden palm frond, riders in chain mail, feathers swaying above their spiked helmets, carried standards and flags. Others followed on foot, wrapped in sheets to resemble Arabic robes and headgear. Veiled boys, depicting holy ladies, came last.

Once the actors had settled, a young mullah in the black turban of a *Seyyd*, a direct descendant of the Prophet, sprinted up the steep wooden stairs to the right of the stage. A stocky older narrator followed to sit at the bottom of the stairs. By now, the men, some with backs bloody from self-flagellation, had filled their section.

His dark eyes ablaze with passion, the mullah began speaking in his haunting voice, in the name of the benevolent and merciful Allah. The audience fell silent. He pleaded for the Imam's blessings for the audience and the patrons of the Ta'azyeh, especially the merchant who had provided the lunch. Then, he motioned for the narrator to start.

The crowd rumbled. Women stirred uncomfortably. Qamar whispered that the brazen mullah had neglected his obligation to pay homage to or pray for the shah. Gohar shrugged. She never paid much heed to the monarchs who ruled their country—some benevolently, most not so—from a faraway capital.

The chatter quieted once the enactment began. A series of vignettes showcased the bravery of the Imam's retinue attempting to break the siege of Yazid's army and free the entrapped women and children. The narrator weaved the scenes together. Gohar lost herself in the sounds: the passionate chants, the stirring drumbeats, the airy trumpets, the clattering swords, and the flowing speeches.

The audience sobbed when the heroes died. Their shoulders bobbed.

Gohar cried when the Imam's young daughter grabbed his legs, begging him not to go. Only the Imam's sister, Zainab, remained reticent, even when her sons perished. She cared for the wounded and comforted the bereaved, speaking only to save her nephew from execution and her niece from slavery.

The Imam was the last to die. The crowd howled, raising their fists. They condemned the killer to the eternal fires of hell. At this point, the mullah would customarily denounce a present-day evildoer—a cruel tax collector or a loan shark—as akin to the Imam's assailant. Everyone listened attentively for the name of the local evil.

The mullah's voice boomed. "May the Lord's eternal condemnation be upon the shah's army and its murderous Russian commander, who have besieged Tabriz and are starving our brothers, sisters, and their children."

A deadly silence descended. Ashen-faced players froze on the stage with their hands cupped over their mouths. Women clutched their children. Gohar looked left and right for the shah's soldiers to arrive with drawn swords and drag the audacious mullah away.

Qamar turned pale. "That young man is asking for trouble," she said, trembling.

The excited chirping of Qamar from the adjacent room woke Gohar the following morning. "Ali, you won't believe what happened last night. Imam Hossein came to me in my dream and promised an auspicious future for Gohar. My tears for him must have touched him."

Amoo Ali grumbled.

Gohar stretched her back. The light was already peeking through the curtains. She had missed the morning prayer. But the mullah's tale of hungry children had kept her up all night. She had only a hazy idea of where Tabriz was and knew nothing about a siege there. Nevertheless, the suffering of innocents outraged her. The Imam, who had died for justice, would never tolerate such atrocity.

"You should've seen him," Qamar continued. "Tall, handsome,

round face, trimmed beard, black eyes, connected eyebrows. I didn't know who he was until I heard a whisper. I prostrated myself. He lifted me and told me to find Saleh Mirza and do as he said. Then, before I could ask any questions, I woke up and smelled the scent of roses filling the room."

Who was this Saleh Mirza? And how could Qamar worry about her future when the children were dying now? But could the mullah be misinformed? Or misled? Her tutor would know.

That morning, when Gohar entered the living room, Qamar had already sweetened her tea and smeared her bread with jam. "Gohar, dear," she said. "I want you to compose a telegram to Amoo Ali's nephew in Tehran. Ask him to find the former grand vizier, Saleh Mirza, and request an audience for me and Amoo Ali on a matter of the utmost importance and urgency."

As much as Gohar believed in the Imam's powers, she couldn't think of a single reason a grand vizier—even a former one—would be keen to come to her aid amidst national turmoil. Regardless, Qamar's acquaintance with an aristocrat impressed her.

But before she could respond, Amoo Ali cleared his throat. "We are not going if the countryside isn't safe."

Gohar glanced at Amoo Ali quizzically. He seldom expressed any opinion and never questioned Qamar's decisions. She chewed her bread and wished Qamar didn't have to travel with a man so that she could take Gohar instead.

"That goes without saying, sir," Qamar grumbled.

Gohar hurriedly conveyed the previous day's events to her ancient tutor even before he could take off his shoes.

"I don't patronize Ta'azyeh, my child," said the diminutive man, shuffling toward the straw mat under the tree where Qamar could keep an eye on him from anywhere in the house. "But I have heard of similar incidents. It is all because of the cursed war."

Gohar gulped. "What war?"

"The one between the shah and the constitutionalists." He wriggled to squeeze his body into the shade of the tree. "It has been going on since last June."

She had never heard of the constitutionalists. Perhaps they were one of many tribes who roamed Iran: Afshar, Turkmen, Shah-Savan, Qashqai, Kurd, Lor, and the mighty Bakhtiari. "Who are the constitutionalists?"

He stirred the tea Qamar had put in front of him. "Ordinary folks so fed up with the cruelty and folly of the monarchs that they revolted. The former shah allowed them to elect a national assembly to run the country, just like in England." He beamed, puffing out his chest as though he personally had led the revolutionary army to victory. "They call theirs the House of Commons. We call ours the *Majles*."

"What does that have to do with a siege in Tabriz?"

"Be patient, child. I'll get to that." He put the spoon down, sipped his tea, and winced at its heat. "But when that shah passed, his son, the new shah, didn't want riffraff like you and me to interfere with his God-given right to do as he pleased. First, he haggled with the Majles over his choice of advisors and his trips to Farang. Then he got tired and sent the Russian commander of his Cossacks to shell the Majles and close it down."

What cowardice, Gohar thought. A shah ordering a heathen to attack the house of the people. "And the residents of Tabriz revolted?"

"Exactly."

"But didn't God tell people to obey their rulers?" That was what Qamar always said.

"That's debatable. Some religious leaders, *ulema*, believe we must fight unjust rulers."

A peddler in the alley touted the sweetness of his carrots. "Like Imam Hossein fighting Yazid," she said reflectively.

He ran his gnarly fingers through his hennaed beard. "But other ulema say we don't need the laws of men when we have Sharia, the law of God. They say the constitution is a Farangi hoax, a blasphemy, and the shah agrees with them."

"So, the shah sent his troops to punish people."

The tutor nodded.

But surely the children of the rebels were innocent. "Why starve their children, then?"

"He thinks the mutineers' children are future rebels. Best to kill them while they're young," he scoffed. "But he doesn't understand that times have changed. It is the twentieth century. People won't stand being treated like cattle."

"What twentieth century?" As far as she knew, Muharram was the beginning of the thirteen hundred and twenty-seventh year after the migration of the Prophet—the blessing of the Lord be upon him and his family—from Mecca to Medina. That made it the fourteenth century.

"The Farangi century. If we want a modern country, we must be in tune with Farang."

"What year is it in Farang now?"

"1909."

A frightful thought crossed her mind: shahs were capricious. What if this one decided to attack Gurdan? "What's going to happen?" she asked nervously.

"God knows. But at the end of the day, neither the Majles nor the shah runs this country. The English and the Russians do. This shah dances to the Russian tune. But . . ." he lowered his voice, glanced left and right, and leaned closer. "Don't underestimate the English. They are as crafty as the Russians are brutal. The two of them have already carved up Iran: the north for the Russians, the south for the English, the barren desert for rabble like us."

That evening, Amoo Ali reported that a group of hooligans had beaten the young mullah they had seen on Ashura. Their neighborhood luti had boasted of leading the assault.

4

August 1909, Gurdan

The cool, cave-like basement was a welcome respite from Gurdan's scorching August heat. Gohar sipped her *sharbat* as she examined the latest document her tutor had brought her. The four loose sheets of coarse paper—each as wide as her outstretched hand and twice as long—were printed with news and commentary. It was the first newspaper she had ever seen. The daily publication, read aloud in coffee houses in Tehran, had so inflamed the shah that he had banned the paper and ordered the killing of its editor.

Barely two weeks after they had asked Amoo Ali's nephew to contact Saleh Mirza, the nobleman had sent them a telegram, agreeing to meet Qamar and Amoo Ali. But the civil war had spread by then, making the trip to Tehran more hazardous than usual. Gurdan had remained calm, save for sporadic scuffles between the shah's supporters and his growing opponents. But the tribal unrest in the countryside had spurred Amoo Ali to mount a rare resistance to his wife's wishes. He had refused to travel—until Qamar's threat to go alone had shamed him into submission.

They had finally left in April, leaving their son and grandson to watch over Gohar. She didn't mind. Qamar's son didn't interfere with her, and the seven-year-old grandson picked up fresh bread, ran across town to buy her ink, and even walked to the pits outside the city gates to bring her ice. In return, Gohar taught him reading and writing using the new material her tutor had brought, emboldened by Qamar's absence. The material was primarily political articles and contemporary poems. They were in the language of the streets, devoid of hidden meanings, tributes to kings, moral lessons, and adoration of beloveds—earthly or heavenly. They had stark messages: seek knowledge and justice and beware of Farangis and their lackeys, who seek nothing but their land's treasures.

She wondered what Qamar and Amoo Ali were doing. Since their departure, they had sent only one telegram to let her know they had arrived safely. Had they met Saleh Mirza? Had he found Gohar a suitable match?

Marrying and serving her husband and his family for the rest of her life didn't appeal to Gohar. But for a girl, marriage was not a choice; it was a necessity. Single females were shunned, and without a family of her own, Gohar would have no way of keeping a roof over her head or clothes on her back unless she married. The best she could hope for was a suitor with the means to support her and the benevolence not to mistreat her. Beyond that, she tried not to dwell on thoughts of her future husband. It was too depressing.

Meanwhile, hopeful events abounded. Over the summer, revolutionaries from the four corners of the country had united against the shah. Her tutor's tales of men battling their way to Tehran reminded her of the heroes in Qamar's stories—except that these men were bricklayers and laborers, not princes and nobles. Some were Armenians and Caucasians. In Gurdan, the notables and society ladies now vied to host the mullah she had seen on Ashura.

Finally, the powerful Bakhtiari tribe joined the rebellion to defeat the despotic shah, send him into exile, and crown a new shah. How fortunate Qamar and Amoo Ali were to be in the capital at such a historic moment!

Her tutor snorted when she expressed her excitement. "Don't be daft, child. The deposed shah was a Russian lackey, But the new shah is no better. He is a twelve-year-old tutored by a Russian spy."

A knock at the door spurred Gohar to shove the newspaper under the rug before running upstairs. Qamar haggled with a porter in the courtyard while Amoo Ali carried their trunks inside. Gohar rushed to embrace Qamar.

"Praise be to the Lord who let me see you again," Qamar blurted out, wiping away her tears. "I have so much to tell you."

As anxious as Gohar was to hear about the trip, Qamar's grimy, haggard look dissuaded her. "You must be tired, Naneh Qamar," she said as the two descended to the cellar. "Do you want some *sharbat*? Or some melons." She pointed to the melons stacked by the wall.

"Just some water," Qamar replied. "Your *sharbat* is too watery." She lay down on the sheet covering the carpet in the cellar and leaned on a thick bolster. "You have no idea how lucky you are." She cooled herself with a broken straw fan. "You should thank Imam Hossein with your every breath. Name your firstborn Hossein. Saleh Mirza—may God give him health and prosperity—has adopted you as his daughter."

Happiness bloomed in Gohar's heart. She had longed for a father who loved and supported her all her life. Someone who would answer her questions and solve her problems. Someone she could look up to and respect. "Are you serious? Why would he do that?"

"Because he is munificent," Qamar drained the water Gohar had brought in one gulp. "Your parents were distant relatives of his, and he feels responsible. But if you ask me, it was Saint Fatimah who whispered in his ear to look after you."

"When can I see him?"

"He doesn't want you to travel to Tehran. But he is looking for a suitable match for you."

"Oh," Gohar said, deflated.

Qamar grabbed a fistful of pistachios and dried mulberries. "He is not the grand vizier anymore. But you can't imagine how rich he is. The governor's mansion looks like a hovel next to his house." She grabbed Gohar's knee. "And you have a mother! You remember the princess? Her mother, Noor, is married to Saleh Mirza and is your adopted mother. She sent you a letter and a picture. What a miracle! Even *I* can't believe it."

In the picture, Noor resembled her daughter, the princess. Her short but loving letter warmed Gohar's heart and lessened her disappointment at not being asked to visit them. Having a family, even one far away, was a blessing. She loved Qamar but was always aware that she was not her family. "Do Saleh Mirza and Noor have children?"

"Not together. Saleh Mirza has a son from his earlier marriage who lives in Farang and doesn't get along with his father."

"And Noor has the princess. Did you see her on this trip?"

Qamar's face dropped. "No."

"How come?"

Qamar hesitated. "Noor had to disown her."

Gohar gasped. "Why?"

"Noor wouldn't tell me. But," Qamar lowered her voice, "just between you and me, there is a rumor that the princess left her husband for a Farangi. Noor had no choice. She had to protect Saleh Mirza's honor."

Gohar slapped her own face. How could a pious woman leave her husband for a Farangi? No wonder Noor had banished her daughter.

Qamar's face turned serious. "And that brings us to your behavior," she said. "Now that you are part of Saleh Mirza's household, you must uphold his honor. Once you are married, you must obey your husband and your mother-in-law." She wagged her finger. "No more climbing the tree or sitting on the roof, no more letters from strangers, and no more tutors to fill your head with nonsense."

Gohar's jaw dropped. How did Qamar know about her climbing the tree and the subject of her conversations with the tutor?

As though reading her mind, Qamar sighed. "You think I am old and stupid. But I see more than you think." She reached for Gohar's hand. "If you behave, I'll make your future husband let you play tar as much as you like."

Gohar was aghast. If Qamar knew about the tar, why hadn't she burnt it? Tears welled up in her eyes. She touched Qamar's wrinkled face and tucked a wayward strand of hennaed hair behind her ear. "How can I ever repay you, Naneh?"

"There is only one way: don't make me lose face. Don't be fresh with your mother-in-law like you are with me. Don't talk back to her. I forgive anything you do. She will not. Then your husband will divorce you, Saleh Mirza's good name will be tarnished, and I will die of shame."

Gohar embraced the old woman, promising to behave as befitted a member of Saleh Mirza's household.

A week later, a telegram from Saleh Mirza brought news of his choice of a husband for Gohar. The bridegroom, Haji Mohsen, was a wealthy merchant, a widower with a married son, and the representative of Gurdan in the parliament, the Majles. He had already negotiated the marriage contract. All that was left was for Qamar and the bridegroom's mother to agree on an auspicious date for the wedding. Saleh Mirza advised against an elaborate reception. Many in Gurdan were still suffering in the aftermath of the war, and time was short. Haji was due back in Tehran for the opening of the Majles in three months, and the journey took two weeks.

Of all her future husband's attributes, only one appealed to Gohar: his affiliation with the Majles. After marriage, she would live in Tehran and discuss politics with him. He would be so impressed by her that he would seek her opinion on matters of the state. Through him, she would bring justice and prosperity, assist the oppressed, and punish the wicked. Hers wasn't such a bad fate after all.

5

October 1909, Gurdan

Gohar took in the hustle and bustle of the alley from the roof of Qamar's house one last time. Later that day, she would leave her childhood home for her husband's house, entering in a white chador and leaving in a white shroud, as honorable women did.

As the wedding day approached, her anxiety increased. Qamar's constant reminders of Gohar's obligation to respect and obey her husband *and* mother-in-law didn't help. Neither did her instructions not to speak unless spoken to, not to sit until given permission to, and to walk three steps behind her husband. The cold, judgmental eyes of her future mother-in-law, *Khanum Bozorg*, the grand lady, kept Gohar awake and chased her in nightmares.

Gohar tried to picture her future husband, Haji Mohsen, known as Haji. She had never laid eyes on him. Qamar had described him as "mature, God-fearing, and mild-mannered, not young but handsome, with a full head of hair and smooth skin." But what he looked like didn't matter. Her duty was to please him, even if he had horns and a tail. Disgruntled men divorced their wives simply by declaring their intention in front of two witnesses. Worse yet, they might take another one. Saleh Mirza had negotiated Gohar's right to divorce if Haji took a second wife, but what good would that do? A divorced woman was a blight on her family.

All day long, she had anxiously watched Qamar arrange her wedding setting, beginning with the spreading of silver-fringed *termeh*, a sheet of green brocaded silk, over the rug. Qamar herself had embroidered the termeh with paisleys, representing cypresses, the tree of life. Qamar had then placed other items on the termeh, each representing something

essential for marital bliss. The silver mirror and the two candelabras—
sent by the bridegroom the day before—symbolized light. The saffron
and cinnamon-adorned flatbread next to the mirror embodied
abundance; the tray of herbs and incense beside it warded off evil eyes,
and the plates of baklava and *noql,* almond candy, signified sweetness.
The Quran was left open to an auspicious page covered with rose petals,
conveying Allah's blessing.

The day before, when the porters who had brought the mirror and
the candelabras had taken her modest trousseau, tar, and books to her
marital home, Gohar had cried.

Qamar's last addition to the arrangement was a basket of eggs. "For
fertility," Qamar had said. She then explained what happened between
a husband and wife and what was expected of Gohar on her wedding
night. "Remember, " she had said. "The only pleasure for women is in
bearing children. Nothing more."

Dread gnawed on Gohar's heart. Even her best efforts to please her
husband would come to naught if she couldn't bear a child, preferably
a boy. Was this marriage a blessing or a punishment for her insolence in
seeking the friendship of a boy?

For a fleeting moment, she contemplated sliding down the wall and
disappearing into the desert. She could see the world, meet her heroes,
and make her mark. But how could she? She was indebted to Qamar,
who had raised her, and to Saleh Mirza, who had bestowed his noble
name on her without even knowing her. She would not betray them.

The salutation to the Prophet from the alley heralded the arrival
of the mullah. It was time to face her future. She clutched her charm,
glanced at the setting sun, and recited a silent prayer. She would do her
duty and honor her family.

The guests gasped when Gohar entered the room in the long silk Farangi
dress Noor had sent. Qamar loudly praised the Lord. From under her
veil, Gohar scanned the room. Qamar's daughters, her daughters-in-
law, and her friends chatted on one side while Haji's mother, Khanum

Bozorg, his sour-faced daughter-in-law; his older sister; and a frowning woman Gohar didn't know, sat silently on the other. The sour-faced woman must be Haji's spinster youngest sister. Her hooded eyes and downturned mouth made her look older than her sister.

Gohar sat on a cushion facing the mirror, her eyes glued to the intricately patterned henna on her hands. Qamar's daughter rubbed two sugar cones together over a white cloth held over her head to bring sweetness to the marriage. Men rumbled in the adjacent room, where Haji, the mullah, her tutor, Amoo Ali, and the two witnesses—the governor for her and a Bakhtiari chieftain for Haji—had gathered.

The air was heavy with the scent of rose water and incense. A breeze wafted through the open door, cooling her face. Her reflection in the mirror startled her. With her eyes lined with kohl and a dash of Farangi rouge on her cheeks, she looked as dazzling as the princess. She smiled.

The mullah's voice silenced the chatter. He rattled off a list of items the bridegroom had pledged to her—all to be duly recorded in the contract and acknowledged by the witnesses. A Quran, a silver mirror, two candelabras, a diamond ring and matching necklace, and a *mehrieh* of ten thousand gold English coins. Murmurs rippled through the room. The mehrieh must be substantial, she surmised. It didn't matter. While on paper, mehrieh was payable on demand upon the consummation of the marriage, in practice, it was only paid when the husband died or initiated a divorce.

The mullah asked Gohar for her permission to marry her. She waited for him to ask three times before answering, barely audibly. Women ululated. Qamar wiped away more tears.

A lull prevailed as Haji and the witnesses signed the contract in the next room. Then Haji entered, and women ululated. Gohar scrutinized him from the corner of her eye without turning her head. Short and stout, with a protruded paunch, he wore a long, ornate coat and white turban. His round, wrinkled face, and henna-dyed beard didn't make her heart skip a beat, but they didn't repulse her either.

He sat beside her, lifted her veil, and raised her chin with a hennaed finger. His eyes—small, dark, and surrounded by creases—were kind. She smiled timidly. He put candy in her mouth. Her hands trembled as she reciprocated. Women threw *noql* and rose petals over them.

A female photographer took pictures, documenting the union of Gohar at fourteen with the most prominent citizen of the noble city, forty years her senior. He was rich, good-natured, and a member of a powerful tribe, but he was no Prince Charming.

6

November 1909, Gurdan

Two weeks into her marriage, Gohar received her first visitor: her husband's wetnurse. Longing for company, she warmly welcomed the crotchety old woman.

Haji had been kind, albeit restrained, even in private. He had taught her backgammon, shared his prayer books and religious texts with her, and honored his promise to Qamar to let Gohar play tar despite his aversion to music on religious grounds. His only condition was that the music should not reach his mother's ear. Gohar's mercifully quick and intermittent conjugal duties were limited to the period between the morning prayer and sunrise, so Haji could purify himself with a ritual rinse without taking time off business.

But during the day, he received visitors in *birooni,* the public part of the walled compound, while Khanum Bozorg supervised the army of domestics who cooked, cleaned, and served. Since Gohar's sister-in-law, Belqais, had shown nothing but contempt for her, Gohar had no one to talk to. Belqais was tall and big-boned, with a once-handsome face now hardened and a corrosive tongue that tormented friends and foes alike.

With nothing to do and barred from leaving the house alone, Gohar roamed the compound, at least the part of it open to her: the *andarooni,* the women's quarter. Ruled over by Khanum Bozorg, no males over seven, except for blood relatives, were allowed here.

The austerity of the andarooni in such a wealthy household puzzled Gohar. The rooms were whitewashed and bare, even in the areas where the family gathered, and Khanum Bozorg held prayer sessions. No trees or flowers adorned the tiled courtyard, and the basin at its center was empty.

When Gohar asked the wetnurse about it, she cackled. "You should have seen it when Haji's grandfather, Aqa Bozorg, was alive, *Khanum kuchek*," she said, addressing Gohar as the "little lady." "He had scenes of drinking, hunting, and dancing painted on the walls and flowers everywhere." She extended her arms. "This room was his. His wives and slave girls—all twenty-five of them—lived in the little rooms. His eunuch fetched one each night."

Gohar gasped, picturing women lined up for their nightly duty and sent back when they were done with. "What happened?" she asked.

The shrew pulled up her starched scarf. "When your mother-in-law took over the household, she had the walls whitewashed on account of the Quran forbidding the painting of people, especially the kind Aqa Bozorg had in those rooms."

"And the women?" Gohar asked.

"Your mother-in-law sent them packing."

Gohar felt a pang in her heart, picturing Khanum Bozorg with a club in hand, chasing away women with bundles on their backs and children in tow. She pushed the plate of cookies toward the old hag. "Please, take another cookie, Naneh dear."

The wetnurse took a stack of cookies. "Good thing, too. With Haji's father passing so young, there were bound to be disputes with the offspring of those women and claims to the estate. But she was fair, paid the wives their mehrieh, gave their daughters a dowry, and freed the slaves."

Perhaps noticing how Gohar had paled, she added hastily. "But you needn't worry, Khanum kuchek. Haji was never interested in multiple wives. Not even after his first wife—God bless her soul—passed. If— God willing—you give him a son, you'd live in the big wing for the rest of your life." She pointed to Haji's mother's quarters.

Haji was not sentimental. He never recited a poem unless it carried a moral lesson and didn't express any feelings except for hunger. His fidelity to his dead wife touched Gohar. "Tell me about Haji's first wife," she said.

"What's to tell?" the woman said. "We are born to die."

"What did she die of?"

"A fever. Three days and poof. She was gone, taking her newborn twin sons." She sighed. "Evil eye, if you ask me. Will of God, if you ask Khanum Bozorg."

Gohar closed her eyes. Khanum Bozorg's God was cruel indeed.

Later that morning, Haji arrived with a large, cloth-wrapped bundle. "Come see," he said, preening and placing the package on the windowsill. As he took the cover off, he grinned. "The singing birds I ordered for you."

Gohar squatted by the cage. Two birds perched on a bar, each small enough to fit in her hand. They had orange breasts, yellow throats, and yellowish rings around their eyes. The edges of their green feathers were orange, red, and black. They looked fantastical.

Haji pointed to the paler of the two. "That one is the female."

Gohar held her finger out for the female bird to sit on and caressed its feathers, feeling its heart racing. "They are lovely," she said, keeping her eyes on the creatures. "Where are they from?"

"China. Wait till you hear them sing."

She pictured the pair nesting in a faraway forest filled with exotic flowers. They would brighten her dull room and remind her of the lands she still hoped to see someday.

He continued. "Something to keep you company when I am gone."

Her heart sank. She knew Haji had to be present in Tehran for the opening of the Majles. Still, the imminence of his departure disturbed her. She dreaded being alone with Khanum Bozorg and Belqais. "You are leaving?" she said, barely getting the words out.

"Yes, next week. I must be in Tehran in three weeks, and it takes at least two to get there." He held her shoulders. "Believe me, nothing gives me more pleasure than being here with you. But I have obligations to this city and my family."

Gohar recalled the daily barrage of visitors to the *birooni*. Farmers pleaded for funds to repair irrigation canals. Merchants argued for soldiers to secure roads. Neighbors complained about the erratic mail service. Haji had to fight for their needs in the Majles. But his absence left her under the thumb of her in-laws. "Take me with you," she said, a lump forming in her throat. "Please."

"How can I?" he snapped. "I have to work and can't be with you day and night. And leaving a young woman without supervision in a wretched city like Tehran is akin to setting fire to straw. You don't know what's going on there. It's utter madness."

She burst into tears. Even if she managed to placate her mother-in-law, how could she deal with Belqais?

He offered her a rumpled handkerchief. "We all need to make sacrifices for our country," he sidled up to her. "Qamar is due back any day. I will ask my mother to let her stay with you."

She dabbed her eyes with the coarse cloth and cleaned her nose. "Perhaps in your absence, my tutor can help me with the Arabic phrases in the books you brought me." She had excused her lack of interest in Haji's books with her ignorance of the preponderance of Arabic phrases in them.

"Out of the question. What would people say if a strange man visited my wife in my absence?"

She stared at him in disbelief. "But he is old. He could be my grandfather."

"A man is a man, no matter how old. Besides, I despise the old fool. He is a heathen, known to support those infidels, the Demokraats."

Her tutor was secular, but he never disrespected Islam. "Who are the Demokraats?"

He spat on the ground. "A bunch of fake Farangis in the Majles. They want to replace Sharia with manufactured laws." He frowned, wagging his finger at her. "I do not want to hear any mention of this tutor, ever. Understood?"

She nodded, gazing at the fading traces of henna on her hand.

The noon call to prayer poured from the local mosque.

"It's not the end of the world, my dear." He softened. "Before you know it, I'll be back for Nowruz."

"But Nowruz is four months away, and then you will go back to Tehran again."

"Yes, but God is merciful. Maybe Tehran will be calm by then, and I can take you." He paused. "If you don't like the books I gave you, ask the manservant to buy new ones."

That was a consolation. "Will you write to me?" she muttered. "I want to hear about your work and the Majles."

"I'll write every week. But not to discuss the Majles. Women should not be exposed to politics. Civic discourse ruins marriage." He leaned on his knees to rise. "Now, my dear, it is time for lunch."

She stared at him. "Aren't you going to pray first?"

He smiled and extended his hand to help her rise. "That can wait. I'm famished."

Suddenly, the birds burst into song. Their sound lifted her spirits. In Haji's absence, her tar and the birds would keep her company, the birds singing as she played. She would join her in-laws only for meals and keep her mouth shut.

And this afternoon, while Haji and his mother napped, she would slip to the cellar to mingle with the maids. They were warm-hearted and quick to share juicy tidbits, mostly about Belqais and her spinsterhood, which persisted despite her substantial dowry and family connections. Some claimed Belqais had a deformity that made the consumption of marriage impossible. Others mentioned a betrothed who had left her for a Farangi or a rival clan member who had deflowered her to shame the family.

She followed Haji three steps behind, anticipating new gossip in the afternoon.

7

June 1910, Gurdan

Gohar placed her book on the carpet by her bed and reached for her water bowl. Her lips were parched. The room was sweltering despite the open floor-length windows. The Chinese birds perched silent and still on the bar in their gilded cage. She didn't recall summers being so unbearable. It must be the life growing under her heart that made her so sensitive to heat, the smell of frying onions, the sound of chewing, and the touch of coarse cloth. Perhaps it was a blessing that Haji was away. His scent was bound to sicken her.

She smiled, rubbing her belly. Having a child of her own would make the suffering worth it. In her mind, she could already touch the baby's soft cheek, smell her sweet breath, and hear her sonorous laugh. Had her mother felt her own presence so strongly? Was she the one who had named her *Gohar*: the jewel, the essence?

Her daughter—surely, it was a daughter—would be named Nik Banu, after the princess Kavous had told her about who had thrown herself off a cliff to avoid capture by the invaders.

The bowl was empty, but she didn't want to call the servants. They had been working since dawn and deserved a midday break. There was water in the cellar, where her in-laws napped. But she could not stomach Belqais's snide remarks or Khanum Bozorg's disapproval of her sheer dress, even in the absence of any males. She kept away from them as much as possible. If it weren't for her constant sickness and Qamar's insistence, she would have kept even her pregnancy secret from them.

Nevertheless, the news had delighted the household. Incense had been burned, the poor fed, and prayers of gratitude offered. Even Belqais had become less abrasive.

She yawned. A nightmare had kept her awake the night before. In her dream, a slender, pale girl with green eyes, her auburn hair braided with golden threads, rode toward a mountain amidst a storm, laughing imperviously at Gohar's pleas to return. She had woken up in a cold sweat. Though Qamar had chuckled when she heard of the nightmare and advised Gohar to ease off on the pickled eggplants, she had also burned incense and gone to the neighborhood shrine to light a candle and pray for the child's safety.

Gohar tried to focus on the book, a translated French adventure novel, *The Three Musketeers*. Haji had brought it when he visited Gurdan for Nowruz.

His pledge to send for her rang hollower with each letter he sent. He complained of the difficulty of running a business while representing their city in the Majles and the preponderance of crimes in Tehran. But she no longer cared. Soon, her daughter would keep her company, listening to Gohar recounting the stories Qamar had told her.

She licked her dry lips. It dawned on her that she could fetch water from the tap to the water tank. It was cool down there, too—maybe she could rest there for a while. She put the book back on the carpet.

The clay tiles scalded her bare feet as soon as she entered the empty courtyard. The air scorched her lungs, and a hot wind burned her cheeks and stirred the dry leaves. On the roof, sheets hung to dry flapped. A cat stretched in the tiny patch of shade along the wall, which a lizard climbed. The barren flowerbeds dismayed her. She must ask the gardener to plant flowers before her daughter was born.

A shaft of light illuminated the steep stone stairs to the tap on the water tank. She pressed her hands against both walls as she descended. At the bottom, she sat on the stone platform, washed her face and feet, and drank before leaning back and dozing off.

A loud noise woke her. It was dark. Was it night already? It couldn't be— if she'd been gone that long, someone would have noticed her absence and come to find her. She looked up. The entrance was blocked. For a moment, she imagined a servant coming down to fetch water, but whoever was up there didn't move.

Suddenly, she noticed two blazing eyes staring at her from the top of the stairs. Her heart raced. Was it the baby-eating Djinn who chased pregnant women to snatch their unborn children? Was it a hairy *deev* with sharp horns?

She screamed. The echo of her shout in the stony chamber rattled her. Her heart pounded. She had to get out. But there was only one way—up, toward the blazing eyes. She darted up the slick staircase.

Halfway up, her foot lost its hold. She grasped the wall, but there was nothing to grab onto. Her hands flailed as she tumbled backward. The edge of the stairs punched her ribs. Her head hit something hard. She felt a searing pain, then came blackness.

When she came to, her body ached. Her dress was wet. She was lying on her back. A man with his back to the light bent over her. She couldn't make out his face.

"Don't be scared. I won't hurt you," he said in accented Farsi.

His voice was reassuring. She tried to get up, but pain pinned her down.

"Don't move," he continued. "I will carry you upstairs. Can you hold on to my neck?"

She nodded. He lifted her with his arms under her knees and back. A sudden, sharp stab in her groin made her wince. He held her closer. His smell didn't repulse her.

Halfway up, he stooped to avoid the ceiling, and a ray of light illuminated his face. Gohar gasped. He was the most handsome creature she had ever seen. His chiseled face, straight nose, full mouth, trimmed sandy-brown mustache, and beard reminded her of the princes in Qamar's stories.

Their eyes met. His were blue, the color of the sky and minarets. She had never seen blue eyes before. They looked unreal. She closed her eyes and passed out.

It was dark when she opened her eyes again. She lay on the floor of her room, surrounded by muffled voices. One sounded like Qamar's. Someone raised her head to pour water into her dry mouth. The dampness on her lips was invigorating. Then, the darkness claimed her again.

In her dream, a monster with blazing eyes chased her through endless deserts and countless swamps under a moonless night sky. The air was so thick that it hurt to breathe. Scorpions crawled up her legs. Snakes tangled at her ankles. A young man with piercing blue eyes carried her to safety.

Drifting in and out of consciousness, she lost her sense of time and place. Sometimes, the pain woke her. Sometimes, water wet her lips. Everything was blurred. Nothing made sense. Once, she saw a shadow resembling Belqais smoking a cigarette by her bed.

Finally, one morning, she opened her eyes and could see clearly. A cool breeze caressed her cheeks. Her head was bandaged. She was not in pain. Across the room, Qamar fingered her rosary. When she saw Gohar awake, she cried joyfully and praised the multitude of imams.

"We were all so worried, dear," Qamar said, helping Gohar drink sweetened tea. "You have been out a whole week. The governor sent his physician to look after you. I didn't leave your bedside until Belqais Khanum, God bless her heart, volunteered to watch over you."

"Belqais?" Gohar muttered.

"To be honest, I was a bit cagey. I know she hasn't been kind to you. But I had no choice. I couldn't keep my eyes open, and your mother-in-law needed someone to look after *her*."

Qamar smoothed Gohar's hair. "You lost the baby, dear." She paused. "But we must be thankful. The doctor said the way you hit your head, it is a miracle you are alive and on the mend. It must've been Fatimah herself who grabbed you on the stairs and kept you safe."

Gohar touched her belly. Startled by its flatness, she howled.

Later, as Qamar propped her up with cushions, Gohar probed her. "Who blocked the entrance to the water tank?"

"I don't know, dear," Qamar said. "I wasn't there. When I arrived, you were comatose, and Belqais Khanum was in your room with the doctor. She told me she had heard you scream and found you by the tap."

"You don't think someone in this house would have tried to scare me?"

"Of course not," Qamar said firmly. "Whatever it was, there's nothing to be afraid of anymore. I already got you a talisman to keep the Djinn away, and the servants keep the doors locked—" she stopped midsentence. "Speaking of talismans, where is your gold charm?"

She touched her neck where the charm her mother had left her always lay. "I don't know," she said dispassionately. How could she care about a gold pendant when she had lost her most precious possession, her child?

As her body healed, Gohar's soul remained tormented. The emptiness underneath her heart pained her. Regret gnawed at her. If only she hadn't ventured out that afternoon. If only she had called a servant instead.

She drifted through life as if in a trance. Sequestered in her room, she often remained in bed all day, looking at the blank wall. She stopped crying. Shedding tears felt out of place without a funeral, a grave, prayers for the dead, or the rituals performed on the third and seventh nights of burials.

Qamar pleaded with the doctor for anything that might revive Gohar, but he had nothing to offer. The saints proved equally helpless. It touched Gohar deeply when Qamar brought her the tar, but even the instrument couldn't bring her solace. Haji sent her a long telegram. He understood her loss. He had lost children and a wife. But what had happened was God's will. He would return for Nowruz. The telegram left Gohar cold. What did he know of a mother's empty arms? And

Nowruz was months away.

Well-wishers chafed her. When Khanum Bozorg arranged for a prayer session in gratitude for Gohar's deliverance, she feigned a fever and didn't attend. The commonness of her loss did not diminish its pain; others' misery did not lessen her burden, and the other children she might bear were just that: other children. Children weren't cups to be replaced by another when they broke.

Only in her dreams could she stroll by daisy-filled flowerbeds, hand in hand with Nik Banu, laughing as the wind entangled their identical auburn hair. Her daughter was gone, leaving an unbearable nothingness in her place. She envied Haji's first wife, who had died along with her sons.

Lost in her pain, it was weeks before she remembered the man with blue eyes. "Who was the handsome young man with the accent who carried me to my room?" she asked Qamar one afternoon.

Qamar looked at her askance. "Gohar, dear, what would a young man be doing in the *birooni* in the middle of the afternoon? It must have been an Imam."

"He had blue eyes, Naneh. I have never heard of a blue-eyed Imam."

"Many Imams had Byzantine mothers and blue eyes. But come to think of it, if he were as good-looking as you say, he must have been an angel. Everyone knows angels have blue eyes. Did you say he had an accent?"

"I did."

"That settles it," Qamar said matter-of-factly. "The angels speak Arabic. They are not men or women. But they do grow a beard out of respect for the Prophet."

Since she had never seen or heard an angel—or an Arab, for that matter—Gohar took Qamar's word for it. It was better than the alternative—for if he wasn't a saint or an angel, he must be a figment of her imagination. And nothing—not even being a harlot—was more shameful than being a lunatic.

A few days later, she encountered a servant mending a sheet ripped when the wind knocked it down. Suddenly, it dawned on her that the sun shining through the holes in the torn sheet could resemble the eyes of a demon. Her chest tightened. Her knees buckled. She grabbed the wall to keep steady. The thought of an illusion causing the death of her child was unbearable.

8

October 1910

As summer turned to fall, Gohar remained restless. Her mother-in-law's judgmental God jarred her. She found refuge in Qamar's spiritual faith, with its myriad of saints who protected and comforted her. When the family left to spend the summer in the cool tribal highlands, she remained in Gurdan. Qamar entertained her with stories of her time in Tehran and its attractions: the tree-lined streets, amply supplied shops, and the smoky, horseless machine that took pilgrims to nearby Shah-Abdolazim and Bibi-Shahr Banu.

Gohar longed for her tutor's company and Kavous's letters filled with accounts of Gabr villages and shrines to martyred princesses. The memory of the young man with blue eyes brought her rare solace. She wanted him to be real, to come back to hold her and ease the pain in her soul. But she never mentioned him to anyone. He was an illusion. Even talking about him would make her the subject of ridicule, an embarrassment for the family.

One day, as Qamar gasped in bewilderment, Gohar freed the Chinese birds. They disappeared over the tall walls. Gohar longed to follow them. Nothing kept her in Gurdan. But where would she go, and how?

The "where" part was easy: Tehran. Where magical lights lit the streets, hundreds of newspapers were published weekly, and the twentieth century had already arrived. But how? Haji had already refused to take her.

Noor's invitation to visit her and Saleh Mirza provided the answer. What better excuse to make the journey than to meet her adopted family?

That night, she wrote to Haji. In the letter, much longer than her usual short notes to him, she begged for permission to travel to express her thanks to Noor in person. Three weeks later, he arrived with a bundle of gifts. He had left as soon as he had received her letter. Impervious to his gifts, she implored him to take her to the capital.

Visibly shaken by her pallid appearance, Haji fingered his worry beads. "Gohar, dear, I know travel can help recover from a loss. But the trip to Tehran is arduous, and you are so fragile."

"I am well enough," she said.

"The capital is dangerous," he said. "Only a few weeks ago, the armed militia killed a Majles deputy over a verbal disagreement."

"If Tehran is safe enough for you, it is safe enough for me."

Khanum Bozorg, visiting them in their wing, interjected. "My dear, Haji's household in Tehran is small. You won't be comfortable there. Plus, you don't know the first thing about running a household." She paused. "Why don't you spend some time in nature, perhaps in one of our villages?"

Gohar panicked. What if she was sent to a village instead of Tehran?

"No," she yelped without meaning to, oblivious to Qamar's pleading eyes. "I want to be with my family," she added hastily.

Haji and his mother gaped at her with open mouths.

It was Belqais who resolved the matter. "Mohsen, dear," she addressed her brother. "Why don't you ask our Bakhtiari relatives to arrange the trip? Saleh Mirza is the man of the hour, and our cousins are expert weathervanes. They will jump at the opportunity to be of service to him." She turned to her mother. "Don't worry about the household. Saleh Mirza and Noor will help Gohar settle. It is their responsibility, and it is their fault that Gohar is so useless. Besides, Qamar knows her way around the capital and never leaves Gohar's side when Gohar needs her." She paused. "If three hundred and fifty thousand souls can live safely in Tehran, so can Gohar."

As they prepared to leave, Qamar urged Gohar to call on Belqais to show her gratitude—and to seek forgiveness, as was customary before a long journey. Gohar relented: there was no harm in showing respect. And perhaps Belqais could shed some light on the mystery blue-eyed man.

Belqais was practicing calligraphy in her room when Gohar entered. She motioned to Gohar to sit opposite her at the table. Wordlessly, Gohar observed her dip the pen in the ink, clean the extra ink off the nib, and write without paying attention to Gohar.

"Your penmanship is exquisite," Gohar said after a while.

"This was my father's hobby. I never knew him, though. I was a baby when he died."

Gohar refrained from mentioning the loss of her own parents in infancy. "I wanted to thank you for taking care of me and for convincing Haji to allow me to travel to Tehran."

Belqais put the pen aside and lifted her face. "No need to thank me. Whatever I did was for my foolish brother. To me, you are what you have always been: immature and insolent." She leaned back and continued in a softer tone. "I am sorry about the baby. I know you'd been daydreaming about it and took the loss badly. But this world is full of pain, and life has a way of shattering dreams. You are not the first woman to lose a child and not the first person to suffer a loss you can't mourn."

Gohar felt chided. But the tinge of sadness in Belqais's voice confused her. Was this her sister-in-law's perverse way of sharing her own sorrow? Belqais picked up the pen and resumed writing. Gohar left without mentioning the man with blue eyes.

If any group could get Gohar to Tehran safely through the bandit-infested treacherous terrain, it was the Bakhtiari. The tribe dominated central Iran, their power stemming from a large force of highly trained and well-equipped fighting men. The Iranian central government, lacking a modern standing army, always relied on tribal forces, especially the Bakhtiari, for assistance in times of trouble, and they had played a central role in restoring the Constitution. The discovery of oil in their territory the year before had significantly increased Bakhtiari's wealth and clout. They had secured the oil wells, pipelines, and under-construction refinery in Abadan for the British. In return, they received five percent of the profits of the Anglo-Iranian Oil Company—the monopoly that explored for and extracted oil in southern Iran.

But the Bakhtiari were loyal only to their khans. After joining the constitutionalists the summer before, they promptly disarmed all other militia in Tehran, took over many ministries, and filled the bureaucratic ranks with tribe members. By now, the Bakhtiari were a state within the state.

In late fall, Haji—whose mother and brother-in-law were Bakhtiari—asked them to arrange for Gohar's travel to Tehran. As Belqais had predicted, they embarked on the venture with enthusiasm. On the last leg of the trip, they even provided Gohar with a rare luxury: a car.

Qamar scoffed that the gesture was more to show off their connection to the English than out of concern for their comfort. Gohar agreed. Nevertheless, she was grateful for the miraculous vehicle with its soft leather interior, which replaced the donkeys and carriages they had taken for the previous two weeks. In the capable hands of their Indian driver, they sped through uneven terrain. But the speed unsettled her stomach and pained her body. When they reached the flat terrain surrounding the capital, the car fell into a smoother motion that lulled her to sleep.

When she opened her eyes, she saw a majestic mountain capped with snow rising in front of the car, its peak golden in the last ray of sun. Mount Damavand, she thought with a jolt of excitement. Nestled at its base, Tehran awaited her.

9

January 1911, Tehran

The capital welcomed Gohar with a parade of trees, their red and yellow leaves glistening under the lush autumn rain.

Haji's unassuming house was on an unpaved alley in a modest neighborhood teeming with Gurdan natives. The alley—dusty in the summer, muddy in the fall, and knee-deep in snow in the winter—had a trench that delivered water and drained rain and waste.

Haji and Gohar's bedroom and the living room, where Qamar slept, were at the back of the house, facing a tiny yard with a blue-tiled basin and no trees. Crooked steps led from the yard to the cellar, where the maid slept beside the kitchen. In the front, a narrow hallway separated the tiled formal sitting room with its marble shelf for kerosine lamps from the chamber occupied by Haji's manservant, Mash Qolam. A curtain isolated the front of the house from its back.

Haji could easily have afforded something grander in a more fashionable location. But he was leery of attracting the attention of unscrupulous characters in a city rife with them and where political rivalries often turned into bloody skirmishes. The house pleased Gohar, who cherished being away from Khanum Bozorg but lacked the skills to manage a large home. And the location delighted Qamar, who loved socializing but was wary of strangers.

From the minute she arrived, Gohar yearned to meet her adoptive parents. But it wasn't until a month later that Haji decided to take her to visit them. The news both pleased and concerned her. Ignorant of the etiquette required around aristocracy, she feared coming across as crude. Barraged with questions on the proper protocol, Qamar finally ended the debate: "Ask them, dear," she said, then, noticing Gohar's baffled look, added, "They are not like your in-laws or Haji. They are modern people."

On the Friday they were to visit her parents, Haji left before noon to lead the prayer at the local mosque as usual. Gohar tried on multiple outfits before settling on one that Noor had sent and a gold-trimmed, dark-blue silk chador to wear over it. After lunch, Haji shed his traditional woolen robe, *qaba*, and white kaftan for a three-piece suit and a brimless felt hat to accompany Gohar and Qamar in a droshky to Saleh Mirza's house.

Moving north in the wide, tree-lined Nasseryeh Avenue, Gohar gawked at the shops, each much larger than the alcoves in Gurdan's bazaar, and imagined the exotic goods inside. The enormous dome of Tekyeh Dowlat peeked from behind the five-story-tall, exquisitely tiled entrance to the royal complex, Shams-ol-Emareh.

Even more impressive than the sights were the people. Men in *qaba* walked alongside urbanites in *sardari*—a knee-length, front-buttoned jacket with trousers—turbaned clergy mixed with tribal men in ethnic garb and headgear. Men in suits rode in droshkies or on horseback. A handful of covered women followed their menfolk like ducklings. Some hid their faces under gauzy veils; others covered their mouths and chins with the sides of their chadors. A few wore fashionable belted chadors. Qamar derided those donning the voluminous black pants as old-fashioned.

"Don't gape at people like a villager." Haji scowled.

Gohar ignored him.

Qamar pointed to an alley north of the royal complex. "That is Dar Andaroon, the entrance to the harem."

"Not anymore," Haji said. "The royal harem was decommissioned after the constitution."

Qamar rolled her eyes.

Gohar bit her lip. Since their arrival in Tehran, tensions between Qamar and Haji had been rising. She could see that Qamar was irked by Haji's bossing around and deliberate delays to their visit to Saleh Mirza's house—and while he had no power over Qamar, he could spur her to leave, forcing Gohar to return to Gurdan.

For now, the moment passed, and they reached the end of Nasseryeh: a large square surrounded by identical three-story buildings. Tramlines intersected in its middle.

"This is Toopkhaneh," Haji pointed to six ornate archways, each leading to a broad, tree-lined avenue. "Those go to the grand bazaar, the royal palaces and the ministries, the Majles, the foreign legations, the citadel, and the electric plant."

These were all centers of power in the city. The square was the undisputed heart of the capital.

A white complex dominating the square's east side grabbed Gohar's attention. A dark blue flag with red crosses flew above it.

Haji noticed her gaze. "That is the Imperial Bank of Persia."

"But what is that flag in front?"

"The British flag," he said. "The English own the bank,"

But how could foreigners own "the Imperial Bank of Persia"? She wanted to ask but felt embarrassed to. Her eyes drifted to the rusting cannons in the square, bounties of long-ago military victories.

"That is Pearl Cannon," Qamar said. "When I came to Tehran with Noor to nurse the princess, we used to sneak out to tie a piece of cloth to it and make a wish."

Haji rolled his eyes.

North of Toopkhaneh, the droshky turned into an alley off the wide Ala-O-Dowleh Avenue and stopped at a brown door. This was the entrance to andarooni, the private section of Saleh Mirza's compound. Gohar and Qamar got off, leaving Haji to continue to the birooni, the public side of the house, where a doorman ushered in well-dressed men. A car, much larger than the one that had brought Gohar to Tehran, was parked in the alley.

A maid helped Gohar and Qamar change into house chadors in a hexagonal vestibule before guiding them through a courtyard with an empty, round pool surrounded by boxwood-fringed flowerbeds with burlap-wrapped rosebushes. A short flight of stairs across the yard led to a covered veranda and Noor's reception room entrance.

The scent of jasmine overwhelmed Gohar as soon as she stepped into the sun-filled room. Farangi-style paintings of gardens and a portrait of a dancing girl adorned the walls. Several women sat around on cushions. One of them rose to greet the newcomers. Gohar instantly recognized the slender woman as Noor from her picture. With her smooth skin and a twinkle in her green eyes, Noor looked decades younger than Qamar, who was only a few years older. Gohar stepped forward and bent to kiss Noor's hand.

Noor stopped her halfway and embraced her tightly. "Welcome," she said, motioning for Gohar to sit with her. "Call me Bibi."

Her unexpected kindness and intimacy allayed Gohar's fears and touched her heart.

The room was warm, justifying the lack of a *korsi*, the quilt-covered low table with a brazier underneath that people sat under to warm up. Noor pointed to a black cylinder with a chimney. "We use a Russian wood stove for heating. So much more convenient than a korsi."

After the other guests left, Noor and Qamar took turns reminiscing about their harem days, when Qamar was a lowly wetnurse and Noor a lonely new mother. Gohar silently listened to their stories of intrigues, plots, rivalries, and occasional friendships. Despite its allure, the harem sounded like any other community of women from different walks of life. Noor animatedly recounted how the women's refusal to serve tobacco to the shah had spurred him to rescind the tobacco concession he had given to a Farangi. Her relaxed manner and down-to-earth language surprised Gohar. "Do you miss the palace?" she asked Noor.

"Not for a second," Noor replied. "I'd rather be the sole queen of this house than one of three hundred women seeking the shah's affection. Saleh Mirza is charming and witty, loves me, and has promised not to take another wife. He may be cunning, but his heart is in the right place."

Noor was a lucky woman to love and be loved.

The opulence of the dinner—two stews, yellow split peas and spinach and plum, along with both plain and lentil-laced saffron rice—laid out for just three of them stounded Gohar after hearing that Haji ate with

Saleh Mirza in his study, and the servants had their meal in the kitchen. In her household, everyone shared a single dish in the communal room.

Noticing Noor using a spoon, Qamar commented that the metal would spoil the taste as she shoved food into her mouth with her fingers. The assertion embarrassed Gohar, who, overwhelmed by the prospect of meeting Saleh Mirza, ate sparingly. He was one of the most powerful men in Iran, controlling not only her destiny (married or not) but also the nation's.

After dinner, she followed Noor to the intricately carved doors separating the andarooni from Saleh Mirza's study. Her palms were slick with sweat.

Saleh Mirza stood beside a sizable table at the far end of his large, scantly furnished study, with its tall windows to the formal garden. Despite his medium build and slight pudge, he looked regal in a brown suit complete with a gold pocket watch. A pencil mustache adorned his clean-shaven, handsome face, and curly salt-and-pepper hair peeked from under his skullcap. Haji, hands clasped at his front, stood timidly at his side.

Saleh Mirza motioned for Gohar to approach. Up close, his kind, smiling eyes dispelled her fears. She bent down to kiss his hand. His long fingers did not bear any trace of henna.

Like his wife, he caught her midway and kissed her forehead. "Welcome home," he said. His voice was gentle but authoritative.

Gohar's heart filled with gratitude.

Everyone took a seat at the table except for Qamar, who sat cross-legged on the exquisite Tabriz rug. Noor took a Turkish delight from a wooden box on the table and passed the box to Gohar. "Try the ginger. These are from Haji Bekir, the sultan's confectioner, in Istanbul."

The spicy taste of the delicacy tingled on Gohar's tongue. She watched Saleh Mirza approach a gadget attached to a large trumpet on a small table in the corner and crank it.

"That's a gramophone," Noor explained, noticing Gohar gaping.

Saleh Mirza selected a black disk from a stack and placed it on the gramophone. The sound of tar playing filled the room. Gohar had never heard music played without musicians, nor a tar sounding so heavenly. The notes glided smoothly, fitting together like pearls on a necklace. She closed her eyes and saw the gentle flow of a stream in a forest of poplars swaying in the wind, the dance of fish in a pond. She would give her life to play like that. Soon, a deep male voice evoked the longing of a lost soul. Unconsciously, she hummed along.

"Who taught you to sing like that?" Saleh Mirza said.

She opened her eyes. "No one, Your Excellency," she replied, gazing down. "I taught myself."

"You follow the music like a professional," Saleh Mirza said.

Gohar was emboldened. "I play tar too, Your Excellency," she volunteered, impervious to Haji's darting glances from across the table.

"Amazing," Saleh Mirza said. "And call me Saleh Mirza."

But calling him by his name didn't seem respectful. She had to forge something courteous but intimate, and quick. "May I call you Aqa Mirza?"

"Sure." He smiled mischievously. "I heard you play backgammon too."

"I do, now and then," she said demurely.

He pointed to a mother-of-pearl–inlaid backgammon case on a bookshelf. "Show me."

She beat Haji regularly, but Saleh Mirza was a master. He defeated her twice before she won her first round. Losing, however, did not dampen his mood. He laughed just as heartily as he did after beating both Haji and Noor handily.

Late into the night, Saleh Mirza summoned his private carriage to take them home. As they took their leave, he kissed Gohar's forehead. "Come back the day after tomorrow. I'll have a surprise for you." He winked.

"Saleh Mirza never sends *me* home in his carriage," Haji griped as they passed a flowerpot-filled gallery.

"You are a man, Haj Aqa," Qamar said acerbically, using Haji's honorific name. "You can take care of yourself." She squeezed Gohar's arm as they crossed the torch-lit garden. "They loved you!" she whispered triumphantly.

10

February 1911, Tehran

Paralyzed with fear, Gohar stood at the threshold of the house. One more step, and she would be alone in public for the first time in her life. She wished Qamar were there to accompany her to Saleh Mirza's house. But Amoo Ali's sudden illness had forced Qamar to return to Gurdan, and no one else was around to chaperone Gohar. Haji and Mash Qolam had gone to his *hojreh* in the grand bazaar, and the maid was cooking. If only she had known Qamar would be gone, Gohar would have accepted Saleh Mirza's offer to send his carriage for her.

Not going was not an option. Saleh Mirza had gone to great lengths to convince the foremost master of tar in the country to teach her. He had then overcome Haji's objections to having a man visit his house in his absence and to music emanating from it by arranging for the lessons to be conducted in Saleh Mirza's presence at his mansion.

She smiled, recalling the old master's reaction to her playing. His expression had gone from annoyance to surprise to delight. In the end, he had broken into a toothless grin and declared her talent exceptional—especially for a woman. He would teach her to play music, he had said, tossing back his long white mane. "Not make noise like the *motrebs*."

Working women passed the alley with their shopping baskets. She envied their freedom. But what was holding her back? She was as capable as these women. All she had to do was to walk to the main street and take a droshky. What could happen to her in the daylight with all these people around? No one would attack her. No one would kidnap her.

But what if Haji were to find out? The neighbors might tell him or spread gossip that would reach him. He might beat her, stop her from seeing Noor and Saleh Mirza, send her back to Gurdan to live with his mother, or even divorce her. Women were divorced for lesser crimes than leaving the house alone.

Even stopping her from seeing her adoptive parents would be painful. Since first meeting them a month before, she had spent as much time as possible at their house. Both, especially Saleh Mirza, were warm, passionate, and quick to answer her questions, and their home overflowed with interesting people.

But playing tar as skillfully as the master was tantalizing. Wasn't she willing to give her life to play like the musician she had heard on the gramophone? Artists have always suffered for their art. And as long as the neighbors didn't see her leave, she could tell Haji that Saleh Mirza had sent his carriage to pick her up. With a veil covering her face, no one would recognize her once she was out.

Lying to her husband was a sin. But it was unjust to stop her from learning because no one was available to chaperone her. She stepped forward.

On the surface, the local market seemed normal. Shoppers picked fruit and vegetables from the stalls lining the walls, men lined up to have their beards trimmed and their heads shaved, and women dragged their children to the public baths. But the tension was palpable. The shoppers didn't haggle, men didn't chatter, and women didn't linger. Even the boys conjugating Arabic verbs in the storefront *maktab* sounded agitated.

The news of an attempt on the life of the Isfahan governor had put everyone on edge. The governor had been severely injured. His cousin was dead. But the assailant, a former police official, had fled to the Russian consulate. The Russian meddling in Iran was nothing new, but the killing had rekindled the fear of political unrest in Tehran. She hastened her steps.

A porter with a trunk on his back trudged through the melting snow. By sunset, the alley would freeze and become impassable. It would be prudent to stay overnight at Saleh Mirza's. Without Qamar to keep her company, what was the use of returning to the house, anyway? Haji socialized at the local mosque long after the evening prayer and preferred silence at home. Gohar couldn't even chat with the Turkish-speaking maid: she didn't know a word of Farsi. Dinner with her adoptive parents was lively with banter and stories, and they played cards and listened to Persian, Turkish, and Egyptian records afterward. Before returning home, she could gorge on newspapers and discuss the articles with Saleh Mirza in the morning. She would send a messenger to alert Haji later.

The droshky driver hummed as they made their way through the entangled mess of drays, horses, donkeys, carriages, and pedestrians. *"Tonight, is a full-moon night, and I want my beloved, my healer; Wake her up if she is asleep; Sober her up if she is drunk..."*

Gohar had heard the song before. It was a *tasnif*, a ditty, with a hummable melody and simple lyrics. Everyone in Tehran—from bath attendants to gardeners—seemed to sing similar tasnifs.

Most of the ditties were about love. A love that was neither the mythical courtship of kings and queens nor the vulgar lust of the burlesque. It was earthy, sensual, *and* ennobling. It made the moonlight shimmer, the flowers blossom, and the leaves dance. It made a concealed touch heavenly and a chance encounter euphoric. But it also made the absence of the beloved unbearable, his neglect devastating, and his rejection lethal.

And *this* love, this burning sensation that enchanted and destroyed at once, baffled her. She had never experienced it. It was nothing like her love for Qamar, Noor, or Saleh Mirza, or her fondness for Haji or her Gabr friend, Kavous.

Was she even capable of loving someone like that? At least the music was moving. She wondered what her teacher would think of a song like this.

The driver continued. *"If my beloved is drunk, sober her up, if she is asleep, wake her."* Was he really in love? Or did he sing only to alleviate his boredom?

The droshky's sudden stop jolted her out of her reverie. A crowd was running towards them, filling the street.

The driver shouted to a passerby, "What's happening?"

"They shot the finance minister near Toopkhaneh," the man shouted back, out of breath, "He's dead. The police are searching for the murderers. Two men. Armed."

The driver turned to her. "We have to wait for the mob to pass."

But people were still pouring in. It would be a long while before they could continue. By then, she would be late for her lesson, worrying Noor, who would send someone to Gohar's house, revealing her absence and awakening Haji's ire. There was no choice but to walk back.

She regretted her decision the minute she stepped down. People and animals packed the street, making it impossible to walk in. The sidewalk was no better. Men stood around to see what was happening. She turned to a side alley. It would be easier to move around there.

Once in a quiet alley, she realized she was closer to Saleh Mirza's house than her own. Going there was a better option. She didn't know the neighborhood. But Mount Damavand, visible from everywhere, would be her guidepost.

Deep in the narrow alleyways, however, the sight of Damavand disappeared behind the tall walls. She stopped to ask for directions from a mullah in a brown *qaba* and white turban. But he, like many mullahs hostile to women alone in the street, averted his eyes and hastened his step. She'd have to wait for a woman or until she saw a store.

All the shops in the next market she came to were closed. No hawker was around. Was it lunchtime already? She had yet to hear the call to noon prayer. The thought of being alone in the alleys with assassins nearby jolted her. Unconsciously, she reached for her charm. Its absence disturbed her even more.

Despite the cold, sweat ran down her back. She wrapped the chador tighter around herself. The main street would be safer. She turned around to go back there. But soon, she found herself in the same place she had been before. It was hopeless. Her stomach churned.

She wandered the meandering side alleys, frantically searching for a way towards the main street. With her eyes on her surroundings, she missed a patch of ice, stumbled on it, and twisted her ankle. Pain seared her leg. She grasped the wall for balance. Her delicate slippers were not made for long walks in the winter. A *saqaa-khaneh*, a water dispenser, built into an alcove up ahead caught her eye. She limped towards it.

Candles lit a likeness of Abbas, Imam Hossein's brother and the water-bearer of Karbala, in the tiled back wall of the saqaa-khaneh. The saint's serene eyes comforted her. She drank from the tin water bowl chained to the bars in front, said a prayer, and left some coins for the poor.

The recessed entrance of the house next to the saqaa-khaneh had a deep-set doorway. She descended the stairs, hobbled to the stoop in the back, and sat. Shrouded in shadows here, no one could see her from the alley, but she could observe everything.

As she took off her slippers to rub her frozen feet and toes, screams startled her. "Murderer! Murderer!"

Shortly, a man emerged from the bend of the alley, pursued by a mob. She slid backward and pondered knocking on the door. But without knowing who might answer and how they would react to a strange woman in the chaotic city, it was best to wait here for the mob to pass.

Not far from where she sat, the lead pursuer lunged at the fugitive. Both men rolled to the ground. The pursuer's hat fell, and his sandy-brown hair shone in the sunlight. Then a loud noise echoed in the alley. She covered her mouth to suppress a scream.

The men scuffled for some time as others arrived, including men in the light blue uniforms of the police. Finally, the pursuer overwhelmed the fugitive, sat on his chest, and wrestled what Gohar assumed to be a gun out of his hand. As the police restrained the runaway, the pursuer rose. Astounded, she recognized her angel from Gurdan.

As policemen dragged the fugitive away with his hands bound, a heavyset mustachioed officer approached the stoop. Her heart raced. She pressed herself to the door.

The policeman stopped in front of her atop the stairs. "Get inside," he barked. "This is not a show."

"This is not my house," she mumbled.

"Then what are you doing here? Where are your menfolk?"

"I—I—was on my way home," she stammered. "I—I—I got lost."

A short, thin officer of higher rank approached. "Who is this?" he asked without looking at her.

The first policeman saluted smartly. "I don't know, sir. She says she's lost."

"Arrest her!" the officer snapped. "Be careful. She could be a whore or a thief. Or a rabble-rouser! She may not even be a 'she.' We can't leave her loose in the street. Make sure there's no pistol under her chador, take her to the police station, and send for her menfolk."

Gohar panicked. To be held in police custody with prostitutes, runaways, and criminals would be unbearable. But the police summoning Haji or—God forbid—Saleh Mirza to come for her would be calamitous. This was her punishment for brazenly leaving the house alone. She wished for the earth to open and swallow her whole or a bolt of lightning to strike her dead.

"No, no, please." She burst into tears. "I'm sorry. I promise to go home directly."

The first policeman took a reluctant step forward. "Sir, maybe we should let her go," he said to the officer. "She doesn't look suspicious. I don't see her hiding anything under the chador; no bundles, nothing."

"Do as I say," the officer barked. "It is against the law for women to walk alone in the street."

"But the ban is in effect in the afternoons. I haven't heard the noon prayer.'

The officer's face turned beet red. His nostrils flared. He screamed. "I am the law, idiot. Public morality is in danger."

The policeman shrugged—but before he could move, the soothing, accented voice of her blue-eyed angel stopped him. "We should move on. There is another assassin on the loose. He has already killed five people."

She looked up. Her angel stood between the two policemen, towering over both, resting his hand on the officer's shoulder. Mesmerized, she fought the desire to walk up the stairs and touch him, to make sure he was made of flesh and blood and not ether.

Emboldened by her angel's interference, the first policeman nodded in agreement.

The officer turned to look at the man who had just single-handedly apprehended an armed killer. "Are you sure, Aslan Khan?" he said, with no hint of irony. "She could be trouble."

Aslan nodded without looking at Gohar. The officer stared at her with narrowed eyes. "But you are right, Aslan Khan. We shouldn't waste time on her." He wagged his finger at her. "You are lucky Aslan Khan is here to vouch for you." He turned to leave.

Relieved, she hobbled away under the watchful eyes of the police and neighbors. The first policeman asked one of the children watching the scene to show her the way to the main street. There, she gave a coin to the boy and walked to Saleh Mirza's.

She arrived just as the noon prayer was called. Cold, wet, exhausted, and in pain, she collapsed in the vestibule, smiling triumphantly. The city no longer intimidated her, her angel was a man, and she was on time for her lesson.

11

March 1911, Tehran

The newspapers reported the assassin's capture without naming Aslan. Gohar was relieved. His anonymity would shield him from Russian reprisals. The editorials praised the patriotism of the slain minister and his bold plans to loosen Russia's grip on trade routes to Europe and create an Iranian bank.

The police swiftly apprehended the other killer—but both assassins had to be turned over to the Russians. As Georgians—and thus Russian subjects—they could not be tried in Iran. Their handover spurred public outrage. Gohar wished she could join the demonstrators in front of the Russian legation, but the vigilantes who roughed up known and suspected pro-Russians appalled her.

As Nowruz approached, Haji faced a dilemma. He wanted to spend the holidays in Gurdan but didn't wish to subject Gohar to another long journey or leave her without Qamar in the tumultuous city. For her part, Gohar had no desire to see Khanum Bozorg or Belqais and longed to celebrate the holiday with Noor and Saleh Mirza. Haji pondered, asking Mash Qolam to stay and watch over Gohar, but this solution made Mash Qolam grumble when Haji was not around.

One evening, Gohar made a proposal. "You need to see your family and confer with your constituents," she said to Haji. "And Mash Qolam wants to visit his family. Why don't you let me stay with Noor and Saleh Mirza while you're gone? I can return to the house when you or Qamar return. The maid can watch the house. It's only for two months anyway."

Haji's begrudging consent elated her.

Standing in the doorway to Noor's room, Gohar watched her read. The strands of gray in Noor's hair accentuated its auburn color. Had her mother been as refined and beautiful as Noor?

Noor lifted her head and smiled. "Gohar, dear, is your lesson over?"

"Yes, Bibi."

"You play so well. Come and sit with me. Do you want something to eat?" She pointed to the homemade cookies on a low table.

Gohar sat on her heels. "No, Bibi, thank you."

"Good. It is best not to spoil your appetite. The cook is making your favorite rice with sour cherries and chicken."

The cook's thoughtfulness during the holiday baking season touched Gohar. "That's sweet of him."

"We can go shopping on Lalehzar after siesta."

Gohar's eyes glinted: Lalehzar, the heart of modern Tehran, was home to the most fashionable tailors and boutiques, the best beauty salons, and the finest book and music stores in the country. "I'd like that," she said. "You think the shops will be open?"

"At this time of the year? Of course." Noor showed her the book in her hand. "I was reading my fortune from Hafez's collection. Shall we do yours?"

Gohar didn't want her future foretold by a randomly selected poem from the collection, lest Hafez drop a hint of her daydreaming about Aslan. "No, thank you, Bibi. But if you don't mind, there is something I'd like to know."

Noor squeezed Gohar's knee affectionately. "Of course, dear, what is it?"

Gohar gulped. The question had been on her lips for two weeks—since the start of her stay with Noor and Saleh Mirza—but she had been reluctant to ask. "Do you know where my parents are buried?"

Noor paled. "No. I guess near where they died. Why do you ask?"

"I was thinking of visiting their graves, offering prayers, like everyone else before the new year."

"You don't need to visit their graves to offer prayers, dear."

Noor's pained expression made Gohar regret her question, but now that the subject had been broached, she was reluctant to back off. "Can you tell me anything about them?" she asked.

Noor put the book down. "I didn't know them well. They were distant relatives. My daughter was friends with your mother. But she is gone. It is best to forget them all."

The agony in her voice was palpable. Nevertheless, Gohar persisted. "How about my grandparents?"

"They are all dead, my dear," Noor said, gently clasping Gohar's hand. "We must leave them alone. A typhoid epidemic wiped out your whole family. Thank God you were staying with Qamar. It's the only reason you survived."

This was more than Qamar had ever told her. But she wanted more. "I would give anything to have a memento from them."

Noor averted her eyes. They fell into a long silence broken only by the chiming of the clock in the corner.

"Your father played tar masterfully," Noor said at last. "You have his tar and his talent."

The day before Nowruz, Noor took over the public bathhouse to host her friends. The attendants washed, massaged, threaded the faces, and hennaed the hands and feet of partially nude women. Maids circulated trays of food and drinks. Female motrebs played, and palm readers told fortunes.

Noor asked the beautician to shape Gohar's eyebrows into arches. "You look marvelous," she said, looking at Gohar's face afterward. "Haji will be pleased."

Gohar, Noor, and Saleh Mirza welcomed the new year along with a few loyal servants in the andarooni. They waited for the turning of the year around an elegant arrangement of a mirror, candles, a Qur'an, a tray of sprouted wheat, a plate of bread and salt, a crystal cup of vinegar, garlic, apples, a basket of dyed and painted eggs, gold coins, and large plates of sweets. A pair of goldfish swam in a large Chinese bowl, and the smell of hyacinths filled the room. Once the firing of Pearl Cannon announced the exact moment of vernal Equinox, the New Year, Saleh Mirza embraced Noor and Gohar and gave each a gold coin. Then, the staff, one by one, kissed his hand, received a silver coin, and left. Afterward, the family opened Hafez's collection of poems to a random page so the sage of Shiraz could foretell their fortunes for the new year.

After the ceremony, Noor and Saleh Mirza received well-wishers separately. Gohar sat by Noor as grand ladies arrived with hennaed hair, their ample bosoms squeezing out of too-tight dresses and their cleavages covered with emeralds and rubies. They gossiped, stuffed themselves with sweets and nuts, complained of ungrateful offspring and disloyal servants, and lamented the good old days.

At midday, Noor motioned for Gohar to follow her to a seldom-used storage room. Inside, they ascended a set of narrow steps in the back, partially hidden behind piles of out-of-season clothing, to reach an area large enough for the two of them to sit side by side. Three narrow slits on the sides of the space opened to the reception room, Saleh Mirza's study, and the gallery in between the two. Gohar had heard of similar rooms in palaces used for eavesdropping—especially by women—or by gunmen to protect the nobility from assassins, but she had never seen one.

"Let's see who's here today," Noor said, smiling with a twinkle in her eyes.

In the study, Saleh Mirza sat on his armchair wearing an ornate robe and a brimless hat as his valet ushered people in to kiss his hand, wish him a prosperous new year, and receive a silver coin. A few were invited to sit next to him for a short conversation. The line of men extended to the gallery.

"The man sitting next to Saleh is the German minister," Noor whispered, pointing to a heavyset blond man with a walrus mustache. "Next to him is the English legation's political officer."

Gohar glanced at a cherubic-faced young man in a funny hat.

Noor gestured to a man in a black *qaba* standing in line. "That one is a merchant. Rich as Solomon, stingy as a mouse. Behind him is a French-educated doctor, married to a French woman, but in love with that one." She tittered, gesturing to a handsome young man standing further back, talking to someone else.

Wide-eyed, Gohar listened to Noor describe each and every visitor. These were the city's movers and shakers—politicians, landowners, doctors, writers, editors, major merchants, clergy . . . —and Noor knew each of their peculiarities: sexual preferences, illicit affairs, and affiliations to societies secret or overt.

"I didn't realize so many notables came to pay their respects to Aqa Mirza," Gohar whispered, impressed as much by Noor's knowledge of these men as by Saleh Mirza's status.

"He is the kingmaker. With his bloodline, he could have been the shah, or at least the regent. He's the only one who knows how to keep everyone in their places, Farangis included. A lot of people begged him to take over." Noor sighed. "But he deems the times perilous and himself too old to deal with it."

Gohar had never thought of Saleh Mirza as old.

Noor continued dreamily. "He is sixty years old. He wants us to spend the little time left to him in peace, away from all the nonsense." Her voice trailed off. "But the country needs him."

The merchant slid into his place as soon as the German minister left. But he rose hastily when the valet escorted in a broad-shouldered, bald man of medium height. The man's ramrod stance hinted at a military background. The newcomer took the vacated seat without hesitation.

"Who is he?" Gohar asked, taking in the man's round face, pointed beard, and dark eyes.

"The devil incarnate," Noor replied, spitting on the ground. "Konstantin Smirnsky, the shah's former tutor."

Gohar recalled her tutor's comment in Gurdan. "Is it true that he is a spy?"

"Saleh believes so."

"But he isn't teaching the shah anymore, is he?"

"No. The regent fired him. The Russians offered to send two thousand of their soldiers away if he was allowed to stay. But the regent—God bless his soul—refused."

"What is he doing in Tehran?"

"He is part of the Russian legation. Saleh thinks he is a spy."

"Did the merchant leave because of him?"

"Most likely. Smirnsky knows where the skeletons are buried. And he is known to cause trouble for anyone who gets in his way."

As she scanned the reception room, Gohar noticed a man with sandy-brown hair, deep in discussion with a clergyman. She held her breath. Could that be her angel, the mysterious Aslan? She longed for him to look up—so that she could see his face. Then, as though the heavens were listening, the valet approached, and the man with sandy hair lifted his gaze.

"Aslan," she mouthed with her eyes glued on him.

Noor turned sharply and followed Gohar's gaze. "You know him?" she said.

Gohar cursed her carelessness. "Of course not."

Noor stared at her skeptically. "But you just said his name."

"Oh no," Gohar collected herself. "I–I was saying *Asali* because his hair is the color of *Asal*, honey." She paused. "But he looks familiar."

"You must've seen him entering the birooni. His name is Aslan Madadoff. He helps Saleh with his memoir."

Aslan rose, tall and striking in a tailored black sardari, to follow the valet.

"Is that all he does?" Gohar asked.

"No one knows. There are rumors that he's an adventurer or a spy. I've even heard that he smuggles guns. Saleh doesn't believe any of it. He loves Aslan, thinks he walks on water."

"Where's he from?"

"His name, assuming it is real, is Caucasian. But his Azeri Turkish is abysmal, and he speaks French and Russian like a native." Noor stared at Gohar askance. "Why are you so interested?"

Gohar shrugged. "Just curious."

"Well, don't be," Noor snapped. "You're married, and he's a womanizer."

Gohar paled, but her eyes followed Aslan to the gallery. Just then, Smirnsky exited Saleh Mirza's study on the other side of the gallery. The two men stood eyeing one another like fighters before a wrestling match.

Smirnsky nodded stiffly and continued to descend the stairs. Aslan waited until the echo of Smirnsky's footsteps faded, his handsome face contorted with rage and hatred.

12

April 1911, Tehran

"The American is our best chance to get out of this mess and modernize this country," said the well-dressed, middle-aged writer.

"You think Americans walk on water because your son goes to their missionary school," replied her educator friend. "Besides, if this man is as good and honest as you say, the Russians will never let him succeed."

Silently, Gohar listened to the women at Noor's Thursday gathering heatedly debate the merits of hiring an American to shore up the country's finances. She was shocked to learn that Iran was bankrupt: the rich never paid taxes, what was collected seldom made it to the treasury, and the money already in the coffers was lost to grift, waste, and the shahs' frivolous expenditure. The country couldn't meet its obligations, let alone invest in the future.

To solve the nation's financial woes, the Majles, unwilling to sell concessions or borrow more, had hired an American, William Morgan Shuster, to enact reforms. This was all news to Gohar. No one in Gurdan, not even her tutor, had ever talked about their nation's loans, much less their connection to national independence.

Later, as she mimicked the women's gestures and accents in her bedroom mirror, she pondered the morning's discussion. She understood the pain of unpaid government workers—some of them stranded in foreign countries—and the need for a railroad and a standing army to stop the Russians. Saleh Mirza often gushed about taking the French trains when he had attended the Paris World Expo in 1878, and she dreamt of traveling like Phileas Fogg. But the American wasn't a famous general or a great engineer. He couldn't help them defend their land, cure their sick, or educate their children. She knew of the American missionary hospitals and schools. But Shuster wasn't related to them. He wasn't even an American official. He was essentially a tax collector, someone despised by all.

But she respected these women. They were different from all other callers to the house, who ran the gamut from Farangi-clad women reeking of Parisian perfumes to those who covered their faces from house cats, lest they were male. These women were writers, publishers, and educators. They didn't just talk about social issues; they acted to right wrongs—an innocent freed, a pension restored, an assailant punished, and a dowry supplied. Many had participated in the constitutional war, procuring armaments, distributing clandestine manifestos, sheltering revolutionaries, and even demonstrating in the bazaar and standing in the path of the shah's carriage to give him a petition in support of the Constitution.

While she enjoyed everything at this house—her room, the freedom to play tar, talking to Saleh Mirza, and shopping with Noor— the meetings with these women were the highlight of her week. If they favored this Shuster, there must be something to him.

That afternoon, she stopped by Saleh Mirza's study. "May I come in?" she asked.

Saleh Mirza peered at her from the top of his reading glasses. "Make yourself comfortable," he said, offering her the ever-present box of Turkish delight.

She sat facing him. "Aqa Mirza, what is all the fuss about this American, Shuster? How can he save our nation?" She took out a copy of the influential *Iran-E-Now* newspaper, which had announced its support of Shuster, and told him about the debate that morning.

Saleh Mirza put down the paper he was annotating and explained calmly but passionately in his authoritative voice. It wasn't about Shuster—or any other Farangi, for that matter. It was about Iranian sovereignty.

To support their lifestyle and trips abroad, he said, the shahs had sold the right to navigate the Persian Gulf and explore for oil to the English and the right to navigate and fish in the Caspian to the Russians. They allowed them to bring their armies to defend their "property." When the shahs ran out of resources to sell, they borrowed heavily, then gave the Russians the right to set and collect customs duties and tariffs as interest payments on their loans.

The Majles had hired Shuster to force the rich—not the poor—to pay their taxes and stop the corruption. That way, Iranians could buy back their concessions, fund an army, and build a railroad, schools, hospitals, and factories. But the Russians and the English didn't want to be paid back. They wanted to control Iran, keep it backward and poor, tear it apart, and annex it—the north to Russia, the south to the English colony of India.

"But why an American?" she asked. The only Americans she knew of were George Washington—whom she liked because he had defeated the despicable English—and the young Baskerville, who was killed during the constitutional war.

"Any Persian with the skill and integrity to do the job fears for his life."

She remembered the slain finance minister.

He leaned back. "And why not an American? They helped the Japanese beat Russia. They are fair. They won't take our money and laugh at us behind our backs."

The flag in front of the English-owned Imperial Bank of Persia, the unpunished captured Russian assassins, and the Farangis mocking their country all came to Gohar's mind, inflaming her. If this Shuster, whoever he was, could help them get rid of foreigners, she would support him with her life.

In the pursuing silence, she took a ginger Turkish delight and munched on it. Saleh Mirza took off his glasses and placed them on the table. "On a different subject, do you like your room?"

"It is wonderful, Aqa Mirza," she gushed, picturing the large, airy room with windows to the back courtyard. "I have never had a room like it. I will miss it when Haji returns."

"The room is yours." His eyes met hers. "Even after Haji returns. Married or not, this house is your home. God didn't grant me a daughter—until now. You may not be my flesh and blood, but you are my daughter."

"Thank you," she muttered, casting her eyes down.

"Have you, by the way, heard from Haji?'

In the warmth and the bustle of Saleh Mirza's household, she hadn't thought much about Haji. But his short letters had arrived every fortnight to report on the weather in Gurdan and Khanum Bozorg's rheumatic knees. "He writes," she said without elaborating.

His gaze bore into her. "And you?"

She felt his eyes on her. "I respond."

He paused before asking her in a gentle tone. "Are you happy, my child?"

"I am happy to be with you and Bibi Noor."

"You know you can always come to me if you have a problem."

"I know," she said hesitantly. As much as Noor and Saleh Mirza lavished affection and gifts on her, and as much as she loved them, she was still unsure of her position in their household.

He sighed. "I only wish I had sent for you sooner." He paused. "You should do more than Haji does. Write to him more often."

Amoo Ali's death kept Qamar in Gurdan. Gohar barely knew the man, though she had lived with him for fourteen years. But his passing made her aware of Qamar's advancing age. Sometimes, Qamar became short of breath while climbing the stairs, or had to sit after walking to the bathhouse. Qamar was no longer the center of Gohar's universe, but she was still her most trusted confidante and companion. Despite all her new activities in Tehran and all the new people she had met, she had missed Qamar's unconditional love, easygoing demeanor, and candid advice. To lose her would be devastating.

She longed to write Qamar a long letter. But then Qamar would have to pay the mullah to read it as the only person in her household who could read, her grandson, was in Baku with his father, who had lost his job in Gurdan. She fondly remembered the thin boy with his shaved head. Expressing her feelings for Qamar had to wait.

Instead, she wrote a long letter to Haji, careful to avoid mentioning any activity that he might disapprove of and emphasizing her regular prayer. She omitted that her parents seldom exercised their religious duties, drank a glass of wine now and then, and entertained Farangis, Gabrs, and Armenians often. Every family was entitled to its secrets.

As Shuster's arrival in Tehran approached, the women from the Thursday meetings worried about the Russian lackeys and the reactionaries derailing his hoped-for reforms. The foes of progress were bound to manipulate—and bribe—the poor to create chaos, discredit Shuster personally, and intimidate his supporters. To counter this, the women vowed to increase their aid to the poor, deliver it directly to working-class neighborhoods, and watch for rumors. There were already whispers about Shuster hiring heathens.

Gohar had dreamed of participating in the women's activities for some time. But Haji was sure to disapprove of the women's secular views—and the occasional presence of their male relatives to lecture at their meetings. She hadn't wanted to provoke him. But now, backing Shuster was fighting for independence. Haji, even when he returned, couldn't stop her.

Noor cautioned her that anyone involved in helping Shuster would be in danger. Mobs had already attacked the girls' school run by one member of the group for the third time in as many years and smashed another's office windows. Several women who had already received death threats for their promotion of literacy, women's rights, and freedom, now expected more. The key to safety was secrecy, Noor advised her. If no one knew of their activities, no one would bother them.

The warning made Gohar apprehensive. But the women's courage inspired her, and secrecy suited her. The activities assigned to her—delivering aid, teaching, and writing—were not dangerous, and she could blend in with women in working-class locales better than her peers from more affluent households. She remembered the stories of bravery during the revolution. It was her turn to do what those women had done before her.

Saleh Mirza's approval strengthened her resolve.

13

May 1911, Tehran

Haji returned in early May. Gohar greeted him with open arms when he came to collect her from Saleh Mirza's house. But he stepped back, lightly touching her arm and whispering that she must respect her parents and refrain from showing affection in front of them or the servants.

Gohar froze. After three months of watching Saleh Mirza kiss Noor's cheeks and Gohar's forehead every time they returned from a shopping trip, she had forgotten how Haji abhorred the show of affection. Once in their own house, she was sure he would be more attentive, perhaps even compliment her new dress, notice the kohl around her eyes and Farangi rouge on her cheeks. He would tell her how much he had missed her. She bowed her head, retreated to her seat in Saleh Mirza's study, and politely asked him about his family's health and Qamar's plans.

Stoic and inscrutable as a sphinx, Haji waited for a servant to place a cup of tea in front of him before telling her that everyone was well, Gurdan was peaceful, and Qamar planned to move to Tehran permanently once she had settled her affairs in Gurdan. He then turned to Saleh Mirza to ask about goings-on in the capital, ignoring Gohar altogether.

The news of Qamar's planned move thrilled Gohar. Now, she could take care of her aging companion and shower her with love. She rose to walk to the gramophone and busied herself with selecting a record while Haji continued talking to Saleh Mirza. "No matter how much I tried," he said. "I couldn't convince the governor to send the tax money to the capital."

"Do you blame them?" Saleh Mirza fumed. "What has the central government done for them? Built roads? Jailed bandits? Repaired irrigation canals? No, they have done nothing of the sort."

"I know," Haji responded. "People have a right to be disappointed. But how can we turn the country around without money?"

Gohar turned to glance at the two men. Haji looked flustered.

"Well, let's hope Shuster finds some money," Saleh Mirza replied. "The key is the Majles solidarity in supporting his plans. The Russians will exploit any disagreement there to block Shuster. I need you to keep the conservatives in line."

"I'll do what I can," Haji whined. "But it is difficult."

Gohar silently concurred. Her friends in the women's society also worried about the deep disagreements between the secular and conservative factions in the Majles—although both sides had supported the hiring of Shuster. It was best to keep her affiliation with the women's group—and Saleh Mirza's approval of it—secret from Haji. She didn't want a rift between the men.

"I am counting on you," Saleh Mirza said.

On their way home, Haji glowered. "What did you do to your face? You look like a motreb."

"What are you talking about?" Gohar asked.

"Your eyebrows, the red stuff on your face. This is not how honorable women look."

She swallowed. "My eyebrows are the same style as Noor's."

"That may be suitable for a Georgian, but full eyebrows are God's gift to our women."

Chafed, she bit her lips and kept silent.

The custard-filled cake from the Armenian shop on Lalehzar was as soft as a cloud. Gohar took a bite and washed it down with a sip of the strong coffee served by Noor's tailor, a recent Armenian émigré from Istanbul. She glanced at the loose-fitting white ensemble on the cover of the Farangi fashion magazine on her lap. The outfit was not unlike the traditional shift women wore in Iran—except for the wide-brimmed hat.

In Iran, women were not allowed to wear hats.

A woman's voice caught her attention. "You know what Mahlaqa did to lure Aslan?"

The shop was the favored hangout of Tehran's sophisticated ladies, and the gossip was always about illicit affairs, often with graphic descriptions. The vulgarity appalled Gohar. But the mention of Aslan piqued her curiosity. She lifted her magazine to cover her face as she glanced over the top of it at the two stylish women sitting on the other side of the low table. She had seen them before.

The speaker continued. "She sent him an invitation to their summer house from her husband. But the husband is traveling. She sent the servants away and greeted Aslan alone."

"Mon Dieu," said the other woman. *"C'est incroyable."*

Both women giggled. Gohar flipped the pages of the magazine, unable to concentrate. The woman's audacity jarred her. Surely, any man worth his salt—especially someone worldly like Aslan—would see through the ruse and be disgusted.

"C'est vrai, ma chère . . . " said the first woman, and opened her mouth to continue the story—but Gohar didn't want to hear anymore.

In the fitting room next door, Noor stood on a platform as the thin tailor with stringy, graying hair pinned a chiffon dress on her.

Gohar dropped onto a chair. "The audacity of some women. They would make a harlot look like a saint."

Noor stared at her. "What happened? Why are you so upset?"

"How could a covered woman have an affair?"

Noor chortled. "You are so naïve. Women with means and guile use the hijab to hide their misdeeds."

Gohar recalled a popular poem about a woman meeting her lover naked under the chador. It was rumored to be taken directly from the poet's life. "But why?"

"They want affection. Most of them were married at seven to a fifty-year-old man with other wives and male and female lovers."

Gohar was disturbed. She shared the same predicament. But she wouldn't follow the same route. That was not an honorable way to live. "Shouldn't they seek affection from their husbands?" she said.

"Shouldn't there be tenderness in a marriage?"

"Marriage is not about love and affection," Noor said firmly. "It is about alliances between families. It's the same for men. Saleh was twelve when he married his seventeen-year-old cousin to keep the family fortunes intact."

"What about happiness?"

"Happiness, my child, is an illusion," Noor replied, a shadow passing over her face. "Men fool themselves with pleasures of the flesh."

Gohar glanced at the wooden mannequin in the corner, sporting a half-finished jacket. "And women?"

"Women are the bedrocks of society. Invisible but essential. Even the tallest and most beautiful minaret needs a deep footing to stay erect. If they stray, the family falls apart. Some find fulfillment in children, charity, or friends. Some pursue a hobby. Others seek God." She turned to let the tailor pin the side of her dress. "Those chasing after another man end up with heartache and regret. Eventually, their lover moves on, leaving them to deal with the gossip and shame."

At the mention of children, Gohar unconsciously touched her stomach. Someday, she would have a child, or more. But children came when God willed, and there were already so many children who needed her help. "But you and Aqa Mirza love each other."

Noor sighed. "We do. But Saleh is an exceptional man. He waited years for me to be allowed to join him, and we were lucky." A ray of sun highlighted the lines at the corners of her green eyes. "And we paid a price."

Gohar remembered the sad eyes of the daughter Noor never spoke of—the princess. In her heart of hearts, she knew Noor was right. Marital love didn't exist, not even in the literature. And love always ended tragically—Majnun losing his mind when Layly was married off, Farhad committing suicide, and Khosrow and Shirin being murdered by his son, who was in love with her.

The din of sewing machines from next door filled the lull.

"Will you take the green silk fabric, mademoiselle?" The tailor asked Gohar in her heavily accented Farsi. "I showed Madame Noor a beautiful style with lace on top and roses on the belt. *Très joli, très chic.*

Perfect for you, with your tiny waist."

"I am not a *maadmuselle*," Gohar said, then turned to Noor. "Bibi, do you think I should? I have so many dresses already."

Noor smiled indulgently, lifting her arm for the tailor to take the fabric in. "You can never have too many outfits," she said. "New dresses bring joy. I like the style. She has an Armenian friend who can make lace better than any Irish, and green goes well with your hair."

Green was not her favorite color. But what did a girl from Gurdan know about fashion? Noor had an impeccable eye, and Gohar would never tell her that Haji didn't like Farangi-style dresses. "That fabric is so expensive."

"Who cares?" Noor replied. "She'll add that to my tab, and Saleh's clerk will pay for it."

"You spoil me, Bibi."

"As I should. Why don't you look at the magazines while we finish here?"

Back in the main shop, the scent of coffee and perfume greeted Gohar. The ladies she had overheard earlier were begging the tailor's assistant to tell their fortunes from the grinds of their coffee. Gohar passed through shelves laden with bolts of fabric to reach the window.

Across the street, the massive facade of the Grand Hotel broke the row of three-story buildings on Lalehzar. Above the luxury shops lining the street, professional offices were interspersed with Farangi-style apartments. Gabrs, Jews, Armenians, and a smattering of Farangis lived there, along with progressive Muslims. She wondered what it would be like to live in a place with windows, even balconies, open to the street, with non-Muslims as neighbors and cafes and theaters nearby.

A tall man in a Farangi suit passed by. Despite herself, she thought of Aslan. She wondered what he would think of her in green. But that didn't matter. He would never see her wear the dress, and she shouldn't care about the opinion of a stranger who didn't even know her.

She was married. Her husband was a good man and a devout Muslim. He didn't beat her, smoke opium, chase after other women, or prevent her from visiting her family. Many women would give anything to be in her place. All he required was for her to respect him and uphold his religious standing in their neighborhood. But here she was, imagining herself modeling a new dress for another man.

On the street, a policeman led an urchin by the ear. An emaciated, barefoot younger boy followed them, crying. Beggars were banned from Lalehzar, but hungry young boys always found a way to sneak in and fight for kitchen scraps from the Grand Hotel. She thought of Qamar's grandson, thin and dark-eyed, crying himself to sleep. He should be at school, in his own land, with his own people. Not toiling in foreign oil fields. So should these boys and thousands of others like them.

The rampant hunger, poverty, and disease in Tehran angered her. They needed railroads, factories, schools, and hospitals. They needed doctors, engineers, and teachers. They needed money and modernity. They needed dignity. The key to all of it was the unity between Saleh Mirza and Haji. Her happiness was inconsequential.

She pictured the wind-catchers, the simple structures that turned scorching desert winds into cool air. Without them, Gurdan couldn't exist. That was what she needed to be, changing lives without fanfare. Aslan was a distraction. She would pencil in thicker eyebrows.

PART II
Uprising

If I rise, if you rise, all will rise.
If I sit, if you sit,
Who will rise?
Who will fight the enemy we despise?

H. MOSSADEQ

1

June 1911, Tehran

The local luti was the last person Gohar wanted to see as she entered the working-class area of Chaleh Meydan. But here he was, surrounded by other men and busy kicking something. Her first thought was to bolt stealthily. The man had been hostile to her since she had first set foot in the neighborhood to help the locals, though she had never provoked him. She wondered how he could even recognize her underneath the flowery cotton chador of a domestic worker. Perhaps it was the way she walked, or maybe this was his way of treating all strange women.

But the bloodcurdling shrieks emanating from inside the circle of men stopped her. Someone was being beaten. But who? A thief caught red-handed? A lout leering at a local woman? She could only guess; the wall of spectators blocked her view.

As she watched from under a plane tree, an onlooker moved, allowing her to see the object of the luti's wrath. A hunched figure squatted on the ground with his forearms raised in a futile attempt to shield his face. Blood oozed from his shaved head, staining his jacket and white shirt.

No criminal deserved such savage treatment. Someone had to stop the luti.

But no one seemed to care or dare to intervene. Gohar ground her teeth and bit her lip. If only she was a man, she could step in. But no woman, save for prostitutes and criminals, would get involved in a public brawl.

Her eyes fell on a soiled skullcap, and books scattered on the ground. This was a mere boy, a student from the nearby Elamieh High School.

The blood boiled in her veins. Everything but the boy disappeared.

"Stop!" she shouted instinctively. "You're killing him."

Everyone gawked at her. The luti paused, his bulky, tattooed arm hanging limp by his side. The bystanders shifted nervously.

"What is it to you?" the luti said, glowering.

The crowd sniggered nervously. A man cursed Satan and meddlesome, brazen women in the same breath.

"He's a person," she said, suddenly aware of people gawking at her. She tightened her grip on the chador over her face. "He has a family."

The luti narrowed his eyes and raised one thick eyebrow. "And who might you be? The mayor?" He put his free hand on his hip.

Someone cackled. Another said, "Judgment Day is coming." A third cursed Satan.

"A concerned citizen," she said.

The luti shooed her away with the back of his hand. "Are you itching for a beating?"

The crowd jeered.

All eyes were now on her. Even the boy on the ground stopped whimpering and looked up with large, dark eyes. Blood smeared his smooth, skinny face. He wet his parched lips.

The luti's clowning appalled her. "You should be ashamed of yourself, beating someone half your size," she said, her voice strengthening.

"Whores should be banished from the city," a man said.

"Or stoned," said another.

Her stomach churned. If the luti attacked her, no one would lift a finger to help her. He was not the only one in this neighborhood who was hostile to her. The mullah despised her, too, for bypassing him as the conduit to the poor. And the police—if they showed up at all—were more likely to arrest her for being alone in the streets than stop the luti.

The image of Saint Abbas in the alcove of a *saqaa-khaneh* across the way consoled her. If he were there, he would stand up to the luti. Silently, she pleaded for his protection.

"She's right," said a man from behind. "Why are you beating a poor child?"

A flash of white passed her. The white-haired newcomer in a white tunic and loose pants shuffled toward the luti. She had seen him selling odds and ends at a hole-in-the-wall store. His drooped shoulders and scrawny body were no match for the husky luti.

"Mind your business, uncle," said the luti. He pointed to the boy. "Don't let the puny body fool you. He is the devil's servant. I caught him sticking up a poster insulting the shah and spreading lies about who is starving us." He extended a piece of ripped paper to the old man. Rumors blaming Shuster for the famine had been swirling around Tehran for weeks, attempting to turn people against him.

"And this hussy—" he pointed to Gohar, "is a rabble-rouser. I know her kind."

"So what? Since when does a piece of paper give you a permit to kill someone's son?" said the old man. "And this paper says nothing about the shah. It says people shouldn't be fooled by the agents of the *deposed shah*, that lackey of the Russians we kicked out." He spat on the ground. "And the food shortages are the work of profiteers, not the American.

"And how do you know this woman is a whore?" The old man wagged his finger at the luti. "If she isn't, you are slandering a pious woman. That's a grave sin. If she is, your accusation washes her sins and puts them all on your ledger." He turned to the onlookers and spat on the ground. "You folks should be ashamed of yourselves. None of you were man enough to stop this bully. A covered woman has to speak up to save the boy's life? You are the ones who should wear the chador, not her."

A passerby stepped forward to help the boy to his feet. Someone filled a bowl with water from the *saqaa-khaneh* and wetted a handkerchief to clean his face. Another man gathered his books and dusted off his soiled skullcap.

Gohar silently slipped away, trembling. Shuster had been in the country for only a month, but his zeal in collecting overdue taxes had made him the enemy of the wealthy, who sent their agents to agitate the poor against the American. He also had powerful allies. The young shah had sent his car to Anzali to collect him, and the leader of the Gabr community had housed him in a mansion in Tehran. Meanwhile, ordinary people praised him for repealing the detested salt tax, and civil servants were thankful to have been paid. To facilitate his work, the

Majles had given him unprecedented authority, allowing him to hire a gendarme force to collect taxes.

But in neighborhoods like this, Shuster's good deeds, powerful allies, and glowing editorials in the newspapers didn't matter. Here, people followed their local mullahs and lutis, who often supported whoever paid them more. She would have to be careful, perhaps bring someone along. By now, she navigated the city confidently, sometimes with a servant but often alone, as did an increasing number of women. To curtail women, the police had banned their presence in the streets without a chaperone in the afternoons. But that only spurred them to venture out in the morning.

The explosion of reforms being debated in the Majles kept Haji there, allowing her to come and go as she pleased. Even Qamar's recent return had not reduced her freedom. The old woman might have disliked Gohar roaming around unchaperoned, but since Qamar had trouble walking—the only way to get around most parts of the city—she didn't stop Gohar.

Gohar pressed a handkerchief to her nose to block the pungent odor of refuse as she stopped at a faded green door and pushed it open. Across the small courtyard inside, a thin boy propped up on pillows on the veranda waved at her. A white sheet covered his legs. She waved back.

At the side of the yard by an algae-filled pool, a diminutive young woman was dividing a piece of dry bread among five youngsters. With their faces and hair caked with dirt, it was impossible to guess their genders or ages.

The woman lifted her face as Gohar approached. A black-and-blue bruise circled her left eye.

"Again?"

"I told you not to give me money," the woman whined. "When my husband smells money, he calls me a whore and beats me until I give him what I have."

"He beats you even when you don't have money," Gohar snapped.

"It's not him! It's the opium! He can't help himself." The woman bent her head. "And he has the right. I shamed him, giving him a crippled boy and two girls."

Gohar bit the inside of her lip and squatted to be at eye level with the woman. "Whose children are these?" She pointed to the youngsters.

The woman cleaned the gunk from the nose of one of the children with a piece of burlap. The child squealed. "These three are my neighbor's," the woman mumbled. "She works in Sanguelaj. She pays me."

Gohar scanned the house. It was built for one family but sheltered four—one per room. "Did you take him to the doctor at the American hospital?" She pointed at the boy.

"I wanted to, but I . . ."

"Didn't have the money! *I* will take him if you won't."

"What's the use?" the mother grumbled. "There's no cure."

"What did you do with the money I gave you?"

"I paid the mullah to make him a talisman."

The thought of her money going to a mullah inflamed Gohar. "If I don't give you money, how will you feed him?"

"Just bring me rice."

The boy had brittle teeth and could only eat *fereni*, rice pudding. But the rice was heavy, and coming here in Saleh Mirza's carriage would incense the luti and the mullah even more. Perhaps a good tip could convince a droshky driver to take her to this part of town and help her carry the rice the rest of the way. The effort would be worthwhile if it saved the woman from more beatings. "What should I do with the money this time?" she said.

"I'll take it," the woman said. She squeezed the money between her drooping breasts above her swollen belly. Another child. May God help them.

Back in the alleyway, she hadn't walked more than a few steps from the house when someone called her from behind. "*Khanum, Khanum.*"

She turned to see a woman with her chador wrapped around her waist, leaving her wrinkled face exposed and her hands free. Her knuckles were red and swollen from cold water. A washerwoman. "Did you call me?" Gohar asked.

"You work with the women who back the American?" the woman asked in a Gurdan accent.

Gohar stared at the woman suspiciously. "Why do you ask? Who are you?"

"Sediqeh," she said. "I've seen you around, helping that little boy. I live in the same house. He is sweet, but no one cares about him except you." She paused. "And I saw you stand up to the luti. That was something."

Gohar glanced enviously at the woman's scuffed, untanned boots. Much more suitable for walking in the alleys than her own heeled slippers. "What if I am backing Shuster?" she said.

Sediqeh came closer. "You should know," she whispered. "The luti is offering widows money to show up in front of the American's office and blast him for cutting their pensions."

Old women gathering in front of Shuster's office to accuse him of starving them would be disastrous. If true, it had to be stopped. But who was this woman? Why was she helping? "Why are you telling me this?" she asked.

Sediqeh looked nervous. "You are from Gurdan. Aren't you?"

Despite her diligent efforts, a trace of accent persisted in Gohar's speech. "Is that why?"

"No. I don't care about the Americans, either. A Farangi is a Farangi. But you shamed the pompous luti good. I hate him and his Russian friend."

A Russian? Involved in this neighborhood? That troubled Gohar even more. "Which Russian?" she asked.

"Esmerki? Asmansky? His name is something like that. He pays the luti and the mullah to do his bidding."

Gohar recalled the Russian spy Noor had called the devil. "Smirnsky?"

The woman spat on the ground. "That's it, son of a whore."

Gohar's heart sank. Smirnsky was no ordinary agitator. His involvement meant the Russians were planning something big. "What's he done to you?"

"He is a Russian. I hate all Russians. They took my son away."

"How?"

"He was a weaver in Gurdan. But he went out of business because no one wanted expensive Gurdan silk when they could buy cheap Russian cotton. He moved to Alaverdi, near Yerevan, to work for the Russians in a mine. He sleeps there, too. Never sees the daylight."

Gohar hunted in her purse for a few coins for the woman. "It happened to relatives of mine from Gurdan, too. They are in Baku."

Sediqeh tensed up. She raised her palms and frowned. "I don't need your money," she said tersely. "I clean up people's dirt, so I won't need handouts. Just get rid of the Russian."

2

July 1911, Tehran

Mohammad Ali, the shah deposed by the revolutionaries and exiled in Odessa, returned to Iran in July. On arrival, he was welcomed by loyal tribes before marching to the capital to reclaim his throne. The news jolted Tehran. The residents fl ed the defenseless capital with whatever means they could—droshkies, brays, horses, donkeys, and on foot. Those who stayed hoarded rice and charcoal. Men of all ages patrolled the neighborhoods.

Haji pleaded with Gohar to go to central Iran and stay with his sister until the danger passed. Loath to leave Tehran, Gohar rushed to Saleh Mirza's house to seek Noor's advice.

For months, she had distributed food and money, written petitions for pensioners, and advocated for the accused, while roaming the alleys in working-class locales wearing the faded chador of a domestic. Often, she stayed with her adoptive parents, basking in the attention of Saleh Mirza, who listened and advised, and Noor, who indulged and encouraged her. When Haji complained about her absences, she touted the benefi ts of learning from her worldly family and fretted about the heat in their own house.

Watching Aslan—albeit from the privacy of the observation room—as he worked with Saleh Mirza was an extra reward. By now, she thought of him as a mythical character, a protagonist in a novel, a legend—someone she observed from afar without any hope of ever talking to.

Saleh Mirza's carriage was leaving as she arrived. The maid who opened the door explained that it was taking the cook, who had collapsed suddenly, to the American hospital. Saleh Mirza's assistant, Aslan, had accompanied the cook.

The cellar where Noor napped opened to a hallway with two sets of stairs opposite each other, one to the birooni garden and another to the andarooni yard. A leather-trimmed canvas bag on the stairs to the birooni garden caught her eye as Gohar descended from the andarooni side. She had seen Aslan carrying the well-worn sack and wondered whether it contained anything personal.

After observing him for weeks, she knew he curled his hair around his fingers when pensive and bit his lips when nervous. But watching him didn't give her a clue about his personal life or inner thoughts. With Noor snoring and no one else around, this was her chance to find out more. The prospect thrilled her. She grabbed the bag and ran to the adjacent cellar, where old furniture was stored.

The dust in the storage room made her cough. She covered her mouth and cleared the surface of a low table to place the bag on. Inside the satchel were two stacks of paper, each tied with twine, and a telegram. The string was disappointing—she had expected fancy ribbons binding love letters. But either these weren't love letters, or Aslan was not a romantic.

The telegram was from someone in Astrabad, notifying Aslan of the arrival of someone named Khalil on a Russian steamboat from a small port north of Baku. What did it mean? Baffled, she carefully untied the twine on the larger of the two bundles. Pages handwritten in Farsi alternated with others typed in Russian, all stamped with Russian dates. None were signed. These were copies.

The first sheet was a copy of a letter in Farsi from Smirnsky to the former shah, Mohammad Ali, in Odessa, informing him of the continued support of his loyal subjects and their anticipation of his triumphant return.

Gohar's stomach churned. The letter, if authentic, was evidence of the grandees' sedition. Their opposition to Shuster was well known, but overt support for a deposed shah was nothing short of treason.

The next letter from Smirnsky instructed an aid to Mohammad Ali to send armaments in crates marked as mineral water via train. The third letter contained a schedule of trains from Odessa to the port mentioned in the telegram.

What did these letters mean? She recalled Sediqeh mentioning that Smirnsky was in cahoots with the mullah and the luti in Chaleh Meydan. The women's society had dissuaded the pensioners from rallying in front of Shuster's office. But did Smirnsky have a bigger plan in mind? Looking at these letters, she was glad she had told Noor about what she had heard.

A commotion from the garden alarmed her. In the afternoon's quiet, she could hear Aslan probing the gardener about his satchel. He must have returned from the hospital. She hastily tied up the papers, stuffed them in the bag, and left it where she had found it. Then she rushed to the observation room to wait for Aslan to enter Saleh Mirza's study.

"I should have asked the gardener to bring the satchel to you, but I had no time. Another minute and the cook would have been dead," Aslan said as he entered, looking inside the satchel. "But nothing seems to have been disturbed."

"How is the cook?"

"He will survive. I rushed back to be here on time."

"Thank God," Saleh Mirza responded. "You saved his life. At any rate, I trust my staff, and they can't read."

Up in the stifling observation room, Gohar wiped the sweat from her forehead.

Aslan took out the thicker of the two bundles. "These are the copies of Smirnsky's letters to Mohammad Ali Mirza in Odessa." He addressed the former shah without his title, handing the package to Saleh Mirza. "There is also a list of the grandees and tribe leaders who have pledged their support to him, plus details of his travel plans under the name Khalil. My man watched his ship arrive."

Saleh Mirza cut the twine with a letter opener. A breeze from the open windows ruffled the loose sheets of the stack on the table. He placed a heavy inkwell on the pile.

Aslan handed the other stack to Saleh Mirza. "These are the copies of the responses to those letters. They were all carried in diplomatic pouches. There is no doubt—the Russian government and their legation in Tehran orchestrated the affair."

"We should hurry up before Smirnsky arrives."

"When is he coming?"

"I summoned him earlier. He should be here any minute. "

"Are you going to show him that you have these?" Aslan said, pointing to the letters.

"What choice do we have?" Saleh Mirza sounded exasperated. "If we threaten him with the exposure of these letters, he may be motivated to stop the Russians from bringing back that despot and closing the Majles. He knows that at least some of the grandees would be too scared to join the rebellion if they know we have these."

Her heart sank, grasping the connection between the Russian's presence in Chaleh Meydan and his letters to the deposed shah. Many of the poor were loyal to Mohammad Ali Mirza, considering him, not his young son, the legitimate shah. Money or force could entice others to revolt. An uprising in Tehran would deliver the capital to the former shah on a platter. She shifted nervously. Aslan glanced suspiciously in the direction of the observation room.

Saleh Mirza locked eyes with Aslan. "Where did you get these?"

"A friend in the Russian delegation," Aslan replied with a half-smile. "A kindred spirit."

"The same one who gave you the copy of his letter begging the tsar to annex Iran?"

Gohar covered her mouth in horror. How could a Muslim sovereign agree to become the vassal of heathen foreigners?

"The very same," Aslan replied nonchalantly.

The fleeting exchange of knowing glances between the two men implied that the special friend was a woman. She felt a pang of jealousy. Lucky the woman who could help him.

"Would this be dangerous for either of you, should it get out?" Saleh Mirza asked.

"I am more concerned about your safety than hers or mine. Smirnsky runs a posse of trained assassins." He sat, placing the satchel by his feet.

"This house is a fortress," Saleh Mirza said. "And I seldom leave."

"They are known to poison their opponents."

Saleh Mirza took a Turkish delight from the box on the table. "My household is loyal."

Gohar tasted bile in her mouth. Contrary to his assertion, it would be easy to poison Saleh Mirza. Many mere acquaintances and distant relatives frequented the house.

She loosened her scarf to air out her caked hair and wet her parched lips. Some water would have been heavenly.

Saleh Mirza walked up to the window. "Smirnsky is here," he said.

Silently, Aslan took a pistol from his pocket and placed it on his lap under the table. "Just in case," he said.

Saleh Mirza nodded.

Konstantin Smirnsky was led to the room a few minutes later. Looking dapper in a gray suit with a gold watch dangling from his vest pocket, he bowed, scrutinizing Aslan, who had remained seated.

Saleh Mirza looked out of the window with his hands clasped behind him. "Sit down, Mr. Smirnsky," he said without turning.

The butler pulled up a chair for the Russian at the far end of the table. Saleh Mirza dismissed him without ordering tea.

Saleh Mirza turned around. "I know you speak Farsi well, but I have asked Mr. Madadoff to translate to avoid confusion."

Aslan translated in a flat tone.

Smirnsky wet his lips.

"Do you know why you are here?" Saleh Mirza asked.

"No, Your Excellency," Smirnsky said. "But to be in your presence is always an honor."

The flowery and contrived language of the Russian contrasted with his cold eyes and stony face. It repulsed Gohar.

"My mother was a Kurd," Saleh Mirza growled. "In her culture, a host must protect his guest with his life or lose face. But if a guest betrays his host, the host is obligated to shed the guest's blood. You, sir, are a guest in this country who has betrayed his host."

Aslan pushed a sheet of paper from the stack forward while translating.

"Do you recognize this?" Saleh Mirza asked, pointing to the letter.

Smirnsky glanced at the paper without touching it. He paled. "Where did you get this?" he muttered.

"Thank God there are still patriots in this country," Saleh Mirza said.

"That letter was from me to a friend," Smirnsky said.

"Who happened to be a disgraced former shah whom you have been warned not to contact? Aiding him in a rebellion against the legitimate government of his country," Saleh Mirza said. "Can you imagine how many people would be hanged as traitors if I made these letters public? Even if you leave Iran alive, you will have to deal with your own people."

Smirnsky bit his lips even before Aslan translated. "Should I be concerned for my life?" He glanced at Aslan.

"No." Saleh Mirza rested his left hand on Aslan's shoulder. "Mr. Madadoff is here only to translate."

"I did what I did as a Russian patriot," Smirnsky said, glaring at Aslan with blazing eyes. "Which is more than I can say for others." Vitriol had distorted his face. "What is it that you want? The Russian army to capture Mohammad Ali Mirza?"

"No," Saleh Mirza responded calmly. "Thanks to Mr. Shuster, we have our men to take care of him. What we need is for your government to stop helping him. No guns. No Cossacks. No money."

Smirnsky took out a handkerchief to dry the sweat from his forehead. "And if we don't?"

"Then I will let the world decide." He pointed to the stacks of paper. "I will send the proof of the Russian conspiracy to topple a democratically elected government and install a despotic fool to every embassy and newspaper I can find. The *Times* of London, the *New York Times*, *Le Temps*, *Le Figaro*, *Norddeutsche Allgemeine Zeitung*, *Berliner Tageblatt*, *Vossische Zeitung*, you name it. I don't suppose the French bankers funding your government or your British friends would be amused. Your government won't be pleased either, nor your coconspirator."

She had never seen Saleh Mirza so angry or so regal. Aslan smiled, seeming to enjoy watching Smirnsky squirm.

Smirnsky swallowed. "Will you guarantee Mohammad Ali Mirza's safety?"

"That may be tough. The Majles has already put a bounty on his head," Saleh Mirza said. "But I will do what I can. I don't want his death causing another civil war."

Smirnsky stared at Saleh Mirza. "I will see what can be done."

Saleh Mirza met his gaze. "Then you'd better hurry." He turned toward the window.

Dismissed like a servant caught stealing, Smirnsky rose. "You should be careful, Your Excellency. The times are perilous." He bowed.

"My fate is in God's hands," Saleh Mirza replied.

Gohar tasted the blood from biting the inside of her mouth. He was so courageous.

At the door, Smirnsky barked something in Russian to Aslan, who answered calmly.

"Asshole," Aslan muttered when the door closed.

Saleh Mirza sat, leaving his hand on Aslan's shoulder. "What did he say?"

"That he is looking forward to seeing me hanged like the dog that I am," Aslan said nonchalantly.

"What did *you* say?"

"That I am looking forward to cutting his throat like the pig that he is."

3

October 1911, Tehran

A violent shove from behind knocked Gohar's bundle out of her hand and landed her face down on the pavement. Before she could catch her breath, the man who had hit her picked up the bundle and disappeared into the mob of shoppers, beggars, and pedestrians outside the grand bazaar. People cursed as he cut through the crowd, but no one chased him.

The blow had come out of nowhere. One moment, she was standing on the sidewalk, and the next, she was on the ground, shaken and dazed, with the air knocked out of her.

Women shoppers helped her to her feet. Her companion, the seven-year-old daughter of their new maid, rushed to her side. The girl's face was white as parchment. A merchant brought a stool for Gohar to sit on and offered her water. Her hands trembled as she drank. She had scratches on her hands and knees. Bruises must be forming on her back. But nothing was broken. The attacker's aim was not to harm her but to shock her and steal the package she was carrying. "I am fine," she muttered, squeezing the girl's hand.

She suppressed her anger. Running after her assailant was futile, and she had a mission. "Do you have your bundle?' she whispered to the girl.

The girl nodded. Gohar was relieved. They still had the document they had been tasked to deliver. The attacker had taken the decoy. Her ploy had worked.

She rose, still shaking. "We need to move on," she said.

Earlier that morning, she was in Saleh Mirza's house, taking a break from the crowding in her own home. The former shah's insurgency had devastated parts of the country, forcing many to flee to Tehran. Among the displaced were her in-laws. Khanum Bozorg and Belqais, disguised as peasants, had arrived at Haji and Gohar's house one early morning without warning. They had left Gurdan hastily after the Turkmen had attacked their villages, beaten their tenant farmers, and burned their warehouses. Gohar had welcomed them. They had been at the house in Tehran for three months now. Even after the government forces had defeated the rebellious shah and sent him back into exile, the country remained chaotic.

Meanwhile, the continued Russian opposition to Shuster brought jittery neighbors and merchants to their house to seek Haji's advice. Their presence forced the women into a single room for long hours every day.

Gohar caressed the strings of her tar.

"It was last night that the one who is radiant, graceful, pure-hearted, loyal; Came to visit me; Taking away my heart and my faith…"

Playing tar distracted her from worrying about Aslan. He had left in July to fight the insurgency and was yet to return.

Absorbed in her thoughts, she was startled by the brush of a knee against hers. "Bibi!" she cried. She hadn't noticed Noor entering.

"Continue, dear," Noor said, touching Gohar's knee. "You sing with so much passion. I hope it's your husband you are pining for."

"It is God, Bibi. I am singing about God," Gohar responded. "The composer, Shayda, was a mystic. For him, there was only one lover: God."

"He was also sweet on a Jewish singer," Noor smirked. "At any rate, I came to hear your voice." Noor turned away to gaze out the window. "It is so peaceful here."

"It is. I'm glad you came. I like nothing better than your company when I play." Gohar put the tar down. "You look troubled, Bibi. What is wrong?"

"A lot," Noor sighed. "But I don't want to burden you."

"A burden shared is a burden halved." She reached for Noor's hand.

Noor hesitated, then turned serious. "Whatever I tell you must remain between us. You must tell no one, not even Haji. Lives are at stake, including your father's, Saleh Mirza."

Calling Saleh Mirza her father filled Gohar's chest with love and pride. "My lips are sealed," she said. "You can trust me."

Noor leaned forward and lowered her voice. "You know about the standoff between Shuster's gendarmes and the Cossacks?"

Gohar nodded. The day before, the paper had published a lengthy report on how the Majles had sent Shuster to confiscate the assets of the renegade brothers of the deposed Mohamad Ali Mirza. But a Russian bank had claimed that the outlaw prince had pledged his strategically located properties as collateral on a loan. The properties, therefore, belonged to the bank. Then, the Russian delegate sent Cossacks to stop Shuster from occupying the buildings.

Noor continued. "I can prove that no such loan exists."

Gohar looked at Noor, confused. "How?"

"Islam requires that all debts be declared in a person's will. If there is no mention of a loan in a will, then there's no loan." Noor paused. "I have the will."

Gohar was aghast. "But how did you get it?"

"A friend of mine brought it this morning. She had gotten it from one of the prince's wives, who wanted Shuster to have it. She knows Saleh and I can be trusted, and we may have a way to get this to the American."

Gohar gasped. "She could be killed."

"Indeed," Noor said nonchalantly. "So could anyone else who helps Shuster stop the Russians. But she is a patriot and abhors what her husband is doing."

Gohar's heart raced; her palms moistened. "What are you going to do?"

"I have an idea. The nephew of one of the women at my Thursday gatherings works for Shuster. I was thinking of taking it to her myself, so she can pass it on to her nephew, who can take it to Shuster."

"Can it wait until Thursday?"

"No. That would be too late. Once the Russians take over the properties, they will never give them back. Besides, I don't want this in the house. That bastard Smirnsky has spies everywhere. If anyone finds it here, it will be the end of Saleh and me."

Gohar recalled Smirnsky's threat and Aslan's warning. "Have you talked to Aqa Mirza?

"No, he is visiting a sick friend outside of the city and won't return until tomorrow."

"Can the coachman or your confidante carry it?"

"Absolutely not." Noor shook her head. "They can be bought."

"But if someone is spying on you inside the house, their accomplices will follow you when you leave. And if the coachman is snooping on you, he would know where you are going. So, someone else has to take it, walking or taking a public droshky."

"Then I will ask Qamar. She's the only one I can trust."

"Qamar can't walk. Not even to the main street to take a droshky."

"Then what do you suggest?"

Gohar cleared her throat. This was her moment. "I think you should allow me to take it. No one is watching me. I'll go with a maid."

Noor's eyes widened. "You?" She gulped.

"Yes," Gohar said, her ideas taking shape as she talked. "We can take a droshky to the bazaar. If anyone follows us, we'll lose them in the crowd before going to your friend's house."

"No," Noor said. "It's too dangerous. Too much for a young woman." She gestured to the growing row of books on the mantle. "This isn't like one of your adventure novels. This is real. Plus, I don't like you taking public droshkies or meandering with the riffraff. I can go by myself."

"You can't go." Gohar paused. She didn't want to tell Noor she was much better at negotiating the Tehran streets than her. "You just told me that you are being watched. It's not like I've never taken a public droshky or 'meandered with the riffraff.'"

"I know," Noor said wearily. "Against my will."

Gohar shrugged. Sooner or later, Noor would have to accept that Gohar could take care of herself, and that the world was changing. "Where does she live?"

"Sanguelaj," Noor said tentatively.

"Perfect. Easy to get to from the bazaar."

Gohar jostled through a mob of boys surrounding a peddler of the sweet, gooey *gaz-angabin* on the short passageway to Shah Mosque. Inside the tiled gateway, the calm of the vast deserted courtyard with its reflecting pool soothed her frayed nerves. Before entering the woman's entrance to the mosque, they left their shoes in a trellised vestibule.

Only three people were in the women's section: one praying, another nursing an infant, and a third sleeping. The small space was perfect for Gohar to plan her next move. She had been attacked despite changing plans twice, once to take the tram instead of a droshky after spotting a stranger loitering outside the house and the second time to leave the tram early after seeing a familiar-looking man boarding it. Her assailants were not about to give up. They could have followed her to the mosque and be outside to attack her. The child would be safer waiting here while she delivered her package.

Her body ached. But there was no time to rest. Hastily, she retrieved the rolled-up will from underneath her companion's loose dress, wrapped it in her scarf, and hung it from her shoulder like a swag beneath her chador.

"Stay here," Gohar whispered. "I'll be back soon." Then, remembering the rumors about strangers taking young girls away, she wagged her finger. "Don't go anywhere, even if someone tells you I'm dying and need your help. If anyone talks to you, pretend you are mute." She paused. "And not a word of this to anyone. I'll bring you back some gaz-angabin."

The girl looked scared and confused but nodded obediently.

As she passed through the colonnaded *shabestan,* she looked for a different way out of the mosque. The building had several entrances. But some of them led to the seminary, where women were not allowed, and others would take her out of her way and waste precious time. The stench of urine overwhelmed her as she passed a side corridor.

She covered her nose and glanced at the end of the passage, where a stocky, middle-aged woman sat by an open door leading to the women's outhouse. She must be the janitor.

Gohar approached her. "Excuse me," she said. "Do you have a prayer veil I can borrow? I fell, and my chador got soiled and is impure."

The woman put down the torn straw fan she was using to swat at a swarm of flies and turned to Gohar. Her small black eyes sat deep in her pockmarked face. Strands of gray hair stuck out of her once-white, now-gray scarf. She frowned. "This is not a fabric shop. You should've brought a prayer chador like everyone else."

Gohar took out a silver coin—several times the cost of a satin chador. "Please help me. Last year, when my mother was sick, I pledged that if she recovered, I wouldn't miss a single prayer for a year. She did. Now, if I go home, I'll miss the noon prayers and have to start all over," she paused. "I'll bring it back, washed, tomorrow."

The woman's eyes glinted at the sight of the coin. "You shouldn't have entered the mosque in an impure chador," she chided. "You young people these days, you don't know anything."

"I'm sorry," Gohar said with as contrite a tone as she could manage. "I'll leave my chador and *piche* here."

The woman eyed the expensive silk chador and handmade gauzy veil. "I understand," she said, hastily pocketing the coin. "I keep some chadors in the back. Help me get up."

The janitor hobbled down a long corridor. Gohar followed. They stopped at a padlocked door tucked away beneath a set of stairs. The door creaked as it opened. Gohar stooped to enter the small, unlit storage area.

The janitor handed her a worn-out gray chador from atop a folded stack. Its yeasty smell was revolting. Gohar pointed to a white patterned chador in the middle of the heap. "Can I have that one, please?" White would show stains if there were any.

The woman grumbled but complied. When Gohar took off her chador, she eyed the satchel on her shoulder suspiciously. Gohar gave her another coin. "For your troubles."

When Gohar left the mosque, a slim man in a camel *qaba* was leaning on the wall with his eyes glued to the entrance, chewing on gaz-angabin. He was the same man she had seen boarding the tram. She covered her face with a corner of her chador and imitated the limp of the attendant. He did not follow her.

The grand bazaar covered a quarter of Tehran and was connected to half of its neighborhoods. Its network of covered thruways and alleys connected shops, offices, houses, mosques, *tekyeh*s, warehouses, loading docks, and caravansaries. The bazaar was not only the beating heart of the city but also a microcosm of the country. Here, migrants from the four corners of the land congregated, and foreign merchants kept offices.

She jostled through the paper, jewelry, fabric, and spice markets. People stood in long bread lines, bursting into sporadic skirmishes. A few slept along the shuttered door of stalls.

Once in Sanguelaj, she relaxed. In her worn cotton chador, she looked no different than the throng of domestics who cooked, cleaned, and cared for children in the affluent neighborhood. She was invisible.

The next afternoon, Gohar basked in the autumn sun in Saleh Mirza's study, gazing at the birooni garden, surrounded by tall elms and even taller walls. A long, narrow, reflecting pool ran along the middle. The barefoot gardener in rolled-up breeches watered the Japanese quinces in one of the four large flower beds. Despite the gut-wrenching events of the previous day, she had delivered the documents and bought sugar candy for Fatimah before taking a droshky home, where Noor had greeted them as heroes.

Saleh Mirza raised his head, smiling. "What's on your mind, my child?"

"Just thinking about yesterday."

"You did well."

She blushed.

Saleh Mirza continued. "I have been watching you and listening to you in the past few months. You've done a lot: brought intelligence from the streets and helped people. But what you did yesterday took true courage. I can't tell you how proud I am. You are a lioness, a harbinger of a bright future for this country."

"Thank you." A lump in her throat muffled her voice. "I did my duty."

"You did more than that," Saleh Mirza said. "My mother was a lioness. She rode and fought better than any man I know." He took off the Cornelian signet ring he wore on his little finger. "This is her seal. She gave it to me before she passed. I have never taken this off. But it is time to pass it on." He placed the ring in Gohar's palm. "Put it on."

The ring was heavy. Delicate bands of gold and silver framed the engraved square stone. She mouthed the inscription, *The Kingdom of God*. It was the insignia of someone from a noble family. Was she, an orphan from backwater Gurdan who had never shot a gun and was afraid of horses, worthy of it? Could she carry on the family's name?

"I don't know how to thank you," she said. "But I am not worthy of such an honor." Tears rolled down her cheeks.

"No one deserves it more than you. If this family has a future, it lies with you, not with my hopeless son. I know she would have wanted you to have it."

His son, Akbar Mirza, a gambler, and addict living in Farang, was a source of embarrassment for Saleh Mirza. Perhaps the nobleman was right. After all, she had risked her life and had the bruises on her back to prove it, even if she couldn't ride or shoot.

The ring fit perfectly.

"Do you think the Russians will leave Shuster alone now?" she asked.

"Not likely." He leaned back. "If anything, they'll be more belligerent. But whatever they do, they're no match for you and your friends."

Her heart sank. As determined as they were, a bunch of women were no match for a mighty empire. At least not for long.

She glanced at the smattering of yellow on the stately elms. The cacophony of birds congregating by the pool drowned out the rustle of pen on paper as Saleh Mirza resumed writing.

4

November 1911, Tehran

Fall brought fresh troubles for Iranians. The Russians, with tacit English support, occupied the Caspian port of Anzali and the provincial capital of Rasht. As if on cue, British Indian troops seized the Persian Gulf port of Bushehr and the cities of Isfahan and Shiraz, ostensibly to protect their oil fields.

On a blustery day in late November, the Russians gave the Majles forty-eight hours to fire Shuster, pledge never to hire another foreigner without Russian and English approval, and pay for the deployment of Russian troops. Otherwise, Russia would march on the capital.

That afternoon, Noor dropped by Gohar's room as she read a new installment of the translation of *Les Misérables* in *Bahar* Magazine.

"How is it?" Noor asked.

"Marvelous, Bibi. I just read about Marius joining the student uprising. It's so exciting."

"Well, we may soon have an uprising of our own." Noor looked pensive.

The Russian ultimatum had inflamed people and put the city on edge. Support for Shuster was eroding, and Russian wrath frightened everyone. But it wasn't about the American; it was about their sovereignty.

"I heard the guilds plan to rally in front of the Majles before the vote on the ultimatum," Gohar said, "and I am sure the students will join them. But do you know something I don't?'

"Well . . . I just heard from the women from the Thursday gatherings. Some of them have decided to stop our gutless politicians from caving in to fear or money and voting to accept the Russian terms.

They're going to the Majles tomorrow to implore the speaker to reject the Russian demand."

"A petition?"

"More than a petition." Noor took a deep breath. "They will tell the speaker that they intend to kill any deputy who votes to accept these demands—including their own menfolk—before committing suicide." Noor paused. "They will carry pistols under their chadors to show they are serious."

Gohar gasped. Going to the Majles–where women were not allowed to enter–let alone threatening men, especially their own menfolk, was beyond audacious. It was lunacy. But maybe madness was necessary to get their point across, especially if the men faltered. She wondered how Haji would react if she were to join the women. "Are they really going to shoot the deputies?"

"I don't think it will come to that."

"What will they do if the speaker refuses to see them or sends for the police?"

"They will chain themselves to the gates of the Majles until he does."

"Is anyone actually going to join this mission?"

Noor nodded. "They have more than three hundred volunteers, most of them related to Majles deputies." She paused. "And . . . I am thinking of joining them myself if Saleh allows me.

The idea of elegant Noor joining an uprising in her custom-made clothes and Parisian shoes seemed unreal. "You, Bibi?" Gohar said.

"Why not? I refused to serve tobacco to my master, the shah when he gave away the tobacco concession. I placed manifestos all around the harem during the Constitutional Revolution. You have always agreed with me that women must stand up for themselves if they want to be taken seriously. I think I can do this."

Gohar glanced at Noor. A year ago, she herself would have been scared. But since then, she had braved the street with assassins on the loose, stood up to bullies, been assaulted, and evaded spies. If Noor could do this, so would she. "In that case, will you allow me to join you?"

Noor met her eyes, smiled, and nodded slowly.

Gohar had never been part of a public event, let alone a demonstration with so much at stake. Excited and apprehensive, she stayed over at Noor's and Saleh Mirza's to avoid detainment at home. She slept fitfully. In the morning, Noor gave her a small pistol. It was heavier than she expected. Frightened, she stuffed it in the pocket of her loose pants.

To avoid attracting attention, they took a droshky instead of Saleh Mirza's carriage and got off a short distance from the Majles.

The autumn sun had dried the mud, and the branches of elms, dotted with golden leaves, spilled over the walls of the Negarestan garden. Usually, a stroll on such a delightful day would have lifted Gohar's spirits. But today, she felt nauseous. Her heart pounded so loudly that she was certain everyone could hear it. Her experience of being hit in the bazaar had made her more apprehensive than she cared to admit, even to herself.

Men loitered in the vast Bahrestan Square in front of the Majles. Some squatted on the sidewalk, smoking, while others leaned against sycamores in the middle of the square. Only a handful of policemen supplemented the volunteer militia guarding the wrought-iron gates of the compound, marked with a pair of sword-carrying lion finials. Up ahead, the eight minarets of the stately Sepahsalar Mosque loomed.

A group of women stood by the gate. At the center, a well-known poet recited one of her pieces. The presence of so many women calmed Gohar. She followed Noor to the gate, where the women's leader spoke to a short, thin man. His neat *sardari a*nd slacks marked him as a civil servant, likely the custodian.

The custodian disappeared inside but returned shortly afterward. "His Excellency will receive your representatives—no more than ten— in his chambers," he said with a contrite smile. "The rest must wait outside."

The leader stared at him. "We appreciate His Excellency's willingness to hear us," she said. "But we can't leave our sisters here. They are too exposed. If the Russian-paid riffraff gets a whiff of their presence here, all the militia and police in Tehran can't protect these ladies."

"I understand," he said, unfazed. "But my hands are tied."

The leader discreetly slipped a small bag through the fence. "Listen, brother," she said. "We don't want trouble. Consider us, your sisters and daughters. Would you let thugs molest your womenfolk? Where is your honor?"

He squeezed the bag into his pocket and rubbed his beard. "You have a point, sister. Let me see what I can do."

The custodian returned smiling. "You are all welcome to come in. The speaker agrees with you: it is not proper for the ladies to stay in the open. You can wait in a side chamber."

Inside the gate, the building's façade still bore the shell marks from the Cossacks' 1908 attack. A small group of women, including Noor, were led to the speaker's chamber. Gohar sat with the rest in a large room, listening nervously for gunshots and screams. But the only sound was the gurgling of fountains and muffled voices. Time passed slowly. No one spoke. She wondered what the women were doing in the speaker's chamber. Would the speaker be angry? Hostile? Haji must be somewhere around, too. She wished she was allowed to stroll around the building to see who was there and what was debated.

Everyone relaxed when their representatives returned, beaming. The speaker had listened enthusiastically and promised to take their pleas to the floor without divulging their identities.

As they left the Majles, Gohar was elated. Even confined by chador, they had made their opinion known without harming anyone.

Male relatives met all the women except for Noor and Gohar. The two stood on the sidewalk, looking at the square, now teeming with rough-looking men.

Noor looked for a droshky, but there were none. "I should have listened to Saleh and asked someone to meet us," she muttered. "But I wanted to keep a low profile." She grabbed Gohar's arm. "Let's walk. I don't like the look of these men. The house isn't far."

Gohar agreed. A walk would calm her nerves. The two crossed

the square and entered the maze of narrow, blind alleys. No one was around. Relieved, they slowed to a stroll home.

But just as they relaxed, a group of hooligans emerged from an alley. Out in front was a mustachioed, bald, stocky man in a grimy knee-length tunic and loose pants. They must have followed them from the Majles.

Gohar turned around. Two men on horseback blocked the other end of the alley. She recognized their black fur hats, long collarless coats with red shoulder straps, and the bandoliers across the chest. "Cossacks," she said. They were trapped.

The whips in their hands, the long swords on their sides, and the daggers in their belts unnerved her. Cossacks were known for their brutality and appetite for assaulting women. Beads of sweat covered her forehead. The thought of their hands grabbing at her revolted her.

"Don't be scared." Noor squeezed her hand. "Ignore them. They won't dare to touch us." Gohar wished she believed that. But without a place to hide or run to, they had no choice but to move on. The thugs were bullies, surely paid by the Russians. The women walked toward the men with their heads high.

"*Baha'is*," one of the men shouted.

"Heathens," another hissed.

"Whores," a third barked.

Their leader blocked Gohar. "Farangi flunkies," he grunted.

His hooded eyes, red with anger and hatred, bore through her. The smell of the onion on his breath and the dried dung on his clothing revolted her.

But who were these mercenaries attacking women for standing up to the Russian thugs? How dare they question her motives and chastity?

If they attacked, she would fight. She was young and strong and had a loaded pistol. Granted, she had never used it. But a shot would scare the hooligans and alert the neighbors. She grabbed the gun. She would die before being dishonored.

The glint of a raised knife stopped her momentarily. She gulped but stood firm.

As she and her assailant eyed each other, an unusually tall, broad-shouldered man stepped forward, grabbed the thug by the throat, and pinned him to the side of the alley. Given his size, his agility surprised her.

The knife hit the ground with a clunk. The other thugs stopped, their eyes wide with surprise. One hurled a rock at Gohar. But a tall, slim man with sandy-brown hair stepped forward to shield her. Then he turned, and Gohar felt a lightning strike. Was she dreaming?

"Aslan!" Noor yelped from behind her. "What are you doing here?"

Astounded and transfixed, Gohar gazed at the blood on his cheek where the stone had hit it. Wordlessly, she extended her handkerchief to him, gazing at the vein throbbing on his neck.

"Thank you," he said, pressing the handkerchief to his face.

The hooligans began to retreat. The giant released the man he was holding to give chase to the others, but Aslan grabbed his sleeve. "Let them go."

The large man watched the gang disappear around the bend of the alley.

Aslan yelled after them in accented Farsi. "You scum. You're not man enough to fight men!"

Noor turned to Aslan. "Your face is bloody. We must take you to a doctor."

"No need," he said. "It's just a scratch." He pointed to his companion. "This is Ilych."

Ilych bowed with his hand over his heart. He looked Central Asian, perhaps Turkman or Uzbek.

"What are you doing here?" Noor asked Aslan.

"We were on our way back from an appointment when we saw a large group of ladies leaving the Majles," Aslan replied. "We noticed the thugs following you two and saw the Cossacks. We decided to make sure you got home safely."

Gohar looked over her shoulder and was relieved to see the Cossacks gone.

"Did Saleh send you?" Noor asked.

Aslan blushed, smiling sheepishly. "His Excellency sent a messenger instructing me to fetch some material from the Majles archives this morning. He asked me to take Ilych and wait around in case there was trouble."

"Saleh is so thoughtful, even after I foolishly turned down his suggestion to have you gentlemen meet us at the Majles gate," Noor said. "What happened to the Cossacks?"

"I told them to get lost," Aslan said nonchalantly.

"I don't know how to thank you, gentlemen," Noor said. She pointed to Gohar. "This is my daughter, Gohar."

Even amid the turmoil, hearing Noor introduce her as a daughter delighted Gohar.

Aslan bowed to Gohar, and she nodded to acknowledge him, content to gaze at him from the safety of her chador. The events of the day had left her drained.

Aslan scanned the alley. "We should move on," he said calmly. "The thugs could return. And the Cossacks may discover I am not a Russian officer and decide to turn around."

"I agree," Noor said. "Let's walk to the house."

They rushed through the allies but slowed down once they reached Lalehzar. Despite the turmoil in the city, people were strolling, and the shops were busy. The perennial presence of the police at both ends of the street kept the troublemakers away.

They stopped side by side at a shop to look at a tasteful display of women's accessories in the window, oblivious to the side glances of passersby, not used to seeing a man standing with a woman. Gohar ventured to talk to Aslan without turning her head. "Thank you for your bravery."

"I did my duty. You and Noor are the heroes. You did what most men wouldn't dare."

The sincerity in his voice filled her chest with pride.

A servant awaited them at the entrance to the *andarooni*. Noor hurried inside. Gohar followed. Exhausted and hot, she yanked off her veil and let her chador slide down—but when she turned to close the door, Aslan was behind her in the vestibule. Startled, she stepped back, pulling the chador over her hair.

He seized her wrists gently. "Please, no need to cover up. I have already seen you bareheaded. I carried you last summer in Gurdan."

His touch jolted her.

"I looked for you everywhere," he continued breathlessly. "I wanted to see you again."

Before she could respond, Noor's voice came from behind. "Aslan, dear, Saleh is waiting for you in his study."

He stepped back with a little bow. "I am sorry, Gohar Khanum," he said, loud enough for Noor to hear. "I shouldn't have come this way." He bent down and pretended to pick up Gohar's bloody handkerchief from the floor. "Tomorrow at noon," he whispered as he straightened. "The store we stopped by. Ask the owner for a pair of warm winter mittens. Please."

And then he was gone.

Once Aslan was out of earshot, Noor snapped, "Why on earth did he come in this way? Why didn't you send him away? Why did you take your veil off in front of a stranger? We're lucky no one saw you. Otherwise, there would be no end to the gossip."

Gohar reddened. Noor had never spoken to her this way. It wasn't her fault that Aslan had snuck in behind her, and besides, Noor herself often met Saleh Mirza's close friends with only a scarf covering her hair. So why was she being so harsh now? Hadn't Gohar shown her bravery and maturity already?

But she couldn't make a fuss: it would be disrespectful and only worsen matters. "I'm sorry, Bibi. I didn't realize he was behind me," she mumbled, casting her eyes down.

Noor calmed down. "He should have known better. Honestly, sometimes I don't understand Saleh. Of all the people he could have sent to fetch us, he sent Aslan. Cocky as hell, and with the kind of reputation he has."

Gohar wanted to mention how courageously he had confronted the thugs, but she didn't want to challenge Noor. "You are right, Bibi. At any rate, will you allow me to go home now? I didn't sleep much last night, and I'm exhausted."

"Now? At lunchtime? What's the hurry?"

"I'm not hungry," Gohar said. "Thank you, Bibi. I just need to go home."

"Fine, I'll get the carriage to take you."

"No need. I like to walk," Gohar said, leaving the house before Noor could react.

At home, Qamar chattered away, eager to share the events of her own morning and offering Gohar almond cookies.

Gohar declined. She had no appetite despite not having eaten since the day before. After pretending to listen to Qamar's account of her day and nodding for a while, she excused herself and retired to her bedroom.

All afternoon, she debated whether she should meet Aslan. On the one hand, she had watched him for months and was curious to know more about him, especially why he had been in Gurdan and how he had come to save her. On the other, meeting a strange man, a Russian no less, would be a sin for any woman, let alone a married one, and if found out, cause for shame. Preoccupied with her conundrum, she dropped a cup of water on Belqais's lap. It caused no harm—but Belqais thrashed her regardless.

Haji did not come home for dinner and didn't send word to Gohar. That made her mind up. She was tired of pleasing others and not getting any respect or consideration. It was time for her to do what she knew was right for *her*. Aslan had saved her life and her honor. She owed him gratitude. There was nothing wrong with a short, courteous conversation between a decent woman and an honorable man.

Tomorrow, she would see him face-to-face for the first and last time.

5

November 1911, Tehran

Frenzied knocks on the door woke the household early the following morning. A servant of Haji's cousin had come to warn them that unknown assassins had murdered a pro-Russian friend of the Bakhtiari prime minister before fleeing.

Haji had to go to the Majles, but he told Gohar and the others in the household to stay home. Killers were at large, and with the Majles about to vote on the Russian demand to fire Shuster, public protests were expected.

Gohar was undeterred. Once Haji left, she ordered the maid to carry her bundle to the bathhouse. So many occasions required ritual baths that going to a bathhouse was an ironclad excuse for being away for hours. No one would expect her for the rest of the day. She marched out, ignoring Qamar's pleas to stay home.

The market stalls were closed. A young man urged the crowd in front of the coffeehouse to follow him to a rally in Toopkhaneh, protesting Russian interference. Gohar was surprised to see her conservative neighbors—many of them vocal critics of Shuster—joining the young man.

She dismissed the maid at the bathhouse, changed into a Farangi dress, and sent for a droshky, leaving her bundle with an attendant. The driver looked surprised to hear her destination, but a sizable tip motivated him to head uptown.

The further north they went, the thicker the crowd on Nasseryeh became. People emerged from the alleys like streams joining a river. Some carried banners. Fresh-faced adolescents locked arms with middle-aged, bearded men. Shopkeepers in loose pants and dark vests walked alongside urbanites in sardaris and traditionalists in qabas. A cluster of women wrapped in shrouds formed a white island amid the dark sea of men. She had never seen so many people in one place. The crowd seemed somber and peaceful, but she felt the strain lurking underneath. Even a loud noise could have caused a stampede. A tinge of fear tainted her excitement. She should have stayed home.

The droshky slowed down, then halted. The driver shrugged—he couldn't go any further. Gohar got down.

The crowd closed around her immediately. The smell of sweat, grease, and dirty, wet wool choked her. Unable to elbow her way to the side, she let the mob propel her forward.

In Toopkhaneh, a line of policemen blocked the entrance to Lalehzar. She pleaded with a young officer to let her pass, claiming her husband and their sick infant were waiting for her at the doctor's office. A small donation motivated the policeman to let her through. She declined his offer to escort her.

Lalehzar was jam packed. Even the serene garden of the Sufi lodge overflowed with people. The middle-aged and well-dressed here were as agitated as the young and haggard in Toopkhaneh.

Men passed on the news of the debate in the Majles to one another. Occasionally, she could hear chanting.

"Death to traitors!"

"Freedom or death!"

She slithered through the crowd.

At the store where she was to meet Aslan, the blue wooden shutters were closed, covering the windows. Exhausted, dizzy, and discouraged, she stood under the rolled-up awning, unsure of what to do.

Then a hand touched her shoulder, and a familiar accented voice whispered in her ear. "Follow me."

Instantly, she felt as light as a feather, free as a bird.

The roar of the crowd made conversation impossible. Wordlessly, she followed Aslan to the building next door. At the top of a flight of stairs, he unlocked a glass-paneled door marked *notary* in black lettering and entered. She hesitated at the threshold, taking in the dim reception area, its white-washed walls lined with worn-out bentwood chairs. But she had come a long way and was tired. She stepped through the door.

From the lobby, they passed through another door, into an office with shuttered windows facing Lalehzar. She collapsed onto a chair, leaned on the wall behind it, and closed her eyes.

"Drink this," he said. "Take off your veil and breathe. Don't be afraid."

She opened her eyes. Aslan was kneeling in front of her with a glass of water, looking worried. His closeness unsettled her. She fought the temptation to touch him.

"Do you want me to take you home?" he asked.

"I'll be fine," she muttered, pulling back her veil to sip the water. "I doubt if we could pass through the crowd anyway. We might as well wait until it thins out."

"I agree. Do you want to lie down on the window seat?"

A glance at the coarse carpet covering the window seat made her mind up. She shook her head.

The din of the crowd slipped through from the street below. Aslan disappeared again and returned with sugared water and a plate of cookies. She took a bite. They were tasty, albeit stale.

He sat on the worn leather chair behind the beaten-up desk on one side of the office. A pile of bound register books was stacked on the desk. "I'm sorry I had to bring you here," he blurted out, his eyes avoiding hers. "I only discovered this morning that the shop we were to meet at would be closed."

His deferential manner relaxed her. "No need to apologize. I understand. We can't go to Café Paris or the Grand Hotel anyway. Here is as good a place as any."

"Take off your hijab; make yourself comfortable." He smiled mischievously. "I've seen you uncovered before anyway, and I won't harm you any more than I would hurt a flower."

Recalling her near-nakedness when he saw her in the water tank, Gohar blushed. "Well, you may be tempted to pick a flower you fancy. But the flower may not appreciate that." Nevertheless, she let her chador slip down, revealing the loosely pinned scarf beneath.

"Unlike flowers, people have tongues. They can say no."

"You don't like head coverings, do you?"

"No. It's insulting to insinuate that the mere sight of a woman's hair could make me behave like an animal. Men who force women to wear the veil are weak. Like children, they can't control their impulses." He paused. "And talking to women in hijab is like talking to eggplants. How would you like to talk to an eggplant?"

She had heard similar sentiments from secular intellectuals and politicians. "It's not like we have a choice," she said. "The last Iranian woman who ventured out bareheaded was stoned to death."

"That's barbaric!" The corner of his lip turned up in contempt.

"No, that's reality." She snapped.

An uncomfortable silence crept in. She regretted her harshness. The last thing she wanted to do was argue with Aslan about the hijab during their first and only solo encounter.

But what would be a proper subject of conversation with Aslan? She had never conversed with a strange man before. Even with Haji, all she did was exchange information as succinctly as possible. "Where did you get the cookie?' she said finally. "It's tasty."

"Do you like it? There's a kitchenette next to the reception. I can make tea if you like."

His domesticity impressed her. Most upper-crust men wouldn't know how to fire a samovar and would abhor serving a woman.

"I would have preferred a pastry." She smiled. "But I'll take the cookie."

He smiled back. "Wise choice. I doubt the pastry shops are open now. Maybe next time."

Her chest tightened. There wouldn't be a next time.

He lifted his face. "I was afraid you wouldn't make it today."

She wet her lips. "It wasn't easy."

"I'm glad you came." His voice turned dreamy. "After I saw you in Gurdan, I couldn't stop thinking about you. You were so beautiful, like a Renaissance painting of the Virgin."

She blushed. "Really?"

He locked eyes with her. "Really."

She longed for a veil to cover her burning face.

He continued. "I looked for you everywhere. But I didn't even know your name."

The conversation was becoming uncomfortably intimate. She needed to ask the question she had come to ask, then leave quickly. "What were you doing in Gurdan?"

"Delivering a package. I was there when we heard a scream and found you unconscious and bloody. I carried you up and went to fetch a doctor."

It seemed far-fetched to imagine him delivering something to Khanum Bozorg or Belqais, and even more so to a servant. "A package?" she said. "For whom?"

"You'll have to find that out for yourself."

Outside, the crowd had grown louder, their chants alternating between "God is great" and "death to Russia."

They listened in silence. They could be here for hours. She scanned the drab office with its bentwood chairs, whitewashed walls, and cheap rug, racking her brain for a suitable subject of conversation.

"Are you worried about people attacking Russians?" She motioned to the window.

He shrugged. "Although I am ethnically Russian, I am from Elisabethpol, the city you call Ganja in the Caucasus. Eighty years ago, I would have been a Persian."

She nodded. Ganja was the birthplace of her beloved poet, Nezami. If it weren't for the subject of the poetry, she could have discussed it with Aslan. Nezami's masterpiece was the salacious tale of a Persian king falling in love with an Armenian princess after seeing her naked.

Aslan continued. "Plus, I hate the Tsar as much as anyone here, if not more. I even shaved my beard to look different from him."

"I noticed the beard was gone." She pointed to his mustache. "You look like an Azeri."

"You remembered my beard from last year? I didn't think you could have noticed much, in the state you were in."

She panicked. He must never find out that she had been spying on him. "I saw you in February when you caught the Georgian assassin."

Aslan's eyes widened in surprise. "You did? Were you in one of the houses?"

"No, I was the woman you took pity on."

"See what I mean? I didn't even know it was you under the veil. You could have been a monster, and I wouldn't have known. If I had known, I would have beaten that stupid cop to a pulp for disrespecting you."

"That would have gotten both of us killed," she said. "You did the right thing. I was grateful. How did you end up chasing the murderer, anyway?"

"I was on my way to see the police chief, Yeprim Khan. I saw policemen chasing the assassin and joined them. Did you know the assassins also killed a policeman and two servants?"

"No! That's awful. There was nothing about them in the paper."

"There never is. They're expendable."

And invisible, she thought. "You know Yeprim Khan?" she asked. The man was a revolutionary legend.

"I trained his men and procured arms for them before he marched to Tehran in 1909."

"Is that what you do? Smuggle guns?" Their conversation flowed easier now.

"I am not a gunrunner," he snapped. "I do what is necessary to support what I believe."

"Do you supply the militia?"

"Never," he bristled. "You can't go around killing people you disagree with. It will come back to bite you."

She nodded. In her experience, the militia assassinating their opposition had done nothing but create chaos.

Aslan walked to the window and opened the shutter for a crack. "People are still pouring in," he said. "I doubt there's any room left down there."

She walked to stand near him, his closeness strangely comforting.

Suddenly, the crowd sounded somber and eerie as they recited the Muslim last rites. "I attest that there is no God but Allah . . ."

The Majles must have rejected the Russian ultimatum. She felt a chill in her spine.

As a horse-drawn streetcar approached, someone shouted that it was time to teach a lesson to the Russian bastards who owned the streetcar company. The mob cheered as they surged onto the track to block the tram. Some hurled stones at the compartments, while others urged the occupants to leave.

Gohar's eyes glided over the passengers' terrified faces as they hastily left the tram and vanished into the mass of bodies. When the horses pulling the streetcar reared up, the conductor cut them loose. The animals struggled desperately to navigate through the crowd. A handful of policemen on horseback looked on.

Soon, the sound of breaking glass drowned out the horses' neighing. Further up the street, the mob was attacking a Greek shop with a sign in Cyrillic script. People pushed the tram's empty cars off the track, kicked the wheels, broke the sides into pieces, and set them on fire. Flames illuminated their distorted faces.

Awed and elated, Gohar watched the rage spread through the street like a sandstorm, destroying everything in its path. United, people were powerful, but the unbridled masses were frightening. The dingy office suddenly felt like a safe harbor.

She stepped closer to Aslan.

Finally, overwhelmed by the display of fury, she sat back in her seat.

Aslan glanced at his pocket watch. "Are you hungry? It's almost three."

Wrapped up in the dramatic events of the day and the excitement of being so close to Aslan, she hadn't noticed her growing hunger. "I am, but . . ."

He glimpsed out of the window. "Wait here. I'll be right back."

Kneeling on the window seat, she anxiously watched him leave the building. He fought his way to a doorway across the street, where a sugar beet vendor had sheltered.

Before long, he returned with steaming sugar beets wrapped in newspaper.

She stared at him. "You could've been killed! I don't see much dignity in dying for sugar beets."

"Would it have been more dignified if I died for kebabs?"

She covered her mouth to hide her laugh.

They sat on the window seat, facing each other. She watched him methodically skin and slice the beets with a pocketknife. The silence between them was strangely soothing.

"What will you do if the Russians attack?" she said.

He chewed on a piece of beet. "Same as before. Fight. I am training Georgian and Caucasian volunteers."

"Why are they fighting on our side? Do they want to be part of Iran again?"

He leaned back. "No. They want independence, or at least an end to the tsarist rule. By fighting here, they weaken Russia and prepare for their own battles."

She had never considered this possibility, but it made sense. Why would anyone want to ditch the Tsar only to become a subject of another autocracy? Silently, she wrapped the beet skins in the newspaper and took them to the kitchenette. Aslan was looking out the window when she returned. "Is it quieting down?" she asked.

"Doesn't seem to be."

She sat on the window seat. He settled close to her, drawing his knees to his chest. She didn't mind. He was respectful and easy to talk to. "What brought you here?" she dared to ask.

"I heard about the shelling of the Majles from Iranian refugees in Baku. That is what the Tsar did in Russia: he let people to elect an assembly, the Duma, then he shelled and closed it. So, I decided to help you Iranians."

She met his eyes. "But then you stayed. Why?"

"To make a difference. To uproot the misery, not merely help the downtrodden. I could live in France, Germany, even England. But what difference would I make there? Here, whatever I do matters."

"Do you like it here?" she asked timidly.

"I like the people and their enthusiasm for modernization. But I don't like the corruption. It is everywhere."

"Aren't you afraid of getting injured, or worse?"

"Weren't you afraid when you went to the Majles? Fear is not an excuse for cowardice."

She couldn't agree more.

The commotion outside was fading. She glanced at the darkening sky. It was time to leave. She dreaded the thought of never seeing him again. After months of dreaming about talking to him, the reality had proven even better than her fantasies.

He followed her gaze. "I'll take you home now."

She nodded her thanks and rose. As they passed the reception area on their way out, he stopped and turned to her. "When can I see you again?"

For a fleeting moment, the thought of seeing him again thrilled her. Then reality hit. He must think of her as another floozie at his beck and call. "You realize that I'm married, don't you?" Her voice harsh, offended.

He looked dejected. "I didn't mean to be disrespectful," he said. "I enjoyed your company, and I want to know you better. Saleh Mirza has told me what you've done, risking your life helping the reformists. It's not every day that I meet a Persian woman who has done that, especially one so young. The way he talks about you, I pictured you as someone much older." He paused. "I expect nothing but friendship. You have my word."

He looked sincere and contrite. Besides, if Saleh Mirza had told Aslan about her activities, he must have trusted his discretion and integrity. "Even if I wanted to see you," she said, "how can I? I can't sashay out of the house whenever I want to."

"You came today."

"I pretended to be going to the bathhouse. I can't use that excuse every day."

"I know it won't be easy. But finding you was a miracle, and so was spending a whole afternoon with you in the middle of an uprising. We will manage."

She hesitated. He didn't intimidate her, and his friendship would open a new world for her. She despised deceit but knew dozens of ways to leave the house without raising suspicion. Still, was it wise to risk her reputation, marriage, and life for his friendship?

But wise or foolish, they would all perish if the Russians attacked Tehran. "Even if I agree to see you, how could we? My husband isn't violent, but honor killings are rampant in his tribe."

"I will protect you. Plus, no one would dare harm Saleh Mirza's daughter."

"If there is a scandal, Haji would divorce me, and Saleh Mirza would either disown me or lock me up in a dungeon," she said reflectively, gazing at the ring Saleh Mirza had given her.

"Nonsense. Saleh Mirza loves you and is too enlightened for that." He grinned. "And if Haji divorces you, so much the better."

That was brash. But that didn't deter her. She didn't have much time to think—it was already dark. "Where can we meet?" she asked.

His grin turned mischievous. "I don't suppose you'd consider coming to my place?"

"What do you take me for?"

"Leave it to me. Come to the store where we were supposed to meet, at noon the day after tomorrow. If you are detained, then come the day after, or the one after that. I'll be there. I'll send you a message if there's a problem."

In the droshky home, he instructed the driver to stop before they reached her neighborhood. In the darkness, he took her hand and kissed her palm lightly, then stepped out.

She watched him disappear into the maze of alleys as night fell.

6

November 1911, Tehran

That night, Haji arrived home in a solemn mood. Uncharacteristically, he invited Gohar to sit with him. "My dear Gohar," he said. "Did you hear what happened in the Majles today?"

The question surprised her. Haji never discussed politics with her. "I heard people shouting in the street."

"Well, you knew that today we were going to vote on how to respond to the Russians' demand to fire Shuster?"

She nodded.

He continued. "I must admit, I was undecided until last night. Shuster has helped us. But he has ruffled a lot of feathers. That is not smart in this country. Neither is going against the Russians and the English. God knows I've had my share of troubles with them." He paused when the maid brought in a kerosene lamp. "Yesterday, a lot of people came to me to share their opinions. I had my own worries, mostly for your safety, if the Russians attack the city and round up the Majles deputies. At the end of the day, I went to see Saleh Mirza and ask for his advice."

"What did he say?"

"He agreed that I had a grave burden on my shoulders. But his position was clear: Iran's sovereignty is not negotiable, not even when his or his family's life is at stake."

Gohar could hear Saleh Mirza's clear and gentle voice uttering those words.

Haji continued. "Then he told me what you did. He was so proud of you. I had heard about the women's visit to the speaker, but I didn't realize you were one of them. Right then and there, I knew how I must vote. To die with honor is better than to live with shame. You saved my honor. I'm proud of you, too," he said. "Your bravery showed me your maturity and wisdom. I know that I can trust you." He gave an astounded Gohar a sealed document. "This is my will, in case something happens to me."

Gohar stared at the envelope. Never before had Haji entrusted her with something meaningful.

That night, as Haji snored, Gohar lay awake. Every minute of her encounter with Aslan replayed in her mind: the theatrical way he had served her, his profile in the ray of sun peeking through the shutters, his calm as the world outside went mad. The thought of not seeing him again was unbearable.

But even a simple friendship between them would face insurmountable obstacles.

Then again, they had found and met each other against all odds. Was it because they were destined to be together?

Her mind whirled all night as Haji slept soundly in his bed.

The next day, Gohar planned to stay home. The city was chaotic, and she didn't want to see Noor so soon after being chided about Aslan. But when Saleh Mirza sent his manservant to summon her to their house for her tar lesson, she obliged, telling herself it would be best not to dwell on the incident.

Her tar teacher had a new song by the revolutionary composer Aref. It cautioned that firing Shuster, a guest in the country, would bring eternal shame to the Iranian people. She muddled through the piece, longing to play something more in line with how she felt. A passionate song by Shayda, the crazed mystic hopelessly in love with a Jewish singer, would have been more suitable.

"I noticed you were distant today," Noor said ruefully as they ate lunch after the lesson. "You didn't come to see me before your lesson, and I had to fetch you for lunch. If this is about you being bareheaded in front of Aslan, I didn't mean to be harsh." She paused. "You are astute for your age, but you are not even seventeen. Besides, it's not your integrity that I question. It is other people's gossip. God forbid a servant caught you bareheaded, talking to a man. They'd make a mountain out of a molehill." She sighed. "I've already paid that price. Rumors took my daughter from me."

The agony in Noor's voice distressed Gohar. She squeezed Noor's hand. "You don't need to worry about me, Bibi. I'll never let you down."

There and then, she vowed silently that nothing dishonorable would ever happen between her and Aslan.

After lunch, Noor brought out a pair of drop earrings with diamond-shaped rubies and seed pearls. "I found these in my jewelry box." She handed them to Gohar. "I used to wear them often. Now, I want you to have them."

Gohar had seen Noor wearing the earrings in her pictures. This wasn't a store-bought gift; it was an heirloom. With the earrings on, Gohar looked into a hand mirror. Seeing her face side by side with Noor's startled her. They both had the same pale, oval face—Noor's rounder—the same full mouth—Noor's bordered with tiny lines—and the same eye shape—Noor's green; hers, black. But this was only an illusion, wishful thinking. They couldn't look alike. They were not related, not by blood.

"Do you like them?" Noor asked.

"They're lovely."

Noor held Gohar's hand between hers. "Aslan is not a bad sort. Saleh thinks highly of him. But he doesn't know our customs. He thinks he can talk to you like he does to a Farangi girl. But people talk, especially with him being young. We need to protect Saleh Mirza's honor."

The conversation tore Gohar, but it didn't deter her from seeing Aslan the next day. She felt guilty deceiving Noor, but Gohar was anxious to see Aslan again. She would stay the night at Saleh Mirza's to make getting away the next day easier.

Gohar took Saleh Mirza's carriage home the next day in her new green dress and earrings, covered under a modest chador. The coachman wasn't suspicious when she got out before reaching her house: she often dismissed the carriage early, concerned about being seen in a fancy droshky in her modest neighborhood. This time, though, she waited in a shop until the carriage disappeared.

Janitors were still clearing broken glass and repairing damaged shops in Lalehzar when she got there. She reached the meeting point with Aslan just as the clock on the façade of the Grand Hotel chimed noon, proud to be punctual even without a watch—a luxury reserved for elite men. Someone tugged on her chador as she examined the shop window, prompting her to turn.

An urchin stood behind her. "Gohar Khanum?" he asked.

Perplexed, she nodded.

He continued. "Your husband sent me to fetch you."

A knot formed in her stomach. What was Haji doing here? Wasn't he working in the Majles? Had she been found out?

"Where is he?" she asked.

The boy gestured to a side alley with his head. "There, follow me."

Was this a ruse to kidnap and rape her? She scanned the busy street. If it were, a scream would bring janitors and police to her rescue. On the other hand, if it were really Haji who was waiting for her, disobeying would only make him angry. She followed the boy, struggling to devise an excuse to justify her presence there.

But the man standing by a droshky in the side street was not Haji. It was a smiling Aslan. On the driver's seat, Ilych, his Uzbek companion, lifted his hat to greet her.

Her fright gave way to pure joy.

As they made their way to Dowlat gate, they heard demonstrators chant "independence or death."

The tree-lined road outside the gate led north to the mountains, where the rich maintained summer retreats among the orchards and vegetable farms. No one on the road paid particular attention to them. They were a couple, like many others, leaving the chaotic city for the serenity of the mountains. Midway to the village of Tajrish, they veered onto a narrow road leading to the bank of a good-sized stream. Aslan guided her to a narrow dirt road flanked by poplar trees. The quiet countryside, the soothing murmur of the water, and the warm sun washed away Gohar's anxieties.

At a stone bridge, he pointed to a compound in the distance. "That is the summer retreat of the Russian legation." He motioned to another equally large complex on the opposite side. "That one belongs to the English legation." He pointed to an arched stone bridge surrounded by boulders. "And here is our land,"

He spread a small rug by the water underneath the bridge, in an area sheltered by the boulders from the elements and prying eyes.

"Is this where you bring all your lady friends?" she asked playfully.

"Only you. The others prefer my house."

She swallowed hard, recalling the raunchy stories she had heard. But jealousy had no place among friends.

He sat on a rock and opened the box he carried to reveal cream-filled pastries. Gohar was astounded. "Where did you get these?" she asked, taking a pastry.

He beamed. "You asked for them. My Armenian landlord made them. He has a shop on Lalehzar."

She gestured toward Ilych, who had stayed with the droshky. "Who is Ilych? How do you know him?"

"He raised me from when I was a toddler. My mother was bedridden, and my father was always away. When I was sent to boarding school, he went back to Tashkent. I found him there much later."

"That sounds familiar. Qamar was the one who brought me up in Gurdan."

"I didn't realize that. The way Saleh Mirza talks about you, I imagined he would never let you out of his sight."

"Saleh Mirza didn't know I existed until three years ago. He adopted me." Haltingly at first, but soon as confidently and comfortably as if she had known him for years, she recounted her dalliance with Kavous, followed by Qamar's vision and subsequent trip to see Saleh Mirza, culminating in her own adoption and marriage.

"Naughty girl. Throwing pebbles at a boy? Exchanging letters?

I never would have guessed." He smiled mischievously. "Did you care for him?"

She blushed. "No, no, it was just curiosity. I was bored."

"And for the sake of your amusement, a poor boy got bloodied. That's cruel. Maybe I should get a talisman to keep me safe from you."

She chuckled. "I'm sure you can manage without one. But if you do want one, Qamar can have one made for you at a reasonable price."

Absorbed in conversation, neither of them noticed the time. The darkening sky alarmed Gohar. She'd have to hurry home to be there before dinner.

As she packed, he drew a map of the parade ground where Ilych would pick her up for their next meeting.

Near her house, he kissed her palm and slipped away. Ilych drove her home.

7

December 1911, Tehran

As soon as the Majles rejected the ultimatum, the Russians occupied Qazvin, a city ninety miles west of the capital. People boycotted Russian and English goods, and merchants in Shiraz refused to supply the English, leaving their Indian soldiers to scramble for food. Demonstrators in Paris denounced the Russians and the English, and an avalanche of telegrams from all four corners of the world urged Iranians to stand firm. The Majles unanimously declined Shuster's offer of resignation, twice.

In Tehran, fear reigned. Suspected Russian sympathizers were beaten, their shops ransacked, and their houses burnt. Rumors of attempts to assassinate Shuster and other notables ran rampant. Haji's tribal cousins sent a burly Bakhtiari to guard him as he rushed from one meeting to another, seeking a way out of the impasse with Russia.

Undeterred, Gohar concocted new schemes to get away and see Aslan. Haji's manservant, Mash Qolam, unwittingly helped. He had grown up with Khanum Bozorg and was close to her. His presence in the home kept her entertained and too busy to keep track of Gohar's whereabouts. Belqais kept to herself.

Each time, before they parted, Aslan would tell her where to meet him next. The arrangement was always the same. Ilych, disguised as a coachman, would meet her in a public place within walking distance of her house or Saleh Mirza's. Then, before driving north, they would pick up Aslan as well as food from the street vendors that Gohar had developed a taste for: kebobs, fresh walnuts, steamed beets, or grilled corn.

Like many others in the chaotic city, they escaped the empty trams, ransacked shops, and angry protestors for the peace of the northern countryside: Elahieh, Zargandeh, Nivaran. When it was sunny, they would stroll under sycamores, eat by a stream, and gaze at the fall landscape in the secluded countryside. When it rained, they would stay in the droshky, riding through the tunnel of red and yellow trees. Their favorite place, rain, or shine was their "land": a stone's throw from the English and Russian compounds, yet far away from everything, theirs alone.

They stayed close but never touched, except at parting time, when he'd kiss her palm.

When she got home, a guilt-ridden Gohar would vow never to see him again. But as the next meeting approached, her resolve would give way to anxiety about *him* not showing up. Then, as soon as Ilych appeared to whisk her away, her angst would fade.

Aslan was masterful at depicting the places he had seen and the characters he had known. She laughed at his mischiefs and lamented his mishaps. Paris came alive in his description: wide boulevards filled with cafes and theaters, and narrow seedy streets lined with dancehalls and cabarets, all of them open to women. She heard the trains rumbling underfoot, the commotion in the halls of the Sorbonne where he had studied, and the boring lectures that had spurred him to leave before graduation. When he told her about the swashbuckling oil town of Baku, she saw the jungle of oil derricks that dotted the landscape and heard the cacophony of tycoons, bandits, and revolutionaries arguing—sometimes with knives and guns.

Occasionally, he mentioned his family—an older brother he admired, two older sisters who doted on him, and an ailing mother. One person he never mentioned was his father.

For her part, she held nothing back, not even the loss of her child. "I felt a hole in my heart," she said as he lay on a picnic rug with his hands folded under his head. "An emptiness in my soul," she continued. "I was angry at myself for being careless and at people for being glib. I hated it when someone said I was young and would forget, or that I would have more children. The young suffer as much as the old, if not more."

He looked at her, his sky-blue eyes filled with empathy. "Did you cry?"

"Not nearly enough. Without a body to bury or a grave to cry at, it didn't feel right."

"I know what it means to lose someone you love and not be able to mourn," he said. "When I lost my older brother, I wasn't even allowed to attend the funeral."

He rolled to his side and propped his head on his hand. "I still remember the day I was told about his passing," he continued. "I was sixteen, at boarding school in Paris. I didn't think much of it when the principal called me to his office. That happened a lot. But as soon as I walked into the room, I knew this time was different."

The raw pain in his voice tempted her to brush the hair off his forehead.

He continued. "A man I didn't know sat on the only leather armchair in the office. I remember thinking this fat man with his ornate cane, bespoke suit, fancy shoes, and well-groomed gray beard was out of place at our austere military school."

His face seemed translucent in the light filtering through the leaves. "The principal was unusually kind. He even offered me one of the hardbacked chairs and explained that the visitor was a distant relative of my mother. After he left, the man in the armchair leaned closer to me. I could smell his strong aftershave—a bit too feminine—mixed with tobacco. He told me my brother was dead and already buried. No need for me to travel back to Russia. He gave me his calling card and left, just like that. I waited for a letter from my mother or a telegram from my father. Neither came. They'd sent a pompous old dandy to deliver the news."

He closed his eyes, his grave face attesting to the depth of his agony. Longing to ease his pain, she kissed his forehead.

He looked at her with wide eyes. Then he reached for her hand and kissed her palm.

8

December 1911, Tehran

The porter hobbled on the uneven surface of the alley, impervious to Gohar's prodding to hurry. She shouldn't complain. The mud on the path was thick, and the sack of rice on his head was heavy. But she had to hurry if she was going to deliver the rice to the boy with brittle bones and get to her meeting point with Ilych before noon. Rice—the only food the boy could eat—was scarce since the Russians had occupied the rice-growing regions in northern Iran. He would starve if his mother couldn't afford any.

The sight of the neighborhood luti surprised her. This early in the morning, she would expect him to be lifting weights in *zorkhaneh* or drinking tea in the coffeehouse, not here twirling his handlebar mustache. She ignored him. Covered in another faded cotton chador, he would never recognize her as the woman who had stopped him from killing a teenager.

But the luti blocked the green door when the porter reached it. "Where do you think you're going?" he barked. The porter stepped back, glancing apprehensively at Gohar.

"I'm bringing rice to the woman who lives here," she answered.

"She doesn't need rice," he growled.

"How do you know?"

"Because there is plenty of it in the mosque. Thanks to the tsar."

The Russians and their cronies were feeding the poor to appease the Iranian public. She bit the inside of her lip. "She has a sick son. She can't go to the mosque."

"Then she starves," he said, turning to the porter. "Take the sack and this woman back to where they came from."

The porter shifted from one foot to the other, ready to drop the sack and bolt.

Passersby stopped to watch the kerfuffle.

Anger boiled in Gohar's veins. How dare this man stop her from helping a child? He wouldn't be so audacious if he knew who her father was. "Do you know who I am?" she fumed.

He spat on the ground. "A harlot, a godless rabble-rouser. That's who."

But before she could respond, her eyes caught a man in a brown *sardari* smirking at the back of the crowd. Smirnsky. The Russian spy whom Saleh Mirza and Aslan had accused of colluding with Mohammad Ali Mirza and Noor had called the devil. Was he following her? Was he the one behind the luti's sudden appearance? She hesitated. A misstep from her could harm her and dishonor Saleh Mirza, but to back down would condemn the boy to a slow death.

Just then, someone grabbed her arm. "She's my niece," said a woman with a Gurdan accent. "I sent her to fetch rice."

Sediqeh! The washwoman. Gohar exhaled.

The luti narrowed his eyes and turned to Sediqeh. "Where are your menfolk? Where did you get the money to buy this much rice?"

"We don't have menfolk," Sediqeh said breathlessly. "My husband is dead, and hers is in the provinces. My son works in Russia. He sent the money, thanks to the tsar's generosity. I was planning on inviting you for a meal to thank you for your protection." She turned to Gohar. "Let's go inside, dearie. It's cold here."

The waning prospect of a brawl prompted the onlookers to disperse. The luti scanned the dwindling crowd and darted a menacing glance at Gohar. "If you say so, Mother," he muttered, moving away.

Inside her small but clean room, Sediqeh brought Gohar hot water sweetened with rock candy, *nabat*.

"I don't know how to thank you," Gohar said, still shaking. "I am forever in your debt. My name, by the way, is Gohar."

"I did what anyone would do." Sediqeh paused. "That luti has it in for you."

"But why? What did I do to him?"

"It's not you, dearie. It's our time. In the old days, everyone knew their place. Lutis guarded the neighborhoods, settled disputes, and protected orphans and widows. People respected them. Now, everything is topsy-turvy. Young men scoff at the lutis. Women talk back to them. Now, lutis have lost their way. They bully people to show that they matter. That devil Russian's money doesn't help. You'd better stay away."

Sediqeh had a point. But what would happen to the boy if she stayed away?

As though reading her mind, Sediqeh continued. "You don't have to worry. I'll take care of the boy. I promise."

That solved all their problems.

By the time Gohar got on a droshky, the noon call to prayer filled the neighborhood. There was no time to change before meeting Aslan. He would get a kick out of her outfit.

Gohar gazed at the swallows flying south in an arrow formation. "Winter is coming," she said wistfully. Cold weather would make it hard to meet Aslan. Even in "their land," the ground would be too frozen for them to sit.

Down the valley, blue minarets dotted the red and gold trees in the capital. The walled, hexagonal city resembled a magical castle rising from the barren desert to the south.

"I know," Aslan said, taking a fistful of pistachios from a copper bowl between them. "By the way, you don't need to go back to Chaleh Meydan. I took care of the woman and her son."

Two days had passed since Gohar had arrived, flustered from her encounter with the luti and Smirnsky, and mentioned the boy to Aslan. She wasn't sure whether she appreciated his protectiveness or was irritated by his intrusion. "Why? Didn't you like my chador?"

He chuckled. "*Au contraire.* It gave you, shall we say, a certain rustic charm."

She jabbed him in the side. "Don't make fun of me."

Her punch pushed him off the boulder they sat on. He grabbed at the rock for balance, and the pistachios splattered everywhere. "I wouldn't dream of it," he said. "I meant it as a compliment."

She threw a pistachio at him.

He raised his hands. "Don't waste good pistachios. I meant to help so we can spend more time together. Plus, I don't want you there."

"Because of the luti? I'm not afraid of him."

"He's nothing but a lowlife bully. He won't bother you anymore. I made sure of that."

She gaped at him. "You talked to him already? You move fast. Did you beat him?"

"No! I'm not a brute. But I warned him that I would kill him if he ever dared to disrespect my womenfolk."

She smiled. "Am I your womenfolk?"

He smiled back. "In a manner of speaking."

"Then why can't I go back to Chaleh Meydan?"

"First of all, I don't understand why you're wasting your time helping one boy when you could work on ending the misery."

"Lofty ideas." She waved his words away. "I can't change the world. But I can help this boy." She paused. "And second?"

"There is a Russian working with the luti, Smirnsky. I don't want you near him."

She hadn't mentioned seeing Smirnsky to Aslan, but she remembered his face when he had encountered Smirnsky at Nowruz, and back in July. Curious to know more about their relations, she probed. "I have heard of him. How do you know him?"

"He runs spies and assassins for Okhrana, the Russian secret police." He met her eyes. "He will hurt you if he knows who you are."

The blood froze in her veins. "Why?"

"He probably knows what you've done to support Shuster. He has ears everywhere. And he could kidnap you to force Saleh Mirza to do his bidding." He paused. "Plus, he despises me."

"What did you do to him?"

"He thinks I'm a traitor. I foiled his plot to kill Shuster, caught his Georgian assassin, and witnessed him being humiliated. Men don't forget things like that."

The thought of a Russian master spy chasing Aslan worried her. She recalled instances when a beggar, a shopkeeper, or an urchin had shown up in their agreed-upon meeting places to direct her elsewhere. "Is he following you? Is that why you change our meeting places?"

"No, I do that to keep you safe in a turbulent city filled with written and unwritten rules."

Gohar paused. "Noor thinks you're a spy."

"That's preposterous." He grimaced.

Both fell silent. Wordlessly, he sat beside her.

"What did you do with the boy's mother?" she asked.

"I got her husband a job and had a talk with him. He promised not to beat her."

"And you believe him?"

"Of course not. I asked their neighbor, Sediqeh, to keep an eye on them."

"I thought she hated the Russians."

"She does. But I am from Ganja, practically a Persian." He grinned. "She made me tea, and we chatted about Yerevan. Did you know her son is a Bolshevik?"

"No. Did you see the boy?"

"Yes, I took the American doctor to see him."

"And?"

"He gave him some medicine." His face dropped. "But he is not long for this world."

She gulped. "What do you mean?"

"The doctor said there's no cure. Eventually, his rib cage will collapse." His voice trailed off.

The boy's fate was sealed. The futility of her efforts was a heavy blow. Perhaps Qamar was right, and there was no fighting destiny. Or perhaps Aslan was right, and you shouldn't waste your time helping just one person. She fought back tears.

He took her hand between his. She didn't object. The wind rustled through the birches and poplars. Their shoulders touched as they watched the sun wander down the valley.

"Ilych and I are making a brace for the boy to hold him upright and help him sit and walk," he fi nally said. "That and the rice will prolong his life. And someday, there will be a cure." He stood up, still holding her hand. "Come on. Let's take a walk. "

She squeezed his hand.

9

December 1911

"No one works, Khanum Bozorg. They just yap and yap."

Gohar overheard Mash Qolam talking to her mother-in-law as she applied kohl to her eyes in the next room.

He continued. "One of Haj Aqa's customers, a Greek fellow, owes us money. But we can't collect it because he's a Russian citizen."

Haji had never mentioned trouble collecting debts. But then again, they never discussed his business. Talking about business, like politics, was unbecoming to women, as far as Haji was concerned. Gohar didn't care. Commerce bored her. Ledgers and abacuses were mysteries. Mash Qolam did the shopping, and Haji's clerk paid the bills. Saleh Mirza paid for her clothing and left money in her pocket.

Nevertheless, she sensed trouble. Haji had closed his office in Gurdan and left his son, who managed the business there, unemployed. Saleh Mirza had found the son a job in the post office in Gurdan.

Belqais interrupted her thoughts. "Are you going out?"

Gohar glanced at her sister-in-law standing on the threshold. "Yes. I am taking our neighbors to the Armenian tailor."

"On Lalehzar?"

Gohar eyed Belqais suspiciously. Did she expect an invitation to come along? Her heart sank. She had planned to feign illness at the tailor's and leave early to meet Aslan. "Yes. Do you need something?"

"I wouldn't mind a copy of today's *Iran-e-Now*. I sent Mash Qolam to buy one, but all they had was *Estiqlal*," she said, referring to the conservative daily.

Belqais had never expressed any interest in newspapers, and certainly not in the progressive *Iran-e-Now*, the choice of the smart set in Tehran.

"Surely," she said. "I'll get you one. But we may return late. The city is a mess."

"That's fine," Belqais said without a trace of her usual rancor. "Your generation has so much more than we had: trams, cars, newspapers, gramophones, the cinema." She sighed.

Gohar nodded and turned back to the mirror, expecting Belqais to leave.

Instead, Belqais sat down. "I know you and I haven't always seen eye to eye," she said. "And I know I'm the one at fault."

Gohar was puzzled. The two of them barely spoke, let alone conversed.

"You didn't care for Gurdan or our house," Belqais continued. "But I did. I didn't know how much until the village elder told us that the Turkmen were coming. You don't know how scary it was."

Belqais looked forlorn. Was she seeking sympathy? Or was this a fishing expedition?

"We had our share of troubles here, too," Gohar said.

"We only had an hour to pack, hide the silver, and leave."

Gohar remembered her in-laws arriving in grimy rustic garb. "I can imagine."

Belqais leaned back. "That made me realize how fragile life is," she said wistfully. "There are many things I regret. Being hard on you is one. You have been kind to us."

Gohar feigned a smile. "Our house is your house."

"You have changed a lot. You dress differently, walk differently, sound differently. You are . . ." she hesitated, "beautiful."

"Thank you." Gohar rose. "I am sorry, but I am late. Let's talk later."

Belqais recoiled. Gohar felt guilty. But how could she forgo seeing the man she was drawn to like a compass to the North Pole to appease a petulant foe?

As the last month of autumn—Azar, the month of fire—had advanced, the flame in Gohar's heart had grown stronger. The feel of Aslan's hands holding hers, the touch of his lips on her palm, and the heat of his body when he was close all stirred a desire forbidden to a married woman.

At the same time, the constant fear of being found out ate at her. She felt Qamar's anxious eyes burrowing into her back whenever she left the house. The old woman's loyalty and discretion were not in question but betraying the trust of the street-smart Qamar pained Gohar.

Aslan's eyes told her that her feelings for him were mutual. But to give in to the temptation would be to join the ranks of duplicitous women she disdained. It would dishonor Saleh Mirza, break Noor's heart, and anger her God. And when—not if—Aslan left her, she would be bereft of her honor, dignity, and faith. Life would not be worth living.

They had been seeing each other for only three weeks. But in their every meeting an unspoken question hung heavy between them. What next?

That afternoon, when the two of them ventured to Tajrish village, she visited the soulful shrine of Imamzadeh Saleh while he waited outside. An ancient wishing tree, famous for performing miracles, caught her eye in the courtyard. The branches overflowed with colorful pieces of cloth tied by supplicants. She knotted a ribbon to a bough and pleaded for clarity.

10

December 1911, Tehran

Less than a week later, the Russian troops occupied Karaj, a mere twenty-five miles from the capital. Fear in Tehran rose. That night, Gohar and Noor ate alone while Saleh Mirza entertained guests in his study. This was unusual—he always dined with them. Could the meeting be related to what was happening in the country? After dinner, she slipped to the observation room to watch the study and learn more.

Saleh Mirza sat at the head of a table of men in suits, including the French minister and the cherub-faced English attaché. Aslan was at his side. She recognized some of the guests as members of the French-affiliated Freemason lodge, Awake Iran. They spoke in French. But even without understanding the language, she knew their solemn mood portended doom. Perturbed, she returned to the andarooni to distract herself by playing cards with Noor. An ashen Saleh Mirza joined them after midnight. He sank to the floor and remained silent despite Noor and Gohar's cajoling. Soon, he retired to his bedroom.

Aslan took her hand as soon as he boarded the droshky the next day. "We need to talk."

The stern tone of his voice made her stomach drop. She looked over his shoulder to the solitary policeman guarding the empty street. A tall Farangi rushed by the shuttered door of a shop. Was he the *New York Times* reporter said to be filing news from Tehran? There was no sign of the swarms of urchins that usually followed Farangis.

"Of course," she mumbled.

"If I leave Iran, will you come with me?"

A jolt of pain stabbed her heart. The thought of losing him was unfathomable. "Why would you leave?"

"It's not what I want. But it's what I must do."

"Is it related to last night's meeting at Saleh Mirza's?"

He stared at her, aghast. "How do you know about that?"

She couldn't tell him about the observation room. "I saw you and the others coming in."

He leaned back, letting her hands go. "The French are horrified by the prospect of what the Russians might do after taking Tehran. They approached Saleh Mirza with a proposal to save the city from a bloodbath."

Their eyes locked. "Aren't you training fighters?" she asked.

He avoided her gaze. "I am. But it's hopeless. All we have is a bunch of ill-equipped, untrained men. No match for a well-equipped army backed by the Cossacks inside the city and the Turkmen outside. We need real fighters. But the conservative militia is bailing out."

"Why?"

"They're sore because of the Majles forcing them to disarm."

Members of the conservative militia also lived in working-class neighborhoods, heavily targeted by Russian propaganda and bribery. She thought of Smirnsky's presence in Chaleh Meydan.

"And the Bakhtiari? They always seem ready to fight."

"Not this time. Rumor has it they've already made a deal with the Russians to stay in power and keep their share of oil money. Or maybe they are mad that pro-Demokraat militants have killed one of their bigwigs."

The horses' hooves echoed under the tiled arcade of the city gate. The guard standing at the gate was dwarfed by the mosaic mural of Rostam in battle gear with his shin on the back of the white deev. Where was the hero when his land needed him so desperately? Could he have defeated the Russians? One man against ten thousand?

"What is it that the French propose?" she muttered.

"I can't tell you. But I can tell you that Saleh Mirza thought the price of French peace was too high." He paused. "It is a devil's bargain."

Her hands caught his. "What does that have to do with you?"

"I am a bargaining chip. The Russians demand the handover of those of us who have helped the Iranians. Smirnsky has a list. My name is at the top. Some Russians I knew in Rasht have already been hanged." He swallowed. "I'd rather die fighting than be hanged like a criminal."

His stooped shoulders and forlorn face pained her. She wanted to hold him to ease his burden, to calm his soul. "Can't Saleh Mirza protect you?"

"He's tried to get me Iranian citizenship, but he can't. Not without Russian approval. Smirnsky has already said no. Saleh Mirza wants me to go away until things cool down."

"What about Yeprim Khan? He's the chief of police, for God's sake."

"He can help me hide. But I can't live underground like a rat for God knows how long." He sat up. "If I have to go, I want you to come with me."

She was lost for words. "Do you want me to be your mistress?"

"Of course not." He took her hands. "I want you to marry me. I want us to live together openly." He locked eyes with her. "I know we pledged to be friends. But for me, that is not enough. Not anymore. I miss you the second I leave you. My blood boils when I think of Haji touching you. I am tired of secrecy."

"But how?" she yelped. As easy as it was for a Muslim husband to divorce his wife, it was next to impossible for a Muslim woman to divorce her husband. On rare occasions, a woman would pay her husband for a divorce or petition an Islamic judge to end the marriage.

"Easy. If we leave together, what choice would Haji have but to divorce you?"

The cold mountain wind brushed her face. "But then Saleh Mirza would be disgraced. Noor would never forgive me. I would never be able to return or see them."

"I will talk to Saleh Mirza. Man-to-man. He loves you, and he likes me. He can handle delicate situations. Haji is a merchant; he can be bought, and he doesn't want a scandal. As for Noor, she will come around."

She desperately wanted to believe him. "Easy to say, hard to do."

"Tearing things apart is never easy. It takes courage. But sometimes we must break with the past so we can build the future." He paused. "Do you care for me?" he added timidly.

"How could you doubt that?" she snapped. "Do you have any idea how difficult it is for me to sneak out day after day to see you? I lie to everyone and put my life and reputation in danger just to be with you. Is that not caring?" Her voice softened. "I'm tired of secrecy, too. But what you're asking of me is not trivial. I don't love Haji. But I respect our marriage oath. And I can't leave Qamar dangling in the wind. She's left everything for me."

"Haji is old enough to be your grandfather. He married you to solidify his ties with Saleh Mirza. You are his property, not his partner." He paused. "We will send for Qamar as soon as we settle, and we will come back."

"What about your family? I don't even know them."

He gnashed his teeth. "I don't care what they think. I haven't seen them in six years."

"I don't even know your real name or where you were born. Noor thinks Aslan Madadoff is a fake name."

"Does it matter if my name is Aslan or Andre or Ali? Would I be different if I were a Russian, Georgian, or Persian? You don't know who your parents were. Do I care?"

He had a point. "What about the other women in your life?"

His lips turned. "They mean nothing, only amusements."

The prospect of the two of them living together excited and frightened her. Would she become an amusement soon, too? "Not that I care for money, but how will we live?"

"You don't have to worry about that. I'll find a way. I have my grandmother's inheritance to fall back on."

"I need time to think about this."

"I understand. But don't take too long. The Russians are less than a day's ride away."

By the time they reached their "land," the afternoon had turned windy and cold. They huddled under a blanket by the water. Even with the boulders sheltering them, she shivered.

"I'll warm you up," he murmured. He pulled her to his lap and draped his coat around her. She rested her head on his chest and drew in his smell of pine and earth.

His lips brushed her forehead, and his hands found their way underneath her loose blouse. His touch on her bare skin jolted her. He kissed her on the nose.

His mouth found hers. Their tongues touched. No one had ever kissed her like this. Her worries and fears disappeared instantly. Past and future vanished. Only "now" mattered. Soon, the world emptied of all but the two of them. She straddled him. Their bodies merged, skin pressed to skin, limb knotted in limb. They became one.

Their intimacy was as natural as breathing, as wild as fire.

Finally, blissful at their union, they lay under the blanket, holding on to each other, their breath blended, their hair intermingled. The sound of water echoed under the bridge. The air turned heavy with the smell of rain.

On the way back, she nestled on his chest. In the darkness of the fall evening, his strong heartbeat was soothing.

With his arms around her, he rested his chin on her head. "I was born Nikolai Vasilyevich Rudinov in St. Petersburg," he murmured. "I changed my name not because I am a crook but because I didn't want my father's name anymore. Aslan was the name of an Azeri friend in Baku. It means lion. I took Madadoff from a gravestone there." He paused. "I was born a Christian. But I don't go to church. I could convert to Islam, but I would make a lousy Muslim. I drink, lust after pretty women, and am too lazy to pray five times a day. Happy?"

She lifted her face and smiled.

11

She arrived home disheveled and out of breath. Feigning a cold, she fled to her bedroom. There, she sat in the darkness, dizzy and euphoric, his smell on her body, his taste in her mouth.

Carnal relations were part of married life. Pleasing her husband was her duty. But what she had experienced today was otherworldly. It was the sensation women whispered about in the baths and at parties, and poets hinted at. The pleasure had delighted and frightened her. It felt out of control. What if it was even . . . satanic?

Anxiety ripped through her. She wanted to play her tar to calm down, but that was out of the question. Her in-laws were next door.

A house where she couldn't do what she cherished most wasn't her home, after all.

Light-headed and ecstatic, she hummed. *"If I am drunk, it is of your eyes that I am."*

She already missed Aslan. Their lovemaking had only intensified her desire for him. His absence would be lethal.

He was right about Haji and Saleh Mirza, and even about Qamar. Haji had his mother, and his work kept him occupied. Her departure would cause him no more pain than a bruised ego. Saleh Mirza was pragmatic and fond of Aslan. As for Qamar, she forgave Gohar no matter what.

But Noor, who hadn't forgiven her own daughter, would never absolve her.

And what about her country? Could she part with the only land she knew, with its familiar sights and sounds, the smell of saffron and jasmine, the comforting rhythm of its alleys and markets, the nuances of the faces and gestures, the rituals of Nowruz and Muharram?

In *qorbat*, a foreign land, she would only have him. If he turned out to be cruel, indifferent, or even downright criminal, there would be no one to turn to, nowhere to go.

She had to choose between her beloved and everything she cared for. Was this the price to pay for her sin? She buried her face in her palms.

Perhaps this was the answer to her prayer in the shrine in Tajrish—the cloth she had knotted on the wishing tree there. This could be her chance to break free, hand in hand with her angel, her savior, her soulmate, the man she had longed for all these months.

If he was her kismet, then there was no sin in their lovemaking. Had God not given them bodies to enjoy?

Was this relationship the union of two halves becoming whole? Or a gateway to the abyss?

If she had time, she could talk to Saleh Mirza without mentioning Aslan. She could argue—and it would be true—that she'd never be pious or obedient enough for Haji or his mother. That Tehran had changed her, and there was no turning back. Her marriage was a sham. Deceit had doomed it. Why not end it now, with no children to complicate the matter?

Saleh Mirza would understand. Times were changing. Saleh Mirza himself advocated for being bold and modern. He had praised other fathers who had stepped in to save their daughters from bad marriages, even paying the husbands to divorce them. Haji would never challenge Saleh Mirza. She would beg and cry and give up her jewelry and *mahrieh*. Once she was free, Aslan would ask for her hand. They would be married with Saleh Mirza's blessing.

But there was no time. Any hope for an auspicious ending was a pipe dream. Conflicted and restless, she lay in bed, praying for a sign from the divine.

Throughout her music lesson the next day, Saleh Mirza's concerned gaze lingered on her. Did he suspect something? Nothing escaped his sharp eyes.

In the middle of the lesson, a manservant came to fetch him to see a messenger from the British minister. When he returned, he was pallid and trembling. The Russians had trapped more than a thousand nationalists in Tabriz castle and shot at them. Many were dead or severely wounded. The Russians had also severed the telegraph lines and arrested constitutionalists, including prominent clergymen. The minister, alerted by the consulate in Tabriz, had tried to stop the bloodshed, to no avail.

Gohar's chest tightened.

"This is a warning," Saleh Mirza said. "They will do ten times worse in Tehran."

With that, he left, on his way to confer with other notables and find a way to save the city.

A day later, riots broke out in Rasht and Anzali when Russian soldiers confiscated food. At least forty-two people were killed.

Gohar had to decide. Tomorrow, when she met Aslan, he would expect an answer.

12

December 1911, Tehran

"Where are you going in this weather?" Qamar bellowed in horror as Gohar put on her coat the next day. "What's the rush? Go tomorrow."

Gohar glanced at the snow filling the empty water basin in the yard. "The bazaar will be crowded tomorrow." She pointed to the pair of boys' boots she held. "I have snow boots."

"Suit yourself," Qamar said, taking a fistful of nuts left over from the celebration of the winter solstice, Yelda, the night before. "You're the one who'll suffer if you break a bone." She sank deeper underneath the quilt covering the *korsi*.

Despite her bravado, Gohar was not a fan of winter. She was delighted when an empty droshky stopped for her as soon as she reached the main street. It took her a few seconds to recognize Ilych as the driver. Aslan, foreseeing her predicament, had sent Ilych to collect her. His foresight touched her.

Aslan did not speak when he got on the droshky. She was grateful for his silence as they rode. He expected an answer that Gohar didn't have. Not yet. The road was deserted. In the pearly light, frozen rain glistened on the branches of trees. Cottony flakes of snow fell silently. The world was pure and dreamy.

At their land, he got off first. "Come on out," he said, pointing to a yellow spot across the ice-covered stream. "I want to show you something."

But walking on the slippery riverbank proved impossible, even with Aslan's help and wearing her new boots. She climbed back as he crossed the ice and brought back a branch of wild winter jasmine. She was amazed by the delicacy of the flower that blossomed in the snow.

Even sheltered under the bridge on their land, it was too cold to
be outdoors. They huddled in the droshky for a while, but when he
suggested that they go to his house, she relented. That would give her
a chance to see how he lived. On their way, he put his arm around her
shoulders. "Did you hear about the massacre in Tabriz?"

She nodded and recounted what had happened the day before at
Saleh Mirza's. He pulled her closer. "Russians are known for their cruelty.
They're pressuring Tehran to surrender before Russian Christmas." He
paused. "You know what that means for us."

She caressed the yellow petals on her lap. This was the sign she
had asked for. If the fragile flower could thrive in the winter, she could
survive in a foreign land. Fear was not an excuse for cowardice. Together,
she and Aslan could face whatever was to come.

"I will come with you," she said without hesitation.

He lived near the Armenian church in the southwest of the city. To her
delight, only stiff sheets on the clothesline greeted them in the empty
courtyard. In his sparsely furnished room, up a short flight of stairs,
large windows overlooked the courtyard. A brazier holding slow-burning
charcoal covered in ashes warmed the room. Books, a gramophone, and
a neat stack of records were the only luxuries.

She removed her shoes and drenched chador and stood awkwardly
on the faded rug. Her eyes lingered anxiously on the row of books in
Latin and Cyrillic script on the mantle. "Will you teach me French and
Russian?" she asked.

"Of course." He smiled mischievously as he placed a record on the
gramophone. "But first, I want to teach you something more important."
He cranked the turntable handle.

The sultry voice of a female singer filled the room. Her melancholic
tone contrasted with the cheery music. The words were in French, but
the heartfelt emotion was universal. A bit like a *tasnif*, she thought.

"This is Yvette Guilbert," he said.

He walked to her in his collarless white shirt and suspenders, stood, clicked his bare heels, and bowed. "May I have this dance?" he said, reaching for her hand.

The magazines at the tailor shop were replete with drawings of men in elegant tailcoats dancing with women in flowing evening dresses. But she had never seen an actual couple dancing. "If only I knew how." She giggled.

"Allow me." He rested his right hand low on her waist and placed her left hand on his own shoulder. "We start easy. Walk with me, keep the beat." He held her close, but not tight.

With eyes glued to his feet, mindful not to step on his toes, she followed his lead. Deftly, he moved her around the room. "Let yourself go," he said. "Trust me."

Her steps became more assured as they moved. She let the music and Aslan guide her. He spun her around. Her heart pounded. She laughed. Her scarf fell off.

He pulled her closer and unbraided her hair so that it spread on her shoulders.

They moved as though they had been dancing together all their lives. Over his shoulder, she glanced at the winter jasmine on his desk. How glorious their life together would be. No more mayhem and gloom, no more fear and deception. Their days would be filled with music, flowers, and love.

When the music stopped, he kissed her. Long and leisurely.

Then he stepped back. "Are you ready for a hard one?" He placed a new record on the gramophone. "The waltz is the king of dances, and *The Blue Danube* is the king of waltzes."

He held her waist tightly as they whirled to the sweeping and gracious music. The motion made her dizzy as they turned faster and faster. His eyes sparkled in the afternoon light. She felt like a child: exhilarated, free. Her feet barely touched the ground. This was as close to flying as she could imagine. She closed her eyes and let him carry her.

Flushed, sweaty, and heaving, they dropped onto the narrow wooden bed when the music stopped. Their hands explored each other's bodies; their mouths sought each other's mouths. She welcomed his body on hers. Unhurried and harmonious, they began a new dance. No music needed.

They made love with the windows open to the falling snow. The cold relieved the fever of her body. All doubts had vanished. They belonged together, like fish and water, birds and sky. No one could come between them.

As darkness fell, they made plans. In three days, on Christmas Day, she would leave her house early for the bathhouse, carrying her bundle. Ilych and Aslan would meet her. She would have three letters for Aslan to carry to Saleh Mirza: one pleading with him for help and understanding; one for Noor, begging her for forgiveness; and the last for Haji, asking for compassion and a divorce. Then, Aslan would meet Saleh Mirza before joining her and Ilych on the road to Anzali. Once in that port city, they would catch the ferry to Baku. From there, a train would take them to another boat, this time to Istanbul.

Far from Haji and Smirnsky, life would be a rapturous poem to write, love a glorious song to compose . . .

13

December 1911, Tehran

On the afternoon before her planned departure, Gohar sorted through her belongings to select what she could fit in a bundle. As she wrapped jewelry in a favorite shirt, Haji's voice startled her. He wasn't expected until dinnertime.

She found him slouched on the living room floor with his shoulders hunched and his face in his hands. His white hair jolted Gohar. When he lifted his head, his sallow complexion and sunken eyes frightened her. He looked ghastly and old.

A knot formed in her stomach. His illness could delay her departure. "What's wrong?" she asked. "Are you sick? Shall I send for the doctor?"

"No need. It will pass." His voice trembled.

Dread gnawed at her heart. "Do you want tea?" Tea—Russian and British—was boycotted. But she still had a stash.

He moaned. "Later. For now, let me be."

"Is there anything I can do?"

"Yes. Will you play your tar for me?"

Gohar was aghast. He didn't like music. And it was Muharram—no one listened to music now. But she left to fetch the tar and asked Qamar to brew borage for Haji. That would settle him.

He sobbed as she played. Finally, he calmed down enough to talk. "At the Majles today, Yeprim Khan came with his men, a large contingent of Bakhtiari fighters, and an order from the Regent to end the legislative session. He sent us home, locked the building, and dismissed the militia."

Closing the Majles meant the end of their sovereignty. Suddenly, she understood the French proposal. Freedom and democracy were the price they had to pay to save their capital city from the Russians' destruction. They were a nation only in name. A devil's bargain, Aslan had said.

Anger and despair filled her heart. "What did you do?" she muttered.

"Nothing. What could a bunch of unarmed old men do?" He cursed his fickle tribal relations. "We left quietly."

"You knew Bakhtiari are loyal only to Bakhtiari. Your cousin said as much before the vote to reject the Russian ultimatum," she said, putting her tar down.

"I expected their treachery," he fumed. "But I never imagined Yeprim, our so-called national hero, would put a knife in our back." Yeprim Khan's bravery in fighting Mohammad Ali Mirza earned him the title of People's Hero. "Some people say he must have been paid off," Haji continued.

"You mustn't say things like that," Gohar said, shocked. "Yeprim Khan would never take a bribe. I am sure he didn't have a choice if he wanted to avoid bloodshed. He must have closed the Majles with a heavy heart."

Haji looked at her askance. "How would you know?"

"How could it be otherwise? He has risked his life for the constitution and the Majles on multiple occasions," she said. "The Regent was clever. If he had sent the Cossacks, people would have revolted. But with Yeprim involved, people stayed calm."

He didn't respond. His breathing had become labored. Sweat covered his forehead. When he complained of nausea and weakness in his left arm, she sent for the doctor and made him a bed in the living room.

After the doctor left, Haji asked her to sit with him. "It's not just the Majles that's finished," he said. "I am, too."

Alarmed, Gohar stared at him. "What do you mean?"

"I'm broke, dear. We haven't collected rent from our orchards and villages in months. I have warehouses full of Russian goods I can't sell. When I do, I can't collect payment."

Gohar recalled Mash Qolam's comments about the state of the business. How long had this been going on?

He took her hand. "You, my dear, are now my only reason to go on living. Without you, I might as well die."

His words stabbed her heart. Like Yeprim Khan, she was trapped. Her duty was to care for this broken man in this broken land. She couldn't leave.

Later that night, the doctor gravely reported that Haji was in critical condition. His heart was damaged, a condition the Farangi called *infactus*, possibly triggered by the shock and stress of recent events. He may not survive, but his chances would improve if he could pull through the coming week. It was all in God's hands. He gave Haji a tincture. Gohar kept the news to herself. No need to worry her in-laws.

That night, she vacillated between her desire to break free and her obligation to her family. She had decided to leave a healthy and wealthy Haji for the man she loved. But abandoning a sick and broken man for a foreigner—a Russian, no less—would be unjust and shameful. The rumors would finish Haji off if the disease didn't. If he died, the burden of guilt would poison her love for Aslan. Their life together would be doomed.

Everyone in the country paid a price. Hers was love. A devil's bargain, indeed.

She rose before dawn. A deadly calm had engulfed the city. She washed her face with freezing water from the basin and donned a black dress. Qamar was surprised to see her but didn't question her, considering her black outfit a sign of mourning for the martyrs of Karbala. Together, they performed the morning prayer. In her prayers, she beseeched the Lord for strength, Haji's health, and Aslan's safety.

As they sipped hot, sugared water afterward, Qamar whispered. "So, you stayed."

Gohar gasped. "What?"

"I saw you packing," Qamar murmured.

Did Qamar know of her affair? Since when?

As though reading her mind, Qamar put her hand on Gohar's knee. "You don't have to worry about me. My lips are sealed. I know it's hard on you. But you did the right thing."

Gohar put her head on Qamar's bosom and let the tears roll down her face.

Later, she explained their financial predicament to Qamar. Their maid and her daughter would stay. They had nowhere else to go. Gohar would manage the household finances, selling jewelry as needed. Gohar didn't want to involve Saleh Mirza or Noor, at least not yet.

At sunrise, Gohar walked to the bathhouse to send an attendant to meet Ilych with a note. She couldn't bear the thought of Aslan waiting for her in the cold. Cossacks were already patrolling the neighborhood.

Two days later, William Morgan Shuster resigned.

On Ashura, the Russians hanged forty-two constitutionalists in Tabriz from poles decorated with the Russian flag. That afternoon, Gohar declined Noor's invitation to Tekyeh Dowlat. Instead, she and Qamar attended the Ta'azyeh in their own modest neighborhood. Unencumbered by the fear of losing power and status, locals had dressed Yazid as the tsar—replete with a pointed beard. The crowd vociferously condemned the tsar and his cronies to eternal damnation as soldiers in Cossack uniforms martyred the imam and his retinue in what resembled the castle in Tabriz. A large Iranian flag flew on the stage.

Gohar bawled as the imam in a white shroud bade farewell to his young daughter and wailed as Zainab was told of her beloved son's death. The others urged her on: tears shed on Ashura washed away sins, leaving the heart pure to communicate with the divine. She implored the Lord to grant Aslan peace and joy and pleaded with the martyrs of Karbala to watch over him.

As for herself, her pain was her righteous punishment. She prayed for endurance.

Two weeks later, on the day Shuster left Iran for good, Gohar discovered her pregnancy.

14

March 1912, Tehran

The house, like the city, lingered in foggy gloom throughout the winter. Gohar ran the household, cared for Haji, and comforted his mother, all with compassion and grace. Love was neither required nor on offer.

Smirnsky's reinstatement as the young shah's tutor outraged her. She seethed when the Russians built permanent barracks in the northern provinces and set up road construction headquarters in Qazvin. But it was the pictures smuggled out of Tabriz that inflamed her most. The victims, many of them mere teenagers, had been killed in a gruesome fashion. Some were blown out of cannons. Others were quartered, impaled, or beaten to death while hung by the feet.

She was sure that the true extent of the atrocities would never be revealed.

Prayer became her refuge. In the silence of night, when she felt the presence of the divine in her heart, she pleaded for Aslan's safety and the health of her unborn child. Despite her faith in the Lord's mercy, she was racked with worry about the common belief that a child conceived in sin would be born disfigured. But without the telltale sickness of her first pregnancy, it was easy to keep her condition secret.

She didn't write to Aslan. What could she say to a person she longed for with every breath but would never see again?

One morning, a picture in the newspaper rattled her. It showed bearded, emaciated men chained together, boarding a Russian ferry. The men were Russians who had fought on the Iranian side. In utter panic, she rushed to Aslan's house. The Armenian landlord assured her that Aslan and Ilych had left of their own volition some time ago. She declined his offer to see Aslan's room. She didn't have the heart.

Haji recuperated slowly, sleeping fitfully, eating sparingly, and avoiding people, especially his tribal cousins. He didn't even attend the mosque. His mother and Gohar urged him to return to his *hojreh*, the business place. He did when he felt better, but always complained about the sluggishness of business. Goods were scarce after a prolonged boycott of the English and Russians, and people were suffering under foreign occupation and tribal unrest. On top of that, people's tastes had shifted to foreign merchandise, leaving his skills in domestic trade worthless. These days, commerce was dominated by young men with language skills and overseas contacts.

He announced his plan to sell his *hojreh* and retire.

As spring approached, Gohar longed for the hustle and bustle of the streets. On a rainy day before Nowruz, she ventured to the grand bazaar. The colorful mounds of skillfully arranged oranges, apples, pomegranates, and grapes at the produce market lifted her spirits momentarily.

Only a handful of customers tried on shoes in the cobblers' market inside the multistory entrance, known as the "mouth" of the bazaar. Passersby barely glimpsed at the rows of shoes hung on the wall. People were destitute.

A tug on her chador stopped her in the passage leading to the fabric market. She turned. A barefoot boy in shabby clothing stood holding a small cloth sack. Her first instinct was to give him a coin, but his audacity in touching her irritated her. She pulled her chador away from his grasp.

"Please, lady, stop! I don't want money," he said.

The pleading in his voice halted her.

The urchin raised the bag to her. "This is yours. I saw you drop it,"

The bag didn't look familiar. This was another ploy to extort money. She turned to leave.

But the boy ran ahead to block her. "Please take it." He forced the pouch into her hand.

She hesitated. The pouch was the kind many housewives carried.

"How do you know it's mine?" she said.

"I saw you drop it, and the luti saw me pick it up. If you don't take it, he'll think I stole it and beat me up."

The bag wasn't hers, but the boy's genuine fright softened her. He reminded her of the urchin Aslan had sent to fetch her once. She took the bag. The boy disappeared into the crowd without taking the money.

On the walk home, Gohar peeked inside the bag for anything that might help her locate the rightful owner. In the dim light that shone through the holes in the bazaar's vaulted ceiling, she saw a small white bundle and an envelope bearing her name. Shaken, she swiftly closed the pouch.

At home, she sent Qamar on an errand and retired to her bedroom before opening the envelope. The short letter was in neat, albeit novice, handwriting.

My dear Gohar,

Please forgive my inadequacy in writing Farsi. As you know, I had no choice but to leave Tehran. Ilych, however, has inquired around and watched your house to make sure you are not in danger. I know your husband has been sick but has recovered. Since you knew where I lived and no note or letter has been sent there, I can only conclude that you do not wish to be in touch with me anymore.

I can't say I understand because I don't. But I accept and honor your decision, as painful as it is. I cannot tell you what our brief time together meant to me, or the anguish I feel now. Suffice it to say that it was the best and the worst time of my life. Fate brought us together before. Perhaps it will do so again.

I found the enclosed chain and medallion in the courtyard of your house on the day I saw you for the first time. Should you ever need me, please bring the broken chain to Golestan Jewelry in the gold market of the grand bazaar. Ask for Mr. Dauvoody, the owner. Tell him you have a broken chain and ask him to find the other half. He will find me, wherever I am. I will keep the other half of the chain as the only memento I have of you.

Yours forever,

Aslan Madadoff

She sat motionless for a long while before opening the little bundle. Wrapped in a white handkerchief were a broken chain and the gold charm her mother had left her to keep her safe.

15

April 1912, Tehran

On the first week of the Persian New Year, the Russians shelled the Shrine of Imam Reza in Mashhad and raided its treasury. The attack killed many and injured many more. The audacity of assaulting the country's holiest site on the national holiday shocked even the foreign diplomats.

Later that week, Gohar felt the child moving under her heart for the first time as she shelled fava beans. She had kept the pregnancy to herself until shortly before Nowruz. The announcement had sent Qamar to the nearest *saqaa-khaneh* to light a tray full of candles. Noor and Saleh Mirza had fed the poor for three days, and Khanum Bozorg had praised the Lord for sending them light in the time of darkness. Even Belqais seemed delighted.

Haji, however, remained muted. "I am happy for you, my dear," he had said. "A newborn is a blessing. But bringing up a child at my age, and in my financial situation, will be difficult."

Gohar was chafed. If he weren't so gentle, she would have thought he knew of her indiscretion and was suspicious of the child's paternity. But it didn't matter. The child's possible physical resemblance to Aslan could be explained easily by her own unknown ancestry. Above all, she would make sure that her child was loved.

Belqais's offer to step in and finish the fava beans surprised her. Her sister-in-law had never done anything like that before. But her back was stiff and painful. Belqais squeezed her hand affectionately as Gohar leaned on her shoulder to rise. "May God grant you fortitude."

Gohar arched her back to release the tension. From here, the yard looked neglected. She would ask Mash Qolam to plant some violets, maybe a rosebush.

The goldfish on the mantle—a leftover from the Nowruz ceremony—struggled to swim in its tiny bowl. It would be happier in the water basin in the yard, where it could amuse a little boy with its swimming. She caressed her belly as she walked to the open window.

Outside, a swallow with a red mark on her chest perched on the barely green bough of the mulberry tree. Gohar looked around. There were swallows everywhere, chirping joyfully on the tops of walls, on rooftops, on window seals, and on trees. She breathed deeply, taking in the scent of moist earth and new leaves. Spring had finally arrived.

PART III
Stranger in Her own Land

Leave me—this stranger in his native land—alone.
The envoy of bitter experiences,
Warns my heart.
That you are a lie, lie.
That you are a ruse, rus...

M. AKHAVAN SALES

1

December 1914, Tehran

On the fall day Aslan came to visit Saleh Mirza after three years of absence, the man who was once the most powerful in Iran lay in bed dying.

His illness, which made eating difficult and digesting painful, had baffled every physician, even the American doctors in the missionary hospital. It had progressed rapidly. Not long after he fell ill in the summer of 1913, Saleh Mirza needed a cane for walking. By that winter, he required assistance to stand. When Nowruz arrived in March, he received his well-wishers lying down. By summer, too ill to read, he had listened to Gohar deliver the news of the German attack on his beloved Paris.

That day, Gohar spotted Aslan through the window while she was reading to Saleh Mirza. The shock stopped her mid-sentence.

"What is it, dear?" Saleh Mirza asked.

"You have a visitor, Aqa Mirza," she said, her eyes glued to Aslan as he greeted the gardener. Sporting a fashionably trim mustache and an oversized overcoat, he looked much thinner than before. "It's Aslan."

Aslan had never been far from her mind, but since the start of the war, her thoughts of him had turned morbid. When Tehran cheered the demise of an entire Russian army in Prussia, the image of his bloody corpse in a burned-out forest kept her awake night after night.

"Help me get dressed. I can't receive him like this," Saleh Mirza said. Despite a multitude of servants attending him, it was Gohar who groomed him. Helping him get dressed allowed them to share a moment without discussing his disease. Now, the task gave her a moment to rein in the tsunami of emotions the sight of Aslan alive had unleashed in her—joy, regret, guilt, and fear of accidentally revealing secrets that must never be revealed.

Dressed in his Parisian silk dressing gown, a Sulka foulard wrapped around his neck, his hair combed, and a Japanese quince pinned to his lapel, Saleh Mirza leaned on her to stagger across the room. He leaned back in his yellow wingback chair, crossed his ankles, and folded his hands on his lap. "How do I look?" he said, pleading with his eyes.

She kissed his forehead. "Glorious." Some rouge would have brightened his pallid cheeks, but Saleh Mirza would never go for that. She wondered whether it was the illness that had weakened him or the laudanum the doctors prescribed. "Now I must go," she said, turning to leave. "I will tell the valet to bring Aslan in."

He grabbed her wrist. "Stay."

Since his confinement to bed, Saleh Mirza had defied all conventions and insisted that Gohar remain with him when people visited. Her presence made some visitors uncomfortable, but others didn't mind. The more liberal-minded ones even engaged her in conversation. Participating in even a mundane meeting enthralled her. Afterward, Saleh Mirza would ask for her opinion or explain the background of the conversation. But not today. She couldn't face Aslan in the presence of Saleh Mirza.

"I have to check on Kamal," she said, hiding her face by picking up her son's toy soldiers from the floor.

The boy had been born robust, handsome, and good-natured, befitting the name Saleh Mirza gave him, Kamal—perfection.

"He's asleep," Saleh Mirza said. "With all the servants around, you shouldn't worry so much. Be like other women. Let them take care of him. They adore him."

Indeed, everyone in the house doted on the rambunctious little boy with his easy smile. But Gohar never felt comfortable leaving him with anyone except Qamar or Noor. "Qamar has gone to the shrine of Shah Abdolazim, and Noor is resting," she said. "I am not like other women, Aqa Mirza. I don't want others to take care of my child."

She had even defied her social circle's norm of hiring a wet nurse, instead nursing the child herself. From the moment he was born,

Kamal had never ceased to amaze her with his fierce assertion of his personhood and his canny ability to get his way with smiles and cries.

"I know," he said, resigned.

In the andarooni, Kamal was asleep beside Noor, clutching his stuffed Steiff bear. With his ringlets of sandy-brown hair loose on his pale forehead, long eyelashes, and rosy cheeks, he resembled a cherub from a Farangi painting. Gohar beamed with a mother's pride.

The observation room, unused for some time, was dirty. Gohar cleared the cobwebs from the slots to watch Aslan embrace Saleh Mirza. A flood of memories rushed through her mind: their walks, their dancing, the melancholic voice of the French singer, and the delicate yellow flower wilting on the empty desk.

Aslan and Saleh Mirza spoke too softly for her to hear them. But their animated gestures delighted her. It had been a long time since Saleh Mirza had been this lively. Her heart sank when Saleh Mirza proudly showed Aslan the studio pictures of Kamal on his first and second birthdays, displayed on his bedside. But Aslan put the picture back after a perfunctory look.

Saleh Mirza's shining eyes and glowing cheeks after the visit delighted Gohar. He asked her to jot down a new entry for his memoirs. "You should try the Waterman fountain pen Aslan brought," he said, demonstrating the pen's ingenious screw cap with the guileless smile of a child.

The mention of the memoirs—neglected for three years—pleased her. Perhaps he had turned the corner. Perhaps Aslan had promised to return to work. For a fleeting moment, she fantasized about the three of them collaborating on the book. "Is he back for good?" she asked as casually as she could.

"At least until the war ends." He paused before adding, "He defended Paris, you know," as though he needed to protect Aslan's honor against her judgment.

She nodded and wrote as he dictated:

"The past three years have been a period of devastation and despair for our ancient land. The uprisings, boycotts, assassinations, and rage have gradually given way to apathy and stagnation.

"In the north, the Russians govern with brute force. They monopolize navigation and fishing in the Caspian, confiscate land to settle their citizens, and coerce prominent residents into becoming Russian subjects. They connected Tabriz to the Russian border via rail and rebuilt the Anzali-Qazvin Road as a motorway to link Russia to Mesopotamia.

"In the south, the English have completed the construction of the largest oil refinery in the world on the island of Abadan to supply their navy.

"For years, the Majles had remained closed despite pressure from the press and the threat of strikes by the guilds if it did not reopen. With half the country under foreign occupation, rampant corruption, tribal rivalry devastating the countryside, and an inept, bankrupt government, it wasn't clear whether democracy would ever have a chance to flourish or even a role to play in the country.

"Concerned about possible challenges to the shah's legitimacy if he wasn't sworn in by the Majles, the regent called for an election in 1913. However, lack of funds, foreign occupation, and apathy in the provinces prolonged the process despite the enthusiasm of intellectuals and the press in Tehran. The Russians blocked the election in Tabriz, the second-largest city in Iran. The Majles finally opened in December of 1914.

"The young shah was crowned in the summer of 1914. Two weeks later, Europe erupted in a Great War, pitting an alliance of Russia, England, and France against a coalition of Germany and Austria-Hungary, soon joined by the Ottomans.

"The war did not concern the citizens of our land: Farangis, being Farangis, could fight each other all they wanted as long as they left us out of it. Better for them to fight one another than to meddle in our affairs. Only a few weeks later, however, the Ottomans breached our borders to defeat the Russians in Tabriz. Now, they are the occupiers.

"Like a plague, the war has crept into our home: unannounced and unwelcomed."

That evening, Gohar contemplated returning home. Saleh Mirza seemed better, and she had not been home for weeks. She had spent little time at her marital house since the last month of her pregnancy when she had moved to Saleh Mirza's place so Noor could care for her. The stay had been extended first to let Gohar recuperate, then to help her care for infant Kamal, and finally, to allow her to tend to Saleh Mirza. She didn't miss the house. But Haji had been quietly complaining, despite his usual deference to Saleh Mirza. He wanted to see Kamal and take him to the mosque to show him to the neighbors.

Haji never opposed his father-in-law's wishes to keep Gohar and Kamal at his house. But the child had brought him luck. On the day he was born, Haji had partnered with a savvy young Azeri merchant who had an abundance of overseas contacts and a reputation for honesty. The venture—financed by the sale of Gohar's and her mother-in-law's jewelry—had prospered. Haji's subsequent easy reelection to a newly reopened Majles had only strengthened his belief in Kamal's luck. He wanted the boy close.

But Saleh Mirza didn't want Gohar to leave that night. He was feeling better for a change. They could talk, and he could play with Kamal. Gohar relented.

At dinner, Saleh Mirza asked his valet to open a bottle of Bordeaux the French minister had sent. "You must try this," he said to Gohar. "It goes well with *fessenjoon*." He pointed to the stew of walnuts, pomegranate, and duck the women were eating. "But it doesn't pair well with my *fereni*." He gestured to the bland rice pudding prepared for him.

Gohar felt guilty. *Fesenjoon* was Saleh Mirza's favorite dish. The wine was too bitter for her, but she took a sip.

"You are happy tonight, Saleh," Noor said, sipping her wine. "It must be seeing your long-lost son from your French mistress." That was what Noor jokingly called Aslan.

Saleh Mirza chuckled. "I wish he was. Hell of a lot better than my flesh and blood."

The sad undertone in his voice pained Gohar. His estranged son, Akbar Mirza, was a source of grief for Saleh Mirza. Even knowing how sick his father was had not motivated him to write or come to see him.

"What's Aslan doing here, anyway?" Noor asked.

"Staying out of harm's way," Saleh Mirza said.

Gohar wanted to ask more about him, but she feared raising suspicions. Besides, with Saleh Mirza getting better, she would have plenty of opportunities to inquire later.

After dinner, they listened to music and talked for some time before Gohar kissed Saleh Mirza's cheeks and left him to rest.

A cry of agony woke her early the following day. It sounded like a wounded animal. She ran to the source of the noise, Saleh Mirza's study. There, his burly valet slumped by the door, beating his chest, and wailing. His look told her all she needed to know.

Soon, mourners filled the house. Saleh Mirza's body was washed and wrapped in a shroud blessed in the shrine of Imam Ali in Najaf and adorned with Qur'anic verses written in saffron.

That afternoon at the cemetery, women were kept at a distance as the body was lowered into a newly dug grave. Gohar envied Haji, who was allowed one last glimpse of Saleh Mirza's face before covering him with fresh earth.

"*We are of God, and to Him, we shall return,*" the mullah recited as Noor howled.

Drained and distraught, they returned to a house already transformed. The furniture was draped in black cloth, and the curtains drawn. Noor screamed on seeing a picture of Saleh Mirza, framed in black, on his chair. The smell of saffron and rosewater wafted through the house.

A deluge of people poured in that evening. Teary servants circulated trays of coffee and the traditional funeral sweet, halva. Cooks prepared food on the wood fire in the courtyard to feed the poor lining the alley. The melancholic voice of the mullah drowned the sobbing of an inconsolable Noor.

Gohar mourned quietly. Sitting beside Noor and squeezing her hand, she held her tears back as people paid them their respects. Her loss deepened with every hour. Awake all night, she held Kamal tightly as he slept.

2

January 1915, Tehran

Snow fell silently on the bent boughs of elms, covering the burlap-covered roses and Japanese quinces. In Saleh Mirza's study, Gohar read the note Saleh Mirza had dictated to her six weeks earlier, on the day Aslan had returned. How eloquently he had depicted the predicament of their land in this last entry to his memoirs.

She put the paper down. It was too dark to read. Saleh Mirza had contemplated installing an electric light in his study, but now he was gone, and soon the house would be too.

His will would be read shortly. His son, Akbar Mirza, would inherit the house, for which he had no love. Soon, the compound, covering two city blocks, would be torn down to be rebuilt as a hotel, a movie theater, or a complex of apartments and stores, as was happening to all the grand houses around Lalehzar. This land so close to foreign legations and new luxury hotels was too precious to be left alone. Her chest tightened. The house was her home, her sanctuary, her refuge. Her son had been born, taken his first steps, and uttered his first word here.

She had no delusion of Haji buying the house, even if he could afford it. With its intricate plasterwork, tall ceilings adorned with exquisite wooden tiles, expertly carved doors, and latticed mosaic windows, it was too flamboyant for Haji's taste.

This was the room she would miss most. It was where Saleh Mirza had shared his life and wisdom with her, where she had heard recorded music and learned tar, and where Aslan had once worked. Restless, she walked to the andarooni, where Kamal sat on Qamar's lap in his American-made sailor suit, clutching his stuffed bear.

As though sensing her presence, he lifted his head. His hazel eyes widened. He grinned, wriggling free from Qamar to run to Gohar, dragging the toy. "Bibi! Bibi!" he screamed.

She picked him up, ignoring Qamar's warnings about the child's weight. He wrapped his hands around her neck, burrowing his face into her shoulder.

In the study, she left him to play on the carpet while she put on a record. The music drowned out the cawing of crows outside.

"Yuk," Kamal said, folding the bear over his head to cover his ears. He wasn't a fan of slow tunes.

She sat beside him and held his wrist gently. "Stop that, dear. You will ruin the bear. Grandma will be upset if you tear her gift."

Kamal smiled without heeding her. He knew she didn't have the heart to scold him. The smile reminded her of Aslan's. She felt old. At barely twenty, her only brush with passionate love was to spot the fading reflection of her lover's smile on her son's face.

Kamal climbed into her lap. "*Reng, reng.*" He pointed to the gramophone, demanding dance music.

"Not tonight, dear," she said, kissing his hair. At barely two and a half years old, he knew what a gramophone was—something she had not seen until she had come to Tehran at sixteen. His world would be so different from hers. To appease him, she hummed a folk song.

"Your lips are my flower blossoming in a smile.
Your eyes are my sun, shining even at night."

He giggled, twisting his raised hands. Her youth might be over, but his was only beginning. Despair crept into her heart. Soon, they would have to return to Haji's house to live under Haji's rules. Maybe she could get used to his reticence, old-fashioned ideas, and dislike of music. But what about Kamal? He deserved better.

She didn't want Kamal educated in a *maktab*, entertained in a mosque, and apprenticed at the bazaar. He should play piano, attend the French missionary school, and patronize cafés, theaters, and cinemas. Even if she, as a woman, couldn't.

But she was powerless. Fathers decided their children's fates. Even if she could coax Haji into agreeing to send Kamal to the missionary school, he would never pay for it. She had no money of her own. With the exception of her signet ring and the earrings Noor had given her, all of her jewelry had been sold. Saleh Mirza would have overruled Haji and paid for Kamal's keep. But he was dead.

A maid knocked. "Everybody is waiting," she said. "Shall I take Kamal?"

"No, ask Qamar to come." Then, noticing the maid's dejected look, she added, "You can play with him here."

A smattering of staff, friends, and family were in the reception room when Gohar entered. The middle-aged notary sat quietly in his brown suit, his pince-nez spectacles dangling from a string around his neck. Next to him, Saleh Mirza's first cousin and the executor of his will—a blue-eyed former diplomat—chatted with Haji. The only stranger in the room was a mousy little man in an ill-fitting suit. Noor whispered to Gohar that he represented Akbar Mirza. She side-glanced at the appalling creature wolfing down cookies and appraising the antiques.

The notary put on his spectacles, cleared his throat, and unrolled the will. He started with bequests to staff, relatives, and friends. Saleh Mirza's insight in selecting which objects to leave to whom amazed her. He had left Haji a precious handwritten Qur'an that he had once admired. Aslan inherited Saleh Mirza's papers, his French books, and a few personal items. The choice to leave the papers to him rather than herself disappointed Gohar, but Aslan's contribution was undeniable. She would send the bequest to him before moving out.

When the notary had finished with the small gifts, Gohar felt betrayed. As an adopted daughter, she wasn't entitled to anything. Still, she had hoped for some token to acknowledge her, something to remember him by. But then, he had already given her so much: his name, his insights, his worldview, not to mention the overabundance of gifts and jewelry he had given her and Kamal. What more could she ask for?

Noor was left with several orchards, a large village, gold, silver, and a Swiss bank account. The assembly nodded approvingly. She would never want for anything.

A lull followed. The notary scanned the room from atop his spectacles. The audience wriggled. The agent smiled smugly.

The notary resumed. *"I shall leave the remainder of my estate, listed herewith, including my house and its contents, villages, and orchards, to be divided equally between my beloved daughter Gohar and my grandson Kamal. His share is to be kept in a trust administered by the executor of my will until he reaches maturity at sixteen. A portion of the said trust is to be dispersed annually for his keep and education at the discretion of the executor."*

Gohar gasped. Haji looked bewildered. The agent left hastily.

3

March 1915, Tehran

Passersby were gawking at two blond men leaving a long-nosed car on Lalehzar when Gohar stepped into the street. Two small flags bearing the white, red, and black of the German Empire marked the car as an official ministry vehicle. But it was neither the car nor the men that piqued her curiosity, since a sizable number of Austrians and Germans resided in the area. It was the outfit of one of the two men: the flowing robe and headgear of a Qashqai tribesman.

The two men entered a bookstore, and Gohar stopped to look at a shop window. Shoppers looking for gifts for the coming Nowruz, undeterred by the steep prices, crowded the sidewalk. As she inspected the tasteful arrangement of pipes, lighters, and cigarette holders in the window, the reflection of Haji across the street startled her. What was he doing here in the middle of the day when he was supposed to be in the Majles?

With his head down to avoid accidentally laying eyes on a woman, he hurried across the street and entered the same bookshop the Germans had. Gohar was even more puzzled. Haji was not a bibliophile. His interest in literature was limited to skimming headlines in the papers.

But then again, what did she know about Haji? Not much.

They had been married for almost five years but had lived together for only a fraction of that time. They had not been intimate for years, and their conversation never went beyond necessities. He had begrudgingly moved to Saleh Mirza's house—now hers. But he still ate lunch at their old house with his mother every day and attended the mosque in the old neighborhood.

She had given up on fostering a relationship with him. But seeing him out and about had piqued her interest. Perhaps it was worth trying to be congenial again. For Kamal's sake, if nothing else. While Saleh Mirza's inheritance had emancipated him financially, Haji remained his legal guardian. She didn't want romance. Her heart was cold, and he was too old. But they could be companions, even friends. With Saleh Mirza gone, she needed a male presence and harbored no illusions that Aslan would ever return to her. He had not attended Saleh Mirza's funeral, memorial service, or the reading of his will, and had not acknowledged receipt of the papers and books Saleh Mirza had left him, which she had sent.

Finding out what Haji was up to would be a step toward getting to know him better and forming a relationship. She sent her attendant home with her shopping and followed him.

In the bookstore, there was no sign of the Germans. But at the back of the store, a clerk was blocking a staircase. As Haji approached, the clerk moved aside to let him up. Upstairs was a publishing house known for promoting progressive literature and pro-German books. The Germans must be meeting supporters there. But most German sympathizers were members of the secular Demokraat party—the only formal party in the country. Many of them had spent time in Berlin or Istanbul. Whereas Haji, like most merchants, favored the alliance of England, France, and Russia in the ongoing war because of the traditional trade links and the dislike of the German ally, Sunni Ottomans.

As she awaited her turn at the counter, two manservants carried trays of teacups upstairs—enough to serve at least two dozen people. She took the book she had requested to an area set aside for women. Surrounded by tall bookshelves, it offered the perfect amount of cover to keep an eye on the stairs without being seen.

Suddenly, the din of the crowd from upstairs fell silent. Then a slightly accented, velvety voice rose. She caught a few words: Hafez, Goethe, Nietzsche, Zoroaster. Was this a literary event?

The voice spoke for some time, broken at times by clapping. Finally, there was a long round of applause, just as a thin man in *sardari* hurried downstairs and out of the store. Of medium height with a pencil mustache, he was remarkable only in his ordinariness. The commotion resumed upstairs. The gathering would end soon—time to leave.

Outside, the sidewalk was packed with men on their way to cafés, movies, and playhouses. The food vendors were busy. The thin man was chatting with the driver of the German car. The only other woman in the street was an Armenian with her family. Men pulled aside to avoid touching them. In the path cleared in their wake, Gohar rushed home.

At dinner that evening, Haji was more talkative than usual. "Were you aware that Germans revere our culture? Their greatest poet, Goethe, has even written a book about Hafez."

"I didn't know you were so pro-German," she said.

"I'm not," he grumbled. "But I am fed up with the thieving English calling us smelly and ignorant while stealing our oil to fuel their war machine. Did you know that the British government owns half of the shares in the Anglo-Persian Oil Company, and we own none?"

"Well, your Bakhtiari cousins do."

"My cousins are whores," he fumed. "And I am talking about our government, not individuals. At any rate, until today, I didn't know how treacherous the English are."

Undoubtedly, this was related to that afternoon's meeting. "What happened today to make you so aware?" she said nonchalantly.

"Some German officials showed us the eye-opening documents they had intercepted. One report from an English cabinet secretary even admitted that the number-one English objective in the East is to hold on to Persia's oil." He paused. "They also showed us a telegram from an English admiral to their prime minister, proclaiming that nothing should prevent Britain from enjoying the fruits of *its* Persian oil. Can you believe the audacity of the bastards?"

She didn't share the pro-German sentiment in Tehran. To her, Germany was yet another European empire looking for gain. "Do you believe the Germans?"

"Why wouldn't I? They built us factories and trained our engineers without asking for anything. They can help us get rid of the Russians and the English."

Iran was awash with German merchants, military and technical advisors, and instructors—not to mention the Austrians who had escaped the Russian war camps.

But Gohar didn't believe in German munificence. Once, she had asked Saleh Mirza about the Germans' role in the war. "I don't understand why they would go to war over the death of a middle-aged Austrian prince," she had bristled.

"The assassination was an excuse, my dear," he had said. "The empires had been itching for a fight for years. The Austrians couldn't let Serbia incite a revolt in their Slavic citizens, so they attacked Serbia, and the Germans eagerly supported them."

"What's in it for the Germans?" she had asked.

"Respect. European dominance. Paris. But they miscalculated. Now, they're pinched between the Russians in the East and the French and English in the West."

With Iran in their camp, the Germans could pressure both the English and the Russians and take over Iran's oil. The Germans didn't love Iran. They liked its geography.

But arguing with Haji—who would surely disagree with her—was futile. She retired to her room to read her new book.

4

March 1915, Tehran

Two days before Nowruz, Kamal was playfully tugging at Gohar's earring when Haji entered her study.

"Don't let him do that," he barked. "He'll tear your earlobe."

She smiled. "He's a baby."

"He is not a baby. You are spoiling him."

Gohar stared at him. This was not the first time Haji had criticized her lenience with Kamal. While he had doted on the boy as a baby, he had become strict recently.

"What's wrong with showing affection?" she said. "You visit your mother every day."

"That's different. She's lonely. Besides, I didn't sit on her lap when I was three."

"He isn't even three yet," she said. Nevertheless, she put Kamal on the carpet to play by himself and glanced inquisitively at Haji. He never visited her study. "What are you doing at home?"

"There isn't much going on at the bazaar, and the Majles is on break." He lowered his gaze. "I thought to come and see what you're up to."

She softened. "Of course. Please sit. Would you like some chamomile tea? Belqais is coming over to help me pack sweets for the poor." She pointed to the mound of cookies on the table. "But we can play backgammon until she arrives."

"Maybe later." He sat across from her. "I didn't get you a gift for Nowruz."

"I understand. We are still mourning. It hasn't even been six months since Saleh Mirza passed."

"I thought we could go to a bookstore on Lalehzar together and buy something you'll like."

She looked at him in utter disbelief. They had never gone anywhere together, not even on a pilgrimage to the nearby shrine of Shah Abdolazim. Was he turning into a Demokraat?

"That is very sweet," she said. "I'd like that."

He tousled Kamal's hair on his way out, but Kamal wriggled free of him, running to Belqais, who had just arrived.

Gohar had not planned to celebrate Nowruz that year, but many people came to pay their respects to her and Noor. Uplifted by the presence of old friends, she agreed to help them raise money for the refugees flooding Tehran. Fighting between the Russians and the Ottomans on Iranian soil had uprooted many villagers, who had fled to the capital.

Midmorning, curious to see how Haji was faring receiving guests as the male head of the household, she snuck to the observation room. Haji sat brooding next to a large portrait of Saleh Mirza. His business partner, Hosseinqoli, kept him company while a smattering of Saleh Mirza's friends chatted with each other. This was a far cry from the crowd of dignitaries who lined up to see Saleh Mirza every Nowruz. She missed her father.

She was about to leave when the German she had seen in the Qashqai robe on Lalehzar entered. This time, he was in a well-cut suit that accentuated his powerful build. The thin man she had seen chatting with the Germans' driver followed him. Haji sprang to his feet to embrace the much taller blond German. Hosseinqoli left immediately, leaving the newcomers to sit on both sides of Haji and engage him in animated conversation.

Who were these men, and what did they want with Haji? They looked too cunning for her liking. Haji had never been friendly with Farangis. Something was not right. She could feel it in her bones.

Later that day, Haji stopped by her study. "I am going to my mother's house. I'll eat dinner there."

Gohar narrowed her eyes. "Tonight? You won't find a droshky." She had sold Saleh Mirza's carriage after her coachman retired. "Why don't you wait until tomorrow? We can go together and take Kamal. Your mother misses him."

"I will walk. I have a duty to visit my mother on the first day of Nowruz."

"Then please wish her a prosperous new year from me."

As he turned to leave, she asked casually. "By the way, who was the blond Farangi I saw leaving?"

He squirmed uncomfortably. "Oh, he was no Farangi. Only an Azeri merchant."

His touch on her shoulder woke her late that night. The stench of alcohol on his breath was revolting. Where had he been? Her religious mother-in-law abhorred drinking. She feigned sleep, expecting him to leave. But he lingered, caressing her side. She stayed motionless.

His hands glided under her loose nightgown. He groped her breast, forcing her to her back, and straddled her.

She bolted up, shoving him back with all her might. "You are drunk."

Her heart raced.

He landed on his haunches. Moonlight illuminated the folds of puffy skin bulging under his watery red eyes, his disheveled short hair, and his slack mouth. White stubble covered his cheeks. His *qaba* had fallen off his shoulders, revealing his stained kaftan. He reeked of vomit.

She scanned the room for something to throw at him. "Do you want to beget a devil's child?" she said, playing on the common belief that children conceived in drunkenness were wicked. "Shame on you." She spat on his face.

He stayed motionless. Then, wordlessly, he stood up and left the room. She bolted the door and curled up on her mattress. Shaken to the bone, she stayed awake all night.

5

June 1915, Tehran

The sensual and mournful voice rose into the warm, late-spring night. *"From the blood of the nation's youth, tulips bloom."*

The scent of Parisian perfumes and sweat filled the canvas-covered veranda packed with bejeweled women. Gohar peered through the sheer curtain that separated the porch from the makeshift stage. The ruggedly handsome singer, with his turban tilted rakishly, caressed the tar on his lap as three other musicians played the flute, santoor, and goblet drum on the stage behind him. Beyond the platform, intellectuals, aristocrats, and gendarme officers sat, mouthing the lyrics to this tribute to the martyrs of the constitutional war.

Gohar fanned herself. Attending charity events in private homes was not usually part of her routine, but Aref, the revolutionary performer, was her idol, and this concert was a much-needed distraction. For months, Haji had been leaving home at dusk and returning at dawn, reeking of alcohol and opium.

She was neither naïve nor a prude. Men drank. Even Saleh Mirza sipped wine now and then. But Haji was a devoted Muslim. He disdained alcohol. Had her actions driven him to vice? But she wouldn't have refused him if he hadn't been drinking in the first place.

Neither of them had spoken of what transpired between them on the first night of the New Year when he'd come home drunk. Gohar felt justified and guilty at the same time. A woman's refusal to fulfill her marital duty was not only an offense punishable by beating but also a sin. But so was drinking, punishable by public flogging.

Perhaps it was the house. He had been ill at ease there, reluctant to deal with the servants. If that were the case, he would settle in time. She had to be patient. But his behavior raised eyebrows. Noor and Qamar looked concerned, and the servants whispered behind Gohar's back.

Midway through the concert, the ladies were treated to roasted lamb, three rice dishes—one plain, one mixed with fava beans, and one with green beans—and four sauces. The opulent meal, at an event intended to raise money to feed the poor, dismayed Gohar. Rice and charcoal were scarce again as the Russians had stopped their supply to Tehran in retaliation for the Iranian rebels' burning of the Lianozov and Khoshtartia factories in Gilan. She returned to her seat early.

The tips of men's cigarettes bobbed like fireflies in the dark garden. The glint of blond hair in the light of a passing torch caught her eye. Few, if any, Farangis appreciated Persian music. Squinting, she recognized the enigmatic German friend of Haji. "I didn't know Farangis liked Persian music," she whispered to the woman beside her.

The woman snorted. "He speaks Farsi better than you and me. Quotes Hafez and Mawlana left and right."

"You know him?" she asked, watching a well-known politician approach the German.

"He is the German consul in Bushehr." She looked around, covered her mouth, and lowered her voice. "Rumor has it that he is an agent provocateur known as Wilhelm of Persia. He makes trouble for the English and is close to the Tangestani leader."

Gohar's stomach churned. Was this the man Haji had been spending time with? The prospect of Haji associating with a German spy frightened her. The English and Russians might have their hands full, but they had powerful allies in Iran. To aid their enemy would be sheer folly.

As darkness claimed Wilhelm, the melancholy voice of the singer soared, *"From the palm of my hands breaks free, the rein of my restless heart."*

The death of Haji's mother in early summer shocked them all. A day earlier, Mash Qolam's visit had alarmed Gohar—the old servant who lived with Haji's mother seldom called on her.

"What is the matter?" Gohar had asked Mash Qolam while she watched Kamal play with water in a large copper bowl.

"Nothing to worry about, Gohar Khanum," Mash Qolam said. "I came to tell you that Haj Aqa will stay at his mother's house tonight." He paused. "This morning, Khanum Bozorg woke up with heartburn and nausea. If you ask me, it was the yogurt and pickles that did it. But when Haj Aqa came over for lunch, he told me to fetch the *hakim*."

Calling for a *hakim* instead of a real doctor dismayed her. Over the years, she had grown fond of her stern but frank mother-in-law. "What did he say?"

"He ordered castor oil. She'll be good as new tomorrow. Haj Aqa is staying over."

Gohar was concerned, but not overly so. Khanum Bozorg was robust and healthy, and most likely Haji was simply using the excuse to spend time with her.

But the next morning, Mash Qolam returned with news of Khanum Bozorg's passing. Gohar, Noor, and Qamar were stunned. Qamar blamed the death on the evil eye and burned incense. Noor sent a servant to buy Kamal a charm engraved with the names of five holy bodies to keep him safe.

At her mother-in-law's house, Gohar found Haji distraught and shaken. Hosseinqoli had taken over the funeral arrangements. Gohar helped Belqais send telegrams to the family.

Haji kept his composure throughout the funeral but burst into tears on the ride home. His sorrow touched Gohar. Flouting the custom barring the public display of affection, even between husband and wife, she reached for his arm as he held his head in his palms. He recoiled, side-glanced at the droshky driver, and glowered. Embarrassed, she retreated.

No one spoke or ate at dinner, save for the mullah, who ate with the other men in the front room. Gohar was worried about Kamal, who had been left with the servant, and she missed her house, her tar, the moonlight from her window, and the scent of roses in full bloom. Was she heartless?

She was ready to leave even before the dinner plates were cleared. But Haji was incredulous when she asked for permission to go. "How can you ask that?" he said tersely. "I can't leave Belqais alone. We need to prepare the house for the memorial service tomorrow."

"Should I send for Kamal and stay the night with you?" she asked half-heartedly.

Haji closed his eyes and sighed. "No need," he said at last. "A house in mourning is no place for a noisy child. Do as you wish."

She asked Mash Qolam to flag a droshky.

Wilhelm attended Haji's mother's memorial service briefly the next day. But his Persian companion remained by Haji's side through the service. Gohar didn't bother to ask Haji about either of them.

Haji's nighttime absences continued throughout Ramadan, but Gohar kept her peace. His mother's sudden passing had been hard on him, and picking a fight would only lend credence to the gossip in the household. But a remark made by Belqais—who now lived with them—stung her. Haji, she commented, must have gotten dispensation from a mullah to break his fast with *araq*, the potent domestic liquor. Gohar winced. Even Haji's sister was now criticizing his behavior publicly. That surely would reflect badly on Gohar herself and affect Kamal's future.

That evening, she stopped Haji as he was leaving. "May I ask where you are going?"

Haji snapped. "Don't you see the country is on fire?"

She winced.

His voice softened. "Do you think I *want* to go out every night? No. But people are suffering. I'm meeting with other notables to solve the country's problems."

It sounded plausible. People were frustrated by the government's inability to stop warring armies from committing atrocities—attributed to either the Russians or the Ottomans, depending on the political bent of the paper reporting them—in their neutral country. Successive administrations had resigned after failing to satisfy the conflicting demands of the shah, the Majles, the English, the Russians, and the Germans.

But were drinking and smoking opium parts of political discourse? "I would be more understanding if you confided in me," she said.

Haji stared at her long and hard before leaving without comment.

Finally, his refusal to join the family on their month-long trip to their village in the mountains—after asking for it so he could spend time with Kamal—spurred her to take action. She decided to have him tailed.

Following Haji would require a trusted male. As luck would have it, Qamar's son, Ahmad, had come to visit. The English had shut down the parts of the oil fields where he worked after a series of Tangestani attacks. Rumors of German involvement—and the tribe's audacity in attacking the British residency in Bushehr—had compelled the English to close some operations and summon the Indian cavalry.

Plump like his mother and no taller than Gohar, Ahmad was blunt when he heard her account of Haji's behavior. "Do you think he's seeing a woman?"

The thought of ugly, old Haji chasing women despite all his claims of religiosity vexed her. "I don't know," she said. "He's sixty years old. Who would want him?"

"He is well off. Some women care for money."

She cringed.

Ahmad agreed to follow Haji. But since he didn't know the city, Gohar decided to accompany him. Once they knew where Haji was spending his time, Ahmad could investigate further. In a perverted way, she looked forward to her outing with Ahmad. She missed roaming the streets freely without an army of attendants.

The next evening, covered under a tattered chador and an old-fashioned veil, she joined Ahmad. They followed Haji to Ala-o-dowleh and took a droshky when he did. The middle-aged driver smirked when Ahmad told him to trail the other droshky. But he complied.

They moved south. Bulky doormen kept vagabonds away from the entrances of the new Farangi-style hotels. She wondered where Haji was heading. Udaljan, where they used to live? Sanguelaj, the hotbed of intellectual movements? The bazaar, teeming with activist guilds and mosques? They were all in this direction.

Near the bazaar, they turned west toward Qazvin Gate, where migrant workers lived in rooming houses. She had never been to this part of the city. Charcoal fires glinted in braziers on the sidewalk. Smells of grilled meat and corn mixed with tobacco and opium. Working men squatted in circles in the scant light of lanterns. Some ate, while others smoked clay pipes or fat domestic cigarettes. Still others played dice. A young boy hawked shelled walnuts. A snake charmer entertained the crowd.

Their droshky stopped abruptly as soon as they passed the Qazvin Gate. The driver turned. "Excuse me. But do you realize where the other droshky is headed?" he asked anxiously. "Straight to Qajar Alley! That's not a place for a decent woman."

She gasped. Qajar Alley was where houses of ill repute served soldiers, travelers, and laborers. Officially known as the New City, the place was nicknamed after a former shah who had relocated taverns and gambling parlors there to shield the burgeoning community around the royal compound of Baq-e-shah from vice.

Ahmad looked at her hesitantly. "I don't think it's safe to continue," he whispered. "But you're the boss."

"No, no," she murmured, glad for the veil covering her burning face. "Please ask the driver to turn around."

The droshky dropped them off near the Hotel de Paris. They waited for it to disappear before heading home. She walked with her head down, bearing Haji's shame on her shoulders. No political meeting would take place in Qajar Alley. Whatever he was doing there was vile.

Had she driven him to patronize houses of ill repute? Was it retribution for her infidelity and defiance? But wasn't forsaking the man she loved penance enough?

"There are orchards on Qazvin Road, too," Ahmad said gently as they neared the house. "Maybe Haji has gone to a meeting there."

She glanced at his soft features. "Perhaps," she muttered. In her heart, she knew where Haji had gone.

A faint scent of rosewater wafted through the cool, dark shrine of Imamazadeh Saleh. Cocooned under her chador on the threadbare carpet, Gohar drew her knees to her chest. In the week since she discovered Haji's jaunt to Qajar Alley, she had contemplated canceling the trip, despite the stifling heat and rampant typhoid in the city. But Ahmad had convinced her to go. Haji or no Haji, Kamal needed the fresh mountain air, and she needed time away. He would watch Haji in her absence. She had relented and left with Kamal, Qamar, Noor, and Belqais, stopping at the shrine.

If she were sure that he patronized brothels, she would leave Haji. Saleh Mirza had secured her right to a divorce in case Haji took another wife or committed adultery. She didn't love him, didn't need his money or protection, and his public infidelity humiliated her. His patronizing houses of ill repute could also endanger her life. Women died or went insane from the diseases their husbands caught in brothels. She would find a way to get custody of Kamal.

But what if the seedy joint was simply a place for a clandestine meeting? Backing him then would be her marital *and* patriotic duty.

How could she act when she knew so little?

She remembered the day she'd tied a cloth to the wishing tree outside, pleading for clarity while Aslan waited. Should she have left with Aslan? Regret gnawed at her heart.

She glanced at Kamal taking a sugar candy from Qamar. He needed a father. Haji hadn't been much of one. But in a country where the reputation of fathers determined the fate of their sons, she had to do all she could to keep Haji's name untarnished.

A worshiper with wavy gray hair standing by the latticed cage over the saint's tomb reminded her of Saleh Mirza. She missed him, his wisdom, his calm, his acumen. Now more than ever. What would he have advised her to do?

In the last month of his life, Saleh Mirza told her the story of his falling in love with Noor, then the shah's concubine—a crime punishable by death for both. For years, they had both braved danger by corresponding secretly and meeting rarely from behind a curtain, while he endured his unhappy marriage to an irascible older cousin without taking another wife or even a mistress. Finally, they were allowed to marry, long after Noor was widowed.

Patience was what Saleh Mirza would have advised.

6

October 1915, Tehran

The month in the countryside revived Gohar. The primitive living accommodations brought back her sense of adventure. She played hide-and-seek with Kamal and shared everything—including a mosquito net at night—with Noor, Qamar, and Belqais. They ate fruit right off the trees and played cards by the streams. At night, they listened to the portable gramophone. Gohar visited the women in the villages, praised their crafts, tasted their cooking, and promised to repair the drinking well.

The idyll evaporated the minute they reached the outskirts of Tehran on their return. Many armed men, some in tribal outfits, others in uniforms without insignia, had camped outside the city wall. The gendarmes—the closest the country had to a regular army—had pitched their tents at the city gates. Gohar had never seen this many armed men in one place.

Ahmad greeted their carriage at the city gate. Once on board, he explained that the gendarmes were seeking their back pay. The tribesmen, militia, and Turkish volunteers were there to support them. He reported that Haji had been away from the house almost every night.

When they reached the house, he hesitated to get out. "The English have killed the Tangestani leader," he said. "The oil fields are operational. I can go back. But I don't want to leave you in the lurch if you need me."

Gohar was pleased. Ahmad was honest and loyal. He could be her confidant and act as her eyes and ears in places she couldn't go. "I would be pleased if you would stay," she said. "I need a trustworthy man, and you are as close as I have to a brother. Naneh Qamar would love to have you around, too."

He beamed and said shyly, "If it would be helpful, I'd be glad to."

As the fall began, seemingly spontaneous pro-German demonstrations erupted throughout the city. The papers argued that an alliance with Germany would force the Russians out and compel the Ottomans to evacuate the towns they had occupied. Rumors swirled that the prime minister was negotiating a military pact with the German minister.

Ahmad mentioned the preponderance of guns and ammunition popping up in the neighborhoods. Qamar cited the mullah's emphasis on Islamic unity with their Sunni Ottoman brothers despite the public outrage over the Ottoman occupation of Tabriz. The infidel Russians and the English, the mullah declared were the real enemy. Pro-Germans fed the poor in the city.

Gohar joined a mob of spectators to watch the daily drill of gendarmes at the parade ground. Initially formed by Morgan Shuster and trained by the Americans, now they had Swedish instructors. The gendarmes' immaculate uniforms, discipline, and skill with precision German weaponry impressed her. As skeptical as she was of all foreigners, she could see a beneficial collaboration with Germany that would boot out the English and the Russians and help them modernize. Iranians could manage them. After all, Germany was far away. Russia and English India were neighbors.

On the first day of Muharram in November, the gendarmes took over Shiraz, Yazd, and Kerman. They occupied the telegraph offices, government buildings, and the local branches of the English-owned Bank of Persia in each city. In Shiraz, they detained all British citizens, including the consul, and incarcerated the men in the fortress of an Arab chieftain.

Tehran was euphoric at the news. But the joy quickly turned to fear when the rumor of a Russian attack circulated. Stationed in Qazvin, only ninety miles to the west, the Russians could preemptively strike the gendarmes camped in Tehran, or lay siege to the city. Once more, people fled the capital and hoarded staples.

Gohar had planned to feed the mourners during Muharram—the holy month of mourning—and the month after. But considering the situation, she called on Belqais, Qamar, and Ahmad to reassess their arrangements.

Belqais suggested curtailing the scope of their plan, to save rice and charcoal. "Right now, a lot of people are giving out food for Muharram," she said. "We need something to fall back on if the Russians attack."

"I agree," Gohar said wearily. "But if we do that, we will need armed guards to protect the supplies from the mob." The house was strong. But even a fortress needed defenders, and the servants were no match for hooligans paid by the Russians or the Cossack Brigade under Russian command. Any rumor of Haji's collaboration with the Germans could make the house a prime target for looting by pro-Russians.

Frantic knocking on the birooni door interrupted their meeting. Gohar looked out the window to see Haji rush in, push the gardener aside, and cross the courtyard. She followed him to his bedroom, where he was hastily loading a trunk. "What are you doing?" she asked.

"The Russians are coming," he said as he packed. "I must leave."

Her heart sank. How could he flee, leaving her at such a perilous time? She ground her teeth. "Why?"

"I am leaving with the Majles deputies and city notables to join the gendarmes and fight the English and the Russians." He stopped and turned to her with his hands on his hips. "The shah, the prime minister, and the cabinet will follow us in a few days."

Her knees buckled. This was a full-fledged rebellion. She sat on the bedroll. "What happens if the Russians attack Tehran?" Without the gendarmes, the city would be defenseless.

"They won't. The Germans and Ottomans are also coming with us. Without them or any government in Tehran, the Russians will have no reason to attack the city."

The logic was understandable. Without the rebels and the Germans and Ottomans, the Russian had no excuse to trample the city. But it didn't guarantee the safety of her household. "What about us?"

"Nothing will happen to you. I will send for you once I am settled."

Gohar would have to hire people to defend herself and her household. "Where are you going?"

"First Qom, then Isfahan."

These were the areas the gendarmes controlled. Haji's actions must be part of a well-thought-out larger plan. "What if the Russians attack *you*?" she asked.

"The gendarmes, the Turkish irregulars, and the tribes will protect us."

She remembered the camps outside the city.

He sat beside her. "The German minister is a seasoned general. He will lead the charge."

"What if—God forbid—the gendarmes are defeated?"

"They won't be. Once the shah is in Isfahan, he will call for national mobilization. People will join us in droves—even the Persians in the Cossack Brigade are planning to join." He reached for her hand. "I am doing this for your future and Kamal's. I am not young. But I would rather die with dignity than live in shame."

His white hair and beard glowed in the sunshine, resembling a saint ready for martyrdom.

He continued. "I have been working on a treaty with Germany for months. I wanted to tell you sooner. But I was afraid that spies would stop us."

The news shook her. How could she have doubted his integrity? Her heart filled with affection, pride, and foreboding. "I am proud of you." She touched his face tenderly.

He released her hand and rose. He looked taller, his shoulders broader, his posture more erect. He was a new man.

"When will you be back?" she asked.

"I don't know, but I will keep you informed." He embraced and kissed her forehead before calling for a servant to carry his trunk. "Take care of Kamal and Belqais."

"Shall I fetch them?"

"No, no," he said. "People are waiting for me."

She followed him to the front door and saw Wilhelm's Persian companion helping Haji into a waiting carriage. She wasn't surprised.

The sound of hooves and wheels in the street kept Gohar awake all night. In the morning, Ahmad went out and reported that the shops and stalls in the grand bazaar were closed. Most of the Majles deputies, government officials, and well-known nationalists were gone. So were all the Germans, Austrians, and Ottomans. The gendarmes and pro-Demokraat militia had commandeered all available horses, carriages, fodder, and baggage animals to transport them, and taken over the telegraph and toll stations on the road to Qom.

That evening, Qamar returned from tekyeh excited. The mullah had called the rebels *Mohajeron*, in honor of those followers of the Prophet who had left Mecca for Medina to invigorate Islam. Gohar rejoiced; people were united. Victory was within reach.

Hamadan was the next city to fall to the rebel gendarmes—now widely known as the Mohajeron. A large contingent of Cossacks there broke rank with their Russian commanders and joined the rebels, as Haji had predicted. Newspapers lionized the young gendarme commander, comparing him to the hero of Gallipoli, Mustafa Kemal Pasha.

The renegades, now controlling central and western Iran and challenging the Russians and the English, formed a Committee of National Resistance in Qom. Soon, the papers leaked a document from the Ministry of Foreign Affairs to foreign consulates announcing the capital's move to Isfahan. Another of Haji's predictions had come true.

In the city, fear of a Russian attack grew.

Two days after the leak, the shah announced his plan to stay in Tehran. Swiftly, the prime minister officially dissolved the Majles, declared martial law, and banned Muharram processions and rituals.

Cossacks assumed positions everywhere. Only two newspapers were allowed to publish: one pro-English and one pro-Russian. Fear and confusion engulfed the capital. The tide was turning, and it alarmed Gohar.

A week later, both newspapers in Tehran reported an uprising in Gilan. The rebels called themselves *Jangalis*, men of the forest. They demanded the expulsion of *all* foreign forces and the restoration of the constitution. Papers branded them and their leader, Mirza Kuchek Khan, bandits. But people in the alleys, mosques, and coffeehouses knew better. They hailed the Jangalis as their last hope.

Gohar only hoped that their rebellion would strengthen her husband's cause.

7

December 1915, Tehran

The Russians spared the capital but captured the rebel stronghold of Qom. Then both Tehran newspapers stopped reporting on the renegades.

Gohar had received a telegram from Haji reporting his safe arrival in Qom but heard nothing since. Her telegrams to her sister-in-law in Isfahan and Haji's son in Gurdan were futile—neither had heard from him. She rejected Ahmad's offer to go seeking Haji. Sending him to a war zone would be madness.

The news of the rebels forming a government in exile allied with Germany in Kermanshah rattled Gohar. Haji was now a traitor and an enemy of the English and the Russians.

Only close friends and relatives came to the cemetery to commemorate the anniversary of Saleh Mirza's passing. Even fewer joined them at home. Those who came carefully avoided any mention of the gendarmes or the rebellion. No one inquired about Haji's whereabouts.

Undeterred, when Gohar heard of the former rebels trickling back to Tehran, she rushed to question them. Most refused to see her. Some denied having been in Qom or ever harboring pro-German sentiments. The few who agreed to talk to her mentioned the chaos after the Russians' attack. Some people had sheltered in the shrine of Saint Massomeh. Others had fled to the countryside. None had seen Haji or knew where Wilhelm of Persia was.

As winter began, the food and fuel shortages worsened in Tehran. Riots erupted. To save fuel, Gohar sent dough to the neighborhood bakery. She gave half of the bread away. Her agents dispersed the food set aside for Muharram. The rituals were banned, but no one could ban hunger. Mullahs inflamed the conflict between Sunnis and Shias. When they forbade taking food from pro-Germans, the poor flocked to pro-Russians. The tsar's ruble was as good as the Kaiser's geld.

On Christmas Day 1915, a prince of the highest pedigree, an Anglophile with substantial holdings in the London Stock Exchange, became the prime minister. It was rumored that the British minister had personally carried a bounty of precious gifts—including orders for a new Rolls-Royce—to the shah to secure the appointment. The pro-English makeup of the new cabinet dashed Gohar's hope of clemency for the Mohajeron, including Haji.

That evening, a man called on Gohar. His embossed calling card introduced him as Sadeq Isfahani. When she entered the reception room, she found a mousy little man with beady eyes and an ill-fitting Farangi suit. He rose from his seat and bowed.

She was surprised to recognize him as the man who had represented Akbar Mirza at the reading of Saleh Mirza's will. He plopped back on his seat and crossed his legs before Gohar invited him to sit.

As soon as he unleashed a series of flowery flatteries and endless pleasantries, she interrupted him. "Please, Mr. Isfahani. Get to the point. I am busy."

He cleared his throat. "Please forgive my impertinence. I am only a humble messenger from His Excellency Homayoun Mirza, who, as you know, is a cousin of your late adopted father, Saleh Mirza. May God bless his soul. He is also a relative of the prime minister." He lowered his voice. "Some people expect him to be a minister in the new cabinet."

"Isn't your client related to Saleh Mirza's son, Akbar Mirza?"

He put three lumps of sugar in the cup of tea before him. "You are so perceptive, my lady. Just like the late Saleh Mirza. Yes, Homayoun Mirza is Akbar Mirza's uncle, the brother of his sainted mother. At any rate, it has been brought to His Excellency's attention that you are in trouble."

"That's news to me. I dare say your client is ill-informed."

"No, my lady. Perhaps you don't know. But His Excellency has it on good authority that your husband Haji Mohsen is wanted by the English and the Russians as a German spy."

"I don't know where this information comes from," she responded calmly. "But it is easy to accuse someone of a heinous crime, and hard to prove it. It is no secret that Haji supported the Mohajeron, but that doesn't make him a German spy. He joined the group only after he was assured that His Majesty the Shah would lead the movement. He is not even a Demokraat."

"My dear lady, this is not idle chat," Sadeq said, his spoon clicking the glass teacup as he stirred his tea. "Thanks to the English, who have eyes and ears everywhere, the government has ample evidence of Haji's treason. He collaborated with a known German agitator, Wilhelm of Persia, to incite violence against His Majesty the Shah." He sipped his tea, wincing at its heat. "I don't need to remind you that the punishment for treason is hanging and confiscation of property."

"Is there a witness?"

He smirked. "As a matter of fact, there is."

She pulled the white chador tighter over her face. "Who, if I may ask?"

"An honest businessman and the owner of a tavern in Qajar Alley. He has seen Haji and Wilhelm together with his own eyes and heard them plotting against His Majesty the Shah with his own ears. All as they consumed alcohol and consorted with females of ill repute. Both crimes are punishable by fines and lashing."

Haji meeting Wilhelm in Qajar Alley and drinking alcohol were not news to her. But did he also consort with hussies? The image of him in the company of a harlot appalled her afresh.

"Even if Haji is guilty," she said, "he must be tried first. At any rate, he is not here, and I have no knowledge of his whereabouts."

"He is not here." Sadeq put his cup down. "But *you* are. You could be implicated as his collaborator. You'd be jailed, and your son would enter into the custody of your closest male relative. Which, may I remind you, is your adoptive brother, Akbar Mirza."

She ground her teeth. No degenerate addict like Akbar Mirza would touch her son while she was alive. "That's preposterous," she bristled. "How can I be accused of something I didn't even know about?"

"His Excellency agrees with you." He leaned back. "He is appalled by Haji's actions and knows you are innocent. Out of respect for Saleh Mirza—may he rest in peace—and knowing how dear you were to him, he is offering you and your son his protection." He poured his tea into his saucer, blew on it, and then slurped.

The sound chafed her. "That is very kind of him."

"But the German agent has damaged English property and forced the Russians to send troops to liberate Qom." He took a cookie.

Gohar wished she had instructed the servant not to serve this creature.

"The English are reasonable," he continued. "They want fair compensation for themselves and the families of those who have lost their lives because of your husband's actions. But the Russians are another matter. Especially since there had been bad blood between them and Saleh Mirza."

"Saleh Mirza is dead," she snapped.

"I know. But the Russians hold grudges for generations. Plus, it is well known that you share your adopted father's anti-Russian sentiment."

"My father was a patriot, so am I," she said.

He leaned forward and lowered his voice. Instinctively, she moved as far back as possible. "Just between you and me, there's a Russian, Smirnsky—a nasty piece of work, if you ask me—who has a personal vendetta against your family. He has hooligans in his pay and Cossacks at his command. All savages." He stared at her. "You, my dear, *need* English protection."

She cringed at hearing him call her "dear" but played along. "And how might I avail myself of that?"

"With His Excellency's backing and a modest gift to show your gratitude to the crown." He pulled a dirty handkerchief out of his pocket and blew his nose loudly. "I don't have to remind you of the mayhem and damage the Cossacks caused in 1908. You may have to hire Indians to guard your person."

"I do not know this Wilhelm." She suppressed a burning desire to slap the man. "But I understand the predicament my husband has put me in." She straightened her shoulders. "His Excellency's benevolence and concern about my welfare are most appreciated. No doubt, the protection of the mighty British Empire is priceless. But I need to think."

"I understand. English protection is not cheap." He put the handkerchief back in his pocket. "But think of what might happen to you and your son without it. At any rate, I am authorized to give you a week to come up with the money." He continued with a contrived look of concern. "Given the circumstances, Akbar Mirza is prepared to make a cash offer for the house to keep it in the family."

"I will keep that in mind," she said, grateful that the chador shielded her from the eyes of the despicable vermin.

He rose. "May I offer you a piece of brotherly advice?" He continued without waiting for her response. "I haven't seen your face, but it is known that you are young and very beautiful—may God bestow his protection upon you. In my humble opinion, there is only one solution for a woman in your predicament: to divorce your disgraced husband and marry a powerful man to protect you and give you more children. No point in wasting your youth for a traitor who would never dare to return. You can close the city gate, but not people's mouths. The longer you live without a man's custody, the more they will gossip about you."

He then promptly offered his services to secure a speedy divorce through a sympathetic religious judge and find a suitable match for a modest fee. It took all her restraint not to bash the little man's head with the heaviest object in reach.

Once Sadeq was gone, Gohar rubbed the thigh she had been pinching to contain her screams. She cursed Sadeq, Homayoun Mirza, Akbar Mirza, and Haji, all in the same breath. There was no question that the scheme had been concocted by a leech, Akbar Mirza, and a sleazebag, Sadeq, to extort money. But she could not ignore the threat. Though she was loath to admit it, Sadeq had a point. A young woman with substantial wealth was vulnerable in a country without proper courts. Haji's participation in the rebellion—undoubtedly motivated by patriotism—had exposed her. Worse yet, his repudiation of his powerful Bakhtiari cousins had robbed her of their protection.

Furious and restive, she sent for Noor, Belqais, and Qamar. There was no time to waste.

In her study, Gohar recounted Sadeq's visit to the women.

Noor slapped her knee. "How dare they threaten us?" She bristled. "Saleh did so much for that snake Homayoun and his family. He didn't know he was breeding scorpions. If Saleh were alive, these people would never have dared to send that weasel to insult us."

"Homayoun Mirza isn't the problem, Bibi," Gohar said. "It's Akbar Mirza. He is taking advantage of the situation to avenge being cut from Aqa Mirza's will."

"I agree," Noor responded. "The truth will eventually come out. I don't think we should pay him or that weasel, Sadeq. If we do, they will never stop asking for more. But it may be prudent for you, Gohar dear, to leave Tehran. If you aren't here, Akbar Mirza can't hurt you or Kamal."

As much as she disliked the thought of abandoning her house, the prospect of leaving the chaotic city behind appealed to Gohar. "But where could I go?"

Everyone agreed that following the Mohajeron would be futile and dangerous. Noor suggested one of the villages Saleh Mirza had left her, perhaps the one they had spent the summer in.

"The lodging there is not suitable for winter," Gohar said. "And Akbar Mirza could easily bribe the village head to hand us over to the Russians. I don't even trust our agent."

Qamar proposed going to Gurdan, but Belqais shook her head. "Bad idea. Haji has a lot of enemies there. Plus, his son and daughter-in-law are not keen on Gohar or Kamal." She turned to Gohar. "I think you should go to Istanbul. A lot of exiles live there, including some of the Mohajeron. The Ottomans are German allies and will protect you."

"I like that option," Gohar said. "But we don't know anyone there."

"I can find contacts," Noor said. "But how will you get to Istanbul with all the fighting?" A fierce battle between the Russians and the Ottomans raged at the Iranian-Ottoman border.

She remembered the plan she and Aslan had devised that winter's day a lifetime ago. "If we can get to Anzali, we can take the boat to Baku and then the train to Batumi, where we can take a boat to Istanbul."

"Not anymore," Noor said. "First, you have to pass Gilan to get to Baku. The Russians control the province, and they are fighting the Jangali bandits. It would be lunacy to go there. Second, Baku itself is Russian, as is the rest of the Caucasus."

Belqais interjected. "The Russian hold on Baku is shaky. Azeri oil barons run the city. Plus, lots of Persians live there and in the rest of the Caucasus. If we can get to Baku, we can circumvent the battlefield and get to Istanbul safely."

Gohar was astounded by her sister-in-law's knowledge of that area. But she was right. Baku, while nominally Russian, was autonomous. Aslan, who had trained Iranian revolutionaries there, had told her a lot about the city. He had described the mansions of the oil barons—most of them Azeri Muslims—that lined the boulevard that ran along the Caspian. The multi-ethnic, oil-rich city also housed thousands of Iranians—as many as one in ten residents—who were active in anti-tsarist activities. Farsi was spoken as widely as Azeri-Turkish and Russian in the South Caucasus. Even the founder of the progressive *Iran-e-Now* newspaper in Tehran was from Baku. He now led Baku's dominant political party, *Musavat*. Meanwhile, the South Caucasus's borders with the Ottoman were porous and easy to cross. Going to Istanbul through Baku could work.

"How do you know all that?" Gohar asked Belqais.

"My maternal first cousin lived in Baku. He used to write to me about the area."

Gohar had never heard of a cousin in Baku. But the idea of going to Baku, known as Paris on the Caspian, was appealing. She pointed to the map Saleh Mirza kept in his study. "Unless we go to Gurdan, we'll have to pass Gilan no matter where we go." She turned to Belqais. "Can your cousin help us?"

"He is dead. But I can try to find his contacts," Belqais responded.

"My son lives in Baku. He can help us there," Qamar intervened.

"You can't travel alone, no matter where you go," Noor said. "You need a man. Someone who won't sell you to the highest bidder."

The only person Gohar could think of was Hosseinqoli, Haji's partner. But he was in Odessa and not expected for several months. "We can take Ahmad," she said.

"Ahmad is trustworthy," Noor said. "But he is no match for the bandits. You need someone with fighting skills."

Qamar nodded in agreement.

"We need to move quickly," Gohar said. "That cretin is coming back next week for his money. If we can't find someone more suitable, we'll have to make do with Ahmad."

Noor agreed to call on her friends for contacts in Istanbul. Qamar volunteered to inquire about convoys destined for Gurdan, while Belqais would look for connections in Baku.

They agreed to keep their efforts secret from the household staff. Any inkling of Gohar's plan to flee would prompt their enemies to pounce swiftly. They would regroup the following evening.

Before dispersing, Gohar turned to Noor. "Will you come with us?"

"No," Noor said. "I am too old. I would slow you down. Besides, no one would dare to bother me. Times may have changed, but I am still the widow of a shah and a kingmaker. You should leave Kamal with me."

"Wherever I go, my son goes," Gohar said resolutely.

"Gohar, dear," Qamar interrupted. "With Noor's permission, I want to come with you. I am old, but I can still care for Kamal and keep you company."

Gohar hadn't considered taking Qamar. The trip would be dangerous and challenging, and Qamar was in poor health. But she was delighted that Qamar had volunteered. She looked to Noor for affirmation, who nodded. Then, to Gohar's surprise, Belqais asked to join them. Gohar hesitated. She and Belqais had become friendly but not close, and her past snide remarks still haunted Gohar. But Belqais's passion and sincerity touched her. She relented.

Alone, Gohar ruminated on her plans to escape with Aslan. What would her life have been if they had followed through?

But she had to focus. There was so much to do, so much to arrange. Noor was right. They needed someone more capable than Ahmad to take them on the perilous journey. But who? She felt lonely and discouraged.

If only she could talk to Aslan. He would know how to get through the Russians and get to Istanbul. But it had been a year since she had even laid eyes on him, and he could have married or moved. Then she remembered his letter. She had never doubted his sincerity. But the offer had been made long ago, in the throes of passion. She didn't expect him to interrupt his life for her. Contacting him was a long shot. But she had nothing to lose. Akbar Mirza was not going to go away. Meanwhile, hastily marrying someone for protection—even if it was possible—would be no guarantee of salvation. She could end up trapped in another joyless marriage. Worse yet, her new husband could mistreat Kamal.

Hurriedly, she rummaged through her trunk to find the broken chain, wrapped in its white handkerchief, where she had left it.

8

December 1915, Tehran

Golestan Jewelry was a narrow shop with a single counter in the grand bazaar. When Gohar entered, a scrawny teenager in a yarmulke arranged gold jewelry on a tray. Gohar asked to see the owner.

The assistant kept his eyes on the tray. "He's not here. Can I help you?"

"I need to talk to him."

The boy raised his head. "What are you looking for, sister?"

"I have an item for repair. But only he can take care of it."

"I can give you an estimate if you like," he said, placing a pair of earrings on the tray. "I do all the repairs."

"No, no, I need to see him. Please."

He shrugged. "He won't be in until noon. You can come back then, or I can take what you have and show it to him when he comes in. You can come back tomorrow."

"Can you send someone to fetch him?" she said. "I'll pay for it."

The boy placed the tray inside the glass case. "We don't have an errand boy." He gestured to the jewelry around him. "And I am not allowed to leave until he gets in."

Her gaze drifted to the earrings and necklaces artfully arranged on green felt in the case. Typically, she would have enjoyed wandering around the bazaar for a few hours. But it was cold, and too early for most shops to be open. She asked if she could wait in the jewelry shop.

The boy scrutinized her before offering her a chair. When the waiter from the nearby coffeehouse brought tea, he had a cup for her.

Shortly before noon, a plump, bespectacled man arrived. Curly gray hair poked from under his yarmulke. The shop assistant pointed to Gohar and whispered in his ear.

The older man's inquisitive black eyes burrowed into her. "I am Dauvoody, the owner. How can I help?"

After sitting in the shop for hours, she felt foolish. This must all be a cruel joke—Aslan's way of humiliating her in revenge for her leaving him in the lurch. For a moment, she considered making up an excuse and leaving. But she had come too far. "May I have a private word?" she murmured.

Mr. Dauvoody eyed her suspiciously before dispatching his assistant to fetch lunch. When she was alone with the jeweler, she showed him the chain and explained what she needed. He examined the chain impassively. She held her breath, expecting him to burst into laughter.

Finally, he lifted his head and put the magnifier down. "Were you, by any chance, referred to me by Aslan Madadoff?"

She nodded.

"Do you have a message for him?"

"I need to see him urgently. Today, if possible."

Mr. Dauvoody shrugged. "I can only send a message; the rest is up to him. How can I reach you?"

"Please. Can you send someone right away? I will pay for the time and the droshky."

Mr. Dauvoody raised his open palms. "No need to pay. I will try. But I can't promise anything. Is there a place he can send a message to or meet you?"

Meeting at her house, with its sea of prying eyes, was not an option. But there were no cafés, parks, libraries, or other public places where a man and woman could meet discreetly in Tehran. "No, but he can suggest a place. I can come back for my answer."

The jeweler glanced at her with attentive eyes. His face softened. "Come back after the midafternoon call to prayer. God willing, you'll have your answer."

Aimlessly, she wandered around the bazaar. In a passage, a migrant family huddled under a tattered quilt. Their colorful assortment of household items attested to their once middle-class status. The thought of herself and Kamal as homeless migrants rattled her. She left them all the money she was carrying.

When she returned to the jewelry store, Mr. Dauvoody was alone. Silently, he motioned to the door at the back of the space.

Behind the door was a room not much larger than a closet, lit by the pale winter sun peeking through a narrow window close to the ceiling. There, seated behind a beaten-up wooden table, was Aslan Madadoff.

9

He rose to greet her. She stood motionless, her hands aching to touch him, her lips hungering for his. Blood rushed to her face. Not for the first time in his company, she was relieved to be wearing a veil to cover her burning face.

Calm and composed in a long tunic and trousers, he circled the table to pull out a chair for her. An authoritative detachment had replaced the passion that had once burned in his blue eyes.

He leaned against the back wall. A narrow beam of light lit his crossed arms, leaving his face obscured. "Can you take your veil off?" he said flatly. "I'd like to see who I am speaking with."

Gohar felt foolish. She pulled up the veil and let the chador slip down her shoulders. "Thank you for coming. I—"

He interrupted. "I don't mean to be rude. But I don't have much time. It is best to do away with the pleasantries."

She flinched. But what did she expect? It was a miracle that he had come at all. She swallowed hard, folded her hands on the table, and recounted her predicament.

He glanced at his wristwatch once she had finished. "What is it that you want from me?"

His icy tone cut through her heart.

"I need someone capable and trustworthy to take me to Anzali and help me to take the boat to Baku," she muttered. "From there, Qamar's son can help me get to Istanbul."

"And you expect *me* to drop everything and come to your rescue?"

"No, no," she said hastily. "I was hoping you'd know someone who would. Maybe Ilych? It shouldn't take that long. A week at most."

"Do you have any idea how difficult and dangerous it is to travel north now?" he snapped. "First, you must pass Qazvin, which is filled with Russians. The road from there is reserved for the Russian military. You'll need a special permit—which I doubt you'd be able to get—or someone to smuggle you." His voice rose as he spoke. "Ilych is too old for all that."

"I can pay."

"You can, if you find someone suicidal enough to do it, and with the scruples not to rape you and hand you to the Russians to rape and kill you."

She bit the inside of her lips. His anger was easier to take than his sarcasm. "Is there an alternative route?" she asked calmly.

"In the summertime, there is. Through mountain passes. But now the trails are buried in snow." He put his right foot on the empty chair and leaned on his knee. "Even if by some miracle, you make it to Gilan, you won't be home free. The Russians have relaxed their rule in the province, but not in Rasht or Anzali. And you'll need a passport to go beyond Anzali."

This was hopeless. She rested her face on her palms.

"Can't friends of Noor or Saleh Mirza persuade the English to leave you alone?" he said in a more conciliatory tone.

"No." She looked at her hands. "We are toxic. My husband is a German sympathizer and part of the Mohajeron. He is accused of treason and espionage. People refuse to see me."

"Why don't you pay Akbar Mirza and be done with it?"

She erupted, staring at him unblinking. "I'd rather set fire to the house and kill myself and my son than be protected by the pompous British and their corrupt agents from the even more despicable and brutal Russians. They'd milk me until I was penniless. Then I'd be their whore, and my son their slave."

He didn't respond. The weight of his stare lingered on her. He sat down, burying his head in his hands. She watched him wordlessly. On the other side of the door, the jeweler haggled; a woman laughed; the outside door opened with a jingle; a glass clinked on the glass case; coins jangled; papers crinkled.

The trickle of sun through the window narrowed and notched higher on the wall. The darkness masked the outline of his body. The teenage shopkeeper brought in a kerosene lamp and left it on a shelf without looking at the two of them. The light bounced off the glass on Aslan's wristwatch. She dared not speak.

Finally, he raised his head. "Listen," he muttered. "I'll take you." His voice, barely audible above the din, was firm.

The flood of gratitude overwhelmed her. But she couldn't accept that. It would be asking too much. "I don't want to disrupt your life," she said.

He dismissed her with a brusque hand gesture. "No need to concern yourself with my welfare." His voice was flat. "I'm not doing it for you. This is for Saleh Mirza. I owe him so much. And it's to honor my word, foolish as it may have been."

"I don't know how to thank you," she murmured. "I will be forever in your debt."

"No need." He leaned back. "I need time to plan and arrange my affairs."

"I don't have that much time," she cried. "We must be gone before the agent comes back. That gives us less than a week."

He mumbled something in a language she didn't understand—a Russian curse? —before switching back to Farsi. "You're not making this easy. Is it just you?"

"No. There are four of us: me; Qamar; my sister-in-law, Belqais; and my son, Kamal."

"And Noor?"

"She is staying. As long as I am not there, no one will dare touch the house with her in it."

"And she can't protect you in the house?"

"No. She can't stop the soldiers if they come for me, or Akbar Mirza from claiming custody of my son."

"Even so, you should leave the infant with her," he said. "It's winter, and we may have to walk across the mountains. He will slow us down, and he could get hurt."

"He's not a baby. He turned three last summer." She met his eyes through the dark. "He is coming with me. We live together, we die together."

"I see." He hesitated. "Where can we meet tomorrow night?"

"My house, Saleh Mirza's old house, at midnight. I will leave the door to the andarooni open." She paused. "Do you need money?"

He turned red. "Who do you take me for? A mercenary?"

"No, no," she blurted out. "For travel arrangements. I don't want you to spend your own money. You are already doing much more than I ever hoped for."

"Bring it with you." He rose. "Bring a mix of rubles, English pounds, and Persian coins." He crossed the room and stood beside the closed door.

"One more thing," she said reluctantly. "No one in my party knows about us. I want to keep it that way."

He turned around and placed his hands on the table. His cold eyes bore into her. "My dear Gohar," he growled. "You have nothing to worry about. In case you have forgotten, there is no 'us,' and there never will be. I will take you to Gilan. There, we will part for good, never to see each other again. Understood?"

She nodded in agreement. A lump blocked her throat.

That evening, Noor shared the contacts her friends had provided. Belqais had sent telegrams to her cousins. Qamar had nothing; no convoy was leaving for Gurdan any time soon.

Gohar was last. She summarized her meeting with Aslan, omitting the part about needing passports or permits. In time, money would solve such problems.

Noor paled. "Oh my God," she yelped. "Traveling with someone with Aslan's reputation for debauchery? That would be ruinous."

"What choice do we have?" Gohar said. "I don't see others rushing to help us. Aqa Mirza trusted him with his own life and ours, and he has saved us before. What more could you ask?"

Before Noor had a chance to object, Belqais intervened. "I agree that we don't know much about this man," she said in a measured tone. "But let's not be hasty. Let's assume that the gossip is true, and he is an adventurer and a ladies' man." She held her right index finger with her left hand. "On the first count, who but an adventurer would take a bunch of women on a crazy trip like this?" She took her middle finger. "On the second count, we all promise to exercise self-control and remain immune to his charms."

Belqais's defense of Aslan surprised and delighted Gohar. Did she know him?

Noor darted a glance at Qamar, who nodded. She grudgingly agreed.

10

January 1916, Tehran

The knock on the door was so soft that Gohar would have missed it if she hadn't been expecting it. But any louder and the sound would have woken the household staff and spoiled her plan to leave covertly. Aslan stood outside in the milky dawn light. A green truck with Cyrillic writing on the side idled in the alley. Beside it, Ilych and a shorter man warmed their cupped hands with their breath.

"Here's your magic carpet to Qazvin," he said.

His friendly mood relieved her. They had a long journey ahead. "A Russian military truck?" she whispered.

He smiled smugly. "It's safer and less conspicuous than traveling in a car with three covered women and a child. Not to mention bigger." The truck, he explained, was part of a daily cargo between Tehran and the Russian army headquarters in Qazvin. "Our good Chechen driver believes it is his religious duty to take a sister to see her dying mother while carrying vodka for his asshole imperial masters. In the process, he can make some money. Come see for yourself."

She touched her chest to ensure the vest she wore under her blouse was secure. It was a gift from Noor. The gold coins sewn expertly into its seams could be retrieved easily. She followed Aslan.

Ilych took off his hat and bowed when they reached the vehicle. Not wanting to acknowledge her familiarity with him, she nodded.

"Allow me to introduce my friend, Petrus," Aslan said, pointing to a bespectacled man with a handlebar mustache and wavy brown hair. A foot shorter and a good decade older than Aslan, he looked pleasing. "He teaches French and is from Gilan. He'll be your guide there."

Petrus bowed with his right hand on his chest.

Aslan pulled back the canvas cover in the back of the truck. A small, carpeted area was visible through a narrow opening between the cargo boxes. "Once you're in, we will rearrange the boxes to conceal the compartment, in case we're stopped, and the truck is searched. I've left cushions, food, and water for you."

His choice of transportation was wise. "Is this a military uniform?" She pointed to his great coat and Astrakhan hat.

"No, only a winter coat in the right color to reinforce the illusion." He paused. "If we are caught, I don't want to be shot on the spot for impersonating a Russian officer."

A chill ran up her spine. There was a truth to his words, though he spoke them lightheartedly. She was unable to express her gratitude for all he was risking for them. "You move quickly." It had been only three days since their meeting at the jewelry shop.

He shrugged. "Friends helped."

Belqais and Qamar left the house, followed by Ahmad carrying Kamal. Gohar introduced the women, then pointed to Kamal clutching his Steiff bear. "This is my son, Kamal."

Aslan took a perfunctory peek at the child. "We must move."

Gohar handed him the black bag she carried under her chador. "Money for our expenses," she murmured.

"Keep it," he said, helping her climb onto the truck. "It is safer with you."

With the women and Kamal on board, Aslan poked his head in. "Petrus has to ride with you ladies. But no need to worry. He doesn't bite and won't go crazy at seeing your faces and hair."

"We promise to keep our hands off him." Belqais smiled, took off her veil and chador, and made room for Petrus next to herself.

Her sister-in-law was full of surprises.

"At roadblocks," Aslan said, "I will knock on the side three times. When you hear that, stay silent until the car moves again."

Gohar clutched Kamal on her lap. This would be no joyride.

Ilych rearranged the boxes. Shortly after, Gohar heard the car door close and water splash on the ground. Ahmad had poured it to wish for their safe return. The truck lurched forward.

They drove through the quiet streets, the engine echoing as they passed beneath the barrel ceiling of Qazvin Gate. Once they reached a smooth, open road, Gohar dozed off, exhausted after three nights of packing while the servants slept.

Three knocks woke her. Next came the sound of Aslan speaking in Russian and men laughing. Inside, Kamal sat on Petrus's lap, covering his mouth with the stuffed bear. Petrus must have invented a game to keep him quiet. Nobody moved. She didn't exhale until the truck rolled again.

The vehicle stopped several times as Gohar floated in and out of sleep. Once, a conversation in Russian woke her up while they were stationary. The sight of a Russian soldier holding a rifle through a tear in the canvas rattled her. She exchanged a glance with Belqais, who was holding Kamal. More Russian voices followed. She heard Aslan laugh. It sounded contrived, but all the same, they were soon moving forward again.

Belqais resumed talking with Petrus in a low voice while feeding small pieces of cheese and bread to Kamal. Gohar fell back to sleep.

A sharp turn slammed Gohar to the side. They were climbing a bumpy road. A row of leafless poplars flew by, visible through the tear in the canvas. Once they stopped, Ilych rearranged the boxes to let them out.

Gohar was the last to leave the truck. By the time she emerged, Kamal was already running through a field lined with sycamores, making galloping noises. Five villagers and a convoy of donkeys stood beside a wide path that led to the mountains through the woods. Gohar stretched her back. The cold air was refreshing.

As the villagers piled the luggage onto their donkeys, Aslan gave the driver an envelope and embraced him. Ilych lifted Kamal to his shoulders and led the group up the path on foot as the truck drove off in a dust cloud. The villagers made room for Qamar—as wide as she was tall and with painful knees—on a donkey. After the tense drive in the cramped truck, the walk in the pale midafternoon winter light was rejuvenating. No one spoke. Kamal started singing.

At sunset, they reached a vast orchard surrounded by tall walls. Four men in loose white pants, sheepskin coats, and hats stood by the wooden gate. One of them, a thin, middle-aged man with a drooping mustache, stepped forward when they arrived. He bowed deeply to Aslan and embraced Ilych.

Aslan acknowledged him with a nod and introduced him to the group as the estate's caretaker, Mash Baqer. The caretaker apologized profusely for not sending buggies or enough donkeys to carry them all. He had been given too short a warning to procure enough animals, he said. He led the group through a wide, tree-lined, pebbled path to a large, ornate, Italian-style villa. As they walked, Gohar overheard Mash Baqer tell Aslan that "Her Ladyship" had instructed him to give Aslan full access to the property. The ladyship's bedroom was ready for Aslan. The bathhouse was warmed up, and the cook was preparing Aslan's favorite dish, *tahchin* with chicken and yogurt saffron rice. But the cook could make grilled chicken if Aslan or his guests wished for something else. Mash Baqer's manner and decorum denoted his experience with serving the nobility. Gohar wondered who "Her Ladyship" was; she must be close to Aslan. She suppressed a pang of envy.

The guests left their shoes in the vestibule and entered a marble foyer. To their right was a Farangi-style library with huge bookcases and an unlit fireplace. Ahead was a living room occupying the entire back of the villa. The doors to their left were closed.

The mother-of-pearl inlaid in the wooden ceiling tiles glinted in the light from tall windows on three sides of the living room. The carpet, custom-made to cover every inch of the floor, was velvety soft. A Russian woodstove warmed the room. The room was impressive, even by the standards of Tehran.

The guests settled on cushions behind the low tables laden with sweets and fruit and arranged in a horseshoe at the far end of the room. Then the maids served them tea in dainty gold-rimmed glass cups. Gohar asked Mash Baqer to take her to the bathhouse.

Gohar did her best not to gawk at the white marble covered walls and vaulted ceiling of the women's bathhouse as a maid helped her undress and wrapped a thin sheet around her. She declined the servant's offer to wash her and sent her to fetch Kamal and the other women.

When the others arrived, Gohar was floating happily in the pool at the far end of the bathhouse. Qamar declined a bath sheet, pointing to her ample stomach that folded over her private parts. Washed and relaxed, the women lay on soft towels by the marble fountain in the middle of the room, snacking on almonds and pistachios while Kamal jumped into the pool. Qamar mentioned that Noor had considered building a bath in the house in Tehran, but the prohibitive cost of upkeep had deterred her.

Once Qamar and Kamal had departed, Belqais and Gohar lay side by side on their backs. The intimacy of their half-nakedness emboldened Gohar to ask Belqais whether she had known Aslan previously.

"I met him in Gurdan almost five years ago," Belqais said matter-of-factly.

Gohar gazed at the darkening sky through the hole in the ceiling. "What was he doing there?"

"He brought me my cousin Saman's writings."

"Is Saman the cousin who lived in Baku?"

"Yes."

"How come I've never heard of him?"

Belqais sighed. "It's a long story."

Gohar was intrigued. "We have all the time in the world." She turned to her side, rested her head on her palm, and gazed expectantly at Belqais.

Belqais remained silent for some time. When she spoke, her voice was barely audible. "Saman and I grew up together. In our tribe, boys and girls—especially cousins—mingle freely. Since my father died when I was very young, Saman's father acted as my own.

"Saman and I were thick as thieves. We learned reading and writing together, practiced calligraphy together, rode and hunted together, and got into mischief together. We were inseparable. I worshiped him. To me, he was the essence of perfection, a god, a beautiful face paired with a beautiful soul. A Rostam who painted and wrote poetry. When we were betrothed, I was on top of the world. Everyone commented on how well we got along. A match made in heaven, they said. My uncle was particularly keen on our union."

Through the mist in the darkened bath, Belqais looked much younger. "Summers were the best," she continued. "We played music, roamed the land, and laughed. Then one day, as our mothers planned our engagement in the fall, he asked me to ride with him. Atop our favorite hill, he told me he was in love with someone else, not a woman but a man. He wasn't like other men, he said. Never was and never would be. He wanted to call off the wedding."

Gohar squirmed. This wasn't going to be a happy story.

Belqais turned to face Gohar. "I was devastated. It was true that with all the talk about our marriage, calling it off could have been a black mark on my reputation. But it wasn't me that I was worried about. It was him. In our tribe, a man loving another man is against our honor code, a sin to be washed away by blood. I couldn't let him die."

Belqais inhaled. "I suggested that we get married. To live with him would be enough for me; he would be free to love whomever he wished. Many men did. But he rejected the idea. He cared for me too much to ruin my life, he said. I deserved better: a happy marriage, children, that sort of thing. Plus, he didn't want to live a lie, and there was no place in our tribe for him. He had to leave."

A maid brought a kerosene lamp and lit the candles in the wall niches. Belqais waited for her to leave. "So, we agreed on a plan. He would leave, and I would tell his parents and my mother that I had broken off the engagement. That's what I did when Saman left. My mother and uncle were furious. But I didn't care.

"A few months later, my uncle came to see me, raving mad. He had discovered the truth and wanted to find Saman and wash away the stain of disgrace with the blood of Saman and his lover.

"I emphatically denied everything. I even went as far as claiming that Saman and I had been lovers for years. But my uncle didn't buy that. He said that if that was true, Saman was even less of a man than he thought. Finally, he denounced Saman. No one, not even Saman's mother, was allowed to mention his name. He threatened to kill anyone who did."

Belqais fell silent. Outside, the sky had turned black.

Gohar sat upright, gazing at her sister-in-law. Her heart ached for Belqais, suffering alone with a judgmental mother like Khanum Bozorg. No wonder she was so bitter. Gohar was lucky to have Qamar in her life. She reached for her sister-in-law's hand.

Belqais continued. "Saman moved to Baku. There, he met Aslan while they were both training Iranian revolutionaries. He died there of typhus. Aslan brought me Saman's diary and poems. That was the day you fell. You know the rest."

She remembered Belqais's words in Gurdan, commenting on Gohar not being the only one unable to mourn for a loved one. "We'll visit his grave when we are in Baku," she said, squeezing Belqais's hand.

Belqais nodded.

They rested on their backs wordlessly. The stars shone through the hole above. The mother-of-pearl inlaid in the ceiling glinted in the candlelight, the sky inside competing with the one outside.

Gohar broke the silence. "Were they lovers?"

"Who?"

"Aslan and Saman."

Belqais smirked. "No, Aslan likes women, and they like him back. Look at how he's treated here, under orders from our mystery hostess."

Gohar felt a tightening in her chest. Luckily, darkness hid her discomfort from Belqais's sharp eyes. "How do you know he's her lover?"

"He sleeps in her bed, for God's sake." Focusing on someone else seemed to have distracted Belqais from her own painful memory. "This house is their love nest. Look at how sumptuous it is. Mash Baqer knows what's going on—he treats Aslan like a sultan, bowing left and right, ordering his favorite dish. What's next? Feeding him with a silver spoon?"

Gohar swallowed. "You have a point."

"Now it's your turn. How did you get Aslan to take us on this trip?"

Gohar decided to tell Belqais about how she had met Aslan, him recognizing her after seeing her by accident, and his letter offering help. It was true, albeit incomplete.

Belqais bolted upright. "Rascal! I knew he was smitten. He carried you like you were a China bowl. I didn't tell him who you were. But he made me swear on Saman's grave that I would personally look after you."

"Is that why you stayed up with me? You said you did it because of Haji."

"I couldn't tell you the truth, could I? To be honest, I was a bit jealous."

"You like Aslan?"

"God forbid." Belqais sniggered. "He is far too young and cocky for me. But I was jealous of his affection for you. I wished for someone to care for me that way. He must still have a soft spot for you—look at all the trouble he's gone to for you."

Aslan's words in the jewelry store rang in Gohar's ear. "Well, even if he fell for me then, he certainly doesn't care for me anymore. As you aptly pointed out, he is the sultan of our hostess's heart, and she is the queen of his. In any case, I am married."

Belqais stared at her. "I wouldn't be so sure. Being smitten like that doesn't go away, my dear. He isn't married, and you may not be for long."

Belqais came to dinner with her hair wrapped in a colorful turban. Everyone complimented her. From inside the horseshoe, maids served them spinach and plum stew, saffron rice, roasted lamb, and lentil soup, in addition to Aslan's favorite, *tahchin*, in porcelain dishes with silver utensils.

"They don't seem to have heard of the war here," Belqais whispered to Gohar.

Gohar smirked. "I suppose not."

Aslan, relaxed in an ornate silk robe, played the gracious host—

ordering servants to bring the next dish and urging the guests to try it.
Gohar ate sparingly. Being close to him, breathing the air he breathed,
walking the road he walked, and eating the food he ate had disturbed
her more than she had expected.

After dinner, she took Kamal upstairs to their room. He was asleep
when she heard a knock, barely audible over the chatter and laughter
from downstairs.

Ilych stood in the hallway. "May I come in?" he asked.

His visit surprised her. Ilych seldom talked to her. But knowing how
close he was to Aslan, she moved aside to let him in.

He closed the door behind him. "What are you playing at?" he said
curtly.

His rudeness vexed her. She glanced nervously at her sleeping son.
"What do you mean?"

"Don't be coy with him." He lowered his voice, wagging his finger
at her. "You left him in bad shape. I don't want to see him like that
again, ever."

There was no point arguing with the old man. Ilych was not subtle,
but he loved Aslan. "You have nothing to worry about," she said calmly.
"I have no plans for him."

"Frankly, I was shocked when he said we were going to travel with
you. He'd sworn never to talk to you again. Then he moved heaven and
earth to arrange this trip."

"I'm grateful." She paused. "If you must know, he's helping me
because I'm desperate." She fought the tears forming in her eyes.

His face softened. "Look, I didn't come to yell at you. I came to
warn you. Be careful here, especially with Kamal. Never leave him with
the servants, or mention you knew Aslan."

His tone disturbed her. "Why?"

"Our host is jealous and vindictive. She'll make trouble if she
suspects anything going on between you and Aslan or gets wind of your
history. The servants are watching."

"I never leave Kamal with anyone except for Qamar and Noor," she
said defensively.

"You can leave him with me. I'll guard him with my life." He turned.

"Don't mention what I told you to Aslan. He won't believe it."

She grabbed his sleeve. "Tell me one thing, please," she asked anxiously. "Is he happy?"

He pulled his sleeve away. "He is at peace. That's all you need to know."

After he left, she felt confused, restless, and lonelier than ever.

11

January 1916, the hunting lodge

Weeping willows surrounded the ornate stone fountain in the formal garden behind the villa. Gohar inhaled the cold, crisp air as she passed through burlap-wrapped rose bushes in tidy, boxwood-edged flower beds. After tossing and turning all night, the stroll outside was invigorating. She took the path through the orchards beyond the garden to reach an enormous reservoir surrounded by stone benches.

At the villa, Petrus was reading, Belqais was playing with Kamal, and Qamar was drinking tea. Aslan and Ilych were out. Gohar didn't mind. Being alone in the silence of the mountains gave her a chance to think.

She sat on a bench at the water's edge. Soon, the intense mountain sun warmed her. With no one in sight, she removed her jacket and headscarf and unbraided her hair. She pictured Noor's teary green eyes as they bade each other farewell. Would she ever see Noor or her own house again? Would Haji ever come back to clear his name and hers? If not, she would have to find a way to clear her name before Akbar Mirza could strip her and Kamal of their rightful inheritance, or accuse her of treason, send her to jail, and take custody of her son. She ground her teeth. It wasn't losing money that enraged her. It was the injustice—and her powerlessness to fight it.

Absorbed in her thoughts, she didn't hear the footsteps approaching. Aslan's voice startled her. "Beautiful, isn't it?"

Quickly, she pulled her scarf up and turned around. He stood by the bench, gazing at the snow-covered mountains beyond.

"Is that necessary?" He turned to her.

"It's for the benefit of the servants," she explained, pleased by his friendly mood.

"Servants are nosy." He sat at the far end of the bench. "But here, they are used to uncovered women mingling with men."

She remembered the maids' indifferent attitude toward them dining together the night before. "Still, it's good to be careful," she said. "Where were you this morning?"

"Qazvin."

"What did you find out?"

"Can you wait a bit? I'd rather report to all of you at once."

She felt chided. "Certainly."

They sat in silence.

Finally, she asked. "Do you come here often?"

"I hunt with our hostess's husband and stepson now and then and attend their gatherings here. I even hid here for six months once."

Had he come here after their breakup? Curiosity overwhelmed her. This was as good an occasion as any to find out more. "And who is this hostess?" she asked nonchalantly.

"Nosrat-ol-Saltaneh, the only daughter of a princess and a wealthy man." He opened his arms wide. "The owner of this villa and the land around it, plus many others."

"I've heard of her. How do you know her?"

"We are mutual admirers of fine things." He paused. "Why do you ask? You're not jealous, are you?"

She swallowed. "Why should I be? Just curious. I'd like to know whose generosity we should be thankful for."

"You can thank me."

"That I do. What did you tell her about us?"

"That you are the daughter of an old friend who needs shelter. What else is there?" He sounded annoyed. "She didn't probe."

"And her husband?"

"He does as she commands." He turned his gaze to the water.

She watched his profile against the blue sky. Neither one of them spoke. Then, against her better judgment, she pushed. "What were you doing here when you stayed here?"

"Growing up," he said, his voice suddenly bitter and terse. "Being disabused of romantic notions, hiding from the Russians, thinking about what to do next." He rose before she could ask more questions. "We need to go. Lunch should be ready soon, and I want to tell everyone what we have learned."

She followed him silently.

In the house, a fire roared in the Farangi-style library. Aslan leaned against a bookcase next to the fireplace. Gohar joined others on the sofa, facing him. At a different time, she would have enjoyed exploring the overabundance of books in the library, at least those written in Farsi.

"Qazvin is swarming with Russian soldiers," Aslan said. "More are coming daily to fight the Mohajeron and the Germans in the west, the Ottomans in the south, and the Jangali guerrillas in the north." He put his foot on a chair.

"What about the Russian road?" Petrus asked.

"Where is that?" Belqais asked.

"Sorry, I forgot you ladies are not local," Petrus said. "That's what the locals call the road connecting Qazvin to Anzali. The Russians built it."

"No civilian traffic is allowed," Aslan replied. "Not even with a permit. It is now the only motorway the Russians can use to move troops and supplies. They are terrified of the Jangalis and the Germans damaging the road. Anyone caught sneaking in is executed summarily. So, smugglers won't take the risk, not even for large sums of money."

Gohar gazed at the fire. It sounded hopeless.

"Is there an alternative route?" Belqais asked.

"Yes, we can take the old trail," Aslan replied. "But we are on our own. No convoys operate this time of the year, and I don't trust local guides. Ilych found a Tajik friend of his, an army surveyor who knows this area like the back of his hand. We wanted to hire him as a guide, but he has broken his leg in a brawl and can't ride. He is drawing a map to help us cross the mountains on horseback."

"I can't ride!" Gohar yelped. "I'm afraid of horses. Neither can Qamar, and what are we going to do with Kamal?"

"Let's not be hysterical," Aslan said. "Look at the alternatives. We can stay here until the Russians let civilians through or the snow melts, or we can take a convoy of donkeys." He glanced wearily at the door and lowered his voice. "But here, we're a stone's throw from the Russians' military hub. They are actively looking for German spies. Sooner or later, they'll hear about us. Maybe a blabbermouth says something, or someone wants to make some money. Plus, there's a rumor that the Russians will stop civilians from traveling on Baku ferries by the end of January."

If the previous night's conversation with Ilych had not convinced Gohar that they needed to move on, the proximity of the Russians and the urgency to catch a ferry to Baku did. They might be looking for her, but an attack on the compound would endanger Kamal and Aslan.

Aslan stared at her. "Everyone here can ride except for you and Qamar. No one is looking for Qamar. She can stay here until Mash Baqer finds her a safe passage to Rasht, where Petrus's family lives. They can help her catch up with you if you are already gone. And I am sure the Russians will not stop an old widow from joining her son in Baku. I can teach you how to stay on the horse and then lead you through the mountain passes."

The prospect of going to Baku without Qamar troubled Gohar. But there was no other option. "And Kamal?"

"I considered advising that we leave him here with Qamar," Aslan said. "But Ilych was adamant that we'd take him. He has volunteered to carry him throughout the journey."

Gohar turned to glance at Ilych in the back. He acknowledged her with a slight nod of his head. Aslan invited the group to chime in.

Petrus spoke first. "I agree, we need to move on. But not to Rasht. Because of the Jangalis, the city is under martial law. The Russians burned a whole section of the city as a warning after finding rebel leaflets there."

"What do you have in mind?" Aslan asked.

"Somewhere further east," Petrus replied. "The guerrilla leader,

Mirza Kuchek, is from western Gilan. Any fighting would be centered there. I have a friend in a small town near the Mazandaran border, less than a day's horse ride from Rasht. You can stay there. I will go to Rasht by myself to assess the situation before we all move on."

Aslan exchanged a glance with Gohar, who nodded. "Sounds reasonable," he said.

"I've been riding through the mountains all my life," Belqais interjected. "I can take turns with Ilych to carry Kamal."

Qamar, who had no affinity for cold and snow, not to mention heights, enthusiastically agreed to stay behind.

Gohar spoke last. "As much as I loathe the cold and horses, this is the only viable option. I'll do my best not to be a burden."

Aslan shifted his weight and moved his foot to the ground. "We will leave as soon as is practical."

Aslan and Ilych disappeared after lunch and returned a few hours later, carrying a bundle of men's clothing: pants, fur vests, jackets, and round felt hats. Aslan explained that the clothing was to enable Gohar and Belqais to travel as men. Covered women on horses were impractical and conspicuous. He encouraged them to try the clothes on.

"Belqais, dear, you look better as a man than a woman," Petrus quipped when he saw them in their new outfits.

"And you, dear Petrus, would be ugly as sin as a man or a woman," Belqais retorted.

Petrus laughed and turned to Gohar. "You, Gohar dear, are too handsome as a boy to be left alone anywhere in Qazvin," he said, alluding to the reputation of men in that city for preferring young boys to women.

Everybody laughed except for the befuddled Gohar. When Belqais explained, she blushed bright red.

The conversation at dinner was lively. Petrus discussed the challenges of teaching French to pubescent boys. Aslan recounted his pranks at school in Paris. Belqais raved about a book of miniatures she had found in the library. Even Qamar recounted stories from her childhood. Only Gohar remained silent. As soon as the meal ended, she feigned fatigue and took Kamal upstairs.

Kamal fell asleep quickly, but Gohar lay awake. The sound of a male singer crooning in a language she didn't recognize wafted up from downstairs; it must have been from the gramophone she had seen in the library.

"*O sole mio*," she hummed with the singer. Even without knowing the meaning of the words, their mix of joy and longing moved her. The language had the perfect vowels for singing and poetry, like Farsi. A wave of nostalgia rushed over her as she recalled evenings in Saleh Mirza's study, listening to music, singing, talking, and laughing. How happy she had been.

But wallowing in the past was useless. She decided to explore the house, hoping this would tire her out and help her sleep, or at least distract her. In the hallway, light peeked from a slightly ajar door. She tiptoed to the light and pushed the door open. A massive walnut four-poster bed with pulled-back red damask curtains dominated the room. Aslan's clothing was neatly stacked on a shelf beside his grooming kit. Two kerosene lamps with red glass chimneys bathed the space in a soft glow. This must be their hostess's bedroom.

She stepped to the bed, admiring the carved headboard inlaid with exotic wood that matched the spiral posts. Her finger glided under the crimson velvet coverlet to the crisp white sheets. It was sensual. She had seen similar beds—though none this ornate—in the Farangi consignment store but had never slept in one. On her return to Tehran, she would have to buy one.

Books in Cyrillic and Latin were stacked on the bedside table. They must be Aslan's. A slender silver cigarette holder and a matching ashtray sat beside a framed picture on the opposite bedstand. The woman in the photo was in her thirties. With her hair pulled back, almond eyes gazing provocatively into the lens, and full lips partially open, she was beautiful. This must be their hostess, Nosrat. Gohar felt a knot in her stomach.

The reflection of her own pale, gaunt face in the mirror atop the massive vanity dismayed her. She picked up a bottle from the assortment of containers on the vanity and pulled the cap off. A heavy, flowery perfume wafted through the room.

Their hostess smiled seductively from another picture by the mirror. Gohar picked up the heavy frame for a closer look. In this one, Nosrat was much younger, perhaps Gohar's age. She wore a white dress with a matching wide-brimmed hat. Her hair cascaded down to her shoulders. She carried a parasol. In the background was the base of a slender iron tower Gohar knew well: the Eiffel Tower, the symbol of the modern age. Saleh Mirza had a picture taken at the same place when he attended the World Expo of 1900.

Suddenly, Gohar imagined Nosrat naked, her skin softened by the potions in these jars and scented by her musky perfume, lying on the bed with Aslan. His hands groped her breasts. Hers were on his back. She laughed like a harlot, whispering to Aslan in French.

Enraged, she tossed the photo as if to chase away the demons. The frame hit the bedpost and tumbled on the carpet. Mortified by what she had done, she rushed to pick up the picture. Luckily, the glass was intact, but a corner of the frame was chipped. Hastily, she placed it back on the vanity, arranged the bottles, and ran out.

Ashamed of her actions, she squatted by the door inside her room. The depth of her hatred for their hostess disturbed her. Why envy a woman whose generosity had sheltered her and her family when everyone else rejected her? How could she question someone else's morals when her own were so questionable?

She closed her eyes and breathed deeply. It wasn't Nosrat she was angry with. It was herself. She had nothing to say, couldn't ride, didn't speak a foreign language, and was too naïve to comprehend a mildly erotic joke. The extent of her reading was newspapers and the translated adventure novels of second-rate European authors. Her talk was not peppered with French words and phrases thrown in for their *effet*, and she hadn't traveled, not even to the holy cities of Qom and Mashhad, let alone Paris or Istanbul. She didn't wear her wealth like a custom-made glove the way Nosrat did.

It was her desire, her longing for him, and his indifference that had inflamed her. The craving she believed was dead and buried had resurfaced: she wanted him to want her, to touch her, to hold her, to yearn for her as he once had.

But that was folly. She had walked out on him, broken his heart, leaving Nosrat—sophisticated, seductive, and rich beyond imagination— to comfort him and shower him with all the luxury he deserved. Now, he was at peace. Wasn't that what Gohar had prayed for every night?

There was no turning back. He had made that crystal clear by bringing her to the house of his beloved. It was unrequited love that she was feeling. The kind of sensation that brought ruin, and which a sane woman, let alone a pious one, should never entertain.

She remembered the comfort prayers had brought her before. Determined, she abluted with the water in the jar in the corner, donned a prayer chador, and faced Mecca. With all her heart, she implored the Lord to purge her of evil thoughts and temptations.

Her heart lightened, and she fell into an untroubled sleep.

12

January 1916, The Hunting Lodge

Early the next day, Gohar dressed in men's clothing, tucked her hair under a brimless felt hat, and met Aslan in front of the villa for a riding lesson. By noon, she could stay on the horse while it walked and mount and dismount unassisted. She was ready.

When they returned to the house, Ilych, pretending to be a monster, chased a giggling Kamal around the front fountain.

Aslan smirked. "Finally, Ilych has found a playmate his own age."

She covered her mouth to hide a smile.

Bathing was her reward for the morning's riding. She would miss this bath. A nap afterward soothed her aching body.

When she came downstairs, the house was quiet, the living room empty. Aslan was writing in the library. She glanced at the closed door across the hall and overwhelmed with curiosity, opened the door. Instantly, she was dazzled. Thousands of tiny, mirrored pendants on the walls and the ceiling reflected the sun shining through narrow windows, giving her the illusion of entering the forty thieves' cave in *One Thousand and One Nights.*

Three sides of the vast room were lined with platforms covered in red velvet cushions. At the far end, another platform covered in white cushions formed a tiny stage. Next to it, a shelf housed a tar, an *oude*, a *kamancheh*, a *santoor*, a goblet drum, tambourines, and finger cymbals. She imagined guests sitting all around, sipping wine as musicians played and a slender dancer with fancy headgear and cymbals on her long fingers twirled on the tiled floor.

She took the tar from the shelf, carried it to the stage, tuned it, and played.

When she raised her head, Belqais and Petrus were sitting on the cushions.

"Don't stop," Belqais cried. "It sounds heavenly."

"I agree," Petrus said, before adding hesitantly, "Do you by any chance know the song 'From the Blood of the Nation's Youth Tulips Bloom'?"

"Of course." Gohar smiled. "Would you like me to play it?"

"If you don't mind," Petrus said.

She changed the key and played the overture. Petrus's deep, pleasing voice filled the room before she could open her mouth to sing. She joined in, forming an impromptu duo. As they sang, Gohar noticed tears rolling down Petrus's cheek. This was not unusual. Many veterans of the constitutional war teared up listening to this tribute to their fallen comrades.

When they finished, Belqais clapped. "You two sound divine. If we fall on hard times, you can sing at weddings."

"And you will be the band manager," Petrus said.

"Of course," Belqais said. "Otherwise, the two of you will squander the money and end up in the poorhouse."

Gohar complimented Petrus on his voice and played a few cheerful *reng* to dispel the gloom. Petrus sang along, and Belqais kept the beat with a tambourine. The household staff trickled in, and Qamar took a seat at the front of the room—but Kamal was not with her. Gohar stopped. "Where is Kamal?"

"How should I know?" Qamar replied with a puzzled look. "Ilych took him out after lunch."

Gohar glanced at the windows. It was dark out. The light in the room came from candles placed in hollow openings and slits on the walls. The staff must have lit them while she was playing. Her chest tightened. Ilych and Kamal had been gone for hours. Could they have encountered bandits or Russians? Ilych was brave and trustworthy, but he was one man. He could have been subdued, injured, or killed. The image of her helpless child left in a ditch—cold, lonely, hungry— inflamed her. She scanned the room suspiciously. Could one of the servants be responsible for their delay?

Her heart pounded. Her face burned; her temples throbbed. Voices became dissonant; faces were blurred. She dropped the tar, stormed down from the platform, and grabbed Qamar by the shoulders. "Why did you let Ilych take him?" she shouted, oblivious to the servants' inquisitive eyes. "Who gave him permission?" She shook Qamar hard.

"Please, Gohar, dear, I'm so sorry," Qamar whimpered. Her eyes were wide and filled with fear. "May God send a lightning bolt to kill me this instant. I thought you knew," she sniveled.

"What seems to be the problem?" Aslan's voice came from the door.

Gohar let go of Qamar to turn to him. "Where is my son?" she fumed.

"With Ilych," he said calmly.

His composure only inflamed her more. "Who gave him permission?"

"Calm down," he said, approaching her. "Get a hold of yourself. You were asleep, Belqais and Petrus were out, I had work to do, and Qamar couldn't cope with a spoiled boy who doesn't listen to her. So, I asked Ilych to take him."

Suddenly conscious of all the eyes on her, she side-glanced at Qamar rubbing her arm. Her eyes drifted to her reflection in a mirror: disheveled, braid undone, eyes red and crazed. The image terrified her. Was she going mad? She wished she could vanish. "But it's winter," she whined.

"So what?" he growled. "The boy needs discipline, fresh air, and male company. Now, he's getting all three."

The room spun around her. Neither Qamar nor Aslan were at fault; she was. She had left her child at the mercy of strangers while she bathed, napped, and played tar. Her hands trembled.

"Mash Baqer, ask the servants to return to work," Belqais's authoritative voice rose from the side. "This is not a spectacle. Qamar, go upstairs and finish unpacking. Kamal will be home soon and will need a change of clothing." Belqais stepped forward. "Aslan, dear, please go back to your work. Petrus will keep you company." She took Gohar's arm to lead her to a platform.

Gohar sat, holding her face in her palms and sobbing. "I know something bad is going to happen to Kamal. I abandoned him. God is punishing me for slacking in my religious duties."

"Nonsense." Belqais sat beside Gohar. "God is merciful. He wouldn't hurt a child to punish you for missing a prayer here and there. And you are not vile. You are generous and kind." She put her arms around Gohar.

Gohar rested her forehead on Belqais's shoulder. The warmth of Belqais's body comforted her. "No. I am despicable. I lost control, hurt Qamar, made a scene, and embarrassed Aslan."

"Qamar will forgive you. She always does. Aslan had no business meddling in the first place, and I am sure this is not the first row the servants have seen."

"That's what I'm afraid of," Gohar said. "Their whispers."

"Gossip is a poisoned well. You don't have to drink from it."

Gohar regretted listening to the vicious rumors the servants in Haji's house had spun about Belqais. "I'm losing my mind," she murmured.

Belqais stroked Gohar's hair gently. "You are not. There is too much on your shoulders. If my brother hadn't left you in the lurch, we would be in Tehran now, warm and cozy under a *korsi*." She paused. "I know we haven't been close. But you should know you can count on me. I wouldn't side with my brother just because he's my blood. Have faith. Kamal will be back soon."

As though the gods were listening, a grinning Kamal rushed in carrying a pair of winter boots and mittens. "Look what Ilych bought me," he yelled. Gohar's teary eyes and bloated face stopped him. His eyes widened with apprehension. He glanced at Belqais.

"Come show me what you got," Belqais said. She turned to Gohar and whispered. "You'd better go wash up. Put some blush on. You look like a corpse."

On her way upstairs, she overheard Kamal excitedly recounting a visit to Ilych's friend, who had drawn a cat for him. On the way back, he had held the horse's reins.

13

January 1916, the hunting lodge

"O sole mio," Gohar hummed as she watched snowflakes floating outside her window.

The night before, Aslan had translated it as "Oh my sunshine." He claimed the singer, Enrico Caruso, was the best in the world. Gohar didn't believe that, but she didn't challenge him.

Belqais had compelled Gohar to join them in the library after dinner. "You shouldn't be alone. It isn't healthy," she had said. Gohar had complied, especially after seeing Kamal rejoice at Qamar's promise to tell him some new stories. In the library, she had asked Petrus to play the song, and everyone had savored dainty, sweet *paderazin*s and sipped tea.

When Gohar came down the stairs the next morning, Ilych was leaving. Kamal asked Aslan's permission to go with him.

Aslan side-glanced at Gohar. "No, my boy. Ilych has a lot to do. And you should ask your mother for permission, not me."

When Aslan left to work in the library, the women tried their best to entertain Kamal in the living room.

Qamar started a story. "Stop, Naneh," Kamal said, covering Qamar's mouth. "I am not sleepy. It is daytime."

Belqais offered to bounce him on her lap.

Kamal shook his head from side to side and contorted his mouth. "I am not a baby."

Gohar handed him his stuffed bear. "Your bear misses you."

Kamal sat the bear down in a corner and piled his toy soldiers in front of it. "You play," he commanded, wagging his finger at the bear. "I go kill the white deev." He ran around the room, pretending to be

Rostam riding his steed. Belqais and Qamar cracked up while Gohar pleaded with him to stop.

The commotion brought Aslan in. "May I take Kamal outside to play in the snow?" He looked at Gohar, who had followed Belqais's lead and wrapped her hair in a turban. "I could use a break myself." He grinned sheepishly.

Kamal looked at her pleadingly. She glanced at the frost-covered windows. The snow had stopped. Powerless to contain her son, she nodded. Once they left, she cleared a patch of the fogged-up window with her sleeve to watch them. They threw snowballs at each other, ran around the snow-buried fountain, and wrestled. Kamal sat triumphantly on Aslan's chest, both of them beaming.

Aslan was right. The boy needed male company. His world, filled with horses, guns, and swords, was foreign to her. His need to run, wrestle, and be in constant motion was beyond her. How could she guide him to manhood in a rapidly changing world? What did she know about the realm of men? It was as mysterious to her as hers was sure to be to them.

She watched Aslan lift the child to his shoulders to walk up the path, a ray of sun breaking through the clouds to light their matching light-brown hair. Kamal flailed his arms like a bird, the sound of his laugh echoing in the valley.

At lunch, Kamal begged Gohar to come and see the snowman he and Aslan had made. He told her about the snowshoes Aslan had fashioned from a broken basket. The two of them had made her a stick to help her climb the hill.

As afraid as she was of slipping and falling, Gohar didn't want to disappoint her son. Once they reached the frozen reservoir, Aslan cleared the snow from a bench for the two of them to sit and watch Kamal dance in the new snowshoes.

"I noticed that Kamal didn't take any sweets until you nodded," she said. "And then he took only one. Usually, he takes a fistful."

"I told him too many sweets will make him fat," he said. "I hope you don't mind."

"No, I don't." What did she, the product of Qamar's childrearing school of benign neglect, know about the restraint a young boy needed? "I know he should have discipline. But as you aptly pointed out, I am no good at it."

Tired of snowshoeing around the reservoir, Kamal climbed onto the bench and sat on Aslan's lap.

"Did your father teach you how to make snowshoes?" she asked, watching him take the shoes off Kamal.

"No, Ilych did. My father was a brute."

The bitterness in his voice didn't surprise her. His father had always been a sore subject. "At least you knew who he was," she said. "I have no clue about mine."

Kamal nestled on Aslan's lap. He covered the child gently with the flaps of his overcoat. Soon, Kamal fell asleep.

She glanced at the smoke rising from the houses in the village below. "You are good with him. Do like to have children?" she asked.

"I'm not married." He managed a sad smile. "The last girl I proposed to, left me in the cold—literally."

She reddened. "Perhaps she had a good excuse."

He shrugged. "No need to get married, anyway. Wives are like summerhouses. Unnecessary to own one if your friends do. You have all the pleasure and none of the hassle. Plus, you can visit as many as you can handle."

She pictured the ladyship's sumptuous bedroom. "I'll take your word for it."

They watched ravens dig into the snow in search of food. Neither spoke as the setting sun turned the tops of the mountains gold.

It was Aslan who broke the silence, his voice barely audible when he asked, "Is he my son?"

This was the question she had dreaded most. She didn't know how he would react to either answer—affirming or denying his paternity—or what it would mean for the future. "Why do you ask?" she said without looking at him.

"Ilych thinks he looks like me when I was that age." His voice grew firmer. "And I put a few things together myself. One is the timing. We had an affair; nine months later, you gave birth. Then there are the pictures."

She turned to look at his profile. "What pictures?"

"Pictures of Kamal on his first and second birthdays. They were inside the book Saleh Mirza bequeathed to me. He had written the dates on the back. I thought he must be sending a message."

Her eyes welled up. Nothing had ever escaped Saleh Mirza's sharp eyes. "What if he is?"

"I want to spend time with him, take him hunting, camping, teach him riding, shooting, languages," he said. "I don't want him fat and spoiled, glued to your skirt for the rest of his life."

"And if he isn't?"

"He still deserves a better father than a disgraced old fool like Haji," he snapped. "A father is not the one who sires a child, but the one who rears him."

"What would people say?"

"About what?"

"Me, you, him. You said it yourself. He resembles you. What if others see it too?"

"I don't give a rat's ass what people say. There are plenty of rumors about you."

"Me?"

"Yes, let's face it. You, raised by a peasant woman in a remote town, were adopted by one of the most influential men in Iran. He married you to a prominent member of a powerful tribe. Then he left his fortune to you instead of his flesh and blood. You are the beloved companion of his widow, whom you resemble like a twin. Shall I say more?"

His words shocked her. It had never occurred to her that Saleh Mirza had adopted her for anything but to fulfill an obligation to his kin. She glanced at Kamal, happily ensconced inside Aslan's coat. The prospect of Kamal spending time with Aslan didn't bother her. It would make her life more complicated, and she didn't like the thought of her child mingling with Aslan's floozies or being harmed by their fits of jealousy. But Aslan was good for Kamal, and Saleh Mirza had taught her that every challenge presented an opportunity.

She bit the inside of her lip. "Kamal would approve of your plan. But I need to think about it."

"Take your time." He glimpsed at the sky. It was turning purple. He rose, holding the sleeping child to his chest. "We need to get back. The path will get icy soon."

She buttoned his overcoat over the child and followed him down the hill. As darkness fell, the threesome passed through the orchard in the silent intimacy of a family.

PART IV
Legends & Heroes

Oh, you, the pure land,
With the first blossom of every year
In the prairie of your eyes, awakens,
The flowering garden of my thoughts

—F. TAMIMI

1

January 1916, the Hunting Lodge

A massive snowstorm trapped them in the hunting lodge the next day, but that didn't deter Aslan and Kamal from roaming the countryside together. They brought back a dead rabbit one day and a branch of winter jasmine for Gohar the next. One morning, Gohar found her son bouncing gleefully on the four-poster bed while Aslan clapped. One evening, Aslan carved a dog out of wood that Gohar found in Kamal's pocket the following day.

Kamal's happiness filled her with joy. But she dreaded the possibility of Aslan abandoning the child at the end of the trip.

The weather calmed down after three days, allowing Aslan to teach Gohar to use the pistol Noor had given her in a clearing in the woodland. As they walked back, Aslan slowed down for her to catch up. The morning's unexpectedly bright sun had melted much of the snow. Still, even dressed in pants and boots, she had difficulty keeping up with him.

"How are the French lessons going?" he asked.

Petrus had been tutoring her and Belqais in French every morning. Gohar reciprocated by teaching him tar in the afternoons while Belqais painted alphabet cards, each depicting a Latin letter and a picture of something that started with it: a lark, *alouette* for A; a boat, *bateau* for B . . .

"It's hard at my age," Gohar told Aslan. "Especially the pronunciation."

"You're not that old. What are you? Twenty?"

"Twenty-one."

"I was twenty-four when I went back to Paris to finish my studies."

"But you were halfway done," she said ruefully. "I never went to school."

"You don't need to go to school to learn. I'm learning English by reading the same book in both Russian and English."

She glanced at him as he stepped firmly on the mud, his hands clutched behind his back. "That's clever." She paused. "Saleh Mirza was my school."

"Then you had the best of the teachers. No money can buy that kind of education."

"I know. I miss him every day," she said reflectively. "Speaking of Saleh Mirza, you didn't come to his funeral or memorial."

"Why should I? He wasn't there."

"But his family were. You could have come to honor him."

"I came when it counted. When he was alive."

"And it made him very happy. Still . . ."

"Noor doesn't like me."

He could have come for her. But that could have been awkward. "I noticed that. Why?"

"How should I know? Women are fickle."

They strolled through the leafless birches. The smell of burning wood wafted in the air. She locked eyes with a rabbit peeking anxiously from behind a bush.

"What do you do in Tehran these days, if I may ask?" She broke the silence.

"Nothing exciting. I help merchants deal with Farangis, mostly Russians. I negotiate contracts, get export licenses, visas, that sort of thing." He sneered. "Poor sods, they're clueless but they refuse to hire a Russian. I'm their best bet."

She nodded. Haji depended on his partner for similar matters. "Do you like it?"

"It pays well, and I can pick who I work with." "Do you still see your old associates?"

"No. They are all pro-German. Being a Russian makes it complicated, and I don't believe the Germans are the solution to the Iranian problem."

"Do you think the gendarmes were wrong to revolt and join the Germans?" she asked hesitantly.

"Not wrong, only misguided. They fought bravely and succeeded early on. But it is hard to fight a massive army with a few men, no matter how well trained."

"Then there is no hope for us," she said bitterly. "The gendarmes were our best chance."

"There is a way. The Americans showed it. They trained farmers to be soldiers, the Minutemen. They came out of nowhere, attacked the British, and vanished."

"So, we need our Minutemen?"

"What do I know?" He smiled. "I'm just a lawyer, avoiding politics like the plague."

The lodge came into view through the bony branches of elms. The quiet of the mountainside was broken only by the crackling of their feet in the snow. A grouse darted from a tree and soared in the cloudless blue sky.

"How come you didn't go to war?" she asked at last.

"I was exempt from conscription and didn't volunteer." He paused. "I am not a coward. I defended Paris against the Germans. But this war is not about right or wrong. It is about empires grabbing land. How can the English tell the Germans to leave Belgium when they have occupied Ireland for a thousand years and India for one hundred and fifty? Is it better for the Egyptians to be under the rule of the Ottomans, who worship the same God, or the British, who insult them? The English send Indians and Irish to die in the war but refuse to give them independence. It is a travesty when they force a cultured Indian to call a farm boy from Yorkshire *sahib*—master!"

His rage was the sign of his passion to end misery in a world bursting with it. "Saleh Mirza would have agreed with you," she said.

"And you?"

"I do. But I don't know much about the world."

He stopped to face her. "Don't sell yourself too short. Bringing up an amazing child, like Kamal, takes wisdom. He makes me a better person. The other day, he offered me his bear so I wouldn't be lonely at night. Can you believe it?"

She chuckled. "That shows how much he cares for you. He loves that bear."

"He was the one who wanted to bring you that winter jasmine the other day."

Disappointed, she lowered her head. "He is thoughtful."

"He made me realize what a blessing a child is, and why someone like Nosrat, who has everything, would spend a fortune to have a baby."

She could see why Ilych was alarmed. Children, especially the offspring of a beloved, disturbed some barren women. "I can't imagine life without Kamal."

"I know. I saw the way you panicked when I sent him out with Ilych."

They locked eyes. For the first time since their encounter in the jewelry shop, she saw the clear eyes of the young man she had fallen in love with. "I am sorry I embarrassed you in front of the servants," she said.

"I wasn't worried about them. I just didn't want Qamar to get hurt." He smiled. "You scared me."

"I am paranoid when it comes to Kamal. I never leave him with anyone except Noor or Qamar, and occasionally Belqais."

"I'll never let anything happen to him. Neither would Ilych. You have my word."

She grabbed at his sleeve as they parted in front of the villa. "For what it's worth," she said, "I don't think you are a coward. I'm glad you didn't go to war."

2

January 1916, Alborz Mountains

Six days after their arrival, the group of three men, two women dressed as men, and a child left the hunting lodge. Aslan led them, holding the reins of Gohar's horse. Behind her, Belqais and Petrus exchanged barbs while admiring the scenery. Farther back, Ilych carried Kamal on his back, bundled in a blanket, oblivious to Petrus's teasing, likening him to tribal women. Mules laden with baggage and provisions brought up the rear.

All of the adults carried weapons. Gohar touched the pistol in her pocket and the dagger in her sash. Earlier, Ilych had loaded the horses with rifles wrapped in wool cloth. "There are wolf packs in the mountains and tigers and bears in Gilan," Aslan had explained. They now faced a different kind of beast. As frightening as the wild animals were, she preferred them to the political ones. They were more honest.

She glued her eyes to Aslan's back, grateful for the early morning fog that obscured the bottomless crevices either side of the path. They zigzagged up a steep, narrow, slippery, and deserted track. Around them, boulders sprouting from the snow formed a forest of stone. The higher they went, the colder it got. Gohar's frozen fingers made it hard to hold on to the reins.

Despite the perilous road and the unknown destination, she was happy to leave the lodge. The constant anxiety in her ladyship's house had been exhausting. The night before, Gohar had given Mash Baqer a coin out of her vest and a silk prayer mat with silver fringe and added a generous gratuity for the servants. Mash Baqer's eyes had glinted. The coin alone was worth more than a year's salary. But the gifts were an investment in cultivating a friend in the house of a foe. He had bent down to kiss her hand.

"This is a token of my gratitude and a sign of my friendship," she had said, before inviting him to visit her in Tehran.

A pale sun was struggling to break through when they stopped to rest. From atop a knoll, she looked at the sliver of the White River shimmering in the valley. The blue minarets of Qazvin were visible in the distance. Aslan handed her the binoculars he carried around his neck. "That is the Russian road." He pointed to a wide road that ran parallel to the river.

The motorway was shrouded in a cloud of dust. A long convoy of trucks moved alongside men, on horseback and foot, and machine gun-mounted drays drawn by mules. Every now and then, a motorcycle weaved through. Through the powerful binoculars, Gohar could see the ruddy faces of soldiers. "They're so young," she said.

"A bunch of conscripted peasants marching to their deaths," Aslan replied. "Five million of them, along with only four and a half million rifles."

"Are they going to fight the Mohajeron?" she asked.

"Some. Others are heading to Mesopotamia to help the English fight the Ottomans."

The war that had seemed abstract in Tehran suddenly became real. "The ones going north, are they going home?"

"No, they're going to fight the rebel Jangalis." Aslan pointed to where the valley narrowed. "That's Manjil Bridge, the only river crossing wide enough for a vehicle or a convoy of men. Blow it up, and no Russian soldiers can get to Tehran, Isfahan, Mesopotamia, or anywhere south or west of here."

Heavy enforcement around the bridge attested to its importance. "That's why the Russians don't want civilian traffic anywhere near it," Aslan continued.

After a lunch of bread and cheese, Belqais volunteered to carry Kamal. Gohar had never seen her sister-in-law so lively. After her, Petrus and then Aslan took turns carrying the child. When it was Aslan's turn, he let Kamal take the reins, to Gohar's chagrin. The child's laughter only made her more nervous.

At dusk, they reached a cluster of flat-roofed huts clinging to the side of the mountain. The hamlet was too small to have a mosque or a bathhouse, but it looked inhabited. Aslan decided they should spend the night there. It was too cold to camp outside, and any larger village close to the motorway would have Russian guards who would be suspicious of travelers in the dead of winter. The group had already agreed on a cover story: the brothers Gohar and Kamal were on their way to visit their ill father. Their uncle Aslan and friends Ilych, Belqais, and Petrus accompanied them. But Aslan wasn't sure if that would pass muster with the soldiers and didn't want to try their luck. They took the narrow path to the village.

The village elder placed the oil lamp on the earth-packed floor and bowed to Aslan. "I hope this is satisfactory."

The mud and hay hut reeked of sweat, dung, and woodsmoke. A smoke hole above a smoldering pit was its only opening to the outside apart from the door. But it was warm. Gohar glanced at Aslan, who had to bend his neck to stand.

Aslan nodded. They were tired and hungry, and this was the best the village could offer. The elder had evicted its occupants to house them, pocketing the money Ilych gave him.

A young boy brought a tray of freshly baked bread, yogurt, and tea. Once he was gone, Aslan and Ilych blocked the front door with a piece of wood. Ilych took the first watch. The others piled the straw mats and dirty bedding in the even smaller side room, wrapped themselves in their blankets, and slept by the fire. Gohar didn't think she could sleep on the hard, uneven floor. But, dog-tired, she drifted off as soon as she lay down. Kamal was already asleep in her arms.

Petrus was on guard duty when she woke up to use the outhouse. Its filth and foul smell revolted her. She scanned the tiny yard. The shadow of poplar trees in the moonlight was frightening. She stooped and walked towards a crumbling shed that looked promising, standing next to the external wall.

The village elder's voice startled her as she entered the shed. "Thank you, sir. I appreciate it."

She peeked through a crack in the wall. Nobody was there. The voice must have come from farther down the path. Sound carried a long way on a clear, cold, windless night like this.

"No, thank *you*," a gruff voice responded. "Now, we'll all be rich. The Russian captain promised me good money for the Farangi. He thinks he's a German spy. But he wants him alive this time."

Someone said something indecipherable. The gruff voice responded, "Yes, dumbass. You can beat him, but don't kill him like last time. The captain doesn't like dead Germans. Corpses don't talk, no matter how much you beat them."

The voices hee-hawed. The gruff one must be their leader. She wondered who the Farangi was. Was there anyone besides them staying in the tiny village?

The gruff voice continued. "I want the two brothers. They're worth money, especially the little one. I know folks who would pay a fortune for him. The older one isn't bad, either. He'll bring in good money. But kill the rest, the Uzbek first."

Suddenly, her confusion gave way to panic. *They* were the group these men were about to attack: the two boys were herself and Kamal; the Farangi was Aslan; and the Uzbek, Ilych. She covered her mouth to suppress a scream. Her first thought was to run back and alert the others—but more information could save their lives.

"Should we wait for the Russians?" a third man said.

"No, no, no, you idiot," the gruff voice barked. "They won't be here until dawn, and the captain won't let us take the boys or the horses. We need to move before he gets here." He paused. "We can have some fun with the boys first. I don't like the little ones. They squeal too much. But you can have him. He's going to get used to getting fucked anyway."

He cackled. The others aped him. The men took turns describing the various lewd acts they would perform on the brothers. Gohar shuddered.

"Do you want to wait for Hassan and Qasem?" This voice was new.

"Yeah. It shouldn't be long now. We'll go as soon as they arrive."

"What do you want me to do?" the village elder asked.

"Nothing," the leader responded. "Go back to your hut, close the door, and don't come out until I tell you to."

Soon, she heard footsteps and then saw the silhouette of the village elder in the moonlight. Stealthily, she rushed back.

In the hut, she breathlessly told Petrus what she had heard.

"How many are there?" Petrus whispered.

"I heard five voices besides the elder. But there could've been more. Adding the two who are coming, that makes at least eight."

Petrus woke Aslan up and asked if they should leave immediately.

"No," Aslan replied. "Our horses are in the stable, and we can't find our way in the dark. Even if we could get the horses and leave, the bandits would block our path." He paused. "We need to set a trap." He turned to Gohar. "You, hide Kamal in the side room and lie on the floor. Pretend you're asleep. Ilych and I will wait in the corner and charge the bandits when they enter. Petrus and Belqais will be outside to close the trap. Got it?"

Everybody nodded. Belqais and Petrus each took a rifle and left stealthily. Ilych hid by the door with his dagger in hand. Aslan crouched in a corner with his sidearm drawn. Gohar carried Kamal to the next room and covered him with straw and blankets as best she could. The child stirred but fell back to sleep.

Lying on the main cabin floor, she touched her pistol and clutched her dagger. If the worst were to come, the weapons could save her and Kamal from the indignity of capture. Wide awake, hands slippery with sweat, blood pounding in her ears, she said a silent prayer.

Before long, the sound of footsteps was followed by muffled blows on the door. Gohar prayed that the commotion wouldn't wake Kamal. Soon, the wood holding the door gave up with a thud. Pieces of it hit the ground just above her head. A gush of frigid air burst in.

She opened her eyes a crack. A burly man with a pistol stood at the top of the stairs. More men stood behind him. He glanced at her and entered.

Suddenly, Ilych lunged from the side. The two rolled to the ground. The sound of a gunshot from behind startled her. The smell of cordite filled the room. A second assailant bent down and grabbed his chest. Shots were fired outside.

Quickly, she skirted the fighting men. Crouching down, she rushed to hold a fully awake, crying Kamal. "Hush, I am here, baby," she whispered. "Don't be scared."

He folded his arms tightly around her neck, burrowed his face into her shoulder, and sniffled. She felt the throbbing of his heart. In the front room, shadows whirled violently in the scant light. Gunshots and screams echoed.

The stench of a body alerted her to the presence of someone in the room. When a hand touched her shoulder, a primal instinct took over. Fear turned to anger. She swiftly drew the dagger and stabbed him in the thigh with all her might. The man screamed and kicked her.

A searing pain immobilized her momentarily. She curled into a ball, letting go of Kamal. He screamed as the man grabbed him. She crawled to her side, slid to a seat, and pressed her back against the wall. Taking the pistol out of her pocket, she did as Aslan had instructed: clutched the weapon with both hands, slowed her breathing, and squeezed the trigger.

The kick of the weapon slammed her into the wall. The sound of the shot deafened and disoriented her. She shot once more. The man let go of Kamal, grabbed his stomach, and uttered an obscenity. As he stumbled out, Kamal crawled to Gohar. She picked him up and dashed out of the hut, relieved to find the front door unguarded.

The mother and child huddled on the damp ground by the crumbling wall. A man staggered out of the hut and disappeared into the dark just as another came up the path with a rifle. She searched for Petrus or Belqais, but there was no sign of them. She whispered to Kamal not to move under any circumstances; Aslan was in danger. To her surprise, he obeyed without resistance. She followed the new man, stooping to remain hidden.

At the hut door, he aimed his rifle inside. Shouting would only draw the attention of more bandits. She looked for the pistol but couldn't find it—she must have lost it in her haste to flee the cabin. It would do no good anyway. Shooting a man from this distance was well above her skill level. A sliver of the man's bald head below the brim of his hat glinted in the moonlight. Her fingers searched the ground for a rock small enough for her to handle but large enough to do damage. With the right stone in hand, she aimed at the nape of the man's neck.

The stone hit the spot. Blood trickled from the wound. He grabbed the back of his neck and screamed obscenities, then turned around to look for his assailant. Gohar lurched backward.

He aimed the rifle at her, and she heard it cocking. There was no escape. "*I attest that there is no God but Allah.*" She recited the Muslim Last Testament and closed her eyes. Her time had come. May God protect her son.

The shot deafened her, but she didn't feel any pain. Cautiously, she opened her eyes. Aslan stood in the doorframe with a pistol. Her assailant lay motionless on the ground. She put her head on her knees and threw up.

When she lifted her head, Aslan stood in front of her. Blood soaked his shirt. "Are you hurt?" she almost screamed.

"Nothing serious." He shrugged. "A stab wound."

Soon, they all gathered in the yard. Aside from Aslan, no one was seriously hurt. Three of their assailants were dead. Others moaned on the ground, one foaming from the mouth. Gohar regretted nothing. These men deserved their fate.

"You did well," Belqais told her.

Ilych kicked the injured men and warned them to be quiet. The villagers had ignored the commotion and stayed holed up in their huts. Aslan asked Ilyich to fetch the village elder. He broke down the man's door without knocking and dragged him out.

The elder pleaded for mercy and tried to kiss Aslan's feet. The bandits didn't give him a choice, he said. They would have killed him and his family. Belqais spat on his face. Ilych kicked him and threatened to break his neck.

Aslan was about to let Ilych do as he pleased when Petrus intervened. "We need to move on. The Russians will be here shortly. We are not in a position to fight trained soldiers."

Aslan sent Ilych to saddle and bring out the horses.

3

January 1916, Alborz Mountains

They stopped at an area hidden from the main road by tall rocks. Aslan collapsed on the ground as soon as he dismounted. Ilych kneeled beside him. "You need a doctor," he muttered.

"We won't find a doctor in a village," Aslan snapped. "And in towns, the Russians looking for us will shoot first and ask questions later. *You* need to stop the bleeding."

Ilych helped him take off his coat, then looked at Gohar. "I need some clean cloth."

The blood on Aslan's shirt alarmed Gohar. She glanced at Ilych. He was frowning. The euphoria of surviving the bandits was all but gone. Wordlessly, she went to get her clean prayer chador and cut it up into strips for a bandage.

When she returned, Petrus was examining two maps spread on the ground: the one drawn by Ilych's friend and the one the British surveyors had made, and Aslan had won in a game in Baku.

"We have to change course," Petrus said.

"Why?" Belqais asked.

"The village elder knows where we are headed. He could send the bandits to block our way or alert the Russian captain to chase us." He turned to Aslan. "Do you remember our trip with the Englishman to Simorq Castle?"

"I don't think we have time to hunt treasure," Aslan replied without raising his head.

"I think we should shelter there," Petrus said. "It's on the ancient road to Gilan, so it's not much of a detour, and it's only a half day's ride from here. No one would look for us there."

Gohar wondered if the castle had anything to do with the mythical she-bird Simorq—the wise creature who had lived forever and knew everything. Her eyes drifted to the wound on Aslan's side, open as an evil eye. Simorq had healing powers, too. She had revived a mortally wounded Rostam with the touch of her wing. Could she do the same for Aslan?

"What is Simorq?" Belqais asked Petrus.

"A Sassanid-era fortress built on a cliff that locals believe Simorq once nested on," Petrus said.

"In other words, it is inaccessible," Belqais said.

"It is," Petrus said. "No army has ever taken it, not even the Mongols."

"Bottom line: it's a pile of stones on a remote mountain," Belqais said.

"There are still intact structures there," Petrus said. "Ismailis lived there."

Belqais smirked. "Ismailis lived—what, eight hundred years ago? So, the castle has all the amenities available in the Middle Ages."

"It's not the Grand Hotel, I grant you that," Petrus snapped. "But it's better than being hanged by the Russians, slaughtered by bandits, or eaten by wolves."

"We must get there before dusk," Ilych interjected warily. "We can't scale the cliff in the dark." His support for the plan assured Gohar and ended the squabble.

Aslan exchanged a glance with Ilych, then turned to Petrus. "Can you lead us there before nightfall?"

Petrus briefly consulted the maps again. "That shouldn't be a problem. We're not that far. And riding on the Shahrud riverbank will be easier than on the mountain trails."

Gohar gently put a blanket under Aslan's head. "Thank you for saving my life," she said. He looked ashen in the pale predawn light. The white of his bandage had already turned red.

Ilych interrupted. "*You* saved both of us! If you hadn't distracted that bastard, he would have killed both me and Aslan."

She allowed herself a moment of levity. "That was easy. The back of his neck was practically glowing."

"I always knew you had a talent for hurling stones." Aslan managed a wan smile.

It was the first time he had mentioned their past.

The sky lightened as they rode eastward. They took the first path off the main trail to the foggy riverbank. Ilych, on foot, guided Aslan's horse down the steep and slippery track, with Aslan shivering and dizzy on its back. Gohar followed, holding onto the face of the mountain, and reciting every prayer she knew. Petrus, coming behind her, slipped and screamed. Only Belqais navigated the trail easily, carrying Kamal on her back and dragging the remaining horses and mules.

It was considerably warmer by the water. The slanted, smooth shore was wide enough for Gohar to ride unassisted. By now, blood had soaked through Aslan's bandage, and Petrus's sprained ankle had swollen.

When they stopped, Ilych boiled water in a metal flask on the fire the women had made from dried bushes. He then soaked a needle and a cord of thread in a tumbler of vodka, cleaned Aslan's wound with warm salt water, and stitched it with the serene proficiency of a trained doctor. Aslan passed out.

The sun burned through the fog as they journeyed through the red–brown river valley. Peak after snow-covered peak, each higher than the last, loomed as far as the eye could see. Only the clatter of hooves and the rolling of the river broke the silence. Aslan lay pale and motionless on the back of a mule.

By noon, they came across a rope bridge with many missing planks. Despite its sorry state, they decided to take it. There was no knowing when they would encounter a more solid crossing. Ilych tried the bridge before leading the mule with Aslan on its back across it. Belqais, Kamal, and Petrus followed on foot. Gohar was last. She slowly climbed the narrow path to the bridge, grasped the rope, and took a cautious step. The bridge wobbled. She stopped. The next plank was missing, revealing the water rushing underneath. Its sound deafened her. She thought of going back, but to what end? Finally, Ilych came back to hold her hand and help her cross.

Once they all had crossed, Ilych returned to guide the animals over the bridge. Gohar sat by an unconscious Aslan strapped to the contraption Ilych had made to carry him on the mule. She scanned the valley, picturing Simorq flying in the cloudless, blue sky, her feathers shining like rubies and gold in the sun.

Suddenly, a horse's neigh alarmed her. She looked at the bridge, where the lead horse was thrashing frantically. Ilych was kneeling, trying to free the horse's leg from a gap in the planks. Belqais ran back to take the load off the horse. Still, Ilych couldn't control the animal.

In horror, Gohar watched him take his rifle from his saddlebag. Suddenly, all she could see was the pleading eyes of the lamb they had sacrificed when Kamal was born. The animal was tied up. The butcher's shin was on its back. A knife glinted in the sun, and the slayer shouted, "God is Great." Next, the metallic smell of blood filled the air. She had run away.

A shot echoed in the valley. Blood flowed from the bridge's side, painting red strips in the water. On the bridge, Ilych and Belqais struggled to push the carcass into the river. Gohar was nauseated. Beside her, Aslan lay motionless with Kamal at his side while Petrus nursed his injured ankle. There would be no running away. She ran to the bridge to lend a hand.

Later, they ate dried bread and cheese and listened to Petrus recount stories about collapsed bridges. Gohar caught Ilych looking warily at the lengthening shadows. "How far are we from Simorq?" she asked Petrus.

"I would have said no more than a couple of hours if we had fresh animals," Petrus replied. "But we don't. Plus, one horse is dead, which leaves the rest of the animals with heavier loads to carry."

She touched Aslan's forehead. It was burning. He wouldn't survive a night in the mountains. "What can we do to speed up?" she asked

Ilych.

"Lighten the load. Leave what we can behind." Ilych pointed to the trunks and provisions lined up on the riverbank. "We don't need all the food. I can hunt and shop in the village. The last time we were there, they took me for a Turkman from Gorgan. Nobody batted an eyelid."

"We'll leave my trunks," she said. "I'll carry a few essentials for Kamal and myself in my saddlebag."

Without a second look at her stack of fancy dresses, belted crepe de chine chadors, and precious prayer mats, she wrapped the bare necessities in a chador. With her tar slung over a shoulder and dressed as a young man, she could have been a bard, an *asheq*—lover—as the Azeris called them. She smiled wistfully. That was what she was, an *asheq*, hauling her ailing beloved from village to village in search of shelter, making merry at weddings and circumcisions.

As they rode away, the wind scattered colorful pieces of clothing, depositing them on leafless bushes like strange wildflowers.

4

January 1916, Simorq Castle

Late that afternoon, a tall, almost vertical cliff rose above the river valley as though by magic. Three villages gripped the mountainside, appearing as islands of leafless trees, earth-colored huts, and blue minarets in the sea of rocks. Clouds obscured the summit, making it impossible to guess how long it would take to reach the top. It was Ilych who found the steep path buried in the bushes. Everyone but Aslan ascended on foot, dragging the animals behind them.

Rocks blocked the trail here and there, and pomegranate trees and grapevines dotted the face of the mountain. When the path became too difficult for even riderless horses in fading light, they left them on a knoll for Ilych to fetch in the morning.

At the summit, fog shrouded the castle's thick stone and mud-brick walls. As they walked along the intact southern wall, Petrus yelped, "There! We can get in there!" He was pointing to a set of broken steps, barely visible in the semidarkness.

Atop the stairs, a stone gateway, wide enough for a single rider, was flanked by two towers, one erect, the other in ruins. Another set of steps on the other side of the gate took them to an opening two stories higher.

The upper gate opened to a vast, gently rising area. Shards of broken pottery covered the ground. In front of them, the silhouettes of structures were barely visible under a rising moon. Up above, stars dotted the sky.

Halfway up the slope, they entered a single-story brick building with a veranda and a few trees in front. A circular entryway led to two identical rooms, one on each side. Gohar entered the room on the right. The vaulted ceiling was intact, the walls bore traces of plaster, and there were still visible holes where doors and shutters had once hung. At the far end, moonlight spilled in through a narrow window above a raised brick platform. The dwelling smelled stale but not foul. She let out a sigh of relief. They could stay here.

Hastily, they made the dwelling habitable, covering the windows and the entrance with blankets and cleaning the grime and dust from the floor to reveal geometrically patterned mosaics. Soon, a fire was burning on the veranda. Gohar made Aslan a bed with blankets on one room's raised platform. Ilych examined his wound and exchanged a furtive smile with Gohar. The bleeding had stopped.

Too exhausted to eat, she rejected Petrus's suggestion that they take turns caring for Aslan. "You all need the rest, and I'm too wound up to sleep. I will stay up. I will wake Ilych if something changes."

Belqais volunteered to care for Kamal. Then they all left her alone with Aslan.

Moonlight shone around the edges of the blanket that hung in the window as Gohar dried the sweat from Aslan's forehead. His face was ashen, his breath shallow. His body burned, but his hands were chilled. His heart raced. She could feel his life draining away.

Losing him would be too painful to imagine. Why had she dragged him into her misfortune? Despair gripped her soul. Could she exchange her life for his?

"Sing for me," he said, his voice barely audible.

"What?" Was she dreaming?

"I am cold and in pain," he whispered. "If I die, I want your voice to be the last I hear."

A sharp pain stabbed her heart. "You can't die," she said, a lump growing in her throat. "I won't let you."

He managed a crooked upward turn of his lips. "Sing for me . . ." His voice trailed off. "Please."

She cradled him on her lap and stroked his hair. *"If I am drunk, it is of your eyes that I am . . ."* she hummed softly, not wanting to wake the others.

The darkness deepened. The wind howled. She sang every tune she knew. Folk ballads blended into classics, wedding tunes into mourning chants. Songs of devotion followed those of betrayal. Her voice turned hoarse from dust, fatigue, and grief. She crooned of promises kept and oaths broken, of good fortune and cruel fates, of hope and despair. Without knowing the words, she hummed the French song they had danced to, then uttered the perfect vowels of *"O sole mio,"* though they might never see the sunshine together again.

She stopped only to wet her parched throat with a sip of water. Praying that her voice might be the thread that joined his body and soul, the bind that tied him to this earth, in a rasping whisper, she sang to block her sobs.

Finally, he fell asleep. She balled up on the floor facing him and dozed off.

In her dream, a beautiful young woman with long white hair, dressed in red and gold, entered the room. Her scent of jasmine and roses filled the chamber. She touched Aslan's side with long, shapely fingers, then turned to Gohar. Her eyes were the color of water, the color of dawn, a blue lighter than Aslan's.

Gohar woke up with a jolt. Ilych had covered her with a blanket. Aslan was asleep. But his breath was deeper and steadier, his heartbeat calmer, his skin less pale. She dared to hope.

5

January 1916, Simorq Castle

A single dried rose adorned the leafless bush in the garden in front of the building, and a jasmine vine embraced the pomegranate trees. Someone planted this tiny garden with love and care. Was it a Gabr growing grapes, unaware of the advancing Arabs? Or an Ismaili tending to roses, heedless of the Mongols besieging the castle? The compound had sheltered so many. She wished to stay on this timeless rock forever, far from the war, Russian brutality, German intrigue, and British conspiracy. Here, they would be free from deception, famine, and typhoid. But their presence in the ruins was bound to pique the villagers' curiosity and attract the attention of the Russians. And she had a ferry to catch.

The day was sunny and warm, and the river rolled soothingly in the ravine below. Aslan rested, and Kamal, Belqais, and Petrus explored the castle. After weeks of turmoil, the solitude was welcome.

She leaned on the wall of the veranda and squeezed the leathery shell of the pomegranate she had picked off the tree. It would be foolish to read too much into his words as he lay dying. Holed up in a crumbling fort in the mountains, with perils abounding and the future unknown, it would be unwise to let her imagination run amok. She punctured the softened pomegranate's skin and sucked the sweet and sour juice that trickled out.

A commotion from Aslan's room prompted her to check on him.

He looked up when she entered. "Can you get me some water and help me sit?"

He winced when she lifted him. The worst might be over, but he was far from fit.

"How do you feel?" She propped him up with a rolled-up blanket and gave him water. "Do you want to stand up?"

He shook his head. "I need to sit first." He sipped the water. "I'm too heavy for you anyway. Where is Ilych?"

She draped a blanket over his bare shoulders. The brazier Ilych had bought from the village had warmed the room, but Aslan was too weak. A cold could quickly turn to pneumonia. "Washing your clothes," she said.

He smiled. "At least I won't be buck naked when the village ladies arrive."

She hid her smile with a cupped hand. "I don't see any villagers around." She was delighted to find him in a good mood.

"You don't know those ladies. The minute they find out I'm here, they'll come running."

"Don't worry, I'll shoo them away. "

"How did I get here?"

"On the back of a mule." She hoped he wouldn't remember her cradling him on her lap. "You were unconscious most of the way. Ilych pulled the mule. We arrived the night before last, and you have been sleeping since." She paused. "Are you ready for the saltwater Ilych left for you? He said you must drink it."

"It tastes vile." He frowned. "What's wrong with your lips? They're bleeding."

"It's just pomegranate juice."

"Where did you get fresh pomegranate?"

"From the trees outside. There is a garden patch with roses, grape vines, and jasmine. I can mix some pomegranate juice with the salt water to make it more palatable."

"Maybe," he said, drawing his knees to his chest. "Where is Kamal?"

"With Petrus and Belqais."

"Ah, our lovers!"

"They don't act like lovers. They insult each other and giggle."

"People express affection in different ways." He adjusted the blanket on his shoulders. "So, how are *you*?"

"Fine," she said, disregarding the nasty bruise on her side.

He stared at her. "You like wearing men's clothes?"

"I don't mind. They're easier to get around in and warmer than dresses." She smirked. "Plus, I have nothing else to wear."

"How come?"

"I left my trunk on the road to lighten the load and get here quicker."

"I'm sorry about that. I'll buy you new clothes when we get back to civilization."

"I don't mind. They were just clothes."

He met her eyes. "I know women who wear a suit and tie to go to the theater in Tehran."

"That is wicked!" She pictured Nosrat sitting next to him in a dark theater.

"It's necessary if you want to go to the theater. At any rate, you look good."

She tightened her shawl around herself and sat cross-legged. "Petrus seems to be enjoying the castle," she said, changing the subject.

"He loves history. He was over the moon when we came here looking for the Ismaili treasures."

"And you?"

A gust of wind blew through the window, lifting the blanket from his shoulders. He pulled it back to cover himself. "I enjoyed being outdoors and the chance to understand our new masters."

"And who might that be?"

"The English. I know Iranians are scared of the Russians, but Russia is poor and backward, with a repressive government. The Germans have military might but pigheaded leaders. The English will win the war and rule the world."

Not liking that prediction, she changed the subject. "Do you want something to eat? We have some leftover soup."

"Not yet." He slid down to lie flat, folding his arms under his neck.

"Are you tired?" she said. "Shall I leave you alone?"

"No, no, please stay. I like the company. It distracts me from the pain." He smiled. "Maybe there's still some Ismaili hashish around that's potent. I could use it."

"You seem to be in good enough spirits without hashish."

He beamed. "Why shouldn't I be? I'm alive, and I have everything a man needs: flowing water, a jug of wine, and my beloved."

She chuckled. "You *are* becoming Persian. Happy in the middle of calamities and worried at the height of bliss. But I see your point. There's plenty of flowing water here." Petrus had shown her cascading stone tanks that stored water from distant springs and the pulley system that carried water up from the river. "I don't see any jug of wine, but I suppose vodka can substitute for that. Still, your beloved is not here."

"What makes you think that?" He gazed at her mischievously.

Her face burned. "I'll get you some food," she said, rising.

He grabbed her wrist. "Your voice is angelic. You would be an opera singer in Europe, maybe singing with Caruso."

"You remember me singing?" She didn't pull her hand away. "I thought—"

"How could I forget?" He kissed her palm. "I wasn't dead, yet."

6

January 1916, Simorq Castle

"Pick me up," Kamal whined, extending his hands upwards. "Let me see."

"There's nothing to see, dear," Gohar said. "Just a big drop." All afternoon, they had gone from one watchtower on the castle's west side to another so Kamal could shoot imaginary arrows at the Mongol army.

The wind was picking up. Darkness had already obscured the valley. They should get back. Aslan would worry.

"Can we see one more?" Kamal asked.

"No." She tugged his hand. "We have seen them all. Uncle Aslan is waiting for us."

Swirling flurries blinded them as soon as they stepped out. The snow was already ankle-deep. She took a hesitant step and slipped, falling on her back. Pain seared her ankle. Kamal squatted beside her, watching her with wide eyes.

She pulled herself up to sit. A faint howl reminded her of the gray animals they had seen earlier at the edge of the compound. Their pointed ears and long muzzles had frightened her, but Aslan had laughed. Nothing to worry about, he had said. They were wolves, a mating pair. They hunted at night and never attacked buildings. Now, she was out in the open, and night was approaching. Sweat ran down her spine.

They needed shelter. Her ankle was swollen, the building they'd been staying in was far away, and the snow was blinding. Even if she could walk, she couldn't see where they were going. They could easily fall off the cliff. Screaming would be futile—everyone except for Aslan had gone to the village, and in his condition, he'd never make it through the heavy snow—if he even heard her. It was best to return to the watchtower and wait out the storm. By then, everyone would be back.

The wind slapped her face as she rose. She blinked to clear the snow from her eyes and took Kamal's hand. They hobbled back to the tower together. Inside was tolerable, though not warm. It was quieter, too. She sat on the ground beneath the partially collapsed ceiling, pulled the child onto her lap, and covered him with her coat. Her fingers were numb, but at least the cold dulled the pain in her throbbing ankle.

"I'm hungry," he whimpered, burying his face in her chest.

The last of the dried mulberries she had packed as a snack were still in her pocket. "This is all I have," she said, trickling them into his hand. Her teeth were chattering so much she could barely get the words out.

He chewed on the snack and didn't complain. She wished they had brought a candle, but they weren't expecting to be out in the dark. She wouldn't have left the compound if Aslan hadn't needed rest and Kamal hadn't been so restless. She pocketed a broken brick in case animals attacked.

The howl of the wind was deafening now. She imagined the yellow eyes of wolves flickering in the dark. Kamal fell asleep. She was glad. If they were to die, at least he wouldn't be scared.

"*I bear witness that there is no god but Allah . . .*" she recited before dozing off. In her dreams, she was reading on the veranda in Gurdan, where it never snowed.

A faint voice woke her. Someone was calling her. Was it the ghosts of her parents welcoming her to the beyond? Suddenly, a beam of light blinded her. They didn't have a lantern, and a torch would not have lasted in the blizzard. Was it an angel lighting their path to heaven?

The light bobbed up and down. She carefully put the child down and staggered to the entrance. It took a few minutes for her to see Aslan behind the glare of light emanating from a device in his hand.

"Here," she shouted, shielding her eyes from the light and the gale.

"Are you all right?" His voice was tight with worry. Pearls of ice glistened on his newly grown beard. "I've been looking for you."

"The storm caught us by surprise," she said. "Then I slipped on the way back." She showed him her swollen ankle. "I can't walk. Take Kamal. I will wait for Ilych to get here."

"Nonsense, I can't leave you. I don't know when Ilych will be back. The blizzard must have closed the trails." He gave her the tubular brass device, which she had seen in his knapsack. "Hold the flashlight," he said. He picked Kamal up, then lifted her by the armpits. "Lean on me." His coat covered all three of them.

She held onto his waist. Every step she took sent stabs of pain up her leg, but he whispered, "Put your weight on me. Don't be scared."

They trudged toward another flashlight Aslan had hung outside the building. The snow was getting heavier. She could hear animals growling. The weight of the brick in her pocket was reassuring.

It wasn't until they were inside, nestled in blankets, that she let her tears fall.

"It's ok." He offered her a handkerchief. "We're all safe."

She let him examine her ankle.

"Nothing's broken," he said. "We still have some bandages. I'll wrap it."

She stared at his pale face. "You could have caught your death."

"Would you have preferred me to let you freeze?" he said. "You need to lie down."

She glanced at Kamal, flipping the little switch on the flashlight to turn the light on and off. "I need to feed him."

"I'll take care of him," Aslan said. "Be careful, son," he added, turning to Kamal. "I can't replace the battery if it runs out."

"What are you going to do with him?"

"Simple: I'll get him clean clothes and something to eat. Then we'll share some brandy, and I'll teach him how to play dice so I can win his toy soldiers."

7

January 1916, Simorq Castle

The next evening, Aslan decided to stroll up the ramparts and see the castle in the light of the full moon. He urged the others to join him. Ilych was tired after hunting during the day, and Petrus was still limping. Belqais wanted to stay back. Gohar, worried about Aslan tripping and falling on the crumbling walls, decided to accompany Aslan despite her own sore ankle. Kamal stayed with Belqais.

The night was windless but cold. The snow glistened in the moonlight. From atop the ramparts, the cascading water tanks on the east side resembled an enchanting ancient temple. Gohar sat on a flat stone, rubbing her shoulders for warmth. Aslan took off his overcoat and gently draped it over her shoulders.

"You'll catch a cold," she objected.

"We can share," he said with an impish smile.

She wiggled to the side to make room for him. The warmth of his body was comforting. "I heard the story you told Kamal about the she-bird," she said.

"The firebird?"

"Yes. We have a similar fable. But in our version, Simorq guides the prince to rescue the princess."

"Stories travel, and Russia isn't that far," he said, then added wistfully, "My mother told me the story of the firebird when I was young. She was bedridden, so I used to crawl into her bed and listen."

"Where is she now?" Her heart ached for Aslan as a young boy.

"In Petrograd."

"Do you see her?"

"We exchange letters once a year, on Christmas."

"Is that your choice?"

He avoided her gaze. "It suits us both. I can't do what she wants me to: go back and apologize to my father. And she won't do what I want her to: stand up to him."

"What did you do to your father?"

His face hardened. "I refused to see him when he came to see me graduate in Paris."

She didn't probe. His father was always a tricky subject. It was best to let him talk when he wanted to. "Well," she said, "I doubt it was your mother who told you that Prince Ivan had an 1873 Winchester or that the firebird carried a machine gun."

"I was modernizing the story," he smiled. "Kamal liked it." He folded his arm around her waist to pull her closer. She didn't resist.

As they sat cocooned in his coat under the canvas of a sky painted with brilliant specks of light, a comfortable silence enveloped them. Soon, his hands found their way under her loose shirt. His familiar touch on her skin awakened the sensation she had so often dreamt of. The contour of his body enfolded hers. He kissed her temple. She kissed him on the mouth.

Finally, she pulled back gently. "We should go back. They'll be worried."

"Join me tonight." He winked. "Alone."

Gohar lay awake in her bed, listening to Kamal's soft snores. What had spurred Aslan? Lust? Gratitude? Boredom? It didn't matter. She wanted him, even if it was only for one night.

They didn't have a future together. That much was clear. He had a life, a job, a home, a lover. She was a homeless fugitive, married to a disgraced traitor. A fleeting affair would complicate her life even more, further ruin her reputation, and destroy what little was left of her marriage. But this was an old debate with a new twist. Fate had brought them together, only to show her how easily she could lose him forever. They didn't have a future, but they could have a moment of bliss.

She cursed Satan.

Stealthily, she rose, tiptoeing barefoot past the sleeping figure of Petrus in the entrance hall. At the threshold to Aslan's room, she stopped to watch him reading in the light of a candle, his bare shoulders peeking from the blankets. As though sensing her presence, he raised his head, made room for her in the bed, and snuffed the candle.

Later, she rested her head on the hollow of his shoulder and folded her arms around him.

He kissed the parting of her hair. "I missed you," he murmured.

She tightened her clasp around him.

Outside, the wailing of the wind masked the howling of the wolves.

At dawn, she stepped out. The first rays of the sun had turned the snowy-white caps of the distant mountains to gold. The air smelled lusciously of moist earth. She stepped to the veranda's edge and lifted her face to greet the new day. A speck of yellow on the jasmine vine in the garden patch caught her eye. It was much too early for blossom; it must be a piece of cloth from the wash.

Nevertheless, she moved closer. The delicate petals of a single winter jasmine saluted her. Stunned, she picked the flower and carried it inside.

Soon, the gentle scent of jasmine washed over the stale smell of the ancient abode.

8

January 1916, Simorq Castle

As the sun set in the valley, the haunting sound of the evening call to prayer from the village below merged with the gurgle of cascading water. Atop the castle, Gohar watched the fog roll up, hiding the compound from prying eyes. A breeze ruffled her hair. She would miss this place.

The dilapidated castle had been a happy home. She had greeted the rising sun every dawn and marveled at the endless skies every night. With Kamal perched on his shoulders, Aslan had explored the area with her. Sometimes, the two of them talked up a storm; sometimes, they kept a contented silence. Often, she caught him observing her.

At night, they lay on the ramparts, him describing Zeppelins gliding silently amid the stars and her dreaming of traveling in one. They had made love, playfully and leisurely, muffling giggles, cries, and whispers, exploring the boundaries of passion and pleasure. Belqais and Petrus turned a blind eye. Ilych smiled approvingly.

Neither of them had talked about the future. A trunk full of unknowns was best kept locked. *Now* was to be cherished. She was sure of only one matter: divorcing Haji. Her marriage was a sham. Divorce was the only honest path forward. The rest, she would leave to fate. Their destiny, after all, had been written on their foreheads long before they were born.

But now the future was upon them. They would leave the castle the following day. She had only two weeks to catch the ferry to Baku.

"Our last sunset in Simorq," Belqais said, quietly standing beside Gohar. "I'll miss it."

"Me too," Gohar said wistfully, watching the darkness cover the riverbank.

"What do you think of Petrus?" Belqais asked.

Gohar could guess what was coming. "Well, he's mild-mannered, rational, trustworthy, and has a good voice." She smiled. "Why do you ask?"

"We want to get married and open a language school in Gilan."

The news was bittersweet. Her sister-in-law deserved love, happiness, and a new start. But her marriage would leave Gohar to face foreign lands in *qorbat* alone. Would this and their new intimacy spur Aslan to stay with her and Kamal? "Congratulations," she said. "But how will you marry an Armenian?"

Belqais shrugged. "Easy. We'll pay a mullah to 'convert' Petrus and marry us."

"But you've only known him for a couple of weeks."

"How long had you known my brother before you married him? Ten seconds?"

"I wasn't allowed to see him until the ceremony."

"That proves my point. I don't want anyone else to decide my future. I trust him and care for him. We are not young. If I want a family, I'd better hurry."

Gohar never knew Belqais could be maternal. She looked at her in surprise. "Do you?"

"If God wills it." Belqais shrugged. "I see the joy Kamal brings to you. I'd like that."

Gohar embraced Belqais. "I am delighted for you. Thank you for sharing the news."

Belqais pulled back. "Well, I need something more," she said. "Your permission."

"Permission? For what?"

"As a woman who has never been married, I need the consent of my eldest male relative, Haji, to marry," Belqais said. "In his absence, according to tribal traditions, you speak for him."

Gohar cackled. "Then Petrus must obey me, pay a large *mahrieh*, and ask for no dowry."

Belqais looked at her askance. "In that case, Petrus will send Aslan to negotiate. I am sure he will get a better deal out of you!

9

January 1916, Alborz Mountains

Early the next day, their guide, dressed in loose pants and the stiff sheepskin coat of a local, waited by the pile of stones that had once been the north gate of Simorq. Ilych had urged them to hire the short, thin man more for his skills in dealing with bandits than his knowledge of the trail. Petrus had endorsed the idea. Aslan had acquiesced grudgingly.

A shabby band of three bandits blocked the trail not far from the castle. Two of them were smoking clay pipes atop boulders overlooking the pass. A third, armed with an ancient front-muzzle musket, negotiated with their guide, and collected the money.

"We could have blown their heads off," Aslan fumed as they continued.

"Then what?" Petrus replied. "More would have come out of the woodwork to kill us, for our rifles if nothing else."

The mountaintops glowed in the morning sun. The ride through the deep, narrow ravine in the fresh air was pleasant. Though Gohar had to stay silent to avoid betraying her identity, the ease of riding in men's clothing made up for the inconvenience. When she returned to Tehran, she would attend the theater in a suit and tie.

Tiny hamlets perched on the rocks as the gorge widened. Simorq, still visible, was now miles away.

As they left the gorge, a colorful bundle of fabric on a boulder caught their eye. When they got closer, the profile of a young girl emerged from the folds of the ragged cloth. She looked angelic, with a straight nose, long lashes, and ringlets of light brown hair peeking from under a red headscarf. Then she turned, and Gohar gasped. Pockmarks covered the other half of the girl's face. The eye on that side was white and dead. The girl gazed at them with her one green eye.

Their guide averted his eyes, denounced the devil, and veered away. But Aslan stopped and dismounted. He kneeled by the child and ordered the guide to ask the girl who she was and what she was doing there by herself. After a short exchange, he reported that the girl, Assyeh, came from a mountain village and spoke a dialect he could barely understand. Her mother had died a few days ago. Her father's other wife, who considered Assyeh cursed, had blamed her for her mother's death and ordered the father to take her away. Her father had left to her fate with a loaf of bread.

The guide pleaded with Aslan to leave the child with some food and water, maybe a blanket, and move on. With a pockmarked face and a dead mother, she would bring bad luck to anyone taking her.

"I am not leaving a child alone to starve, freeze, or be eaten by animals," Aslan snapped. He instructed Ilych to feed the girl and put her on a mule.

As sympathetic as Gohar was to the child's plight, she objected. What if the girl was a leper? She could be contagious and infect Kamal. To allay her fears, Aslan pledged to carry him as far away from Assyeh as possible until they knew what was wrong with her.

At noon, they arrived at a large village. The sight of Assyeh caused instant uproar among the men eating on the carpeted wooden platforms of a roadside coffeehouse. The commotion brought out the owner.

"Please, we have children with us," the guide pleaded at Aslan's urging. "We only need food and a few hours' rest."

But the owner didn't budge, insisting that they leave even after Aslan offered him extra money. Seething with anger, Aslan threatened to beat the owner and implored the group to move on.

By now, a crowd had gathered around them. Gohar anxiously implored Petrus to intervene. An altercation here would cause delays and could be dangerous. Just then, a young, bearded, bespectacled man of medium height stepped forward. Though he was dressed like the locals, his well-made boots and confident walk made him stand out. The coffeehouse owner bowed to him.

The man took Aslan's sleeve. "Good day, sir. May I be of service to you?" His voice was calm but authoritative. "My name is Esmail Hashemi. I am a doctor. Perhaps I can examine this young lady and determine whether she is afflicted with a disease harmful to others."

Aslan stepped back. Esmail helped Assyeh off the mule and squatted down to be at eye level with her. Gohar noticed the young doctor's longish, curly dark hair poking out of his brimless felt hat.

The doctor questioned the child in her dialect, touched her forehead, and thoroughly examined her eyes, tongue, and neck. "Except for needing a bath and suffering from malnutrition," he declared, "the child is healthy. The smallpox that disfigured her is no longer contagious."

Gohar breathed a sigh of relief. Aslan smiled smugly. The villagers dispersed.

"Unfortunately," Esmail continued, "folks here are too poor and superstitious to care for her. But if you bring her to Lahijan, where I live, I'll find her a home. I would have taken her with me, but I have a long journey ahead."

"We will keep her until a suitable home is found," Aslan said, eyeing Gohar, who nodded reluctantly.

The doctor bowed. "Your kindness toward the unfortunate child is truly commendable. You mustn't think badly of the villagers. They are not unkind, just uneducated. What is truly outrageous is that our government squanders money on shahs' lavish foreign trips but cries poor when it comes to vaccinating children. Will you honor me and be my guests for lunch?"

Aslan agreed. Esmail instructed the coffeehouse owner to take them somewhere suitable. Bowing repeatedly, the owner led them through the smoke-filled, noisy coffeehouse to an enclosed, carpeted porch in the rear. Colorful cushions were scattered about the floor, and the soothing sound of the river drifted through the trellised walls. A servant brought a brazier and told them that, while no women, not even female children, were allowed inside the coffeehouse, Assyeh could eat with the group if they stayed out there.

The doctor did not comment on their reason for traveling. Aslan introduced Gohar as his nephew and explained that dust and the harsh winter air had caused him and their other friend to lose their voices. Esmail's eyes lingered on her, she wriggled uncomfortably. After a lunch of rice and grilled meat, Gohar and Belqais left the men to talk and took the children to the riverbank. The warmer weather had brought village women to the shore to wash clothes and chat. The two sat on a boulder at a distance from the villagers while Assyeh and Kamal squatted by the water and built a tower with pebbles, unencumbered by the cold or the language barrier.

Belqais turned to Gohar. "The doctor has his eyes on you."

"Whatever for?" Gohar said. "He thinks I'm a young man."

Belqais snorted. "That is what some men like."

Gohar blushed. The doctor didn't seem like that kind of a man.

Esmail was speaking when the women returned. "You do not know what it's like to live under occupation, living in constant fear of being jailed or killed. My family in Mazandaran was spared. But I saw the Russians in action in Rasht, where I went to high school. Seeing foreign soldiers on the streets of your city, taking what they want without paying, bullying the elders, assassinating the leaders with impunity, is like watching your sister being raped while your hands are tied behind your back." Bitterness was palpable in his voice.

"If it is of any consolation," Aslan said, "the tsars did the same wherever they conquered."

"That is why people are rioting, burning the Russian factories, beating Russian soldiers when they can."

"Why now?" Petrus asked.

"The Russians are busy with the war," Esmail answered. "And we have leadership, the Jangalis."

"The papers in Tehran say that the Jangalis are bandits. Is it true?" Petrus probed.

"No, sir," Esmail said emphatically. "They are farmers, teachers, shopkeepers, workers, clergymen, you name it."

His description of the rebels reminded Gohar of the American Minutemen Aslan had mentioned.

"Don't they kidnap people for ransom?" Petrus pushed harder.

"That's Russian propaganda," Esmail snapped. "The Jangalis don't need ransom money. People give them money voluntarily."

"Does the leader, Mirza Kuchek, want to be the shah?" Petrus asked.

"No, no. He has sworn allegiance to the shah," Esmail responded. "He wants to get rid of the Russians without German or Ottoman help. He wants to bring back the constitution."

"Is he a Bolshevik?" Aslan asked.

The doctor was unfazed. "No! He is a devout Muslim. Merchants are his biggest supporters."

Petrus stared at him provocatively. "Are you one of them?"

Esmail smirked. "No, sir. I am just a simple country doctor."

After lunch, Aslan invited Esmail to join them. They were going in the same direction and had much in common.

Esmail brightened. "It would be an honor. I rarely come across cultured folks such as yourselves in this area. Would you allow me to guide you?"

Aslan readily accepted, paid the guide in full, and dismissed him.

Once they descended into the valley, the weather warmed up, the vegetation increased, and tilled and terraced fields appeared on both sides of the river. Esmail explained that the moisture from the Caspian Sea moderated the climate. That afternoon, they reached a large village with a mosque, a public bath, and multiple coffeehouses. Esmail suggested that they spend the night. The village elder was his relative, and he had patients there. At the elder's house, Esmail asked the first of the host's three wives to take Assyeh for a bath and give her some clean clothing. She put the host's second wife in charge of dinner and left with the child.

The word of the doctor's presence in the village brought in a crowd. Patients lined up outside the house. Those who could stand, stood. Others squatted on the ground. A few were carried in chairs or wheelbarrows. Most brought baskets of eggs, small sacks of rice, or live chickens to pay the doctor.

Esmail set up a makeshift office in the yard. He arranged bottles of medicine, a stethoscope, and other medical instruments on a small, wobbly table. Ilych and Aslan gave him a hand, moving infirm patients around. Others watched him from a veranda.

As they entered, the patients gave their offerings to the host's teenage son. If a patient looked too poor, Esmail motioned to the boy to give the donation back. In a few instances, he gave the patient some of the provision others had brought.

"Do you always get paid with chicken and eggs?" Aslan asked.

"Sometimes I get fish and fruit." The doctor smiled. "I don't mind. But it gets tricky when I have to refer them to a specialist in Rasht. They want real money, and these people don't have any. I am the only option for people here, no matter what ails them."

Esmail spoke to each patient at length, examined their eyes and mouths, and listened to their hearts and lungs, no matter how dirty and revolting they were. At the end of each visit, the patients received medicine or, infrequently, a prescription.

"Do you carry medicine for everything?" Aslan asked.

"No, I give them what I have," Esmail said. "I am always short of Farangi medicine, like quinine." He sighed and spread his arms. "Half of my patients have malaria. How can I help them without quinine?"

He only showed frustration when two young men carried an old woman on a broken chair. "They brought her to me when she's at death's door," he said after the woman left.

His gentle, tireless treatment of the sick mesmerized Gohar. Belqais jabbed her. "Stop gawking."

Gohar blushed, side-glancing at Aslan, who didn't seem to have noticed. "I am only admiring the doctor's skill and humanity," she said.

The return of Assyeh caught everyone's attention. With her ginger hair in a single, thick braid, she looked adorable, even in the ill-fitting clothing of their hostess's older children.

Belqais gazed at her. "Without the pockmarks, she would have been a great beauty someday."

The line of patients thinned at sunset. As Gohar turned to go inside, three young men entered the yard to see the doctor. None of them looked sick.

Over dinner, their host engaged Esmail jovially. "So, doctor, dear, when will we dance at your wedding?" He pointed to his infant daughter. "At the rate you're going, she'll get married before you do."

"I don't have time, Uncle," Esmail said. "I have to choose either medicine or looking for a wife."

"You don't have time, Esmail Khan," their host's first wife said. "But your mother and sisters do. That's their job, not yours. A good-looking young man like you could marry any girl."

"Are you and my mother in cahoots?" Esmail laughed. He turned to Aslan. "Auntie and Uncle tease me every time I stop here."

Their host smiled. "Don't be so fussy. You're getting long in the tooth. It goes against nature, against Islam, to remain a bachelor. Marry someone. If you don't like her, take another one." He pointed to his three wives. "Better for you, better for them. They keep each other company."

Gohar glanced at the host's elder wives. The harsh glances they exchanged with each other and the way they scowled at the adolescent third wife belied their husband's words.

"The doctor has time," Aslan interjected. "He's not much older than me."

"But you already have a son." Their host pointed to Kamal sitting beside Aslan. "He looks so much like you."

Aslan looked uneasy. "He is my nephew. I am not married."

"Maybe it's different where you come from," the host said. "When I was your age, my eldest was already married, and I had a second wife and was looking for a third."

"I am different, Uncle," Esmail said. "For me, there is only one God and one wife. So, I've got to get it right."

"That's the nonsense philosophers cook up because they can't afford a second wife," the host said.

As the women cleared the dishes, Esmail excused himself. Bedridden patients were waiting for him. He would see them in the morning.

In the guest room all four of them shared, Aslan whispered to Gohar, "You seemed enchanted with the doctor."

She looked at him in disbelief. "Are you teasing me?"

"No, just making an observation. You do as you please."

The exchange made her uncomfortable. She wanted to explain that it was the doctor's passion and skill that she found admirable. But without privacy, a lengthy conversation was out of the question.

Someone knocked as they were getting ready for bed. Belqais answered and returned with a mug for Gohar. "Compliments of the good doctor." She sneered. "A brew to soothe your throat."

The gurgle of the river woke Gohar in the morning, tempting her to explore the area. The sun had yet to reach the riverbank when she left the house. Mist lingered over the water. Across the river, a shepherd led his flock through the purple rocks that rose from the brown earth.

As she stepped on the slick rocky shore, she lost her footing but regained her balance quickly.

"Be careful," Esmail shouted from behind. "You could break your neck on these stones."

She turned to see him watching her from the shore.

"Do you need help?" he asked.

She shook her head, hoping that he would go away. But he was still there when she returned, extending his hand to help her to the shore.

"Thank you for the potion," she mumbled in a deep voice.

He smiled. "Hope it helped."

She nodded and rushed to the house, uneasy with his obsessive attention.

10

January 1916, Alborz Mountains

The next evening, they stopped at another village teeming with Esmail's admiring friends and adoring patients. One of them offered the travelers the use of his brother's house for the night. Esmail mentioned that a famous storyteller would be performing in a neighboring village that night as they walked toward their accommodation. The man was famous for his eloquence and devotion to *Shahnameh*, the book of kings, and his aversion to superfluous embellishments. "The performance will be exceptional," Esmail said. "Most of the *Shahnameh* legends have their roots in this area." He planned to attend, as did their host, Mir Hassan. Everyone was welcome to come along.

Gohar was anxious to see the storyteller up close. Happy memories of listening to *Shahnameh*'s stories from the rooftop in Gurdan still lingered in her mind. The book, nominally about kings, was full of the gallant deeds of warriors, most prominently the noble Rostam. Petrus and Belqais declined the invitation but offered to entertain Kamal if Gohar wanted to go. The boy missed Assyeh, who had been left with Esmail's relatives. Ilych, not fond of storytellers or coffeehouses, decided to stay behind. Gohar whispered to Aslan that they should go. He relented.

They walked through the mountains to the next village in the moonlight. The coffeehouse where the performance was held had a low ceiling and reeked of sweat and tobacco. Men drank tea and smoked clay pipes and hookahs on rows of wooden platforms arranged in a horseshoe. The middle was left open for the storyteller.

The owner came to greet Esmail as soon as they entered. He vacated the front row for the group and ordered fresh tea for them. The doctor whispered that the story that night would be "Rostam and Sohrab."

As they sipped their tea, several men came to talk to Esmail in hushed voices.

"Crowded tonight," Mir Hassan commented. "Even Sardar Khan is here." He pointed to a burly, mustachioed man sitting across from them.

"Who is he?" Aslan asked.

"The owner of most of the area villages."

Sardar, like many in the audience, wore loose pants and a knee-length tunic under a vest. But his well-made, tanned leather boots distinguished him from peasants wearing *charoq*—untanned leather strapped over knitted stockings with colorful woolen threads. From the corner of her eye, Gohar caught Esmail looking askance at Sardar.

The stocky storyteller had a bushy beard and graying, shoulder-length hair. He embraced Esmail warmly and exchanged pleasantries with Mir Hossein. The chatter, the gurgle of hookahs, and the clinking of cups stopped as soon as he took his place at the center of the horseshoe.

He saluted the audience as the true descendants of their ancient heroes, living among the mountains where their idols had once lived. "This, my brothers," he said in a deep voice, "is a precarious time for our nation. It is time to denounce evil and stand with those fighting for justice. You must follow the path of righteousness, no matter the cost. Every one of you is a Rostam. You can protect the weak and slay deevs in the guise of humans."

The spectators nodded, mumbling in agreement.

He began the story with the conception of Sohrab during a night of passion between Rostam and Tahmineh. He continued, describing young Sohrab's longing to meet his famous father and vow to shower him with the glory the wicked king had denied him. Gohar felt a kinship, knowing the pain of growing up fatherless. The narrator recounted the son's search for his father, meeting beautiful Gurdafarid disguised as a warrior, and finally coming across a formidable challenger without knowing that he was his father, Rostam.

The storyteller's skillful variation of pitch and volume mesmerized her. His voice turned soft when he talked of romance, rose in battle scenes, and became grave during moments of sorrow and pain. Agitatedly, he described the battle between father and son, treachery keeping each from knowing who the other was. When the father mortally wounded the son, his voice turned mournful. Throughout the performance, the poetry he recited stirred emotions, and hand-painted scrolls enlivened the story.

Like the rest of the audience, Gohar rejoiced at the lovers' union and grieved Rostam's loss of a child he would never know. The old king's refusal to provide the elixir of life to save young Sohrab angered her. The painting of Rostam with hay on his head, leading Sohrab's funeral procession, became bleary through her tears. At times, she mouthed the lines of the poetry along with the storyteller.

Esmail whispered in her ears. "You know the lines! How unusual for a youth. I love these verses."

She wished they could talk.

After the performance, people left coins for the storyteller in a copper bowl before departing. Many acknowledged Esmail with a nod or an embrace. A few gave him small sacks that he squeezed into his satchel. The storyteller handed the night's takings to Esmail as they were leaving. "For your patients," he said, embracing the young doctor.

On the road back, Mir Hassan wondered aloud why all the good men in *Shahnameh* died young: Sohrab, Siavash, Esfandiar, Iraj.

"This is how it has always been, my friend," Esmail said ruefully. "The righteous have no place in a land of corruption and compromises."

Gohar expected a wisecrack from Aslan to lighten the mood, but he offered none. Only then did she realize that he had been silent all evening.

A large rock across the mountain pass blocked their way back.

"Where did this come from?" Mir Hasan said. "It wasn't here when we came."

Aslan pointed to a tight gap between the rock and the cliff beside it and whispered to Gohar. "Can you squeeze through that gap and find the house we're staying at?"

She looked at him, perplexed.

"This is an ambush," he said. "We need Ilych and the guns in a hurry."

Abruptly, torches illuminated the road from behind them. She turned to see Sardar Khan leading a group of armed men to block the way they had come.

"Good evening, Sardar Khan," said Mir Hassan. "What happened here? Why is the road blocked?"

Sardar spat on the ground. "I want a chat with the fake doctor, the shameless Bolshevik."

Aslan handed Gohar his flashlight. "Go. Now." He pushed her through the gap. Much as she wanted to stay with him, she obeyed wordlessly. The path was steep and uneven, but she ran fast, grabbing the mountainside once or twice to avoid falling.

Ilych was smoking a clay pipe outside the house when she arrived, panting.

"You. Come. Now," she said. "Aslan, ambush." She pulled Ilych by the wrist.

He took his rifle from under his blanket and followed her. Near the roadblock, they heard Mir Hassan's voice. "Please, Sardar Khan, these gentlemen are my guests. I am responsible for their safety. If anything happens to them, I will lose face."

Ilych pointed to a goat path leading to a ledge above the blockade. They climbed silently. From here, they could see a dozen men with various weapons, all aimed at Esmail, who faced Sardar. Mir Hassan stood between them. Aslan was further back.

"He's a liar, Mir Hassan. Don't you see?" Sardar lashed out. "He's not here to see patients. He is here to recruit men and collect money for that bandit Mirza Kuchek. If you don't believe me, ask him where he was last night." He paused. "I'll tell you where. On my land, plotting with my ungrateful farmers. I can't allow it."

Gohar recalled the three young men who had come for the doctor.

Ilych lay on the ground and pointed his gun downward. "Can you throw a pebble to alert Aslan without hitting anyone else?" He whispered.

She squatted to fetch a pebble large enough to reach Aslan without hurting him.

"Sardar Khan, the doctor is doing God's work," their host said. "We need him. He even saved your father's life."

Her stone hit Aslan on the shoulder. He looked up and raised his palm to signal that they should wait.

"If I had known what a snake this doctor is, I would have taken my father to Rasht," Sardar ranted. "He's better dead than left alive to poison my farmers with his ideas. He teaches their children to read! What do they need reading for? Study Bolshevik propaganda? He says medicine must be free. What next? Free houses? Free food? Please move, Mir Hassan. I don't want your blood on my hands."

Mir Hassan didn't budge. "Can you wait till morning? I'll gather the elders in my house to sort things out."

"I've had enough of him and that bastard storyteller talking about fighting deevs," Sardar barked. "And who are these deevs? Me and my family? After everything we have done for this village. These rascals die tonight. The storyteller is history as we speak. The doctor is next."

Sardar took another step forward. "Take your other guest with you. This is not his fight, and Farangis don't have the stomach to watch me cut the head off this dog."

As though on cue, Aslan went around Esmail and Mir Hasan to face Sardar. "But when someone tries to harm my friend, it *is* my fight."

"And who might you be?" Sardar smirked. "What are you going to do? Fight me? With what army? Or maybe you're a magician who can turn rocks into soldiers."

"I am a friend of the doctor," Aslan said, calmly pointing to where Ilych was. "I don't have an army. But I do have a few good shooters with excellent rifles aiming at your head right now."

This was Ilych's cue. His bullet pierced Sardar's hat without harming him.

Sardar paled. He looked up, then glanced at the sidearm in Aslan's hand. "I see the Farangi is backing you," he addressed Esmail. "What is he? German? I knew you and your rascal leader were German lackeys. Good thing the Russians have all your ringleaders trapped." He motioned for his men to lower their weapons and ordered two of them to move the boulder. "Out of respect for you," he said to Mir Hassan. "I will let your guests go tonight. But if I see anyone recruiting in my villages ever again, I will deal with it my way, Farangi friend or not."

Esmail was loading his bags on his horse when Gohar stepped out in the morning,

"I can show you the thermal springs if you want to freshen up," he said. "The water there is warm and clean." He smiled. "And there's no chance of slipping."

She glanced back nervously. Esmail's constant attention unsettled her.

"It's a short walk," Esmail said. "We'll be back before your uncle wakes up. I owe you my life. It's the least I can do."

Then again, he didn't seem dangerous, and her companions were close enough to hear her if she screamed. Tempted by the prospect of seeing the area's famous spring, she followed him up a narrow path to a cave. The pristine natural pool surrounded by greenish boulders was inviting. She longed for a dip but knew the best she could hope for was to wet her toes after he had left. To her surprise, he kneeled by the pool, filled up a small copper bowl, and offered it to her. The tingling of the effervescent water in her mouth was strange but pleasant.

"You must think I'm a bandit or a Bolshevik after last night," he blurted out. "I am neither. I am a patriot fighting foreign occupiers. People like Sardar want the Russians to stay and help them keep their farmers in shackles. They're the ones pushing the Russians to kill our leader, Mirza Kuchek. They know that without him, we are a body without a head—dead."

He reached for her hand. "You must believe me. All I want is to help our leader escape the Russian trap, so our movement survives."

She gently pulled her hand away. His cause may be just, but she didn't want any part of it. Footsteps from behind made her turn. Aslan stood at the entrance to the cave, glaring. Gohar could see the look of hurt beneath the anger.

The men eyed each other. Esmail spoke first. "I'm sorry. I insisted that your nephew come to see the mineral springs. We should have asked for your permission. I didn't want to wake you up, and I was in a rush to leave."

"No need," Aslan said. "I just didn't know where he was." The ice in his voice cut through her heart.

Esmail darted a glance at Aslan and Gohar. "I must be going."

Ignoring him, Aslan turned to Gohar. "I'll see you back at the village," he said before turning around and rushing out.

Gohar hurried after him.

The road out of the village cut through leafless walnuts and poplars. An eagle swooped down on an unsuspecting rabbit as they resumed the journey. Esmail's absence relieved Gohar. She had enjoyed his company, but his presence complicated her relationship with Aslan, and his affiliation with the rebels was troublesome. She trotted to catch up with Aslan, who had not spoken to her since the incident in the cave.

"How was the mineral spring? Therapeutic, I presume." He sneered.

She stared at him. "Are you jealous?"

He kept his gaze on the road. "Should I be?"

"Of course not," she bristled. "What do you take me for?"

"The way he looked at you was scandalous."

"That's ridiculous. He didn't even know I'm a woman."

Aslan cackled. "And the way you looked at him when he poked at his patients, I'd say, was lascivious."

"I admired his humanity. He treated all his patients with care, no matter how poor they were. People respect him."

They rode in silence as the mountainous terrain turned into a forest of chestnuts, walnuts, and pomegranates. The moss-covered ground muffled the sound of hooves. Only the pounding of a woodpecker was audible.

"Did you know he is with the rebel Jangalis?" he said. "He was recruiting men and collecting money, just as Sardar said."

"I gathered as much. He mentioned the Russians trying to kill their leader."

"Yes, they have him trapped in the forest."

She felt a knot in her stomach. "Did he ask you for help?" Aslan getting involved with a rebellion was the last thing she needed.

"Me? No. I told you; I'm done with revolutions."

Gohar exhaled with relief. "But you saved his life."

"Yes. Because I don't like bullies like Sardar."

Soon, women in colorful dresses appeared, working in tilled rice fields, and carrying baskets of eggs and vegetables on their heads. Gohar was surprised to see them covering their hair with headgear and scarves instead of the chador.

They stopped atop a ridge to see the Caspian. The sight of the endless water shimmering under the afternoon sun took Gohar's breath away. Waves foamed, breaking onto the shore. Colorful fishing boats dotted the sea. "I never imagined so much water in one place," she said. "It's majestic."

Aslan pointed to the horizon. "That is Russia."

The proximity startled her. She had always thought of Russia as far away, but here it was. Her chest tightened. Across the sea—where she was going—was *qorbat*, the land of strangers speaking foreign tongues and practicing alien customs. Here, even people who spoke different dialects looked to *Shahnameh* to recount their past and Hafez to tell their future; they all rejoiced on Nowruz and grieved on Ashura. But not there.

She side-glanced at Aslan. He had not spoken to her about his plans, and she, afraid of the answer, had not asked. As a Russian—at war with the Ottomans—he couldn't go to Istanbul. But she would go anywhere with him if he stayed with her and Kamal. But then, what could she offer him that Nosrat couldn't?

The future—unknown and murky—was finally upon her. She gazed at the horizon, suddenly more frightened and lonelier than ever.

11

January 1916, Ahmedabad, Gilan

Petrus's friend's two-story house, stood away from the modest center of Ahmedabad, at the edge of the forest, surrounded by walnut and chestnut trees. By the time the travelers arrived that day, dusk had cloaked the thatched-roofed houses of the neighborhood, and kerosene lamps glowed on their open porches.

Too tired to linger in the large living room, Gohar hurried up the narrow staircase to the bedrooms. Aslan followed, carrying Kamal.

"You and Kamal can share a room with me," he said, standing on the landing between the two bedrooms. "Belqais can have the other one."

The statement unsettled Gohar. In her mind, to share his room would be to accept her role as his mistress. It was demeaning. "What about Petrus?"

"He's leaving early in the morning for Rasht and will sleep with Ilych tonight. He and Belqais will marry when he comes back." He paused. "He knows about us."

"What about Belqais?"

"She knows about us too," he bristled. "In fact, everyone here knows about us."

"And the neighbors?"

He rolled his eyes. "The closest neighbor is a cannon shot away."

Gohar hesitated. At some point, she would have to talk to Belqais about her relationship with Aslan and her decision to divorce Haji. But it was crucial to clear the air with Aslan after the encounter with Esmail—and fast. They had only ten days left before the last passenger ferry would leave for Baku. Even if they were to part, she didn't want to leave him in acrimony.

She entered his room.

Drops of salt water glistened on Aslan's naked body as he stepped out of the sea. She glanced at the long scar on his side. He was lucky to be alive. They both were. Their union the night before had been blissful. They had talked in whispers late into the night, the fatigue of the long trip all but forgotten. Esmail was never mentioned. But she told him of her decision to divorce Haji, and he mentioned his powerful friends and contacts in Baku and how they could help. His own plans remained vague, and as much as Gohar wished for his firm commitment, she hadn't pushed. For now, the hope was still alive.

Then, in the morning, out of the blue, he had taken her and Kamal for a ride. They had ridden along the shore on horseback, crossing narrow streams that widened into shallow pools where ducks paddled. A fisherman repairing his net had given Kamal a red toy boat.

They had stopped at a deserted beach where the tree-covered mountains met the sea.

A gentle breeze, fragrant with sea salt, caressed her cheeks. The water, blue and calm, mated with a cloudless blue sky. Rays of sunlight speckled the sea with gold. Heaven must look like this, everything round and soft, the air mild and moist.

She watched him approach. "You must be freezing," she said, handing him a towel.

"It's refreshing," he said, pelting her with water droplets. "You should try it. No one is here to see you."

The icy drops felt hard as pebbles. "Stop that!" She giggled, side-glancing at Kamal, balled up on the rug. A seagull pecked at breadcrumbs by the sandcastle Kamal and Aslan had built earlier.

She burrowed her toes in the velvety sand. "I can't swim, and it's too cold." She handed him his shirt.

He sat beside her. "You're like my brother. He swam once a year: on July fifteenth."

Gohar held still for a moment. Aslan only spoke of his brother when he felt extremely safe. "Were you close?" she ventured.

"As close as two brothers seven years apart can be. He was at university when I left for boarding school. I admired him."

She glanced at his profile. "What was he like?"

"Passionate, popular, brilliant."

"And you?"

"The second fiddle."

"He died when he was—what? Twenty-two? Twenty-three?"

"Just about."

"What of?"

His face darkened. She had gone too far.

"Shot," his voice trailed off. "By the tsar's soldiers." He gazed at the water.

She wished she could take the question back, but he continued. "My father ordered shooting the crowd. But it was his aide-de-camp Smirnsky who gave the soldiers live ammunition."

Her breath caught in her throat, but she held back from gasping in shock, instead squeezing his hands gently. "How did you find out?"

"My sister wrote to me from Siberia. Her fiancé was with my brother when he died."

"But why?"

"She thought Smirnsky's target was her fiancé because she had rejected his marriage proposal." He turned to meet her eye. "But it didn't matter. I swore to kill the bastard."

Fear filled her heart. Here was the hatred that had been driving him all along.

"Now you know everything about my family," he said with a sad smile.

But the knowledge didn't comfort her.

12

January 1916, Ahmedabad, Gilan

"What are you writing?" Gohar asked, glimpsing at Aslan writing feverishly in the early morning light. "A book?" She stretched her back trying to wake up.

"A letter," he said without lifting his head. "To Nosrat."

She was offended. It was disrespectful to write to his lover while sitting next to a bed that still smelled of their lovemaking, especially after their magical outing to the seaside. Was he informing Nosrat of his imminent return after dumping Gohar? Was that why he still wouldn't discuss his plans with her, even as their parting grew precariously near? Had their outing just been a pleasant farewell?

To be left abandoned, disgraced, and humiliated in a foreign land was her worst nightmare. The thought of being deceived and slighted angered her. "And tell her how much you miss licking her hand and kissing her feet?" she snapped.

Aslan put the pen down. "What has gotten into you? Do you want to read the letter?" He extended the paper to her.

She bolted upright but was taken aback when she saw the Latin alphabet. "How can I?" she snapped.

"I'm sorry," Aslan said, suddenly aware of his blunder. "I—I can translate."

His composure outraged her even more. "Why bother? You'd lie."

"When have I ever lied to you?" Aslan burst out. "Between the two of us, you are the manipulator, leaving me dangling when it suited you and begging for my help when *you* needed me. Nosrat picked up the pieces you left broken. I owe her."

"You think I'm not grateful enough?" She picked up the black bag and threw it at him. "Then that should cover your time."

The bag hit his hand and fell on the writing table, overturning the inkwell.

"Out!" he shouted, pointing at the door. "Now. Before I do something I'll regret."

She felt like a cheap whore, snubbed by a drunk customer. But before she could react, her eyes fell on Kamal awake, his eyes wide with fear and confusion, clutching his stuffed bear. She rose, put her nightgown on, and carried her son downstairs.

Gohar was helping Kamal eat breakfast when Aslan came down later that morning. She heard him tell Ilych that he wouldn't be back for lunch. Then the door slammed.

When Belqais came down, Gohar avoided her gaze. Undoubtedly, she had heard the quarrel. Gohar declined her sister-in-law's suggestion that they visit the women they had met at the bathhouse but asked her to take Kamal with her.

Alone, Gohar wallowed in anger, shame, and regret. What had she done? What demon had possessed her to insult Aslan after all he had done? True, he had berated her--writing to his lover in front of her and dismissing her like a whore was disrespectful. But she was the one who had demeaned herself, given rein to passion, and become the mistress of a foreigner.

And the timing couldn't have been worse. She should have kept her mouth shut. Didn't Noor and Qamar say that God had given people two ears and one mouth so they could listen more and talk less?

Restless, she sought solace in Hafez. A randomly selected poem advised her that the beloved must be considerate and kind, not cruel. She tossed the book aside. Easy for a poet to dispense advice six hundred years after dying.

But what was done was done. She had to find a way to mend their rift and win his respect. Perhaps Ilych could help. She wandered to the kitchen.

Ilych put his knife aside when she entered "You look sickly," he said, as he poured her a cup of tea. "I'll make you an egg."

She couldn't eat—not with this lump in her throat. "I'm not hungry."

Ignoring her remark, he picked two eggs from a basket. "Wait 'till you taste my *khaguineh*."

She watched him beat the eggs in a bowl. "Have you ever been in love?"

"Who hasn't?" he said, pouring milk over the flour he had folded into the eggs.

It was impossible to imagine Ilych writing a love poem or bringing a bouquet to someone. "When was that?" she asked.

"When I went back to Tashkent after Aslan was sent away."

"What happened?"

"We married." He watched the oil sizzle. "She died, so did our children. End of story."

She gasped. "How?"

"Whooping cough." He expertly flipped the *khaguineh* in the pan.

She felt guilty. It had never crossed her mind that Ilych might have had a family or suffered a loss. "I'm so sorry."

He took the pan off the fire. "I was in my yard with a pistol, ready to join my family, when Aslan showed up. At first, I didn't recognize him. The last time I'd seen him, he was a boy, and here was a man, almost as tall as I am." He stood with his hands on his hips. "Do you want *sardeh berenj* with the eggs?"

People in Gilan ate cold rice with everything. "No, thank you."

He plated the eggs and sprinkled sugar on them. "You know he loves you, don't you?" He placed the plate beside her and sat down. "I am an old, ignorant soldier. But I know that those we love hurt us the most. Let him know you didn't mean what you said."

That afternoon, she heard Aslan enter the house and climb the stairs. She followed.

"Would you like some lunch or a cup of tea?" she asked, standing in the doorframe.

He kept rummaging through his bag with his back to her. "Ilych can bring me tea."

"I'll bring it. Where do you want it?"

Aslan turned to look at her quizzically and shrugged. "Downstairs is fine."

When he came downstairs, he looked distracted. She placed the tea in front of him. "Three sugar cubes, no?"

Aslan nodded, staring at her, stirring the tea. "I can do that," he said.

She smiled sweetly. "I want to do it."

"Is this an apology for this morning?"

"Yes," she said. "I was wrong. You have done so much for me and Kamal. I am forever in your debt." She paused. "For what it's worth, I never meant to hurt you."

"I don't think you're deceitful," he growled. "But you manipulated me." He kept his eyes on the tea. "We should let bygones be bygones." He lifted his head. "But we need to talk."

The sadness in his eyes and the gravity in his voice frightened her. Had he already decided to leave them? "Tonight," she said tentatively, wishing to delay the news.

But before long, Belqais returned with severe stomachache. Fearful of the rampant cholera in the area, Gohar saw no choice but to send Kamal to stay with Aslan while she tended to her sister-in-law. The discussion with Aslan would have to wait.

13

January 1916, Ahmedabad, Gilan

The thin, dark-skinned farmer Aslan was chatting with at the edge of Ahmedabad market looked familiar to Gohar. Had she seen him loitering around the house before? It was hard to be sure. The town was full of thin, dark-skinned men with scraggly beards and droopy mustaches, dressed in tunics and loose pants wrapped in puttees. The town's population had more than doubled amid the flow of refugees from the fighting between the Jangalis and the Russians in western Gilan.

The cloth peddler handed her the folded fabric he had just cut. "Wear it in good health."

She envied a Kurdish woman in an embroidered outfit and regal headgear. No bigger than a large village, Ahmedabad had little to offer. Even finding the peddler was a lucky break. The puny general store sold little besides cones of sugar, cans of tea, and packs of coarse domestic cigarettes. Now, she needed a seamstress to make her a loose blouse and a full skirt. Even that would be a welcome change from the ill-fitting dress she had borrowed from Belqais.

"I'll pay for it," Aslan said from her side. "I promised to buy you a dress. This is not up to your standards but consider it a downpayment."

"Thank you," she said. "Who was the man you were talking to?"

"A stranger. He asked me if I knew how to get to Baku without a passport."

"I think I saw him outside our house this morning."

"Did you? I didn't notice."

She glanced at him skeptically. Normally, nothing escaped him. But since their quarrel two days before, he had been preoccupied.

"Can we talk tonight?" Aslan asked as they took the muddy road back home. "Belqais is better and can take of herself." He paused. "And Kamal and I miss you."

Her humiliating dismissal from their room still irked her. But this was as close to an apology as she could expect. A lover's tiff was a luxury they could little afford. "Yes, I'll join you," she said.

They arrived home to find Petrus, his mother, aunt, and a Georgian friend who had accompanied him to celebrate the wedding. Suddenly, the house brimmed with activity.

But Petrus had troubling news. Rasht and Anzali were under martial law, and ferries to Baku were no longer carrying civilians. The situation could change any day. Meanwhile, Gohar could wait with Petrus's aunt in Rasht, or stay in the house in Ahmedabad, where he and Belqais also planned to stay. They would be safe here while the Russians had their hands full elsewhere.

The news disturbed Gohar, but she took it in her stride. Despite its lack of many amenities, the quiet town, with its inviting houses and friendly people, was not a bad place to shelter as long as the Russians stayed away. It was still Iran. And the delay would give her time to convince Aslan to stay with them.

A friendly mullah married Belqais and Petrus the next day. He didn't fuss over whether Petrus had converted to Islam out of conviction or love. Belqais looked radiant in the gown made by Petrus's aunt, a well-known tailor in Rasht. Gohar gave the bride two gold coins as a dowry and wedding gift. Aslan gave Petrus his gold cufflinks.

After the ceremony, Gohar played tar, Petrus's mother sang, and Kamal danced. The Georgian wine complemented the fesenjoon with duck that Ilych had prepared. Aslan didn't drink and barely ate. He retired early.

Gohar fell asleep listening to Petrus's mother and aunt's stories. By then, the bride and groom had gone to their room. Kamal snored on the carpet.

She woke to an eerie silence. It was too late for a serious discussion with Aslan. But remembering how troubled he had looked throughout the festivities, she decided to check on him. She tiptoed up the stairs and pushed the door open.

The room was empty. The mattress was rolled up neatly in a corner beside the folded writing table and the black money bag. Her first thought was that he had gone out for a nocturnal ride. But his clothes, his books, and his sidearm were all gone.

She ran downstairs in panic. Ilych bolted upright as soon as she touched his shoulder. He didn't know where Aslan was. He had woken Ilych to leave an envelope for Gohar and asked him to stay and watch over Gohar and Kamal.

In the envelope, she found a gold-framed cameo brooch, Aslan's pocket watch, and a letter. Gohar opened the note with trembling hands, but her eyes couldn't focus. Belqais, who had come downstairs, grabbed the letter and read it aloud:

My beloved Gohar,

Enclosed is a small gift to apologize for not treating you with the respect you deserve. Unfortunately, the local branch of Fabergé was closed, so I didn't have much choice. The brooch is from my grandmother and, as such, is precious to me. I want you to have it as a sign of my affection and remorse. The pocket watch is for Kamal when he is old enough.

I have fulfilled my promise to you. Petrus will help you settle in Gilan or move on as you wish. Ilych will be at your disposal for as long as you desire. My presence is no longer needed. It can only confuse everyone, especially Kamal, whom I love more than my life.

I tried to speak to you several times, but you did not seem interested. So, this letter, as inadequate as it is, should suffice. Embrace Kamal for me and keep me in your prayers.

Whatever happens, Simorq was the best thing that ever happened to me.

Forgive me.

Yours forever.

Aslan

PART V
Home

Thousands of vocal eyes and silent mouths;
Call me the guardian of their hope;
Thousands of trembling hands and restive hearts;
At times pull me back; At times, urge me on

S.KASRAII

1

February 1916, Gilan

No stranger to pain and loss, Gohar had never been blind to the fleeting nature of her affair with Aslan. Nevertheless, the abruptness of his departure shocked her.

As sleepless nights blended into foggy days, she grappled with a whirlwind of questions. Why the haste? Why not wait a few hours for her to wake up? Why not soften the blow with a sweet lie or two or a vague promise of a reunion? What was he rushing to or from? A lover? An adventure? A threat?

Ilych and Petrus believed Aslan had left for battle. He had taken weapons and maps but left the money and valuables for Gohar, Kamal, and Petrus. Belqais did not buy the men's argument. Aslan didn't need money to return to Tehran, the maps were his to take, and the presents were parting gifts. Gohar didn't know what to believe. The memory of his sad eyes and the finality of him leaving all his possessions behind frightened her.

But it was Kamal's forlorn face that truly devastated her. He stayed by her side all day long, clutching the wooden dog Aslan had made him, perking up whenever someone knocked and falling apart when the familiar footsteps failed to materialize.

With a heart heavy with regret, she struggled to come to terms with her own culpability. Had she been too coy, too dependent, too naïve, too much of this and not enough of that? Every night, she hunted for his smell in the darkness of the room they had once shared.

Shock morphed into anger, anger to despair. Eatin[...] burden; grooming, an agony; friendship, a drain. She rea[...] letter over and over, searching for signs of hope.

After his friend and relative's departure, Petrus spent most of his time outside the house, taking Belqais with him. Ilych ran the household. He cooked, shopped, and tended to Kamal. On the rare occasion that Gohar ventured out, he accompanied her. Once on her way to the public bathhouse, a drunk Russian deserter—one of an increasing number in town—grabbed her chador. Ilych kicked him. She watched dispassionately as blood gushed out of the soldier's mouth. Afterward, he found a Farangi tub and improvised a bath, so she didn't need to leave the house if she didn't want to.

By now, she was certain of the life growing under her heart. The awareness magnified her anxiety: What was she to do with not one but two fatherless children in a land where a father's status defined the destiny of the child? She longed for Qamar.

Ilych cursed "that boy" when he heard. He would give Aslan a good thrashing as soon as he saw him. But he promised to care for her and the children through thick and thin. One afternoon, when he found her searching for rat poison in the kitchen, he said matter-of-factly, "Don't look for poison. I threw it away." That comforted her.

He regaled her with his life stories while chopping vegetables as expertly as he would kill a man. Born Izzat in the vast steppes of Turkestan, the wild and free youth was forcibly conscripted to the tsar's army. The Russians had changed his name to Ilych, subjected him to brutal discipline, and jailed him for disobeying an officer.

He was about to risk his life to flee slavery when a high-ranking officer offered him a better way out: a chance to move in with his family and care for the officer's young son, Aslan.

Noor's letter arrived shortly after Aslan's disappearance.

The light of my eyes, my daughter Gohar,

Your safe arrival in Gilan filled my heart with immeasurable joy. I count the days until I can lay eyes on you and Kamal. As usual, Tehran is filled with intrigue and rumors, not to mention famine and typhoid. The government has ordered all Germans, Austrians, and Ottomans to leave the country, undoubtedly under pressure from the English. We have received no news of Haji, and no one seems to care about the fate of the Mohajeron anymore.

As you suspected, Akbar Mirza has bribed the village elders and government officials to dispute your ownership of your villages. He and his uncle Homayoun Mirza are busy spreading rumors that Saleh Mirza was poisoned by you and me, of all people. Preposterous, I know.

Our cousin, the executor of Saleh's will, is fighting Akbar Mirza's claims through legal channels. I am doing my best to counter the rumors. Meanwhile, we believe it is best for you to stay away from Tehran. Unfortunately, there will be no income from your villages until the dispute is resolved. But I trust that you have enough to carry on.

Ahmad sends his regards and kisses your hands.

Your devoted Bibi, Noor

The letter angered her. As skillful as Saleh Mirza's cousin was, no judge would dare to rule against someone backed by the English as long as a pro-English government was in power. It would be years before an independent government came to power, clearing the way for her to secure an impartial judgment and win back her property and good name.

2

February 1916, Gilan

As her pain dulled, Gohar craved company. Her wishes were granted two weeks after Aslan's disappearance. She was still in bed when Ilych informed her that Esmail was there to see her. She wasn't sure who he expected to see—a man or a woman. But he didn't seem surprised to see her in a chador.

Attired in a tailored sardari and trousers, his beard and hair neatly groomed, he greeted her in the living room. She was thankful that the chador covered her unkempt hair and the sloppy dress she had hastily thrown on.

She invited him to sit and positioned herself at a respectable distance as Ilych fetched tea and stayed close. "What brings you here?"

"I was seeing a patient in the area when I encountered Petrus. He told me of your disguise while traveling and mentioned that you are not well. With his permission, I took the liberty of coming to ascertain if I can be of service."

This report surprised her. Petrus had expressed his mistrust of the doctor on several occasions. But Petrus had been acting strangely as of late, and regardless of his affiliation with the rebels, Gohar was impressed by the way Esmail treated his patients. "I hope you don't think badly of me for traveling in men's clothing," she said.

"It was prudent," he said. "Although I guessed the truth from the beginning."

"Thank you for your discretion."

He moistened his lips. "Petrus told me about your husband. It must have been difficult for him to leave his family. But we all need to make sacrifices. I have a lot of respect for him."

Gohar glanced at Ilych sharpening knives on the veranda by the open door. His closeness comforted her. "I do, too."

Esmail inquired about her symptoms, took her pulse, and examined her eyes and tongue. "I believe your condition is nothing more serious than the fatigue of a long journey. All you need is rest. If the symptoms persist, I can examine you more thoroughly."

The last thing she wanted was for him to touch her. "I agree," she said hastily.

"I don't know of any medicine suitable for a young lady that alleviates weariness. But the company of friends, walks in nature, and reading help. I saw you carrying a tar. Do you play?"

"Yes."

"That will help too."

"I'll try," she said. "You seem much more relaxed than in the mountains."

"You are perceptive. I am. You remember I told you about our leader being trapped by the Russians?"

"Yes, you were seeking help to rescue him."

"Indeed. But salvation came, just as all hope was lost. A miracle happened. A true hero broke through the blockade and rescued our comrades. And not a minute too soon. Our leaders were freezing and reduced to eating grass."

"I am happy for you."

"You should be happy for our country. Folks are joining us in droves, giving us money and inviting us to defend their towns. It is good to see vile people like Smirnsky defeated."

The mention of the Russian master spy jolted Gohar. "Smirnsky?"

"Yes. Do you know him?" Esmail said. "He runs the military intelligence in northern Iran. He was the one who set the trap for Mirza. Not his first attempt to kill our leader, either."

She tasted bile in her mouth. Did Smirnsky have anything to do with Aslan's vanishing? "I know the name. Wasn't he the shah's tutor at one time?"

"Yes. He is behind every assassination in Gilan."

She didn't probe. But being so close to Aslan's arch-nemesis was terrifying.

He hesitated at the door as he departed. "I know you don't have many acquaintances in the area. Would it be acceptable to Petrus if I called on you as a patient next week? With your permission, of course."

It miffed her to think that she required Petrus's permission to receive a visit, but she kept her peace. "If it's not too much trouble. I am sure Belqais and Petrus won't mind."

"It would be no trouble at all. If it weren't for you, Sardar would have killed me. His people killed the storyteller."

"It was Aslan who saved your life," she said. "I only followed his lead."

Another letter from Noor arrived shortly after Esmail's second visit.

The light of my eyes, my dearest daughter, Gohar,

The sight of your handwriting and the news of your health instantly turned my cold winter into a warm spring. We are well. The news may have already reached you, but we heard that the Russians had recaptured Kermanshah, and the Mohajeron had scattered. Some fled to Qasr-e-Shirin or to exile in Berlin and Istanbul. But some have returned to Tehran secretly. I sent Ahmad to make inquiries about Haji, but to no avail.

I completely understand your desire to dissolve your marriage swiftly. Marriages do fall apart, especially when one party has disappeared under suspicious circumstances. No one would blame you for moving on.

Luckily, Saleh Mirza—may God shine light upon his grave—believed in negotiating hard before the start of a relationship rather than fighting once it had soured. With the utmost foresight, he secured your right to divorce under certain circumstances as part of your marriage contract. One such circumstance is if Haji became incapable of providing for you and your children for any reason. In this case, you also maintain custody of your children.

I had no doubt that Haji's abandonment of you and Kamal would qualify as grounds for exercising your right. Regardless, I consulted with the notary. He advised locating two witnesses to Haji's intentional dereliction of his duty as a husband and father. Ahmad successfully tracked down two people who were with Haji in Qom. They have both signed affidavits attesting to Haji arriving in Qom, accompanied by a man and a woman associated with the Germans, and leaving with them of his own accord before the Russian attack. Based on that, the notary has secured a favorable ruling and a divorce decree from a religious judge on your behalf. You are entitled to your mehrieh, and you retain custody of Kamal.

I am counting the days until I see you again.

Ahmad kisses your hand.

Your most devoted Bibi, Noor

Once again, Saleh Mirza had saved her. Even so, a married woman with an absent husband had more freedom than a divorcee. Liberated and frightened at the same time, she shared the news only with Ilych.

3

March 1916, Gilan

Esmail was not the only caller to the house. A steady stream of shady characters visited Belqais and Petrus at all hours of day and night. Some arrived in worn uniforms and scruffy boots but departed in respectable civilian clothing. Others came in dapper and left in rags. A few came dressed as farmers and departed in full Russian uniforms. All were armed, some with pistols, others with knives, and a few with both.

Those who stayed argued constantly in a mix of Farsi, Turkish, Armenian, Georgian, and Russian. They called themselves Bolsheviks, Social Revolutionaries, Mensheviks, and Social Democrats and discussed Marx, Lenin, and people she had never heard of. All of them claimed to champion the downtrodden and know the way forward. But she knew of only one man who had saved the life of a boy with brittle bones and a girl with a pockmarked face, and that man didn't subscribe to any labels. The burden of his absence weighed on her heart even heavier.

These visitors troubled her. After Ilych caught one of them stealing rice from a neighborhood grocery, she asked him to safeguard the black bag and sleep outside her bedroom. Meanwhile, Esmail's friendship provided her with some protection. The Jangalis now ruled most of the province, confining the Russians to Rasht and Anzali.

When Esmail visited, Ilych stayed close, but Kamal shied away. One time, Esmail brought along Assyeh, who now lived with him. Kamal greeted the little girl excitedly. His laughter as he played new games with Assyeh warmed Gohar's heart. After that, Assyeh accompanied Esmail on all his visits.

He brought Gohar reading material they would discuss: a poetry collection, a translated Farangi novel, articles cut from newspapers.

His ease in debating literature and philosophy as aptly as science and medicine awed her. Once, she praised the breadth of his knowledge.

He smiled. "I owe my paltry knowledge to my solitude. I had no choice but to read."

Gradually, their dialogue became personal. He mentioned a problematic patient and lamented his struggles to learn German from a book. One day, as they discussed the story of Rostam and Sohrab, she sighed. "You can't imagine how much I long to know my parents. Don't get me wrong, I love Qamar, but growing up, I always felt like an outsider."

"I felt alone too, even with five sisters," he said. "But I didn't know the true meaning of isolation until I went to study in Tehran. There I was, not knowing a soul, subject to constant ridicule about my accent, my clothing, even the books I read."

The plight of the young man moved her. "What did your family say?"

"I never told them. As it was, they wanted me to quit, take over my father's business, and get married." He paused. "I almost gave up. Once, I even thought of forsaking life altogether."

"But you kept going."

"Yes. I did it for the love of medicine and those I could help. I pledged to excel—I even wrote the pledge down." He lifted his head. "And it paid off. I graduated at the top of my class. I still dream of studying in Berlin."

Belqais welcomed the doctor's visits. "You are too rigid with Esmail," she once told Gohar. "Be softer, more feminine. Nothing too obvious, just enough to keep him around. You should drop the chador when he comes. The local women do."

"Whatever for? I don't cover my face here anyway," Gohar said.

"Let's face it. You need a husband. Haji is gone, and Aslan has disappeared. The doctor is nice, handsome, and a good provider."

Gohar was fond of Esmail. She even missed his gentle tone, shy smile, and keen observations when he wasn't around. But marry him?

"I enjoy his company. But there's no fire in my heart."

"So what?"

"Both Esmail and I need more than that," she said. Walking away, she wondered if there would ever be a fire in her heart again.

Qamar's arrival answered one question: Aslan was neither in Tehran nor with Nosrat. The knowledge disturbed Gohar even more. She would have preferred him alive with Nosrat than dead in a ditch.

According to Qamar, a few weeks after they had left the hunting lodge, the lady of the house had turned up unexpectedly. "Nosrat dug into my arms with nails sharp as knives," Qamar said. "She scowled like the shah's torture master and shook me like a mulberry tree."

"What did she want?" Gohar asked.

"To know if something was going on between you and Aslan."

"And what did you say?"

"What *could* I say? The truth. I told her that you wouldn't dream of having an affair, not even with a prince, let alone with the likes of Aslan. But I was trembling like a willow. I packed my trunk to return to Tehran. But Mash Baqer stopped me. He said Nosrat was upset because of a letter from Aslan Khan. She was worried about his well-being."

This must have been the letter Gohar had seen him writing. Had he told her where he was going?

Qamar sampled the rice cookies Esmail had brought. "These cookies are tasty but dry, if you ask me," she continued while munching. "I told Mash Qolam that a married woman shouldn't worry about a man young enough to be her son."

Nosrat wasn't that old, but Gohar appreciated the sentiment. "What happened next?" she asked impatiently.

"Be patient," Qamar said, giving Kamal a cookie. "What have you been feeding this boy? He's skin and bones."

"He's fine, Naneh." Gohar glanced at Kamal on Qamar's lap. "Just getting taller."

"It must be Ilych's cooking. He doesn't put enough lard in his stew," Qamar said. "At any rate. I was mad. That harlot had insulted my family to my face. I begged Mash Baqer to find me a ride. No point staying to get beaten up. He swore to the holy shrine of Imam Reza—which we both have kissed—that he was trying. But all he could find were convoys of people on foot. He would lose face in front of you and Aslan Khan if he let me walk like a peasant. I took pity on him and stayed. I tell you, that man has a silver tongue."

Qamar tucked one foot underneath her. "Then a letter from Belqais Khanum asked me to hurry up because you were not well after the long trip. In passing, she had mentioned Aslan Khan's disappearance. Mash Baqer read the letter to me and asked for permission to show it to Nosrat. I said fine. The very next day, the hussy was back. All smiles, with a bolt of fancy fabric for me—not that I care for that sort of thing. She asked me to bring you the tar you had played in the lodge. Said she looks forward to hearing you play."

"What did you say?"

"I wanted to break the damn thing on her head and tell her my Gohar was no motreb. But I kept my mouth shut and thanked her. The tar was entrusted to me. I had to bring it to you."

Gohar put the tar aside to give to Petrus. Her own father's tar was the only instrument that could sing the song of her sorrow.

4

April 1916, Gilan

Nowruz that year was the most subdued Gohar could remember. No one bought a new outfit. Qamar knitted Kamal a hat and made Assyeh a doll. Gohar gave the adults small coins for good luck. Even the promise of the return of a beloved Christian foretold in a poem she selected at random from Hafez failed to bring Gohar solace. She didn't believe it.

After the new year, she and Ilych discussed the possibility of moving away. Ilych promised to look for a house elsewhere. Aslan, if he were alive and wished to, would find them.

On the thirteenth day of the New Year, when the household left for the traditional picnic, she stayed home.

That afternoon, Esmail brought her a small bouquet of wild crocuses. "Since you refuse to go out, I brought the outdoors to you."

The gift unsettled her. He had already given her a hand-painted framed mirror for Nowruz that she had found too personal. She excused herself to find a bowl for the flowers.

"You look troubled," he said as she unwrapped the twine.

She busied herself arranging the flowers in the bowl. "It's the house. I need to move, maybe to Rasht."

"Why?"

Unsure of how he would react to news of the characters who frequented the house, she decided not to mention them. "Belqais and Petrus are newlyweds," she said. "They need their privacy."

Esmail squirmed uncomfortably. "So, do you want to move by yourself?"

"Of course not. I'll move with Qamar, Kamal, and Ilych."

"I understand your concerns," he said. "But you can't live without a male relative. People will gossip. Even I would not be able to visit. Here, Petrus provides respectability."

The thought of needing Petrus to offer propriety chafed her. "People can gossip as much as they like. Ilych will be with us. He is a male."

"He is not your relative."

"We will tell everyone that he is my Turkman uncle. End of story."

He squirmed and wetted his lips. "May I speak freely?"

She met his eyes. "Of course. I expect nothing less from a trusted friend."

"Don't you think it's time for you to accept that Haji may never come back? I believe in women's emancipation. But in a country like ours, a beautiful young woman with a child needs a man in her life."

She felt a knot in her stomach. Was he about to proclaim his affection for her? "It is much too soon to consider Haji gone," she said, glad to have kept her divorce secret. "By law, I have to wait five years before declaring him dead."

"I understand." His eyes were fixed on his folded hands. "But the Russians have the Mohajeron by the neck. Some rebels are already here or have gone to Berlin or Istanbul. The rest will be killed or captured and sent to a prison camp in India."

She shuddered, thinking of Haji in a prison camp. No one deserved that fate at his age.

He continued. "The religious authorities in Gilan are compassionate and more enlightened than those in Tehran. They understand that a young woman with a child cannot be left unprotected. If you petition for a divorce, I will see to it that they are sympathetic."

The conversation was becoming uncomfortable. She rose, carrying the bowl of flowers.

He cleared his throat. "I have a confession to make. As much as I try, I cannot stop thinking about you. My intentions are pure. With your permission, I will wait as long as you deem appropriate before sending my family to ask for your hand. Meanwhile, they can provide housing for you and your family."

Gohar valued his friendship and his protection. But she didn't want him to hope for a love she could never give. "Your family will never accept me."

"They will be over the moon when they see you."

She placed the bowl on the shelf. "I am flattered. I have no doubt that you would make an ideal husband. And I would be lying if I said I don't enjoy your company. But I think of you as a brother, not a husband. And you deserve better than a divorcée with two children."

The blood drained from his face. "Are you expecting another child?" he blurted out.

"Yes. So, it will be a while before I can remarry. I can't ask you to waste the best years of your youth waiting for me."

"Congratulations. I considered that possibility when I heard your symptoms. But I didn't want to be imprudent." He sat back. "Two children should give you even more reason to consider my offer. I would love them as my own. You have my word. I can wait until the summer, when the child is born, for you to decide."

She almost blurted out that the baby was not due until fall. But it was best for Esmail to presume Haji to be the father. "I don't know what will happen then." She lowered her gaze. "But I hope we can remain friends."

"I'd be honored to be your friend. I hope you will forgive my indiscretion. Seeing you is more than enough for me."

After his departure, she felt a great burden had been lifted from her heart. Acknowledging the child had miraculously transformed her shame into the grace of a new life. She might be angry at the father, but the child deserved her love. It was time to reveal her pregnancy.

Qamar was the first person she told. "What is done is done, my child," she said, fingering her rosary. "We cannot escape our fate. Thankfully, we are far away from the rumor mill of Tehran. Don't tell Noor. Let's pray to the Prince of Martyrs to show us the way."

Gohar held the old woman tightly in her arms.

5

April 1916, Gilan

"Stay where you are," Ilych whispered, standing in the doorway of Gohar's room. "I'll bring you tea. We have visitors."

Incredulous that there could be yet more visitors to the house even this early in the morning, Gohar peeked around Ilych's solid frame. A short, stocky man in a military-style tunic and scruffy boots stood in the vestibule downstairs. A greasy felt hat perched on his shaved head, and a pistol was visible under his unbuttoned coat.

Ilych continued. "He's here for the newspapers." The newspapers were Berlin-printed Bolshevik publications on their way to Russia through Turkey and Gilan. Their presence in the house put the whole household at risk of a Russian raid. Despite the mild April weather, Gohar shivered.

The man raised his head. His thick eyebrows shaded menacing black eyes that bore into her. She froze. A tiny hand tugged on hers. "Come, Bibi, please," Kamal whispered.

Gohar collected herself, clutched his hand, and returned to her room.

That afternoon, Gohar caught Petrus and Belqais in a rare moment at home without visitors, sipping tea on the back porch. As luck would have it, Qamar and Kamal were out. Though the newlyweds were talking intensely when Gohar spotted them, they clammed up when they saw her approaching.

Gohar seized her opportunity. "Sorry to interrupt your tête-à-tête," she said, sitting beside Belqais. "But I need to discuss your visitors."

"What about them?" Belqais asked.

"I want to know who they are and what they're doing here," Gohar said. "It's very difficult, living with strangers coming and going at all hours. And I'm worried about keeping the newspapers here. If the Russians find out about them, they will arrest all of us."

Petrus stared at her. "Don't you want to get rid of those bastards?"

"Of course. I am a patriot," Gohar responded. "But what does that have to do with the deserting Russian soldiers staying here?"

"Everything, dear," Belqais chimed in. "We don't have a proper army, so we must destroy the Russians from the inside. These soldiers are good people. They have nothing against us, but they must obey their officers. We're helping them go home, and the newspapers tell the Russian people the truth about the war."

"What about the civilians?" Gohar bristled. "Who are they?"

"They come to talk to the soldiers," Petrus said. "To convince them to leave."

"I am sympathetic to your cause," Gohar said calmly. "But I am not a revolutionary. And seeing some of them rob the shopkeepers disgusts me."

"They steal because they're hungry," Petrus snapped. "What are they supposed to do, starve to death?"

Gohar gaped at him. What had happened to the respectful, reasonable, mild-mannered Petrus? "Hunger is no excuse for thievery," she said. "It's not the shopkeepers' fault that soldiers are starving. The merchants are already suffering because the Russian army confiscates the harvest without paying for it. Why don't the soldiers loot the storehouses of the big landowners?"

"Food belongs to the hungry," Petrus said. "When the revolution comes, all landowners will be stripped of their land and grain."

Their increasingly heated conversation brought Ilych to the scene. His presence emboldened Gohar. "What would people say about us harboring thieves?" she fumed. "Or having strangers come and go all the time? This is not a caravanserai."

"I don't understand the fuss," Petrus scoffed. "The house is big enough to share. And speaking of reputations, what do you suppose our neighbors think when they see a well-known Jangali spending so much time here, doing God knows what?"

Gohar reddened. "Esmail is a friend, and no more," she erupted. "We have never been alone together. Plus, you invited him in the first place."

Ilych squatted to be at eye level with them and grabbed Petrus' shoulders. "You ought to be ashamed of yourself, talking to a lady that way," he growled. "Aslan isn't here to teach you manners, but I am. She tells the truth. I was here when Esmail told us you asked him to come."

Petrus winced. "I hadn't seen Esmail since he left us in the mountains—until I bumped into him leaving the house last week. I assumed Gohar had invited him. I decided not to intrude."

Gohar motioned for Ilych to let go of Petrus. "If neither of us invited Esmail, then who sent him and why?"

"Maybe he wanted to be helpful," Belqais said.

"Don't be naïve," Petrus said, rubbing his shoulders. "Jangalis don't do anything to be nice." He met Gohar's eyes. "Could Aslan have sent him? Maybe he's with the Jangalis."

The thought of Aslan being a Jangali was laughable to Gohar. "If Aslan had sent him, Esmail would have told me, wouldn't he?"

"I'm not surprised he knew where we were," said Belqais. "Jangalis are everywhere these days, watching everything."

"I don't trust him," said Petrus. "But we shouldn't antagonize him."

Gohar didn't want a rift with Petrus. "You, Petrus, are my brother," she said softly. "If you see anything improper, you should tell me. All I want is to sleep at night without fear of being raped and murdered or my children harmed."

A look of puzzlement came over Petrus's face. "Children?"

Gohar wondered if Belqais had shared the news with him.

Belqais broke in quickly. "We understand, Gohar dear. Rest assured that from now on, we won't keep the newspapers or let anyone stay overnight."

The conversation made Gohar even more determined to move out. She no longer trusted Petrus, and his influence on Belqais worried her.

Fortunately, neither knew of the treasure sewn into her black vest or the money in the bag. She cursed Aslan. Petrus was his friend, after all.

Petrus was waiting by the stairs when she came down in the morning. "I'm sorry about yesterday. I was out of line. I hope you find it in your heart to forgive me."

She mumbled something about understanding as she walked to the kitchen.

Petrus followed. "Belqais told me about the baby." He hesitated. "Is Aslan the father?"

"What do you think?" she snapped. "You're the teacher. You do the math. The child is not due for another five months, Haji has been gone for six months, and I am not an elephant."

"I don't mean to be disrespectful." He paused. "Does Aslan know?"

"How could he? He left before *I* knew."

"For what it's worth, he told me he planned to marry you."

"And you waited three months to tell me?"

"I was sure he'd be back soon. Ilych was here, and so were you and Kamal," he mumbled. "Truth be told, I was angry with him. You have been his lover for a month, but I have been his friend for eight years. We shared a house. But he left on my wedding night without saying goodbye."

Without looking at Petrus, she carried a plate of bread and cheese to the living room.

Petrus trailed her. "But I didn't stop looking for him. I think he is with the Jangalis. At least, he was in February."

She couldn't believe her ears. What was it about her that made her men join rebellions? "Where is he now?"

"I don't know. The Bolsheviks told me the Jangalis were protecting someone from the Russians. It could be Aslan."

What had Aslan done? Had he been forced to join the guerrillas? She exchanged a worried glance with Ilych, standing in the doorway. "Is he . . . alive?" she asked timidly.

"I'm not sure."

Her knees buckled. "Why hasn't he contacted us?" She sat down.

"Maybe he can't," Petrus said. "Esmail would know. He's a Jangali bigwig, close to their leader. Do you want me to talk to him?"

"No, I will," she said firmly. "You need to keep looking for Aslan."

"Be careful," he said. "The Jangalis are religious fanatics."

Esmail had never expressed any fanatical views. She decided not to mention his proposal.

"Listen, you shouldn't worry about the children," Petrus said as he rose. "Belqais and I can take care of them. That way, you would have more options."

Gohar put her hand protectively on her midriff. She would die before leaving her children with this couple.

On Esmail's next visit, Gohar greeted him in a new dress Petrus's aunt had made, her hair covered by only a scarf. "Can I ask you something, Esmail Khan?" she asked, sitting closer to him than usual on the veranda. "Have you been truthful with me?"

He paled. "Why do you ask? What have I done?"

She glanced at Kamal playing marbles with Assyeh as Ilych planted flowers. "To start with, you told me Petrus invited you here. He denies that. We both want to know why you lied."

He squirmed uncomfortably. "I am sorry for misleading you. I did as Aslan had instructed."

"Aslan? When did he give you instructions?"

He avoided her gaze. "Before he left on his mission, he—he asked me to keep an eye on you." The ordinarily eloquent doctor stammered.

"What mission?"

"To rescue our leader from the grip of the Russians. Aslan is the savior hero I mentioned."

Ilych stopped planting.

"And out of respect for a man who saved not only your life but also your leader's, you lied to the person he asked you to watch out for?"

she said.

"I didn't mean to deceive you. But he insisted."

She burrowed her eyes into him. "How did he end up with you?"

"He joined us." He gazed at his clasped hands. "A few days after we parted in the mountains, he came to see me at my house in Lahijan. I was troubled. Our leadership was in peril, and all we had were inexperienced recruits. He suggested we collect those fighters who knew the area, including two German officers who were staying with us."

Ilych put the trowel down, rose, and approached them.

Esmail gazed far away. "When our men gathered, Aslan produced a map of the area and asked them to mark the Jangalis' locations with pebbles and the position and strength of the Russians with twigs: the larger and more skilled the Russians, the bigger the sticks."

She pictured Aslan prodding the men to mark the map. "He's smart."

"I'll admit that was clever." Esmail swallowed. "Once we had marked out the map, we could see where the enemy was weak, and we could breach the blockades through the back roads. One of our people warned that our attack could backfire. It could guide the Russians to where our leaders were hiding and allow them to raid their hideout."

Ilych leaned against the porch, crossing his arms.

"Aslan agreed," Esmail continued. "He suggested a ruse to divert the best Russian troops from the area. The Russians were afraid of the Germans sabotaging the Russian road. If we made them believe that such an assault was imminent, they would send their most elite troops to fortify the road. He had a map of the mountain trails. He believed if the Russians captured a German officer with the map on him, they would think that the Germans were targeting Manjil Bridge."

"My friend drew that map," Ilych interjected.

Esmail glanced at Ilych. "I thought his plan was suicidal, but the Germans liked it. They volunteered to let themselves be captured but asked Aslan to pledge to get them out. He agreed."

"Brave men," Ilych grunted.

Esmail wet his lips. "He volunteered to lead the raid. True to his prediction, the Russian units moved out of the forest once they caught the German officers. We sent word to Aslan."

Was the farmer Aslan talked to in the market that day a Jangali messenger? She should have spoken to him when he asked. She could have stopped him from pursuing the foolish plan.

"Did you go with them?" Ilych asked.

"No," Esmail said. "We considered it prudent for me to stay behind. That way, if the raid failed, I could help the movement regroup."

"So, you let him attack an army of a thousand with a dozen fresh recruits?" Ilych growled.

"That's how he wanted it," Esmail insisted.

She closed her eyes and saw Aslan riding through the frozen forest under a moonless sky, soft ground muffling the sound of hooves and soldiers dozing. Suddenly, guns erupted, horses neighed, and men screamed in pain. Aslan's voice rose, urging his men to break the siege: to save a life, a movement, a hope.

"Was he wounded?" she asked.

"No," Esmail replied. "He was shot in the shoulder, but not seriously. He was injured later when he broke into the Russian barracks to rescue the Germans."

"What happened?" Ilych asked.

"I don't know," Esmail said. "He was with the Bolsheviks then."

Gohar wobbled. The story was getting bleaker by the second. "Is he alive?" she muttered.

"Last I heard, he was," Esmail said.

"Where is he?" Ilych seethed.

"I don't know. All I know is that the Russians have put a bounty on his head."

She motioned for Ilych to walk away and moved closer to Esmail. "Please find out." Her fingers touched his arm as though by accident. "I need to know."

He flinched. "Have I betrayed his trust by confessing how I feel about you?"

Gohar smiled ruefully. "At least you were honest about something."

6

May 1916, Gilan

Both bearded men in the forest wore threadbare khaki tops, loose pants, and scuffed boots. But their similarities ended there. The taller one had ginger hair and blue eyes and looked Russian. His short, slim companion, by contrast, had black hair and brown eyes and could have passed as Turkish, Persian, or even as an Arab.

"Good evening, comrades," Petrus said, then turned to Gohar and Ilych. "These comrades helped Aslan break into the Russian barracks." He then addressed the tall, ginger-haired man. "Comrade Bahram, please tell my friends what you told me."

The scent of rice paddies saturated the air. Gohar side-glanced at Ilych, drying the sweat off his forehead with a handkerchief. She longed for a breeze.

Bahram eyed Gohar and Ilych suspiciously. "Aslan came to us in February," he said in Gilani-accented Farsi. His voice was barely audible above the din of cicadas.

That was when Esmail had first visited her, Gohar thought.

"He wanted to get into the Russian barracks in Anzali dressed as a Russian officer, with orders to take two German prisoners to Rasht for interrogation. The Russian top brass wanted to know the extent of their collaboration with the Jangalis."

"We knew what he'd done to the Tsarist soldiers to help the Jangalis," he continued. "We wanted to help. We got him the uniform, forged ID and transfer papers, and a carriage to transport the prisoners," Bahram said, motioning to his companion. "Comrade Yuri and I decided to go with him to protect him. We wanted to ask him to join us after the mission. The barracks were half-empty, with most soldiers in the field.

But we decided to go at suppertime when the Russians don't look too closely at the papers. Our people planned to set a fire inside while we were there to distract the guards."

Gohar swatted the mosquitoes away. Prudently, she was wearing pants despite the heat. Malaria was rampant in this area.

"Everything went swimmingly," the dark-haired Yuri said in a thick Russian accent. "When the Russians brought out the Germans, their officer asked Aslan to go with him to sign the paperwork. Aslan whispered to me to be ready to bolt. I pushed the Germans into the carriage and got in myself."

Bahram interjected. "I was chatting with a guard when all hell broke loose. I heard gunshots from the room Aslan was in. Then he came out running and shouted at me to leave at once. He got on one of the messenger motorcycles parked out front."

Yuri picked up the thread. "The minute we moved, a bunch of Russians came out, shooting at Aslan. He sped through the gate. We were at the gate when the fire bells rang, and people ran to put out the fire. The guards waved us through. We cut the horses loose down the road, toppled the carriage to block the way, and ran to hide in the marshes."

"What happened to Aslan?" Ilych asked.

"He drove away," Bahram said. "The Russians chased him, first on foot, then in trucks."

"What happened next?" Ilych probed.

"We swam across the mouth of the river and made our way to our safe house," Bahram said. "When Aslan didn't show up by midnight, we sent word to the Jangalis. We assumed Aslan had gone toward the forest. The Russians don't go there at night."

"The Jangalis sent a search party," said Yuri. "We went with them. Near dawn, we found him in a ditch. He was in bad shape: shattered bones and lots of blood loss. Our doctor didn't think he'd make it. We offered to take him to Baku, but the Jangalis took him away."

Gohar was dizzy. Her knees buckled. Ilych grabbed her arm. "Hold on to me," he whispered. He turned to the Bolshevik. "Do you think the Russians knew you were going to the barracks?"

"That's what the Jangalis asked," Yuri responded. "I don't know. If there was a leak, it was not from us."

"The Jangalis accept anyone," Bahram said, spitting on the ground. "No discipline."

"Even if he survived then, he may not for long," Yuri volunteered. "He shot a bigwig, the chief of Russian military intelligence. The Russians have a huge bounty on his head."

"Smirnsky," Gohar blurted out without thinking. Anger boiled in her veins. He had left to take revenge, leaving them to fend for themselves.

Yuri stared at her with open mouth, bewildered to hear a woman's voice coming from a man's mouth. "How do you know?"

"Doesn't matter," Ilych said, leading her away.

She leaned on Ilych as they walked the muddy path. "We'll find him," Ilych said.

Gohar nodded without conviction, pleading to the Martyrs of Karbala to save his life. Would she at least be given a body to bury?

"Aslan is alive!" Esmail exclaimed as soon as Ilych opened the door. "With Jangalis."

It had been only four days since Gohar had asked him to find Aslan. She hadn't expected to see him so soon. She faced him in the vestibule. "Where is he?"

"With our most trusted people. They won't be tempted by a bounty or bullied into handing him over to the Russians."

"I must see him," she said.

"That's not possible. He can't travel. But I can get him a note. "

"Then I will go to him," she said. "A note will not do."

He looked at her skeptically. "I will let him know."

She glanced at his khaki jacket and long boots. "Where are you going?"

"To the mountains."

"What about Sardar?" she asked, remembering Sardar's pledge to kill him.

He snickered. "I am his honored guest now. He wants an alliance with us."

"When will you be back?"

"Not for a few weeks. But I will get word to you if I hear from Aslan." He took her arm gently, lowering his voice. "And a word of caution. Don't tell Petrus or Belqais where Aslan is. Their friends are all Okhrana informants."

After Esmail departed, she turned to Ilych. "What do you think?"

"We should leave as soon as possible. The Russians are holed up in their barracks and too busy to pay attention to us. We can stay in Rasht or go on to Baku. I'll get us there."

"Will you stay with us?" she asked anxiously.

"What else would I do? You and the children are the only family I have. A man's duty is to defend his family."

She embraced the big man and rested her head on his chest. Would it be wrong for her to tell Ilych how much she loved him?

7

May 1916, Gilan

After Esmail left, Gohar returned to the veranda. Aslan's actions baffled and infuriated her. He had gone on a suicide mission to rescue the leader of a rebellion he didn't believe in, broken into the Russian barracks to liberate Germans he didn't know, and endangered his life to avenge an old vendetta. All without sending her a single word. What was she to do? Look for him? Forget him?

She glanced at the neat rows of petunias Ilych had planted in the yard. Pinning her hopes on Aslan was futile. But was it realistic to live on her own with Ilych, Qamar, and the children? Perhaps she should reconsider Esmail's proposal. The speed with which he'd found Aslan indicated his interest in her and his sway with the rebels who practically ran the province.

Qamar's arrival with tea surprised Gohar. She was usually asleep at this time.

"Do you remember how much you liked my stories when you were little?" Qamar said as she sat. "There's one I'd like to tell you now."

Gohar looked at her askance. "Now?"

"You think I've gone soft in the head, don't you?" Qamar chuckled. "But last night, I dreamed of your sainted father, sitting knee to knee with Imam Hossein."

"How did you know it was my father? I thought you never met him."

"I didn't. But I recognized him from his eyes and hands. They looked just like yours. He thought this tale might help you."

Gohar sighed. There was no harm in listening to a fable if that would make Qamar happy. "Should we wait until Kamal wakes up?"

Qamar shook her head. "This is not a story for children."

Gohar recalled the salacious tales in *One Thousand and One Nights*. Qamar was not in the habit of recounting scandalous stories, but there was a first time for everything. And she could use the distraction. "Go ahead."

Qamar started as she always did, "Once upon a time in an ancient land . . ." then went on:

. . . there lived a green-eyed princess with auburn hair, a slender build, and a face as pale as fresh snow. Her father, the shah, was the absolute ruler of the land. Her mother, the shah's favorite concubine, was a green-eyed Georgian beauty given the title of Noor-al-Saleh, known as Noor.

On her fourteenth birthday, the princess, who had everything, asked her mother, Noor, for one thing: To be taught tar by the court's young music master. He played so skillfully that wild animals gathered to listen, and he could make his audiences dance with joy one minute and cry uncontrollably the next with the change of a single note.

Noor obliged.

Sadly, it didn't take long for Satan to intervene. The princess and the young master, slender and tall, with eyes as black as a moonless night, fell in love. Tempted by Satan—may he burn in hell's fire for eternity—they did what they shouldn't have. Soon enough, she was pregnant.

Noor hollered like a wounded lioness when told of the pregnancy. How could this have happened? Where were the servants, the eunuchs, the ladies-in-waiting, all those wretched creatures charged with keeping the shah's honor intact? Indeed, all of them must be punished. Everyone knew that two young people together were like cotton and fire: all too ready to burn if left too close. The shah would demand blood to wash out this stain.

But what to do with the disgraced princess? Marriage to the musician was out of the question. Even a genius musician was only a lowly motreb, unworthy of being a shah's son-in-law. Noor didn't care if the treacherous musician was put to death—there were so many others to replace him. What she couldn't bear was to lose her daughter, whose sonorous laugh lifted her spirits, and the touch of whose silky hands soothed her pain.

Noor, a legendary beauty, had plenty of smarts. After all, it had taken more than beauty to keep her in the shah's bed for nearly twenty years, fighting off three hundred women determined to kill if necessary. She summoned the grand vizier, Saleh Mirza.

Saleh Mirza, who had an eye for beauty—some would say a roving one—had a soft spot for Noor in his heart and a knack for recognizing opportunity. Being smart—some would say cunning—he quickly found a solution to silence all whispers. The despicable musician and all those responsible for watching the princess must be dealt with severely but covertly.

However, they had to spare the princess. She was not only young and female, which, of course, meant she had only half the brain of a male, but also an asset to the kingdom. Suitors from all over the land, the rich and the nobles, princes, and chieftains, sought the hand of the fabled beauty. Their wooing would keep the shah's treasury full and his army strong. Her beauty was key to securing the loyalty of allies and turning enemies into friends.

With a proper dowry, no one would question her chastity. The wise suitor may even consider the blemish a beauty mark, an enhancement to the bride's allure.

The child was another matter. Noor proposed sending the newborn away. Saleh Mirza objected. Leaving the child alive could complicate the future. True, the shah had many children and grandchildren—but his enemies could exploit this one.

Finally, after many cups of coffee and mounds of burnt almond sweets, the two reached a compromise. The child would live if it were a girl and die if it were a boy. In that case, the mother would be told that the child was stillborn.

You see, my dear, as I always said, our fates are written on our foreheads long before we are born.

The two then hatched a plan to notify the shah. The veterans of the court, well-versed in the art of handling delicate situations, knew how to stage the revelation. After a night of wine, music, and love, Saleh Mirza delicately divulged the nasty work of Satan to the mellowed shah. He blamed the sordid affair on the feebleness of women and the disloyalty of servants, urged compassion, and cited God's mercy for those who forgive. Finally, on cue, Noor threw herself on the floor to beg for mercy.

The shah, pleasant by nature, agreed. He was, after all, modern and had traveled to Farang; he was not an old-fashioned ogre who blinded and maimed his children. Granted, he had ordered the murder of some troublemakers and *disloyal ministers. But killing a young beauty of his flesh and blood would have been barbaric.*

A lover of music, he was sad to lose the musician. But life is bittersweet. To enjoy roses, one has to accept thorns.

It wasn't long before the body of the young musician was found in an alley, and several of the princess's attendants died of accidents and sudden illnesses. The grief-stricken princess was sent to seek solace in a faraway village. She emerged months later, more beautiful than ever. What few knew, and no one spoke of, was that a baby girl had been born in that faraway village.

Shortly after her return to the capital, the princess, ravishing in a Parisian dress and priceless emerald jewelry crafted by the tsar's jeweler, married her Prince Charming, dashing in his finery. The groom, a powerful chieftain, would mend the shah's ruffled relationship with his tribes. Thirty years older than the princess, he would be able to handle the willful young beauty deftly.

The royal feast lasted seven days and seven nights. Rich and poor were fed. Cakes and candies followed lamb, turkey, and saffron rice. Dances, music, and fireworks enchanted the guests. Even the Farangis were impressed.

Amid all the festivities, no one was happier than Noor, stunning in her regalia. If anyone saw her smiling flirtatiously at Saleh Mirza, no one dared to gossip.

On the seventh day after the royal wedding, the princess's old wet nurse, Qamar, watched the sunrise alone on a rickety wooden stand in her freshly swept yard in Gurdan, miles away from the capital. Her decision to take in the princess's daughter tormented her.

On the one hand, she loved the princess and was obligated to the kind and generous Noor, who had saved her family from starvation. On the other, the burden of bringing up a fatherless child in a land where a baker's child would be a baker, or marry one, and a painter's child would be a painter, or marry one, could prove too much to carry.

Qamar could not deny the attraction of the promised stipend. Her husband's grocery store in a poor section of the once-prosperous city could barely feed the family. The money could pay for dowries for her daughters and apprenticeships for her sons. But what if the baby's mere presence was enough to ruin her daughters' marriage prospects?

She was so lost in thought that she was startled by the soft knock on the door. When she opened it, she saw Noor's confidante, accompanied by a woman carrying a baby wrapped in a white shawl. Soldiers carrying a trunk followed them.

Qamar took the infant and opened the shawl. The sleeping child's pale, delicate face, framed by soft auburn ringlets, instantly captivated her. A gold pendant, engraved with a Qur'anic verse to ward off the evil eye, was pinned to the baby's chest. The child's uncanny resemblance to her mother banished Qamar's doubts and warmed her heart.

Once everyone had left, Qamar opened the trunk. Lined with green velvet, it contained some clothing, a tar, and a Qur'an with an inscription on its back cover. Having lived among the highborn, she knew instantly that the writing was the baby's name and birth date. She put it aside to show to the mullah and hid the trunk with the tar in her cellar. The less she saw a satanic musical instrument, the better.

That afternoon, the mullah revealed the child's name to Qamar: Gohar.

Pale, motionless, and hardly breathing, Gohar listened to the horrid tale. Suddenly, everything made sense: Saleh Mirza and Noor's unexpected appearance in her life, their generosity and kindness, her betrothal to a man Saleh Mirza needed to push through his modernization agenda, Saleh Mirza's bequest. Now she saw all the clues she had refused to see: her tar, her charm, the princess's visit, her adoption, her marriage, her inheritance. Here was all she had ever wanted to know. And it was devastating.

She and her mother were pawns in a political game—and Saleh Mirza, the man she loved and respected as a father, was the mastermind. Did he ever care for her?

"Why didn't you tell me this before?" Gohar gasped, barely able to get the words out of her choked throat.

Qamar wiped away her tears. "I had sworn secrecy. And what good would it have done?" She rested her hand on Gohar's knee. "Please, my dear. Don't think badly of Saleh Mirza or Noor. All they did was out of love for you and your mother. They had no choice but to silence the whispers."

Another devil's bargain.

"Where is my mother?" she asked.

"No one knows. Maybe in Farang. She disappeared after visiting you in Gurdan."

Gohar remembered the sad green eyes of the princess. Her heart ached for the teenage mother and young father. How dearly they had paid for their love. "Do I have any siblings?" she asked, hoping for a silver lining to the nightmare.

"Not that I know of. Your stepfather was infertile."

Her chest tightened. She ran out.

A cacophony of birds and frogs greeted her in the forest. She pulled Saleh Mirza's ring off her finger and hurled it. The gold glinted in the light, filtering through the young leaves as the ring flew through the air, disappearing in the forest's darkness. She placed her hand on the trunk of a walnut tree, hunched over, and threw up.

The moss-covered ground welcomed her as she dropped. Leaning on a chestnut, her legs extended among the wild violets and snowdrops, she breathed in the smell of rice paddies. Everything in her life had been a lie. Even her beloved Qamar had lied to her. She could trust no one save for an aging Uzbek.

She bawled for her mother.

8

May 1916, Gilan

Colorfully dressed local women tittered as they watched a lumbering bear climb a tree. The coins on their velvet vests jingled, and their sequined scarves glittered in the sun as they moved. Gohar envied their carefree demeanor.

All week long, she had been tormented by anger and doubt. At last, late into the previous night, she had come to a decision that had brought her some peace. Enough lies and rumors, she had resolved. She was tired of living in the shadows. Whispers had killed her father and deprived her mother of her child and her country. They would not harm Gohar and her children. She would ignore them, settle in Rasht with her children, Ilych, and Qamar, open a music school for girls, and travel to Farang to find her mother. At some point, she would return to Tehran and claim her inheritance. No one could bully her out of what was hers and her children's. But she would never tell Noor what Qamar had divulged. The woman had suffered enough. What she didn't know wouldn't hurt her, and she was her grandmother. As for Aslan, she would not chase him. On that, she was resolute. He was a free man, just as she was a free woman.

But her fragile peace had lasted no more than a few hours. That morning Esmail's housekeeper had brought Assyeh along with a map to a remote cabin in western Gilan. The note on the map was in Aslan's handwriting: *You can find me here.* It rekindled her unease.

The market was lively. Men laughed, betting on a game of *morgāna jang*—the war of the eggs. Women listened to the palm reader telling their fortunes. Girls peeked at the glistening, oiled bodies of wrestling teenagers and giggled. Children ran around. Everyone munched on shelled walnuts and sugar candy.

Everyone, but her, seemed to be enjoying the day. The map hadn't changed her mind—Ilych would be the one to visit Aslan and tell him of their whereabouts, and let Aslan choose to be part of their lives or not. But it had rekindled the pain of losing the love and friendship she and Aslan had once shared. Was that another illusion? Another lie?

Kamal and Assyeh ran to her. Excitedly speaking over each other, they recounted the story of the clever heroine of the marionette show who had outsmarted her greedy father and old suitor to marry the man she loved. Then they dragged her to the long line of people waiting to see the star attraction, the *shahrefarang*—kinetoscope.

The shahrefarang was encased in a tin castle as tall as Gohar and as wide as two men standing side by side. Gohar gawked through the eyepieces. Cars whizzing by, Farangis strolling arm in arm, and contraptions flying distracted her for the one minute her coin allowed her.

On the way home, the children ran ahead with a pinwheel, laughing. In Aslan's absence, the girl had been the only one who could make Kamal smile. Gohar should adopt her, send her to school in Rasht, and teach her music. A third child would be no more trouble than two.

Esmail was a good man, but how could he help Assyeh on her journey to womanhood? What did he know of the world of women? Of accepting the pain of labor to bring the promise of a new life into the world, of being the foundation that shouldered the weight of beautiful buildings, of turning the harsh desert wind into cool comfort like a windcatcher?

She remembered the day they had found Assyeh. It was Aslan who had insisted on bringing her along. How right he had been. Her chest tightened. To live free of lies, she had to know the truth, no matter how painful.

Hell was living in darkness, wondering whether there had ever been light.

She had to see Aslan.

9

June 1916, Gilan

The steep, narrow path branched from the main road that connected
Rasht to Tabriz. Gohar followed Ilych with Kamal perched on his
saddle. As they climbed, the lush forest gave way to tall bushes. The
rocks became jagged. The flowers became scarce. The breeze billowing
her loose dress turned chilly.

The track ended at a clearing, where two armed men in loose
farmers' pants and long tunics guarded a set of narrow steps dug into
the mountain. On one side of the clearing was a steep drop, and on the
other, a flat-roofed mud hut next to a crumbling stable.

The men raised their rifles. One of them stepped forward.

Ilych raised his open palms. "Greetings. We are here to see Aslan
Khan."

"Who are you?" the guard asked, eyeing Gohar in her black tribal
dress and headgear. "What is your business with the commander?"

"My name is Ilych, we are—"

Aslan's voice from atop the stairs interrupted him. "It's all right,
Zafar. This is my Uncle Ilych, the young lad is my son, Kamal, and
the lady is my wife, Gohar." Dressed like his guards, he stood under a
walnut tree. A set of crutches supported his thin body.

One of the men reverently took the rein of Gohar's horse to help her
dismount. The other picked up Kamal to lead the way. Ilych dismounted
and followed. Gohar felt faint. The energy that had carried her across
Gilan was all but gone. What was she doing here? Shaming herself by
chasing a man who had left her? Ilych gently nudged her forward.

At the top of the stairs, Kamal wiggled free and ran to Aslan. He
wrapped his arms around his legs and buried his face in his thigh. Gohar

longed to follow suit, but mindful of the guards and unsure of Aslan's reaction, she stood to the side as Ilych embraced him.

Aslan patted Kamal's hair. "I am sorry, my boy. I can't pick you up." He lifted his head to smile at Gohar. "Apologies for not coming down to greet you. I am not as agile as I once was." His pale face alarmed her.

She wet her lips. "Did you know we were coming?"

"I saw you coming from there." He pointed to the large flat-roofed cabin to the side. "I have a telescope. A gift from the Germans. Shall we go in? My men will take care of the horses and the luggage."

She followed Ilych and Kamal up uneven stone steps to the cabin, taking in the sheer drop across from the dwelling and the mountains behind it. Aslan trailed behind.

The lodging was furnished with only a crude wooden table, a few chairs, and a painted cabinet. A wooden bed was visible behind a half-drawn curtain at one edge of the room. Colorful kilims partially covered the tiled floor. A telescope by the window pointed down the mountain.

A cool, moist breeze welcomed Gohar on the veranda at the far end of the cabin. Bands of red, purple, and blue painted the sky as the sun set. She glimpsed at the cloud-covered peak of Shah-Muallem to the west. The forest, meadows, and rice paddies below ended in a sliver of the Caspian Sea at the horizon.

She heard the click of Aslan's crutches on the tiled floor before hearing his voice. "On clear days, you can see the sea and the village rooftops. You will like it here."

He sidled beside her, resting his hand on her shoulder, and squeezing it affectionately. She didn't react.

"I am sure I would," she said. "If I stayed. But we need to go back in a couple of days."

"What do you mean? You came all this way only to stay a couple of days?" An edge of hurt was palpable in his voice.

"We need to find a house in Rasht. I wanted to make sure you were well. Esmail said you can't travel."

He shrugged. "As you wish."

"What I wish for is the truth. But not now. I'm tired. It has been a long journey."

Before he could reply, Zafar approached and whispered something to him. She was relieved. This was not time for a confrontation, not yet.

Aslan turned to her. "I didn't know you were coming, so we haven't prepared a proper meal. Zafar can slaughter a chicken or make a *pomodor qatoq*. It is a local dish with eggs and tomatoes."

"Pomodor qatoq sounds perfect," she replied. "Kamal loves tomatoes."

"Kamal and Ilych can sleep on camping cots in the small room off the vestibule," Aslan said once Zafar departed.

"And me?" She met his eyes. "You told your men I am your wife. But that is not true."

"How else should I have introduced the woman carrying my child in a conservative area like this one?"

"You knew?" she asked.

"It's not hard to see." He gestured to her protruded midsection. You and Kamal take my bed. I will sleep on the cot."

"What about your leg?"

"No need to worry. I'll manage. As you said, it is for a night or two only." He turned and left.

She washed up behind the curtain and returned to find Kamal on Aslan's lap. He was munching on a sweet cracker, *naan-e-khoshk*. Breadcrumbs covered the table. She envied their easy reunion.

Kamal waved a tiny wooden dog in the air. "Bibi, see what Baba made me," he crowed.

Since when did Aslan become *Baba*? She smiled, taking a seat across the table. "Good, now Doggy has a friend to kiss."

"Kissing is for girls," Kamal said disdainfully. "They fight." He clicked the heads of the dogs together.

Aslan's welcoming manners and evident joy in seeing them had made all she planned to say sound foolish. "How long have you been here?" She sipped the tea Zafar had brought.

Aslan looked up. "A couple of weeks."

"And before?"

"The Grand Hotel was full," he said with a wry smile. "So, I stayed in the cellar of an old mansion. The doctor wanted to amputate my leg, but I told him I'd rather die, so he put me in a contraption." He paused. "I dreamt of you singing to me."

"Do you want me to take Kamal?" she asked, changing the conversation.

"No, let him be. I missed him."

"He missed you too."

He eyed her. "And you?"

She ignored the question.

The smell of garlic announced dinner. Kamal recounted his adventures at the market as they ate, and Ilych and Aslan chatted. Gohar remained silent. Once or twice, she caught Aslan watching her. By the time Zafar cleared the table, Kamal was curled up asleep on a kilim. Ilych carried him to the bed; Aslan must have told him of the arrangement.

She wrapped her shawl tightly around her shoulders. "Do you mind if I close the window?"

"Suit yourself," he said, hobbling to the painted cabinet to fetch a bottle of amber liquor and a glass. "Would you like some tea to warm up? Zafar can make a fresh pot."

She leaned against the wall by the closed window. "No, thank you. I am going to bed soon."

He sat facing her. "You don't need to worry about the child," he said, filling a glass. "I'll take care of both the baby and Kamal. I planned on coming to see you as soon as I could sit in a carriage."

"That's not why I came," she said. "I don't need you to take care of the child."

"Then why *did* you come, if I may ask?" He stared at her. "To bicker and leave me with the thought of another child you're going to take away?" His voice was harsh and pained. "Or is there something else you need me to do for you?"

His raw emotion troubled her. "Please calm down. I didn't come to hurt you." She paused. "I came because I had to ask why you deserted us the way you did. I know you told me that there would never be an 'us.' But it wasn't just me. You abandoned Kamal. Can you imagine how upset he was?"

"I thought he'd forget me quickly. And I never abandoned you. I had to do what I did."

She bit the inside of her lip to keep the anger in check. "You didn't even write to me."

"I couldn't. I couldn't write while hanging from a contraption. Plus, a letter from me would have put you in danger. I sent you a map as soon as I could."

She didn't answer.

Aslan leaned back. Only his hands, clasped on the table, were visible in the light of the kerosene lamp. "Listen, I know you're angry. But hear me out." His voice had turned measured and calm. "You don't need me, but the children do. And I need all of you."

He sipped his brandy. "I'm glad you came. We can clear the air and move forward. I was wrong about 'us.' I care for you. I always did. And I want to be a father to my children. Don't you always fret about not knowing your father? Doesn't my love for them count for anything?"

She winced at the mention of her father. "I would never stand between you and your children or use them to manipulate you. But you should have talked to me before you left."

"I tried," he bristled. "But you sugared my tea and kissed my cheeks but refused to talk to me. I thought you were having second thoughts about us, wanting to take your chances with Esmail. I decided to talk to you after I returned, if I made it back alive."

"Esmail?" She burst out exasperated. "What gave you that impression?"

"The way you looked at him treating patients. The way you mouthed poems with him."

"That's silly. I respected him. But I loved *you*. You could have told me you were joining the Jangalis."

He leaned forward, his eyes burrowing into her. "Is that what he said I did?"

"More or less."

"Well, I didn't. I went to see him because you and I had a silly quarrel and I needed company. Then I saw how desperate he was and offered some ideas. I had no intention of doing anything more. I didn't mind defying the Russians to take you to Gilan. But ganging up with the Germans to save the life of a rebel leader they wanted dead was treason. I wasn't ready for that."

"But isn't that what you did?"

"Yes."

"Why?"

He pulled up a chair to rest his feet on. "I had never met the Jangali leader. But I could see how others—be it illiterate peasants or educated doctors—revered him. Some, like the storyteller we met, even died for him. He advocated for what we all believe in, justice, integrity, and standing up to foreigners and their lackeys. But people believed him, in a way they never did the Farang-educated aristocrats who wrote about *liberté, égalité, fraternité* in progressive papers while living in mansions and owning villages and never breaking bread with farmers."

He shifted his leg. "He had a chance to succeed where others didn't. But rescuing him from the Russian siege would be dangerous. No matter how cunning we were and how incompetent the Russians were, it was still a dozen guerrillas with muskets against a trained army with machine guns. When the Germans offered to let themselves be captured, I asked myself: How could I ask them to put their lives on the line if I wasn't ready to do the same?"

He paused. "We had a better chance of success with me leading the mission than anyone else. Plus, I could minimize the bloodshed. I didn't want poor Russian farm boys to die."

Furious as she was, she understood. Risking his life for his beliefs was his nature. Could she be mad at an eagle for flying or a lion for roaring?

She should have talked to him earlier, to stop him if she could. She suppressed her anger. "Couldn't you have told me sooner? What if I had to leave for Baku before you returned?"

He shrugged. "Ilych would have taken you. I would have joined you if I survived."

He seemed to have an answer to all her questions. "Why didn't you tell Ilych or Petrus where you were going?"

"Ilych would never have let me go alone, and I needed him to stay with you. As for Petrus, he had only just gotten married. I didn't want to disturb him."

"And the farewell letter to me?"

"I didn't want you to wait for me if I were to die and no one bothered to tell you."

"Why didn't you return after you rescued the rebel leader?"

"I couldn't. I had promised the Germans that I'd rescue them. I couldn't break my word."

"Your word to strangers was more important than your commitment to the woman you claim to love, and responsibility to your son?"

"A man who doesn't honor his word is less than a worm." The corner of his mouth turned upward contemptuously. "You were in no danger, and Ilych was protecting you."

"How would you know I was in no danger?" she bristled. "With all the riffraff your friend Petrus harbored."

He paled. "I didn't expect him to become Bolshevik, but I should have known better."

She watched a moth circle the lamp, desperately seeking the flame. "Why did you attack Smirnsky?" she asked. "To avenge your brother?"

"No." He shook his head vehemently. "I had no idea he would be there. He was waiting when I went to sign the paperwork to take the Germans. You have to believe me."

"How did he know you were coming?"

"I don't know. Maybe someone ratted on us. But I don't think he was expecting *me*. He looked as stunned to see me as I was to see him. He hesitated, I didn't," he repeated. "You have to believe me."

She looked out the window. Darkness had obscured the valley. The stars shimmered like jewels dusted on the black-velvet sky. The cabin seemed to float in space. She felt his expectant gaze on her back.

"I need to tell you something." She turned to face him. "I am poor. Akbar Mirza is contesting my inheritance."

He met her eyes. "I expected that. It doesn't matter. I take care of my family."

"There's more. I know who my parents were. My father was murdered before my birth."

He gasped. "Was he a politician?"

"No," she said wistfully. "He was a nobody. A lowly entertainer, a motreb." She paused, remembering Qamar's words. "He died to silence whispers."

"And your mother?"

"She is Noor's daughter, alive in Farang."

He kept his eyes on her as she recounted Qamar's story. "Unbelievable," he mumbled. "Are you sure Qamar was telling the truth?"

She looked at the wall beyond him. "She had no reason to lie."

"No, but she could be repeating a rumor." He patted the chair next to his. "Sit with me. Please."

She didn't move.

He locked eyes with her. "I don't care who your father was or whether you are rich or poor. When I was lying in a ditch in the forest pinned down by a motorcycle, one hope kept me alive: to see you again. Nothing else mattered then, and nothing else matters now."

"My father died so I could live." She could barely get the words out of her choked throat.

"All the more reason for you to make your life worth his."

"What hurts most is that I lost Saleh Mirza twice. Once when he died, and once when I learned the truth."

"He was a complicated man." He hesitated. "For what it's worth, he always spoke of you affectionately and proudly. You may come to see him fondly again someday."

She listened to the waterfall gurgling, the wind caressing the walnut branches, the hooting of owls, the croaking of frogs. He let her be.

With the back of her hand, she wiped away her tears. "Will you stay with the Jangalis?"

"At least until I am well enough to fend off the Russians without their help."

"And afterward?"

"I'd like to." He wet his lips. "When I was recuperating, the Jangali leader came to visit. He is a good man. He cares about people, not power. He asked me to stay."

"To fight?"

"No, to help him govern. The Russians are retreating. The central government is useless, and war is still raging. Nobody is in charge here. Without leadership, there'll be chaos. He needs folks who can plan and deal with Farangis. He wants to build a fair society: schools for all, a free press, hospitals, all run by Iranians."

"Is that what you want?"

"That is what I always wanted: to live in a society where an honest man can live with dignity, where people can think for themselves and not parrot the local mullah." He leaned forward. "But I'll do what *you* want me to. We can leave and build our own world. It's your call."

"I don't know what I want," she said. "I am bitter and confused. My heart is ice-cold."

"Then stay until you know. Stay as a friend. The summers are cool here. The cabin is all yours. I'll have the small cottage repaired and move there with Kamal. You can do as you please."

A flash of light outside caught her eye, and a meteorite burst through the feast of stars. If she walked away now, he would never let her back in his life. But staying meant taking him as he was, a man of principles in the land of compromises, a man of his word even at the expense of his life, an outlaw hunted by the Russians. With him, she would wander from hideout to hideout with her children in tow, fearing for all their lives, craving peace. There would be no return to the life she knew.

There were no half-measures: it was all in or all out, forever.

But their fate was written on their foreheads long before they were born.

She placed her hand on her midriff, said a silent prayer, and then faced him. "If I stay, will you swear on your honor that you will never lie to me?"

He stared at her. "I will."

"And never abandon me or my children?"

"I will." He smiled.

She sat across from him, placing her palms on the table. "And if I am faithful to you, will you be faithful to me?"

He beamed. "I will." He kissed her palm.

Silence lingered like a lazy cat. The howl of a wolf echoed in the mountain.

"It is late," he said. "I will leave you to rest. In the morning, I'll send for Qamar." He put his foot down and leaned on the table to stand. "Can you hand me my crutches?"

Wordlessly, she circled the table and slid her arms under his armpits. "I'll help you."

He leaned on her, his rib cage touching hers. She steered him toward the curtain. He looked at her, confused.

"The bed is big enough for all of us," she whispered.

As she sat on the edge of the bed, Aslan leaned on the wall behind it. His breath smelled of brandy. She watched his neck vein throb. Gently, she brushed a lock of hair off his forehead, then rested her head on his bare chest. His arms enveloped her.

She was home.

GLOSSARY OF PERSIAN TERMS

Farsi	Translation
Andarooni	Private part of a house, Women's quarter
Amoo	Uncle
Aqa	Sir, originally head of a clan within a tribe
Araq	A potent Iranian liquor, normally made from raison
Asheq	Lover, bard in Azeri
Avaaz	Song
Baba	Father
Baq	Garden
Berenj	rice
Bibi	Matron, Lady, also Mother
Birooni	Public side of a house, normally reserved for male visitors
Chaqchor	A
Charoq	A curved untanned leather with holes for wool thread to use to fasten to feet
Deev	A mythical beast with hairy human body and a bull's head
Djinn	Unseen
Droshky	A Russian buggy with room for 2-4 passengers
Farang	West, Europe
Farangestan	West, Europe
Farangi	People from west, European
Fereni	Rice pudding
Fesenjo	Iranian dish
Gilan	A province north of Iran
Haji (female form Hajieh)	Someone who has gone to Mecca for pilgrimage
Hazrat	Saint
Hojreh	A
Imamzadeh	Son of an Imam, also the shrine
Jangali	Men of
Kamancheh	M
Khaguineh	Egg omelet
Khan	Sir, originally leader of a clan o
Khanum	Lady,

Khoshk	Dry
Luti	Tough guy
Mahrieh	Marriage insurance, a sum of money or other property pledged to the bride, normally not collected until a separation by divorce or death
Majles	Iranian parliament
Maktab	Traditional school
Mashdi	Someone who has gone to Meshed for pilgrimage
Mazandaran	A province north of Iran
Mirza after the name	A prince of Qajar family and a direct descendant of Abass Mirza, son of Fath Ali Shah, thus eligible to ascendancy to the throne
Mirza before the name	Learned man
Mohajeron	Immigrants, specifically those who emigrated with the prophet from Mecca to Medina to spread Islam
Morgane-Jang	a game played with eggs
Naan	Bread
Naan-e-Khoshk	Cracker
Nabat	Sugar candy
Paderazin	A type of cookie
Piche	A gauzy veil covering the face
Pomodor qatoq	A dish of tomato and eggs, similar to Shakshuka
qorbat	Foreign land, also being in
Reng	dance music
Rostam	Mythical hero of Shahnameh
Roze Khani	Lamentation
Saltaneh	A title given during the Qajar dynasty
Sard	cold
Sardari	A long front buttoned frock,
Shabestan	underground space in traditional mosques, houses, and schools
Shahname	Book of king, written by Ferdowsi
Shahre-farang	Kinescope
Simorq	A mythical she-bird
Takyeh	A place where they perform
Tangestan	A tribe and a city in Iran
Tasnif	Ditty
Tazieh	Passion play, for martyrs of Karbala, preformed during Muharram
Termeh	A brocaded silk spread

ACKNOWLEDGMENTS

The support of friends and family had blessed me throughout writing and publishing of this book. This venture would not have been possible without the continued advice and inspiration from my friend Gina Vild, invaluable input from my cousin Shiva, and the backing of my family, especially my husband, Lee. The sharp eye, probing questions, and excellent mentorship of my editor, Ellie Robin, has enriched this book and brought its characters and message to life. Arielle Walsh's help with publishing the book and managing its media exposure had been instrumental.

I am grateful for the generosity of Shirin Neshat and Gallery Gladstone for the permission to use the cover photo and Adam Hays for turning the picture into a wonderful cover. The feedback and encouragement of my early readers, especially my friend Homa Taraji, had given me the courage to continue this journey.

A portion of the proceeds of this book will be dedicated to supporting Iranian women and their struggle for freedom and justice.